GW01606078

THE RUNNER

BOOK 1 OF THE RUNNER SERIES

KATIE BAKER

© 2017 KATIE BAKER

ISBN 978-1-7750483-0-5

For Mike

And for the readers of Wattpad,
whose support has meant everything.

contents

contents 3
chapter 1 6
chapter 2 10
chapter 3 14
chapter 4 22
chapter 5 30
chapter 6 35
chapter 7 53
chapter 8 59
chapter 9 66
chapter 10 73
chapter 11 86
chapter 12 93
chapter 13 99
chapter 14 106
chapter 15 116
chapter 16 123
chapter 17 129
chapter 18 136
chapter 19 147
chapter 20 156
chapter 21 161
chapter 22 169

chapter 23 183
chapter 24 196
chapter 25 206
chapter 26 216
chapter 27 224
chapter 28 232
chapter 29 244
chapter 30 253
chapter 31 262
chapter 32 268
chapter 33 276
chapter 34 286
chapter 35 298
chapter 36 312
chapter 37 321
chapter 38 330
chapter 39 335
chapter 40 343
chapter 41 351
chapter 42 365
chapter 43 373
chapter 44 381
chapter 45 389
acknowledgements 392
chapter 1 395
chapter 2 405

chapter 3 411

about the author 418

chapter 1

My fingernails scratch and chip as I grapple to hold on to the building's roof, my feet kicking furiously against the rough stone below me. Finding purchase, my muscles screaming with the effort, I manage to hoist myself up onto my forearms and over the ledge.

I'm sweating from exertion. Without stopping to catch my breath, I push up onto my feet and take off at a run, propelling across the roof toward the next building. The edge is just swimming into view when I hear a latched door flying open. Angry voices shout out as the guards' heavy bootsteps fall into pursuit.

Nearly there. My eyes are trained on the horizon as I recall the impending height and distance. My legs burn and my feet pound across the roof's surface, the reverberation of heavy footfalls at my back spurring me onward.

Finally, my runway ends. Without pausing or slowing down, I plant a foot on the raised ledge and throw myself out across the abyss.

For a single, perfect moment I am sailing through the air, suspended and soaring weightlessly five storeys above the ground. This is it. This is what I chase after: this feeling of utter freedom. The flattened surface of the next roof rises to greet me and I absorb the impact with a practiced precision, landing cleanly.

A grin tugs at my face as I roll out of my crouched position. My legs already feel lighter. I straighten and wince at a familiar pain shooting through my left knee, then turn to look behind me. I push my hair back from where it whips around my face, swirling and tangling in the hot desert air. Squinting into the sunlight, I catch sight of the four guards standing across the gap. The captain is at the forefront, red-faced, his sword raised menacingly toward me as he shouts his threats into the wind.

I raise a hand to my ear, pantomiming deafness while the captain's voice rises in fervour. He gestures madly for his men to return to the ground. Smirking, I turn and jog lightly to the next ledge, swivelling to glance back at the captain standing opposite the divide. Even at this distance I don't miss the daggers in his glare. A thrill of satisfaction runs down my spine and I cheerfully raise my hand to my forehead in a mock salute before I take one step backward and drop off the roof.

Instinctively, my hands shoot up as I fall, catching a window ledge protruding from the building's facade. My feet grip the stone slabs and gradually, brick by brick, I am able to descend into the alley.

Sand kicks up around me as I land on the pathway below. I dust my hands off on my thighs and lower the scarf covering my mouth and nose. Listening for the sound of any pursuing footsteps, I make for the main road, intending to weave my way between the buildings before the guards reach the ground. My worn leather boots scuff through the narrow passageway until I emerge on the busy street, colliding solidly with an older gentleman. His ornately carved pipe clatters to the ground. I bend down to retrieve it with a flourish, smiling graciously. The man, taking in my distinctly ragged appearance, sneers and plucks the pipe delicately from my outstretched hand.

"Apologies, sir." I throw him a wink and take off across the road, smoothly dodging all manner of people, packed tightly together on their way to and from their designated districts. I dart in between a groom and his horse and slip back into the alleyway opposite, changing direction every so often until I am satisfied that my pursuers won't have a hope of finding me.

I finally stop to take a breath when I reach a quiet intersection, sinking down against a cool stone wall until I am sitting with my legs splayed out across the ground. I grin as I examine the woven leather purse clutched in my hand, tossing it from palm to palm and gauging the weight. It's likely that the old man with the pipe will have noticed it missing by now, but a Court dweller such as him can afford to lose a few coins.

The purse is only the icing on top of a very successful heist. Sneaking into the royal stables and raising the outer gate was no simple task, but I managed to release a couple dozen of the army's prized horses into the Wastelands before I was spotted by a member of the guard.

The lost horses will only serve to delay the next draft, but my game is about more than just hindering the war effort. Knowing how furious the King will be when he discovers what I've done makes the risk more than worthwhile.

I drop the purse into the pouch tied at my waist and set off back down the alley, my shoulders angling precisely in the cramped space as I pick a complicated path through the network of rough buildings. The beggars hovering in the crumbling doorways greet me with watery eyes, gratefully accepting the coins I dole out from my stolen coin purse. I offer them a smile and an apologetic touch on the shoulder when the pittance runs out, murmuring promises to return soon.

My pace increases as I race back toward home, crumbling buildings streaking past my peripheral vision. These twisting, narrow streets are more familiar to me than any four walls and when I am in my element, no one can touch me.

Hours later and once again high above the ground, I gaze out from a seat in the window of my single-room haven. The breeze from the desert night cools my skin as I absorb the millions of flickering lights laid out before me, illuminating the dilapidated commoners' sector and drawing the eye toward the grandiose Palace set prominently in the centre of our spiralling City. The glass walls of the Palace reach high above the Court buildings surrounding it; the arched peak of the famous spire appears to scrape the night sky. I imagine the King and Princess tucked away inside, their bellies full of rich food while they toast their gathered members of Court, all of them far removed from any of the worries that might plague us commoners.

My own window is darkened, the lamp empty of oil. My stomach growls angrily as I rise to my feet and toss the old man's empty purse into a dusty corner. I know I'm much too thin these days and it partially accounted for my sloppy antics this afternoon. A wiser girl might take her aches as evidence that she should slow down—perhaps give that old leg injury a chance to heal.

I run a hand through my unruly curls as I cross the small room, grunting when my fingers catch in a snag. My flat is modest, free of any furniture save for the cushions, a small desk and a trunk containing my few personal effects. The landlord rents the attic to me for a reasonable price, and doesn't ask questions when I pay in various pieces of jewellery or some other trinket. I'm not bothered by the tight quarters; I require only a place to sleep and a window large enough to jump through.

Giving up on the knot in my hair, I sink down onto the lumpy pile of cushions that passes for a bed and stare up at the ceiling, releasing a frustrated sigh as I mentally review the chase earlier. That was a close one. Too close. Am I losing my edge? Our never-ending war against the Wastelanders has recently increased the demands that the Court places on the Commons, and I am beginning to feel the pinch along with everyone else. Stunts like the one I pulled at the stables are a stone in the shoe of the King: irritating, but ultimately unimportant.

Rolling onto my side, I shut my eyes tightly against my raging thoughts and the memories that threaten to surface. Eventually, the ache of hunger passes and a heavy wave of exhaustion pulls me under, wrapping me in its folds with the promise of just a brief rest before the daily fight starts all over again.

chapter 2

Morning light pierces like daggers as I ease my eyes open. My lips feel chapped and bruised, dried by the desert air and relentless sun. Through my window float the sounds of the City coming to life. Clanging bells intermingle with the shouts of merchants, the former warning the factory workers they are late, while the latter offers the distraction of cloths and spices.

I roll over, groaning when I am greeted by a dull throb of pain shooting from my left knee down to my ankle. The old hurt has been my constant companion for the last five of my nineteen years. I rub my knee distractedly as I sit up on my bed and wait for the ache to subside. The rich scents of fresh bread and spicy meat float up from the marketplace below, coaxing me to my feet and over to the open window.

I push my shoulders back and breathe deeply, taking a moment to bask in the feeling of the morning sun warming my face. Here we go, again.

I duck through the window and I jump down, then swing to the side and grab the protruding bricks as I drop, floor by floor, and land among the chaos below. Wiping the dust from my palms, I straighten and take in my surroundings.

A bustling crowd kicks up scratchy pellets of sand as it hurries by. The market contains enough colours, fabrics, food and spices to delight every sense. Finely dressed courtiers stroll among the commoners, pausing to speak with the vendors or sidestepping the carts rattling down the street. A great, sweaty horse eyes me picking my way through the swell and I give his rump a friendly pat as I pass.

The market is unusually busy this morning. An airship passes overhead, momentarily blocking the light of the ever-blazing sun as it ferries the City's latest draft of soldiers out into the Wastelands. I slip between a couple of stalls and watch a young mother grip her child's hand tightly as she hurries through the square, pulling the little one away from the beggars at the side of the road.

A beggar man thrusts his arms out toward me and I have to turn my eyes away from the gory sight. The man's hands have been lopped off, the wounds healed into macabre stumps by brutish cauterization. The King's punishment for theft is severe, but every day it seems that more and more of our number grow desperate enough to take the risk. I suppress a shudder at the thought, mumbling an apology to the man and training my gaze on a friendly face up ahead.

Harry's stall is located near the centre of the square, where the crowd is at its thickest. I spot my friend before he spots me; he is rooted to his usual spot and gesturing grandly at his trays of bread and pastries. Everything about Harry is oversized, from his bulky stature and bushy beard to the way he towers above the other vendors.

"Ah, Kay! How is this fine morning treating ya?" Crooked teeth flash behind his flour-coated whiskers.

The delicious smell of fresh bread is enough for me to have to pause and swallow before managing a greeting. "Harry." I say, smiling. "I'm doing fine, thanks. A bit thirsty, though. You wouldn't happen…"

Harry cuts me off, jerking his thumb in the direction of the trough next to the stall and throwing me a wink as he turns to an inquiring customer.

I stoop and greedily spoon out the water with the ladle, choking in my eagerness to ease the drought in my throat.

"Thanks," I say, wiping my mouth with my wrist. "And some breakfast?" I thrust my hand into the pouch I keep tied around my hips, feeling my cheeks turn hot when I find it empty. Stupid, Kay. Couldn't you have held onto a single coin for yourself?

Harry shakes his head and hands me a roll. "No worries. Your money's no good here."

I accept the bread gratefully, my stomach growling its thanks. "Thanks again, Harry. I owe you one."

He grins and raises an eyebrow, leaning in close. "You've done enough for me already. Word around the City is that the Runner caused quite the commotion at the stables yesterday, but I suspect you already knew that." He slips a beefy arm around my shoulder and crushes me against him. "My brother was meant to head out to fight this mornin', but the Runner's given us a bit more time with him."

Harry's eyes appear red and I feel my heart break a little. His brother was part of the latest group of commoners drafted into the King's army.

The Wasteland war has been carrying on to various degrees for as long as I can remember, and the draft has existed for just as long. Some families consider it a blessing if their men are chosen; the soldiers enlisted in the King's army receive some schooling and a small stipend for their family. Commoners and courtiers are both subjected to the draft, but a well-placed coin in the King's palm will ensure that a noble boy's spot will pass to some unfortunate lower-born.

I pat Harry a bit awkwardly on the arm, wiggling out of his grip. "I'm sorry it wasn't enough to keep your brother here for good."

He straightens and grabs two more rolls, shoving them into my hands. "Don't you fret one moment about that, Kay. You do plenty for us. These times we live in, they are...complicated." He struggles with the last word. "Now, get out of here. I have some actual, paying customers that I need to attend to." He rubs his ruddy face before turning away, plastering on a smile and calling out a greeting.

I stuff the gifted bread into my pouch as I wander off, munching on the first piece and savouring the feeling of my stomach finally quieting for the first time in several days.

I survey the crowd as I walk. Many of the vendors and customers wear threadbare clothing similar to mine, rough and undyed but light in this unforgiving heat. The colours here in the Commons district are muted; the buildings are stone, bleached white by the sun, pocked and dimpled by the sand. Men, women and children shuffle past me in tunics and dresses that are patched many times over and faded from countless washings. Colourful scarves adorn the passing heads and shoulders, the many layers providing protection against the elements.

I watch an elderly common man haggle with a fruit vendor over a couple of apples. Beyond him, a plump courtier tosses her coins carelessly to a spice merchant. The rich woman barely gives the seller a cursory glance before strolling off down the street, leaving her common handmaid to accepts the goods and shoulder the heavy shopping bag. The marketplace is the great melting pot between our districts—a shared ground where everyone must gather to stock up on food and goods. Our scant resources have always been controlled, guarded religiously by the monarchy, whose job it is to dole out rations of food and water to the population as they see fit.

The day unfolds before me, long and hot. I wander closer to the centre of the City, moving from the Commons and into the Court. As I stroll I consider various possibilities, sorting through the standard schemes that could earn me a few days' pay. My eyes scan the buildings ahead, eventually landing on one in particular. This home is finer than the rest, with red shutters pulled open to invite in the morning light.

Perfect.

Now I know exactly where my next meal is coming from.

chapter 3

The first rule to successfully robbing a home is to blend in.

I walk around the back of the house with red shutters, slipping into an alleyway and scanning the exterior, my eyes picking out the bricks that will lead me to the top. Silent as a ghost, I leap up and scale the outer wall, bypassing the first-, second- and third-storey windows before reaching the top floor. I pause a moment to take a few breaths, concentrating on slowing my heart rate while I strain my ears to hear any sounds coming from inside.

Hearing nothing, I take my chances and swing over to the window ledge, peering in and scanning the room beyond. Excellent. It is completely empty and I can already see a promising-looking bureau sitting passively against the wall.

Experience has taught me that the top floor is the best place to check for a spare outfit. These rooms are typically used as the servants' quarters and are often unoccupied during the day when the commoners are out performing their chores.

I steal through the window and pad gently across the floor toward the wardrobe, still apprehensive of the sounds of any unwelcome company.

Pulling open the doors, I grin at the racks of maids' simple shift dresses and caps. I select one of the dresses at random and change quickly, re-tying my belt and concealing it behind an apron before I tuck my telltale red locks into a headscarf. I don't bother changing my shoes; my boots are scuffed and dirty, but the skirt hides them well enough. I stash my clothes back in the wardrobe and make a quick stop over at the water basin, frowning at the reflective glass above as I rub a bit of dirt off the side of my too-sharp nose, revealing the scattering of dark freckles beneath. My nose has always made my green eyes appear distrustful, calculating. Which I suppose isn't too far from the truth.

I leave after I've washed the excess dirt off my hands and face, shutting the door to the maid's apartment firmly behind me.

I make my way down the darkened corridor, my eyes flicking up occasionally to glance into the rooms leading off it. My chin stays tucked down low, my every air that of a humble servant. I pass no one in the hall and arrive at the landing of a spiral staircase.

The third floor has to be the living quarters. Bright fabrics of varying patterns and colours decorate the furnishings, a sharp contrast to the muted world outside. What is it with these courtiers? Half the City is struggling to put enough food on the table, while the courtiers spend precious money on making a room look pretty. What a waste.

I am certain that if I were to duck into any of these rooms, I would find some expensive heirlooms. Courtier jewellery would fetch a good price at the pawn shops, but I don't want to take anything that the family could potentially blame on the servants. No, I have my sights set on something else. I bypass the bedrooms and aim for the second floor.

The second rule to successfully robbing a house is to take only the odds and ends; pieces that anyone could put aside and simply "misplace." From the looks of this house, I'll have plenty to choose from.

As I descend the stairs to the second floor, I immediately note a lot more activity. Maids and stewards go about their chores, quietly murmuring instructions and gossip to one another as they work. With my head down and my steps purposeful, I fit right in. I slip into what appears to be a drawing room and grab a discarded rag off a chest. As I dust a shelf, I slip a small silver candlestick and an ebony letter opener into the pouch hidden beneath my apron.

The next room is an office, dominated by a giant, polished wood desk. I pass my rag over its surface, shuffling through the papers and slipping a couple of coins into my palm. A butler walks into the room just as I am leaving and I offer him a swift curtsey before I disappear back into the hall.

My heart beats heavily in my chest while adrenalin courses through my veins. I grow bolder and swipe a jewelled hair comb from the top of a hall table. This piece alone ought to be enough to keep my landlord off my back and deep in mugs of ale for a few weeks.

I find a couple of young maids on the main stairwell to the first floor. They cast me curious glances but say nothing so I continue downstairs, intent on some silverware from the kitchen.

I am heading toward the back of the house, the pouch at my waist clattering softly, when my attention is diverted by a half-open door and the room beyond. Before I can stop myself, my feet are moving of their own accord and I am slipping into the library.

Wiping a rag absentmindedly over the bookcases, I allow myself a look upward to take in the miraculous collection. Books. Books lining every wall from ceiling to floor, in every colour I could ever imagine, their gold and silver bindings flashing cheerily in the afternoon sunlight.

I run my hand over the titles, enjoying the scratchy feeling of the covers beneath my fingertips. One beautiful green spine catches my eye and I reach for it, cracking open the cover and breathing in the familiar, musty scent. Memories swirl through my head as I allow the comforting aroma to return me to a time spent in a tiny flat, listening to my father read aloud by lanternlight. The floor of our flat was always stacked with his books, grouped together in hodgepodge piles on the floor—

"Have you read it?" A voice behind me breaks through my thoughts.

I jump, sending the green book crashing to the ground. My face burns as I stoop to retrieve it, the pouch beneath my apron digging conspicuously into my ribs.

"I, uh, was just putting it back." I struggle to regain my composure, deliberately avoiding looking at the stranger as I carefully place the book back on the shelf. I hear him step closer and turn back around, keeping my eyes trained on the floor. A pair of worn leather boots appear in front of me. The choice of footwear suggests that I've encountered a servant, but as my gaze travels upward, I note a pair of fine leather gloves tucked into his belt, embossed with a kind of crest or insignia. I've been caught by a courtier.

Damn.

"My apologies, sir. I'll just get back to my duties…" I attempt an awkward curtsy and step to the side.

"It's a shame, isn't it?" I detect a note of humour in his voice. "My father keeps an entire room full of books but not a person in this house will read them, much less discuss them."

I halt in my tracks, startled that this man with the dusty boots and handsome gloves would continue a conversation with a servant girl.

"I never read that particular book, but my father owned a copy," I say, the words falling out of my mouth before I can stop myself. *Put a stopper in it, Kay.*

"There we are! Your father is a fan of Tolstoy?" he presses.

I raise my eyes and look up at him, arrested suddenly by a pair of steely grey eyes. The man looks to be only a little older than me, tall and broad, dressed in a plain, collarless linen shirt with the top buttons undone and the sleeves rolled up to his elbows. He sports a short, dark beard and his hair is cropped close to his head in a rough style. I am struck by his grooming; most men of his station pride themselves on their polish, typically opting to shave their chins and oil their hair. I complete my assessment, noting a light sheen of sweat on his throat, which tells me he has recently come from the outside. If it weren't for the quality of his clothes, I would have taken this man for a commoner, perhaps even considered him attractive.

I need to end this conversation and get out of this stolen dress immediately.

"Tolstoy was his favourite." I smile a little at the memory.

The side of the man's mouth lifts in response. Ducking my head, I step smoothly around him and disappear back into the hall. Time to leave; the silverware will have to wait until another day.

Walking briskly toward the stairs and without a backward glance, I spiral upward until I reach the fourth-floor landing. My thoughts continually drift as I run; I am lost in a haze of annoyance and the man's strange half-smile when a sound suddenly stops me in my tracks. I stand stock still, waiting until I hear it again. It seems to be coming from the room up ahead.

I press against the wall and peer cautiously around the doorframe. Two figures are fumbling about on the bed. I catch a glimpse of a woman's tear-streaked face. Her maid's headscarf has gone askew as she attempts to push the man away.

"Please, sir, I don't want—"

The man grunts some threat and she gasps, clawing fruitlessly at his arm as he leans over to suppress her cries.

A strange rushing sound fills my ears and the colour red nearly blinds me. I cross the room in two quick strides and grip the man by the collar, catching him off guard and throwing him to the floor. The girl shrieks, huddling against the headboard and pulling her skirt down around her legs.

"*What* in the eternal Burn do you think you are doing?" the man hisses, enraged yet still mindful enough to keep from alerting the rest of the household.

His silken vest and pressed white shirt tell me I have stumbled upon the lord's private quarters. He's older than I expected, marked with thinning grey hair oiled within an inch of its life.

I glance over at the girl. Her tears are drying and she appears unharmed.

"I should ask you the same question," I say, reaching beneath my apron and smoothly loosing the dagger from my belt. My voice is even, disguising the rage I feel boiling over within.

His eyes follow the dagger cautiously as he licks his thin lips and stammers, "You dare threaten a man of this house, you filthy commoner? The King will have your hands! You are never going to work again, you will rot away on the street, you—"

"Terribly frightening, really, but I'm afraid that neither you nor the King has any say over what I do."

I step closer, my voice steady and my eyes burning into his.

"I am the Runner. I have eyes and ears in every corner of this city, and I can promise that if you *ever* think of harming a member of this household again, I will return. I will come directly and slice your little friend right off from between your legs. Now, how does that sound to you?"

The old man chokes and shuffles back on his hands. "Get out of here at once, you… you gods-damn traitor."

I tilt my head slightly, crouching and bringing the dagger lower. For the briefest of instants, I let the blade hover near his neck, considering the pathetic quivering of his throat. The City would be better off without this noble piece of trash littering up the place and I am not such a fool to think I can protect his servants from his perverted appetites. The red pulsing at the edges of my vision tempts my dagger forward, but instead I drop it several inches, holding the point near his waist meaningfully. "Now, now. There's no need to bring the gods into this ugly bit of business. You've been a terribly ungracious host, but I think the least you could do is offer me a parting gift."

The old courtier scowls but dutifully reaches into his pocket and tosses his purse over.

"Thank you." I pocket my earnings. "And I think that your staff could use a raise, as well. Let's say two silvers a week? See to it, and perhaps your fellow wealthy ingrates won't hear of your shameful hobbies."

The lord's face purples, his white goatee standing out grotesquely. I beckon the maid from the room and step out after her, dipping a bow before shutting the door behind me.

My window to leave has just narrowed considerably. I throw the maid a small wave and she responds with a bewildered stare as I dart off back down the corridor.

I hurry back to the chamber I entered from, depositing my disguise back into the wardrobe and pulling on my own ragged tunic. I make sure to leave a couple of coins in the pocket of the maid's apron before I move to the window.

I step up onto the ledge and swing out, turning and lifting myself onto the roof so I can sit in the sun. The household will be alerted to my presence but I am no longer worried about being caught. The roofs disguise me with a single truth; no one ever looks up.

Once I am settled comfortably, I pull my pouch free of my belt and spread my winnings out before me, grinning when the old pervert's purse tips several coins into my palm. Not a bad haul, considering the slip-up in the library.

I shake my head to clear the image of the young man's smile and instead concentrate on how to avoid making the same mistake again. I shouldn't have let myself become distracted by some silly books. Years of thieving have made me careless. I cannot afford to let my mind wander: a single blunder and I could end up thrown in some stinking gaol. Worse, my hands could be chopped from my wrists and I'd be reduced to a beggar grovelling for scraps. I shudder at the idea.

Of course, the biggest mistake was my dramatics in the bedroom. I rarely reveal my identity when out on a job; maintaining a low profile allows me to move as unobtrusively as possible. The Runner is an identity I use to protect myself, and five years on, the name Kay Knight barely means anything to anyone. That's just the way I like it.

The problem is that my troublesome alter ego has begun to attract attention, either negative or positive, depending on who you're talking to.

Perhaps it was reckless of me to confront that disgusting old courtier, but someone like him deserves a lot worse than I dished out. My stomach churns just thinking about it. How many households are run by these upper-class pricks, taking advantage of the hold they have over the rest of us?

I stand up, scooping my earnings back into the pouch at my belt and checking to see that my dagger is secure. I walk to the edge of the building and glance down, squinting through the glare cast by the sun. An oddly familiar figure swims into view. The young man from the library runs out the front door and into the street. He looks left, then right, seemingly searching for someone. I scoff to myself. He can look all he wants, but so long as I remain up here—

I gasp and step back from the ledge.

Up. He looked up.

No one has ever looked up.

I wrinkle my brow, thinking. I am certain of it. The young man clearly looked in both directions, then turned and stared up at the roof. Did he see me? No, he couldn't have. I'm four storeys above him.

Not wanting to take any chances, I spin on my heel and run at the next roof, leaping across the narrow alleyway, plus a few subsequent roofs for good measure. I laugh a little as I land in a crouched position on the final building, my limbs buzzing from the pure exhilaration of running. The purse jingles happily at my waist when I straighten, affirming a good day's work. I can head down to the tavern and buy myself a congratulatory drink.

Up. He looked up.

chapter 4

Normally I would head straight to the pawn shop, but given the fuss I kicked up back at the courtier's house, I think it would be wise to hold onto my spoils for now. I'll have to try and sell them later once some of the heat has died down.

The dull pain in my knee is all but forgotten as I head in the direction of the tavern. I leap effortlessly from rooftop to rooftop, bypassing the crowds below and travelling with a speed that may as well be flight.

There is beauty to be found among this desolation. The world before the Burn boasted skyscrapers and greenery, but our simple, sturdy structures serve a greater purpose: survival.

The world wasn't always this way—oppressively warm in the daytime and cold at night, harsh with gusting sand and ceaseless drought. Years ago, the earth was rich in variety, ever-changing in season. The way my father told it to my brother and me, the Burn was an inevitable result of humanity being consumed by greed and selfishness. We dug and hollowed out our planet, depleting our resources and spilling toxic chemicals into the atmosphere. Over time, the sun's light grew brighter, gradually incinerating our planet's once-fertile environment until every semblance of civilization was completely eradicated in an event we call the Great Burn.

The harsh climate that settled upon us post-Burn wreaked havoc on our technology and power sources, driving people against one another and forcing them into the desert with all of its murderous intent.

Most of humanity perished within the first few years of the Burn.

Most, but not all.

Some of our ancestors survived by banding together and constructing a settlement, while others chose to remain in the Wastelands and live in roughshod tribes. The first group of survivors built up the walls of their camp into what eventually became the City, while the shadowy Wastelanders retreated further into the unknown, taking up arms and battling us endlessly over the desert's scant resources. It isn't known what originally caused the Wastelanders and the City dwellers to split into two distinct camps, but a couple of hundred years have served only to intensify our differences.

Two hundred and nine years have passed and some semblance of society has returned. The original City has expanded beyond the great, glass Palace and the fine noble homes that were first erected around it, now encompassing what was once a refugee camp. The descendants of the City's first settlers live in the inner district, nicknamed the Court, while the rest of us occupy the crumbling outer area known as the Commons.

Robbed of the old ways, we rely on the history books preserved by our ancestors to learn and rebuild. Our city has long outgrown the reach of its walls and now much of our wood, food and water is provided by traders — brave travellers who make long, dangerous treks into the Wastelands to collect from the nearby oases. The remainder of our materials are extracted from the earth, pried out of crumbling underground caverns. Hundreds of common men make the journey to our quarry every day, armed with their shovels and pickaxes. It is a hard, dangerous job suited only to the City's strongest. Those who venture outside the safety of our wall take their lives into their hands. The peril of sudden dust storms, blistering days and freezing nights pales in comparison to the dangers of coming up against our most dangerous enemy: the Wastelanders.

I roll out of my last jump and stride to the ledge, perching and surveying the endless landscape before me. Miles and miles of twisting alleyways stretch out in every direction, with the low, sun-bleached buildings jutting up between them. From the ground, the City can appear like a maze, full of dead ends and confusing turns, but up here, it all makes perfect sense.

Turning so that my legs are dangling over the edge of the roof, I adjust my grip and climb down to the ground. Landing among a cloud of sand, I push the wayward strands of hair back from my face and stride through the door of my favourite tavern, the Beacon.

The atmosphere inside the pub is a startling contrast to the brightness outside. Here, the air is smoky and the light is dim. The bar's owner, Samus, prefers to keep it dark, as his customers are usually performing a private sort of business. Patrons gather around the low tables, laughing over their pints or participating in riotous, high-stakes card games.

I crane my neck, looking for some familiar faces before I elbow my way to the bar.

"Kay!" Samus' booming voice cuts through the din. "Been a while. Was beginnin' to think you forgot about us." He pulls down a mug, filling it with a foamy, frothy liquid.

Like most of the men in the City, Samus is tall and broad, a build well suited to the miners and bricklayers. The old bartender has been a fixture for most of my life; he worked alongside my father during his quarry days. That was back when Samus still had both his eyes.

"Aw, Sammy, you know I could never forget about you," I tease. "I've just been so busy lately, what with matters of diplomacy to attend to. You know how it is."

Samus throws back his greasy head and laughs. "Yes, that would be time-consumin'." He thrusts a frothing mug of ale at me, the cold liquid soaking my hand as I pick it up. "Thanks for stoppin' by. And don't forget to tip, mind." Unlike Harry, Samus would never neglect to pick up his dues.

I slide a coin across the counter and hold my mug high above my head as I shove my way back through the crowd, concentrating on not spilling my hard-earned drink.

Finally arriving at the back of the pub, I seek out our usual booth near a boarded-up window. Spots of light seep through the gaps, illuminating the two men crowding the table.

"Boys!" I announce my presence obnoxiously, slamming my mug down on the table and slopping its contents onto the rotting wood. "I have arrived. What's the good news?"

Shouts of laughter warm my cheeks. Edmun rises and grabs me a chair while Gordy shuffles to the side to make room. A heavy hand slaps my back as I collapse into my seat and take a healthy sip of my drink, surveying the table and grinning.

"Kay-kay! We were just talking about you." Edmun smiles brightly.

"How many times must I tell you, do *not* call me Kay-kay." I groan. "It was not all right when I was a child and it is not all right now."

A few years older than me, Edmun was the best friend of my brother, Frye. He works as a blacksmith, just as his own father did before him. Despite the fact that he is most often covered in a layer of soot, Edmun's chiselled features and easy sense of humour have always attracted a healthy amount of female attention.

"So you've been gossiping about me, eh? All good things, I suspect. You lot looked very deep in conversation before I came and broke up the party." I take another sip of my drink, raising my eyebrows questioningly.

"Only ever good things. Compliments on your stunt at the stables! That was a feat of beauty." Edmun crashes his mug into mine and throws it back greedily.

I flinch and cast a furtive look over my shoulder, digging my elbow into Edmun's ribs. "Lower your voice, you grease-pile. You forget that not everyone is as friendly as you."

I try to sound strict, but Edmun takes my chiding with typical good humour, chucking me across the chin.

"A bit heavy-handed on the flattery, aren't we, Ed? I heard there was a right embarrassing chase at the end, when they spotted her." Gordy stares right at me, even though his comment is directed at Edmun.

Gordy has always been on the fringes of our little group, but in recent years, with me being away so often, he has become a regular fixture. We have never been particularly friendly; Gordy's snide attitude and general shiftiness have always left me with a lingering sense of distrust. Edmun has only ever laughed and dismissed my reservations as jealousy over his attention.

"There was a bit of a scuffle, but it was nothing I couldn't handle." I rock back in my chair, glaring at Gordy. "Those fat guards couldn't catch a cold."

"Just sayin'." A sneer pulls at his mouth, revealing rotten teeth. "If it were me, I'd have those horses free with none even knowin' I was there."

"So why wasn't it you, Gordy?" A throaty voice breaks through the tavern's din.

I grin as a beautiful, brassy-haired girl, swathed in a traditional white toga, sets her mug on the table and nudges me aside to share my seat.

"Lara!" I embrace my oldest friend, all my frustration at Gordy immediately forgotten.

Lara hugs me back, her heavily made-up face leaving a smear on my shoulder and her gold bracelets rattling when we draw apart. She shoots me her winning smile, fretfully pushing strands of tangled hair back from my face.

"My dear Kay, finally you grace us with your pretty face. You know that I've been worried sick about you." Lara shoots Gordy a look across the table, contempt written across her dainty features. "Has this one been giving you a hard time?"

Gordy has turned as red as Lara's lips. "I wasn't tryin' to give her a hard time—I was just saying if it were me—"

"But it never is, is it, Gordy, darling? Our Kay is taking all the risks and you sit here, criticizing." Lara takes a delicate sip of her drink and crosses one long leg over the other. "Tell me, what have you done for us commoners?"

Gordy grunts. "I can lighten those richies' load as well as anyone. As a matter of fact, just last week I lifted this pretty trinket from a lady down in the market." With a flourish, he produces a soiled handkerchief and triumphantly drops it onto the table.

I snort into my drink and even Edmun has the grace to look embarrassed.

"That's wonderful, Gordy. Handkerchiefs to horses: you are well on your way. Best hold on to that quarry job, though, just in case." Lara bats her eyelashes sweetly and Gordy turns redder still.

The hours pass in an instant, lost among friends and refreshment. I lean against Edmun, laughing until my sides ache and the lantern burns low. Eventually Lara downs the last of her ale and says her goodbyes.

"That's it for me, my loves. I'm off to work." She shoos Gordy away, tugging the train of her dress out from under his feet.

“I’ll walk you out,” I offer, rising somewhat less gracefully; I follow her to the door.

Several catcalls and whistles follow our progress and Lara responds graciously, flashing her trademark smile and winking.

The air outside is beginning to cool, the streets growing dark and the shadows long in the sun’s absence. I stand in the alleyway with Lara as she checks her reflection in a chipped piece of glass, dusting a generous helping of powder over her cheeks.

“You know, Lara, I earned quite a bit today. How about you skip work and we’ll go out for a meal? We can get some of that spicy mutton you like,” I offer, keeping my tone light.

“You are so sweet, darling, but I can’t miss a night’s pay.”

“Just this one time. Come on, I have more than enough for the both of us.”

Lara laughs gently as she tucks her mirror back into her pocket and wraps a slender arm around my shoulders. “I know what you’re trying to do, Kay, but I don’t need you fretting over me. I’m a big girl, you know.”

“It isn’t that, it’s just…”

“Just what?”

I open my mouth to say something, then snap it shut. I know what I would say if I could. I would tell her that I want to take care of her, protect her the way she protected me when I showed up on her doorstep five years ago. I would tell her that she means more to me than anyone in the whole of this city and that seeing her work the streets breaks my already-bruised heart.

I would tell her, but she’s already heard it a thousand times.

Lara smiles a bit sadly and tilts her brassy head. “It’s all right, Kay. You don’t need treat me like one of your charity cases. Why don’t you focus on taking care of yourself, for once?”

Lara’s bluntness was amusing when she was teasing Gordy, but infuriating when it is directed at me.

“I do take care of myself.”

"You're skinny as a rod and taking ever-greater risks." Her tone borders on scolding. "Barely a day goes by now that I don't hear rumour of the Runner. You keep up this routine and you're going to get yourself killed."

"It's not always going to be this way, Lara. I can do more, I can earn more. If I make one big score, I will have enough to provide for us both and you won't need to go out like this." I gesture vaguely toward the darkened alleyway, my meaning clear.

Lara shakes her head, causing her cheap gold earrings to sway back and forth. "It's a lovely thought, but I know you too well. You win some money and then you piss it away on the beggars and the drafted families and all the other bleeding hearts of the City. You aren't capable of saving yourself, Kay. And I won't have you try and save me."

I bite my lip, unable to come up with a retort. Sighing, she pulls me into a hug.

I wrap my arms around her. "Be careful tonight," I whisper.

She squeezes me tightly. "Enough of your fretting—I'm always careful. Now please, step back. You are distracting my customers and I can't have them thinking that a fine lady such as myself would be seen with the likes of you."

"No, we wouldn't want that." I attempt a hollow laugh.

Lara gives me a small wave as she walks off into the alley, rattling the gold bracelets adorning her wrists and signalling that she is available for the first buyer of the night.

My shoulders slump as I watch her disappear into the shadows, an uncomfortable heat burning in my chest at the injustice of it all. Without the luxury of physical strength, we women are left with a city bereft of choices. Unlike the men, we don't have the option of working in the quarry or enlisting in the army. Lara and I are girls of the street and we must do whatever it takes to survive.

Ignoring the sinking feeling in my heart, I briefly consider ducking back into the tavern, but instead turn and stroll aimlessly through the narrow side roads, taking the opportunity to mentally sort through the day's events.

The streets are practically empty at this hour and I enjoy this rare instance of space upon the ground.

I pass an old woman huddled in a doorway and stoop to place my remaining coins in her fist. She looks up at me with sightless eyes but doesn't say anything.

As I walk away, a bout of dizziness reminds me I haven't eaten anything since breakfast. Lara was right: how can I take care of her when I can't even take care of myself?

My patched clothes and the alcohol in my veins are little protection against the cold desert night. I blow on my hands to warm them as I trudge back to the attic, opting to take the long route in order to avoid walking past our old flat. The ash from the fire has long since cleared, but those lost still remain, their ghosts a painful reminder of the commoners' latest rebellion. There was a time when whispers of revolt filled these streets; a time when people grasped onto the hope that the balance of power would be upset and the monarchy would have to pay for what they had wrought.

That hope died in flames.

It is rarely spoken of, now. These days, common people know nothing but hard labour and harsh punishment, while those favoured by the King enjoy riches and leisure. The swift loss of our once-glorious rebellion was enough to bring the commoners back to their knees.

Back to a life where greed is king and nothing ever changes.

chapter 5

The next day dawns predictably: bright and hot.

I pass the morning by first making a quick stop at Harry's cart, quarrelling good-naturedly before ultimately compromising on the exchange of my silver candlestick for a couple of fresh loaves of bread and a handful of day-old rolls. I drift aimlessly for a while, eating slowly and carefully to savour my meal. The remainder of the food, I dole out to the young mothers and handless beggars hanging around the outskirts of the square.

With my stomach filled and my pockets lighter, I decide to head into the Court and see what business I can drum up.

Several blocks of polished stonework and swept streets make up the Court. The wide pathways arc uphill, drawing travellers past increasingly grandiose buildings and ending in the wooden gates and stone wall surrounding the City's grandest testament: the glass Palace. Here, people amble through town clad in rich clothes of vibrant silk, as unhurried and elegant as those from the Commons are rushed and crude.

Fashionable women clasp the arms of distinguished suitors, their genteel voices commenting on this gorgeous hat and those delightful pastries. Their concerns are so vapid, it makes me sick. Not one of them pays me notice and I feel myself a part of the landscape, no more conspicuous than a bench or flower box.

I size up the crowd as I walk, systematically noting the details of my potential targets. I spot two women giggling over a shared joke and wander closer, veering off a moment later when I realize that the quality of their gloves is not as fine as it could be. Most likely these ninnies receive only the barest of allowances.

A gentleman passes me by, his ornately carved walking stick clacking obnoxiously against the brushed stone. I tail him briefly but pretend to become distracted by a shop window when he stops to check his pocket watch and glances in my direction. From the corner of my eye I catch him lifting his lips into a sneer as he regards me. I briefly consider teaching him a lesson in rudeness by taking his watch anyway, but decide against it.

A flash of crimson startles my vision. A young woman exits the shop, pausing momentarily to unfurl her lace parasol before she strolls away.

I pause a few seconds before following, keeping a safe distance as I watch her peering into the windows of various shops. When she stops to consider a display of cakes, I slowly sidle up, waiting until she glances away before I purposefully knock my head against the open parasol, startling her.

"*Ohh...*" I groan, rubbing my head and bending over.

"Oh my goodness! I am so sorry—are you all right?" She steps closer, making to touch my shoulder before she notices my ragged clothes and pulls her hand back.

"It really hurts. I'm not bleeding, am I?" I tilt the top of my head toward her, my eyes completely focused on the pretty little purse dangling from her wrist.

She leans over me, her eyes searching my rats' nest of hair while I seamlessly unsheathe my dagger and cut the string binding the purse to her arm. I catch it soundlessly when it drops into my waiting palm.

"No… I don't see anything…" She moves back and tries to look at my face.

"It's fine, probably just a scratch."

My task complete, I now aim to put as much distance between us as possible. She stands dumbly as I slip back into the crowd and dart away, making several turns for good measure before taking refuge in a darkened alley.

I grin to myself, holding up the purse and examining it. Very finely made, the leather is bleached white and there appears to be some embossing along the hem. There's a promising amount of weight to it, too. I am about to pull the purse open when I am halted by a hand snaking out of the shadows and clamping down hard on my wrist.

"What the—?" I shout in surprise.

On reflex, I bring my elbow up, slamming it into the chin of my attacker. A lightning bolt of pain shoots through my arm but I barely register it, snatching my wrist free at the sound of a man cursing. Immediately, I sprint deeper into the alleyway, feinting left at the end but turning right and tearing down the next street.

I can hear his heavy footsteps behind me, gradually gaining. He is quick, I will give him that. I turn right, left, right again, heading back toward the main street, hoping to lose him in the crowd.

The sound of pounding feet recedes and for a moment I think I've lost him. I am relaxing into an easy jog when suddenly, a body appears from the pathway to my left and we collide full force, throwing me against the wall opposite and sending me crashing to the ground.

My head rings as I struggle to rise to my feet, dimly aware that my pursuer is already up and speaking to me.

"Relax, will you? I just want to talk!"

Blinking rapidly in an attempt to focus, I realize that his voice is stirring some vague memory. I slip my hand into my boot and discreetly withdraw my dagger, then hide the weapon behind my back before I glance up.

My heart pounds with warning while my brain pieces together the information. The close-cropped hair, the squared jaw: it's the strange courtier who confronted me in the library; the man who looked up. I fight to control the increasing panic shuddering through me. This isn't some do-gooder seeking to avenge a lady's honour and retrieve her stolen purse; this is infinitely more problematic. I broke into this man's house, stole his property and threatened his father. There is no doubt in my mind that he aims to see me arrested. Or worse.

The man approaches me slowly, gripping my elbow as he pulls me to my feet. My other hand still clutches the dagger behind my back, carefully rotating it into a precise angle.

"You're not hurt, are you?" His eyes appear concerned, but that could be my impending concussion.

I shake my head and buy myself a few moments by pretending to catch my breath. He retains his hold on my elbow but his grip loosens. I seize my opportunity, bringing the dagger down and raking it across his forearm. He yells in either surprise or pain and releases me, giving me the opening I need to kick out and sweep his feet out from under him. I don't bother to watch him fall and instead take off back toward the main street.

This time I don't take the time to listen for sounds of pursuit and simply throw myself blindly into the crowded intersection. Several people yell out in annoyance as I hurtle into the next alleyway; I turn once before chancing a glance over my shoulder.

I don't believe it. The crazy courtier is *still* chasing me.

Ignoring the tightness in my lungs, I turn again and sprint toward a wooden gate at the end of the street. Redoubling my speed, I jump at the wall beside it, kick off the bricks and sail over the gate. I land in a crouch and take off again, whipping around a corner and pausing to catch my breath. Surely, he can't make that jump.

I glance around the corner just in time to see him land seamlessly.

"What in the Burn?" I curse and start running again. Who is this guy? Is he really that desperate to get his ugly candlestick back?

I glance up the sides of the buildings as I run. Up. I need to go up.

But he knows to look up.

I shove the thought aside and careen around another corner, my lungs burning and my legs shaking. Desperately, I leap at the side of the next building, catching hold of a protruding brick. If I don't manage to get to the roof right now, then I won't have the energy to keep going.

No such luck. I barely make it a few feet up the wall before a hand clamps down on my weak leg and pulls me loose. I feel myself falling backward. I collide violently with his thick chest, crying out as my bad leg sends a spurt of pain up to my hip. Before I can grab my dagger again, he whips me around so that I am facing him, capturing both of my wrists in his hands and slamming my arms above my head back against the wall.

I struggle and kick out, but he easily sidesteps my attacks. We are both breathing heavily, his face so close to mine that I can see the beads of sweat gathered on his forehead.

"Are… you… done?" he pants. His jaw is clenched in anger and his thick eyebrows are lowered menacingly.

I finally stop kicking, my chest rising and falling in frustration. I keep my mouth shut tight and glare at him, feeling my arms going numb from his grip.

This is it. He'll take me to the Palace and turn me over to the guards. I'll be tried and will have to consider myself lucky if they let me keep my life, as I'll most certainly lose my hands. Stupid, Kay. I should have cut his throat when I had the chance.

"I'm going to let you go now. I don't want to hurt you."

I blink up at him, confused.

"Just promise that you won't try and stab me again. I don't care about that purse or any of the things you took from my father's house. I just want to talk." He speaks slowly and carefully, clearly still furious.

I continue to stare uncomprehendingly.

"Well? Does that seem fair or not? Have you gone mute?"

"Yes... I mean no. Let me go. I won't stab you."

The corner of his mouth twitches grimly. "Not that I don't trust you…"

With one hand still pinning my wrists, he reaches around my back. I stiffen, glaring at him. His mouth turns up a little higher as he loosens my dagger from my belt and tosses it down the street.

"All right, Runner. Let's talk like civilized people now, shall we?"

He releases me and steps back, his eyes wary.

I drop my arms and wince when I place my weight back on my bad leg. For several moments, we stand on opposites sides of the shadowed alleyway, considering one another.

After what seems like an eternity, he extends a hand.

"A pleasure to meet you. I'm Will."

chapter 6

I stare at his outstretched palm, noting the vibrant smear of blood soaking the sleeve of his shirt. Numbly, I reach out my own hand and shake, my addled brain still trying to make sense of the sudden turn of events.

"Kay." My voice comes out hoarse and I clear my throat.

His brow twitches and he holds his injured arm as we withdraw. "Kay. I would say that it is an honour to make your acquaintance, but to be honest, the stabbing was a little off-putting." He gestures to his bloody arm and grimaces again.

I am in no mood to dole out sympathy. "What do you want?"

"I want to put a bandage on this. And it looks like you could use something for that leg." He has noticed I am heavily favouring my right.

I attempt to straighten, and wince again.

"Come on, I have a spot nearby where we can patch up," he says. "I'll explain everything once we're there."

"Are you jesting? You just gave me the gods-damn scare of a lifetime, chased me through the streets, slammed me against the walls and wrenched my knee into a *very* unfavourable state, and now you would like me to go to a strange location with you to *chat*? Forgive me, whatever-your-name-is, but we are going to have to establish some trust first."

"It's Will."

"Will. Fine. Whatever. What do you want?"

He casts a furtive glance down the abandoned alleyway. "I don't think this is the best place to discuss it."

"I am sure you are used to being surrounded by marble floors and fine china, but this location suits me just fine for talking."

"For gods' sake, you are a mouthy thing, aren't you?"

"You have no idea. And you haven't answered a single one of my questions. Who are you, what do you want, and how did you find me?"

He takes a step toward me, his grey eyes flashing. When he speaks, it is through clenched teeth.

"My name is Will Cain, I aim to overthrow the monarchy, and I looked up. Now, can we please take this conversation somewhere a little more discreet?"

That's twice now that this man has left me speechless.

"All right," I say, eventually.

I retrieve my dagger and re-attach it to my belt, checking that the stolen purse is still tucked safely in my pouch. Finally satisfied, I turn back to Will and nod. "Lead the way."

I tail him back through the narrow alleyways, noting that he has wisely chosen to avoid the main street. No doubt, our odd pairing and various injuries would attract an uncomfortable amount of attention.

He catches me limping and slows his pace, drawing closer and offering an arm around my back. "Here, let me help you."

"I'm fine." I jump away from his touch.

His mouth twitches up into a half-smile. "Suit yourself."

I expect him to lead me back toward the house with the red shutters, but instead we wind up in the fringes of the Court, adjacent to a rough common neighbourhood. Will pushes open the door of a nondescript building and we spiral up the staircase to the top floor, finally entering a tiny flat.

"This is not what I anticipated," I say, feeling awkward as I regard the few scattered pieces of second-hand furniture.

"The marble floors and fine china not up to your standards?" Will's voice carries from a room at the back of the flat.

"Can't you afford something nicer?"

I hear his muffled snort of laughter before he walks back into the main area, laying some bandages and a bottle of water on a low table between a shabby couch and chair.

"You don't have to just stand there. Please, sit." He gestures toward the couch. "How's the leg?"

"It's fine." It's not, but I accept his invitation to sit and perch on the edge of the couch. "You have a habit of avoiding my questions."

"You have a habit of asking a lot of questions."

"So I'm told." I grab the water and drink greedily, closing my eyes at the sensation of cool liquid coating my dry throat.

He doesn't say anything while I drink. When I lower the bottle, I notice him staring at me, a look in his eyes that I can't quite place.

"What?" I run my fingers over my mouth, thinking I must have spilled water on my face.

"You aren't what I expected," he says, looking away before he lowers himself into a chair and unrolls a long strip of white bandage.

I can feel my face growing warm and concentrate on placing the bottle carefully back onto the table.

"Yes, I think it's time we talk about that." Recovering from my momentary lapse in composure, I straighten my shoulders and stare at him again. "You seem to know a great deal about me. Let's get the reasons for that squared away before we discuss anything else."

"Of course I know about you—there isn't a soul in the city who hasn't heard of the Runner." He tilts his head, studying me. "I've been searching for you for months. You're a difficult person to track down."

I stay silent, tapping my foot impatiently as I wait for him to continue.

"You are the person we need to lead our cause."

"And what cause is that, exactly?"

"I already told you. There is a collection of us, more than you might think, who aim to see this oppressive monarchy gone forever." His voice has lowered and he fairly spits out the last few words. His fists are clenched and I find myself a bit taken aback at the abrupt change from his nonchalant attitude.

"Such a mysterious collective of rebels," I say, my tone dry. "Who have you recruited?"

"Soldiers I fought alongside in the Wastelands. The King has taken too many good men from their families and forced them into battle. We're going to take back the City and put an end to this war once and for all."

My brows rise nearly to my hairline. "End the war? You?"

He looks offended. "Why not?"

"You're a courtier, for one."

"So?"

"So, if you take issue with fighting in the Wastelands, why not just buy your way out?" I lean back in my seat and cross my arms. "Problem solved."

A deep crimson appears above the white collar of his shirt. "You think I should let my spot go to someone from the Commons?"

"Your kinsmen don't seem to have a problem with it." I don't bother to keep the bitterness from my voice.

"Not all of us are like that." The crimson climbs higher. "I've spent five years in and out of the Wastelands, and I can tell you that I've seen courtier blood spilled as well as common."

My stomach churns at the thought. I tilt my head, considering Will. There is an unsettled storminess in his eyes and a grim determination to the set of his jaw. His intensity stirs an old memory and I lean closer, despite myself.

Our war with the Wastelanders has existed since the formation of the City. Desert resources are finite, and controlling the oases means survival. To some, the war is about power. Defeating the Wastelanders in battle and demonstrating City strength is a point of pride, a demonstration of ingenuity over desert savagery. To others, the Wasteland war persists simply because it has always been. It is a constant, as predictable as the setting sun and shifting sand.

I think of the old soldiers occupying the greasy booths in the Beacon. Night after night they sit slumped over their mugs of ale, twitching each time a glass breaks or a door rattles on its hinges. They seem to exist not as men, but as shadows. If Frye had returned from the Wastelands, he might have turned out like them.

But there's something different about Will. Something defiant.

"And how will overthrowing the monarchy change anything?" I ask. "Do you suppose that the Wasters will let us take whatever we need, once they see the King is no longer in charge?"

"Maybe not, but at least it's a start." Will runs a hand over his scruffy head. "If we carry on under this dictatorship, then nothing is ever going to change."

I wrinkle my brow as I regard him, considering his words.

He slumps back in his seat. "You don't trust me."

"I'm not certain, yet."

"Is it because I'm a courtier?"

I shrug. "It certainly doesn't help matters."

"Think of it this way. As a courtier, I can gain access to the King and his underlings. I can move freely about the Palace and I have certain resources that we can utilize to organize a rebellion."

"Resources?"

He stares at me meaningfully. "Money."

One big score. This could be my chance to earn enough to get Lara off the streets for good. It's a tempting thought, but there something else… something even more intriguing than the idea of robbing this rich idealist.

"And where do I factor into all of this?" I ask. "You obviously went to a lot of trouble to get me here."

His eyes light up. "You're the best part. The Runner means something to the commoners. If you and I join forces, then we can knock the King off his perch and rebuild the City into something greater."

"I think you've overestimated my influence."

"But not your skills." Will speaks quickly. "You're quick, stealthy and impossible to catch." He smirks. "Nearly."

I roll my eyes, ignoring the throb of pain in my knee that lingers from when he pulled me off the wall. "So, you want me to recruit the commoners to your cause, is that it?"

"Partly. I actually had something a little more complicated in mind."

His smug expression has softened into something friendlier. When he rolls up his sleeve, I catch a glimpse of the bloody scrape on his arm and grimace.

"Ouch, I really did a number on you, eh?" I bite my lip. "I suppose I should apologize for that."

"No need, I consider myself lucky. I suspect you could have done a lot worse if you'd had a mind to. Besides," he pulls up his other sleeve, revealing a long, ugly scar on his opposite forearm, "now I have a matching set. Thank you for the relative restraint, and for sparing my face." He swabs an alcohol-soaked rag across the cut, barely flinching from the sting.

"I wouldn't want to damage that," I joke back, before becoming suddenly interested in a stray sofa thread.

If he notices my slip, he doesn't say anything. I allow myself a glimpse of his fit physique as he finishes cleaning his arm, bandaging it snugly. Very little blood seeps through the wrapping, which I know is a good sign.

He pulls his shirt back on and looks up at me. "How's the leg?"

"It's all right," I say, abruptly drawing my hand back from rubbing my knee.

"Let me take a look."

"It's fine," I insist, then change the subject. "You still haven't answered any of my questions. How did you find me?"

He looks like he wants to say something about my knee, but thinks better of it. Shaking his head, he regards me and another smug grin escapes him. "You're the one who found me."

"That was only a coincidence," I say, annoyed. "And I don't make a habit of announcing my presence every time I'm on a job. If it wasn't for that old pervert—" I stop myself, biting down hard on my lip and avoiding Will's eye.

His hands curl into fists. Neither of us says anything and I wait while Will takes an audible breath.

"My father." He releases the air through clenched teeth. "I'm sorry you had to see what he's capable of. I do what I can to keep the girls away from that house, but..."

"I know," I say softly. "They don't have many alternatives."

Will stands abruptly, knocking the rickety table between us. Water sloshes from the bottle of water and I grab it before it topples, taking a drink to distract myself.

"All right," I say, watching Will cross the small room. "So, until I wandered into your house yesterday, you had no way of knowing how to find me?"

He ceases his pacing and sinks back down into the chair across from me, then grabs the bottle from my hands and takes a healthy sip. "Essentially, yes. I'll be the first to admit that I had a lucky break." He fairly winks and I feel another jolt of irritation. "That's an incredibly bold trick you pulled, dressing as a maid. Really extraordinary. What did you manage to steal?"

He seems genuinely interested, watching me intently as he takes another swig of water. I am struck at how he doesn't seem bothered about putting his lips where mine have been and momentarily lose track of his questioning.

"Enough to get me through a few weeks' rent," I say, vaguely. "Nothing anyone would miss."

That strange half-smile. "You have a talent for camouflage. I spoke with you myself and didn't have the slightest idea you weren't who you appeared to be."

"Thanks." Will seems oddly focused on the disguise aspect of my heist. "It isn't so difficult. I can rely on people not looking too closely at what's right under their noses."

"Those are my thoughts exactly." He is nodding as though we have just come to some kind of understanding. "With enough confidence and daring, imagine what you could get away with."

"I...suppose." I furrow my brow. "What are you getting at? How did you know to look up?"

"I beg your pardon?"

"Up. You looked up and saw me on the roof yesterday. How did you know to do that?" My impatience gets the better of me.

"Oh, that."

His nerve is positively staggering. I have half a mind to stab his other arm, steal what little this mouldy flat has to offer, and take off out the window straight to the tavern. As it stands, Will is fortunate that I happen to be curious about him and his mad idea for a rebellion.

"Yes, that. How did you know I'd be up there?"

"I didn't know, not for sure. I had a hunch."

"A hunch."

"You have to understand that I've spent a great deal of time searching for you." He studies me carefully, as if memorizing my features. "I spent months aimlessly wandering the City, tracking your accomplishments, chasing rumours, speaking with all manner of people." Shaking his head. "I never came close."

"Good."

"The time spent looking, however, allowed me to come up with some theories."

"I'd love to hear them." I arch an eyebrow, listening.

"I kept coming back to the same question: how does the Runner move from place to place, completely unseen? Once I began thinking about it, the answer became obvious." He extends an index finger, gesturing at the ceiling. "She must go up."

Crap.

"So, when my father came down the stairs, hollering that the Runner was in the house, I knew precisely where to look." He continues, looking at me earnestly. "Seeing you on that roof only reaffirmed my belief that you are exactly the person I am searching for."

"And what person is that, exactly?"

"You're rubbing your knee again."

I am thrown by the sudden change of topic and freeze with my hand on my knee.

"Would you please let me take a look at it?"

"I told you, it's fine." I scoot further down the length of the couch. "What are you, some kind of doctor?"

"Only in the sense that I trained as one and occasionally work in the Palace infirmary."

The half-smile has returned and he moves to sit next to me. I recoil slightly, but he pays no notice.

"Just relax. Is this an old injury?" He picks up my leg gently and lays it across his lap, rolling back my pant leg and slowly rubbing the area with a surprising tenderness.

His touch is so shocking that it takes me a moment to find my words. “Yes. I hurt it five years ago. I was fourteen.” I cringe as he lightly squeezes the sore spot, sending the familiar shot of pain up to my hip.

“Sorry,” he says, not unkindly. “What happened?”

“I was fall… jumping,” I correct myself. “I was jumping and I came down on it and…” I wince again. “It hasn’t been the same, since.”

He nods and reaches across my leg for the roll of bandages, scooping up a small tin in the same motion.

“Let’s try this.”

He brushes his arm across his forehead before applying the balm to my knee. I can feel his warm breath mixing with the cooling effects of the medicine and a pleasant, calming sensation envelops my sore leg. I fall back against the couch, breathing shallowly.

His grey eyes crinkle in the corners as he looks up. “Feels better, doesn’t it?”

“It really does. Thank you,” I say, meaning it.

He screws the cap back on the tin and begins to unroll the bandages. “With an injury like this, you should try and keep the limb stabilized. As your doctor, I do not recommend you go hopping from building to building.” His teasing tone is a stark contrast to the gruff passion he spoke with earlier.

“So, you’re both a doctor and a soldier,” I muse as I watch him lift my leg and wrap it tightly. “A man of many talents.”

“I try to stay busy.”

Looking at Will in his elegant, albeit torn and bloody linen shirt, I can’t help but marvel at what a mess of contradictions he is.

He finishes bandaging my leg, pulling the clasp tight and tapping lightly on the secured knee. “That should do it. I’ll give you this balm and some of these bandages so you can wrap it up whenever you need to.”

"Thank you," I say, again, feeling a bit cold as he lifts my leg off his lap. I am touched by his generosity until I remember that he brought me up here for a reason, not just to tend to my injury.

My head is swimming with questions but I can't seem to articulate one clearly. The cool relief in my knee and the strangeness of Will are proving extremely distracting.

"Are you hungry?" Will asks, making me suddenly aware of how prolonged the silence has become.

"Yes." I am famished.

"Let me see what I can rustle up." He jumps out of his seat, jolting me, then disappears into the kitchen.

"Do you need any help?" I call.

"No, no, I've got it. You relax," his disembodied voice floats back.

I sink back against the cushions and screw my eyes shut, rubbing them in an attempt to make sense of my scattered thoughts.

Will appears a few minutes later, his arms laden with dried meat, cheese and another flask of water.

"Sorry there isn't much." He doesn't look the least bit embarrassed. "I'm due for a shopping trip, it seems."

"It's fine," I say, trying not to appear over eager at a free meal.

I lean forward and grab a piece of meat, trying to chew slowly even though I could scarf the whole mess down in a few seconds.

"So." I swallow. "We have established that you are a rich man who rents a dingy flat, a doctor who can hop fences, and a soldier in the King's army who wants to see the monarchy usurped. Is there anything else I should know about you?"

Will laughs, the warm, genuine sound filling the room. "No, I would say that about sums me up." I notice he hasn't taken any food for himself. "You're one to talk, Runner. There is a great deal that I find strange about you."

I waggle my eyebrows at him, but I'm genuinely curious about what he could know.

"A girl from the streets who has bested the King's forces; a professional thief who gives all of her earnings away. Tell me, Runner: what should I make of that?"

I shrug my shoulders, unable to formulate a response.

"I'll tell you. That you are the person I need to help us end this tyranny." His voice has taken on that low, rough quality again.

I reach forward and grab a wedge of cheese, then break off a bit with my finger. I roll the food around a bit in my mouth, taking my time in answering. "What exactly did you have in mind?"

Will's grey eyes light up as he leans in toward me. "From the way you assimilated flawlessly into my father's house, I assume you are comfortable with sneaking in and among courtiers."

"I can come and go without you even knowing I was there."

"We are in need of someone who can go into the Palace and extract information for us, so we can best plan our attack on its walls."

"Don't you work in the Palace already? Is there a good reason I should risk my neck over yours?"

"I wouldn't risk that neck unless I was positive you could handle yourself," he assures me, looking slightly annoyed.

"So what's the plan, then?" I scratch my neck, thinking. "You want me to work as a servant in the Palace?"

"Not exactly. I was thinking we could get you a little closer to the royal circle than that."

I swipe a slice of bread off the table, raising an eyebrow as I wait for him to continue.

"You are going to the Palace as a lady-in-waiting to the Princess Megra."

The bread seizes in my throat and I choke, coughing loudly. I lean forward over my knees in an attempt to catch my breath, spying Will's dusty boots making their way toward me as he crosses to the other side of the table and pats me sharply on the back.

"Th-thanks," I rasp.

Will hands me the bottle of water and I drain what's left of it. He doesn't say anything, waiting for me to compose myself.

"You want me to pretend that I'm a lady-in-waiting?" I ask when I can finally fill my lungs properly.

"No, I want you to *be* a lady-in-waiting," he replies calmly. "It will be a breeze for you; there's nothing to it but a sense of self-importance and some shiny hair."

I scoff, fingering my own mess of curls, more knotted than ever thanks to our tussle in the alleyway.

"It will be completely straightforward. We'll dress you up and tell you all the right things to say. All you need to do is use that natural stealth and charisma to befriend the Princess."

"But why me? And why a lady-in-waiting?" I rub my temple, struggling to make sense of Will's words. Could it be that less than an hour ago, I was wandering the streets in search of loose coins? I feel as though an entire lifetime has passed since then.

"Recently, an incredibly unique opportunity has presented itself." Will's voice is calm and measured. "One of the Princess' ladies-in-waiting has found herself in a—shall we say—*delicate* condition. I suspect that it won't be more than a month before Miss Tessa will be asked to vacate her position."

He smirks, but I feel an unexpected twinge of sympathy for this girl I've never met. Even in her shiny world of privilege, there is still a distinct unfairness.

"How scandalous," I say dryly. "So, you suppose that any girl should be able to waltz in and take her place?"

“Not just any girl,” Will corrects me. “You.”

I glance down at my sand-smeared rags and dirty fingernails, studying the dried blood crusted in my knuckles where Will knocked me against the wall. I’m about as far from a princess-pleasing courtier as the stars are from the ground.

“Playing a courtier is a touch different from playing a servant,” I say, unsure of whether I’m speaking to myself or Will.

His callused hand appears above mine, hovering for an instant before withdrawing. When he speaks, his voice is gentle.

“If anyone can pull it off, it’s you,” he says. “And you won’t be alone—I’ll be there every step of the way. I’ll teach you everything you need to know: what to say, how to act. If you’re half as brilliant within Palace walls as you are upon those roofs, you’ll have the Princess confiding in you in no time.”

Sighing, I push my knotted mess of curls off my forehead. I feel the weight of Will’s hand on my arm and glance up at him, but he stands suddenly and moves back to his spot in the chair across from me. He leans forward in his seat, forearms on knees, his eyes regarding me and imploring all at once.

“Well? What do you think?” he asks, carefully.

I blow a puff of air out between my teeth. “What possible use could the Princess have to you?”

“She is the King’s only daughter and completely idle in that Palace. If you were to gain her confidence, I think you could learn a great deal about the King and his plans. I want you to relay any relevant information back to me so that I can organize the rebellion.”

“I see.” My head is swimming. The Palace. The Princess. A battle. Just this morning I was a lowly street urchin looking to steal enough pennies to get myself a meal. Now, I am being presented with the opportunity to go directly inside the home of the City’s richest and most powerful. My fingers twitch with the possibilities.

I could go along with Will’s madcap scheme, play his games until I can steal enough to keep Lara off the streets for good. Who knows—with a bit of luck and a lot of guts, I might even manage to give the market beggars a fresh start.

But there's something else...some spark of possibility that draws my interest more than a few shiny Palace trinkets. This plan, as farfetched as it is, could be my chance to do something worthwhile. To do more than just survive. To succeed where my father failed.

From the corner of my eye, I can see Will jiggling his knee up and down, waiting for me to speak.

"It seems like a lot of fuss to take on." I keep my speech to an easy drawl as I look up at him. "Why not just have me help you recruit some commoners? With enough manpower, you could attack the Palace whenever you damn well pleased."

"It isn't enough to attack with brute force—we need to plan our fight strategically." He speaks with the world-weariness of someone who has seen battle. "Real change comes through patience and cleverness."

He's right; every attempted uprising against the monarchy has ended in our blood. I forcefully push aside the memory and concentrate.

"So, you think that you have the answer." I wonder if his arrogance is because he was born a courtier, or if it is a predisposition.

"I believe we can be smart about this. History has shown us that we cannot succeed through fury alone. If we have an ear behind enemy lines, we could learn their weaknesses and exploit them." Will pounds a fist into his palm to emphasize his point.

I find myself nodding slowly. Despite my misgivings, I have to admit I am impressed with his thinking. Unlike previous rebellions, we wouldn't be a hodgepodge collection of miners armed with shovels and pickaxes. We would be an actual army of soldiers, fuelled by the knowledge of our enemy's inner workings.

My heart begins to pound furiously in my chest, and my body buzzes with the familiar static of anticipation. This could actually work.

"Before I agree to put my neck on the line for you, we should first get one thing straight." I lift my bandaged knee out of its reclined position on the couch and place it on the floor, surprised at how much stronger it feels. I stand up, gingerly shifting my weight before taking a few tentative steps.

Will may possess an excessive amount of self-righteousness, but I'll give him credit for knowing something about medicine. I continue my lap of the room; Will turns in his seat to follow my movements, looping his arm over the back of the chair as I walk behind him. I stop in front of the window and cross my arms, fixing him with a withering glare.

"I won't work for you—I'll work *with* you. Your cause sounds promising, but I don't know the full breadth of it. I don't know if you intend to put one of your own in power or how you plan to run the City if you can seize it. You can ask a favour of me and I can choose to help you, or I can choose to leave at any time. Don't think you can impress me with your lofty ideals and fancy plans. I have been running rings around this monarchy for a long time now, and I have never needed anyone to help me." Feeling my cheeks warming from the length of my speech and the intensity of Will's gaze, I fight the urge to turn and look out the window; instead I force my eyes to lock with his.

Will lifts his hands and claps them slowly together. "Well said. Allow me to alleviate your misgivings. Please, tell me what you want for this city."

I ignore his sarcasm and continue my lap around the room, buying myself some time before I return to the couch. I sit back down, careful to keep my body forward instead of slouching.

"What I want…" I start, my brows furrowing and my gaze drifting upward as I think. "I want everyone to have the opportunity to educate themselves. I want my friends to be able to support themselves through their trades, and I want the rich to give up their unnecessary luxuries so that their wealth can be redistributed." I think back to the sea of hungry and wretched faces I walk by each morning.

"Well, I know we could—"

"I'm not finished." My voice comes out more loudly than I had intended. "I want reparations paid to every family of a man injured or killed in the mines. I want the safety of those men guaranteed, and I want our women given the right to take any job that is available to a man." Lara shouldn't have to go out at night, rattling her jewellery.

Will seems to be waiting for me to say something else.

"Is that it?" he asks, after a beat.

"I am sure I will come up with some more later."

"Without a doubt." He scratches the stubble on his chin, a thoughtful grin tugging at his lips. "I can see you've given this some thought."

"The concept, yes," I say, slowly, "but not the execution. I suppose that's where you come in." I admit the last part begrudgingly.

"Well, I *will* tell you that no one can speak to the needs of the people better than the Runner. What you want is fairness and equality, which is exactly what we want as well."

I feel a jolt of irritation at his placating tone.

"I can promise you that, in the new city, no one will want for an education or for the basic necessities. We will all have the same opportunities."

He is an idealist. I've grown up with this type; the kind who believes that removing the monarchy will allow us to rise up as equals. While I admire the idea, I have always failed to see how an angry, under-educated and abused group of people can achieve a thriving nation.

My father always impressed this fact upon us. He taught my brother and me that strong leadership with an ear and voice for the people was what our city needed, and that it was our responsibility as citizens to keep our hearts open to the trials of those around us.

My mind momentarily drifts to the snippets of conversation I would catch as he spoke, huddled with his friends around our kitchen table. That was the first time in my young life that I had heard whispers of revolution.

I stretch my knee again. Under these circumstances I should be wary, but against my better judgment I find myself trusting Will. There is something about this strange man, his unwavering sureness and passion. Somehow, when he speaks of the possibilities, I believe him.

"I have no doubt you have a great many questions about who we are and what we are doing." Will's voice breaks through my thoughts. "There will be enough opportunity for you to meet my friends and consult with us on our plans. Does that help?"

"It does help. Some."

"What I am offering you, Kay, is the chance to be part of something bigger than yourself. Before this, your acts of rebellion have been annoyances, enough to slow the King down, but by going inside, planting yourself right in the middle of the hive—*that* is when the real changes will happen."

It's when his voice takes on that low, burning intensity that I can't help but find myself believing anything he says.

"So, I would have to wear dresses." I wrinkle my nose at the thought.

"Yes." He chuckles. "And wash your face, and brush your hair."

"Bloody Burn." I groan. "I can't run in a dress."

"And you'll have to clean up that mouth of yours." Will raises his eyebrows in mock seriousness. "Don't be so worried about the dress, though. If you can convince the courtiers that you're one of them, you won't need to run."

The afternoon sun is waning in the small room and I can see particles of dust floating through the air, bouncing off Will's dark hair and reflecting in his earnest gaze.

I sigh, but I can't help the smile slowly creeping over my face. "When do we start?"

chapter 7

Two days later, my leg is feeling stronger than it has in years and I am able to leap from my attic window, sidle from ledge to ledge and shimmy down to the ground without issue. I land on the street and stroll toward the main road, aiming to pawn the remaining items I had lifted from Will's house, no longer worried about any impending consequences.

As I walk through the market, I dodge both courtiers and commoners, everyone intent on stocking up on the latest provisions. Our food and water are delivered to us at intervals, sometimes few and far between. Because our resources are drawn from the carefully preserved oases several miles outside the City, we have to ration a fair amount.

The families living in the Court are given a livable amount of rations courtesy of the City, but many of them will come into the market to stock up on extras. This leaves fewer goods for us commoners, but you can't blame a vendor for selling to the customer with the most coins.

I refill my flask near Harry's cart and spend a couple of minutes chatting with him, laughing when he pretends to sneak me one of the burned loaves of bread. I bid my goodbyes when an inquiring courtier couple steps up; I doff an imaginary cap to Harry's rich customers and slip away.

Several twists through the alleyways later, I find myself in a rougher part of the City. Here, the buildings are packed tightly together and appear to loom inwardly over the already-cramped streets. I pass several people huddled in doorways before I locate Mo's pawn shop and swing gaily through the door, glancing about at the new wares.

"Ah, there she is." Mo materializes seemingly from out of nowhere and situates himself behind the counter, drumming his nimble fingers on the knotted wood.

"How are you doing, Mo?" I untie my pouch from my belt and drop it on the counter.

"Been better, been worse. What have you got for me?"

"Straight to the point, as always."

"What can I say, huh? I'm a man of business. You haven't got any of that silverware, have you?"

"I have something almost as good!" I declare, turning the sack over and displaying the odds and ends with a flourish.

Mo pokes through the few scattered bobbins. "Is this it?"

"What do you mean, 'is this it'? I have some really great pieces, right here. Look, look at this." I locate the ivory hair comb and brandish it at him.

The old thief takes the comb from me and turns it over in his hand, squinting.

"Yes, this is quite a nice piece." Mo speaks slowly, ever calculating. "But I am afraid I can't give you more than ten silvers for the whole pot."

"Are you kidding me? That comb is worth ten alone!"

"It may well be, at some respectable shop up in your hoity-toity districts, but down here it's worth three." He doesn't bother hiding his yellowed grin.

"You're a regular burglar—you know that, don't you, Mo?" I sigh and rub my forehead. If there were a better place in the City to take these goods, I would have tried my luck there. Unfortunately, Mo is one of the few shops still operating as a not-so-strictly-legal business.

"I'll tell you what." I chew on my bottom lip, pretending to think it over. "Give me four silvers for that comb, and one for each of the rest. That's fifteen."

"Thirteen."

"Deal."

Mo hands over my pay and I make a show of counting out the coins. I scoop the earnings back into my pouch and wish him a good day, then spin swiftly on my heel and exit the shop.

Out in the alleyway, I look up and consider the bricks protruding out of the side of Mo's shop, plotting my path before I jump and pick my way toward the roof. The sunlight breaks through the shadows, creeping over my back and warming my skin as I climb ever higher.

At the top of the building, I situate myself and head toward the City centre, jogging lightly between each jump, enjoying the newfound strength in my leg and the comforting weight of the coins in my belt. I'm leaping from rooftop to rooftop, losing myself in the pure exhilaration of running, when the familiar sound of rattling jewellery interrupts my thoughts. I draw to a stop, standing stock still as I listen. After a moment, I turn toward the source and walk over to the roof's edge.

Peering into the alleyway below, I spy the top of two heads pressed tightly together, one brassy blonde and one dark. The girl's many bracelets are rattling together with each thrust the man makes between her legs. He shudders and falls against her, grunting.

I step back, my heart sinking and my stomach churning as I recognize Lara.

"Gordy, you can get off me now, you nasty bugger," she protests.

I nearly gag. Gordy?

"One more, Lara. C'mon, for me."

He is repulsive, even at this distance.

"I know you haven't got any more money, so that'll do for now. Off you get, then." Her voice strains and I peer over the wall in time to see her shove Gordy back.

My hands curl into fists at my sides. I am already mentally plotting the quickest path down to them. If he so much as lays another finger on her...

"All right then, gorgeous. I'll be off, but I promise to see you again, very soon." He stumbles as he pulls his trousers up. "'Til next time, then."

"Yea, next time." Lara waves her bracelet-laden arm absentmindedly, straightening her toga as he rounds the corner.

I swing over the edge and drop down to the street, gripping the window ledges to control my fall. When I land and turn to face her, Lara's lips are pressed tightly together.

"So what is it, are you spying on me now?" she demands, coldly.

"I was just passing above and noticed something caught between your legs." I don't bother keeping the disgust from my voice. "Him? Really?"

"Yes, Kay. Yes, him, and yes, any other man who can pay for my dinner." Her brow has cleared and she uncrosses her arms. "Do you really want to have this argument again?"

"As many times as it takes." My attitude softens. "That's enough now, Lara. You can't do this anymore." I fumble for the coins at my belt. "Here, look. Thirteen silvers, and it's all for you. I earned it and I'm not giving it away to the beggars. I want you to have it." I place the purse in her hands. "I can take care of us now, Lara. There is much more of this coming to us."

Lara regards the purse before she looks back up at me. "It's really a lovely thought, but we've talked about this before..."

"I know we have, but it's different now." My mind flashes back to the sight of Gordy pushing himself against her and I speak quickly. "I took a job, a big one. This one is going to change everything."

"What are you talking about?"

I grip her hands and the bag of coins falls to the street. "I'm talking about royalty. I'm going into the Palace and I'm going to pretend to be one of them. We're bringing them down, Lara. The whole vile, corrupt monarchy. We are going to bring them down from the inside and things are finally going to get better."

Her blue eyes blink rapidly at me. "You're...what? Going in? To the Palace?"

"That's right." I nod. "And while I'm there, I'll be able to send you anything you need. Think of it: one big job and at the end of it, everything will be different."

Lara doesn't say anything. She stares down at our clasped hands for a long time, eventually raising her head to look at me. Her eyes are moist.

"I don't want to do this anymore," she says finally, her voice breaking.

"You don't have to."

"I want to believe you, Kay, but this... it's too much. It's too risky, even for you." She releases my hands and swipes a stray tear from her cheek.

"I know it's a long shot, but what other choice do we have?" I kneel down to scoop up the coins, my fingers brushing hers as she stoops to help me. "This isn't a life. This isn't what I want for us. I can fix it. I can make it better." I deposit the last coin in the pouch and hand it to her, straightening.

She laughs wistfully. "Gods, you sound just like him."

I stiffen. "Don't talk about him."

"He used to go on like this as well, you know. How we would be taken care of; how they would unseat the King and bring down the separate sectors." She is ignoring me and her eyes have taken on a glazed, far-off look.

I speak through tightly clenched teeth. "I said, don't talk about him."

"We have to be able to talk about him. He was your brother and he was my..." Lara's voice catches in her throat. I sigh and gather her frail body into a hug, allowing her tears to wet my tunic.

"This is different. I know what he did wrong and I'm going to do it right." I close my eyes as I hold her, my heart breaking at the way her frail shoulders shake against me.

Eventually she draws her head up, keeping her hands clasped behind my neck. "I can see him in you, you know. You have the same eyes."

I nod, not trusting myself to speak.

"Are you really going to do this?"

"Yes," I say simply.

She sighs as she trails her fingers down my cheek. “I don’t suppose there is anything I can say to make you reconsider.”

I give her a small smile. “I’m afraid not.”

“Just promise me you’ll be careful.”

“You must make a promise to me as well.” I dodge her request. “That you’ll take these coins and get yourself a warm meal. Get rid of those godsforsaken bracelets and dump them in the gutter—I never want to hear them again.”

She laughs lightly as she regards the bag of silver, shaking her head. “Gods, I feel like a courtier. Given an allowance and told not to work.”

“I do have a very important job for you, in fact,” I say, watching her tuck the pouch away into the folds of her skirt.

She looks up at me curiously.

“I need you to manage things here while I’m away. I’ll try to send coins and items for pawning as often as I can, and you’ll have to make sure that some money goes to Harry, and the beggars near the market, and yourself, of course, and...”

I am cut off with a firm kiss on the mouth. When she draws back, Lara is shaking her head and smiling.

“Dear, sweet Kay. Always looking after everyone else. Please remember to look after yourself this time, will you?”

“Don’t worry about me.” I grin. “I know exactly what I’m doing.”

chapter 8

While accompanying Lara back to safer streets, I am able to convince her to move into my flat. I figure she may as well, since I won't be using it in a few weeks and there is no sense in us paying two rents.

She hugs me once more and turns to go, leaving me to shimmy back up to the rooftops. I increase my speed as I leap from building to building; the hour has grown late and I have already pegged Will as the impatient type.

I land on the roof of his shoddy flat and lower myself into the uppermost window; soundlessly I swing inside and situate myself into a seated position on the ledge. Will is in the chair with his back turned to me. His head is lowered, intently studying some parchment on his lap.

"Pretty lax security you have around here," I say, then laugh when he jumps in shock.

"Gods." Will clutches his chest. "Ever hear of using the door?"

"Not really my style." I cross my legs and tilt my head.

"You may want to consider it as an option in the future. I doubt the Princess will take kindly to one of her ladies swinging from the rafters. "

I roll my eyes at his seriousness. He places whatever he was reading down on the table and moves toward me. I notice that he still hasn't trimmed his beard.

"You're late," he says, curtly.

Delightful. I've been here less than a minute and have already heard nothing but lectures.

"Sorry, I ran into a friend." Uncomfortable at his proximity, I slide down off the ledge and squeeze around him, helping myself to an apple from a bowl on the table.

"I need you to take this seriously, Kay. I don't think you fully grasp just how different the Court is from what you're used to."

"Would you relax?" I say through my mouthful of apple. Then, swallowing, "I thought you said all I needed was an uptight attitude and good hair."

"As well as manners, tact and decorum."

"I suppose you forgot to mention those. Look, I've been helping myself to goods from your district for a long time—I get the gist of it. Just teach me some fancy phrases and I'll take it from there." I take another bite of the apple.

Will runs a hand over the stubble on his head, his brow furrowed. "You're spewing bits of that everywhere. Didn't your mother teach you to chew with your mouth closed?"

"My mother is dead," I say flatly, making a point of spitting some fruit as I speak.

That shuts him up. Briefly. "I'm sorry. I lost my mother as well."

"Right. Lovely. Tell me, is talking about dead mothers considered good courtly conversation?" I ask, keeping my eyes averted.

I regard the apple core in my hand before polishing it off in two bites. When I look back up, I notice Will has a disgusted look on his face.

"What?" I wipe my hands on my tunic.

"We have a lot of work to do."

Several hours later, my head is aching. Will has been forcing me to memorize the names of nearly every noble, an endless list of useless people.

"And again, Kay. Who is this?" He holds up a printed card showing a fat old man with bushy sideburns.

I squint in an attempt to clear my blurred vision. “Lord Engers,” I say.

“First name?”

“Jorge.”

“And his wife?”

“Carilyn. And his children are Anton and Sebastian.” I squeeze my eyes shut and massage my throbbing temple.

“And who is this?” He thrusts another card at me.

“Lady Emmy Bock. Husband is the deceased Lord Richerd Bock. No children. One lover, Gregory, no title.”

“And this—” He reaches for another card but I lean forward and snatch the entire deck from his hands.

“Stephen Griss, father is Thom Griss, captain of the King’s guard.” I crumple up the card and drop it to the ground. “Here’s Lydia Simons, bit of a hussy. Lady Penelope Haydon, cousin to the Princess. Richie Thaylor. Oren Humber, his brother Louis, and here we have Sam, Kerry, Tomas, Byron, Lyle...” I flick the cards at Will one by one as he ducks and raises his hands to protect himself. “Janit, Peter, Ira, Charles, Lawrence, Rachel, Edith, Sara.” When I run out of cards, I lean back against the couch, satisfied at the sight of Will looking dismayed amid the scattered study materials.

He sighs and stoops to collect the cards. “That was not very ladylike.”

“Forgive me. I never had the benefit of a formal education.” Learning history and literature in a cramped flat from an over-read father doesn’t count.

“I get that you’re frustrated, Kay, but you need to trust me when I say this is important. The people at the Palace are gossipy social climbers and you’ll be expected to keep up with who’s who.” Will scoops up the last of the cards and carefully shuffles them back into place.

I don’t say anything, returning to rubbing my temple.

"I think we're ready for a break, don't you?" He places the deck on the table and stands up. "Are you hungry?"

"Yes, always," I say, brightening.

"I figured."

He disappears into the kitchen and returns a few moments later, a plate of food in each hand. I reach up to take the dish but he shakes his head and motions for me to follow him.

"Not here—we'll go to the dining hall." He places the plates on the window ledge and pulls up a couple of chairs, angling them so they face outside. "I think this feast calls for a formal setting, don't you?"

"I couldn't agree more," I say, sinking into the proffered seat.

Will lowers himself to sit next to me, his shoulder brushing mine in the cramped space. He picks up his silverware and cuts into his meal. "Unfortunately, this is the closest thing I have to a dining table in here. It's a bit tight, but you can't beat the view."

As he chews, he stares out the window at the wide street, coloured bright orange in the late afternoon sun. I tear my eyes away from him and concentrate on my own supper.

"No, no. Not like that." He sighs and reaches for my knife, covering my small hand with his large one and readjusting my fingers so that they rest against the side of the blade. "Like this. You're not stabbing it, you're eating it."

When he releases me, I am left holding the knife awkwardly, rotating myself over the plate as I attempt to slice the meat the way he does. I cut a chunk and raise it to my mouth.

"Stop. Look at what you have there."

I pause and regard the food on my fork. "It looks pretty tasty to me."

"That is much too big a piece. Remember, a lady takes small bites and chews delicately." He demonstrates, smoothly cutting off a minuscule portion of his own food.

I sigh, return the morsel to my plate and slice it in half, biting my tongue while I concentrate on the strange way I have to hold the knife. I brandish the newly cut portion at Will before placing it in my mouth and chewing as slowly as I can manage. Gods help me, it tastes delicious. If I can expect meals like this at the Palace, then perhaps I shouldn't mind the danger quite so much.

Will nods and returns to his supper. We eat in silence as I focus on holding my silverware without struggling, cutting and spearing annoyingly tiny portions of food. It has never taken me so long to finish a meal and I begin to wonder if the courtiers realize how inefficient this method of eating is.

Will chuckles softly and I squint one eye at him suspiciously.

"What?" I ask, careful to swallow first.

"It's nothing. Just the way you look when you're concentrating."

"Isn't it considered a tad gauche for a gentleman to stare at a lady while she eats?" I make a show of dabbing my mouth with a cloth.

"My sincerest apologies—I couldn't help myself. It's been a while since I've had such entertaining company for dinner."

"I am so pleased that you find my struggles amusing," I say lightly, clearing the last of the crumbs from my plate.

He stands to collect our dishes. "Place your fork and knife in the centre of the plate so that the help knows you've finished."

I do as he says. "'The help,' is it? Don't you mean 'the commoners'?"

"That reminds me. You're going to have to keep any commoners you encounter at arm's length. Courtiers, especially royal ones, don't fraternize with anyone they deem socially unacceptable. It's a terrible prejudice, I know, but you'll have to partake if you're going to fit in."

He disappears into the kitchen and I am left staring out the window. I watch the figures passing below, studying the way the street lamps throw long shadows across the front of the buildings.

"You did well today."

I turn at the sound of Will's voice. He is leaning against the doorframe, his arms crossed in front of his broad chest.

"I mean it. I didn't expect you to be such a quick study."

"Why is that?" I don't bother trying to hide the offence in my voice. "Because I haven't been to one of your fancy schools?"

He blinks at me, appearing hurt. "That's not what I meant."

"It's fine. Don't worry about it." I stand and place our chairs back against the wall. When I turn, Will is still reclined in the doorway, regarding me.

"Same time tomorrow?" I ask, sitting on the ledge and swinging one leg out the window.

"You know, we're on the same side, now. You don't have to keep thinking of me as some spoiled courtier."

I pause. My initial impulse is to come back at him with a biting remark, but for once, none come to mind.

"I'm sorry," I say, instead.

He raises his eyebrows, surprised. "You are?"

"You're right. We're on the same side and, apart from throwing me off a wall, you've been nothing but a completely decent person. So, I'm sorry. I'll try to keep the poor-little-rich-guy jabs to myself, from now on."

"Well... thanks." He appears baffled but the corner of his mouth tugs upward. "You continue to surprise me, Kay. And for what it's worth, you've been completely decent as well."

I roll my eyes but can't help smiling along with him. "Oh please, I'm blushing."

Will chuckles and I feel the tension from earlier finally lifting. His laugh is a rich, throaty sound, filling me with warmth despite the cool night breeze against my back.

He walks toward me and the flight instinct flutters in my chest. I force myself to stay in place as he leans past me, his tall frame bending through the window as he looks down at the street. He is close enough that I catch the scent of clean laundry and the slightest essence of sandalwood.

“What is it?” I ask.

“I’m trying to figure out how you climb down there.”

“Oh.” I follow his gaze. “It isn’t that difficult. It just takes a little practice.”

“Could you teach me?” His grey eyes appear dark in the waning light.

I feel a smile tug at my lips. “You’re not afraid of heights, are you?”

“No, only falling from them.” He wrinkles his nose at his own joke.

“Sure. I’ll show you sometime.” I swing my other leg out the window and turn so that my feet are perched on a protruding brick and my forearms are supported on the ledge next to Will’s.

“I’ll see you tomorrow, Kay.”

Looking up, I find myself face to face with him.

“How about an early start?” he says.

“Goodnight, Will.” I raise my eyebrows in mock horror before stepping backward and dropping out of sight.

chapter 9

I awake uncomfortably the next morning, feeling too warm with Lara's arm draped across my chest. I groan and slide out from under her, tiptoeing across the room and pulling my cleanest tunic on over my head. I am attempting to tie my hair back with a length of leather when I hear a soft sound. Lara has her head propped up with her arm on the mattress, regarding me.

"Off so early?" she mumbles sleepily, rubbing her eyes.

I walk back to the bed, sinking down next to her and handing over the strip of leather. She takes it from me and sits up, gently working my hair free of knots with her fingers.

"It isn't that early," I tease, "For those of us not accustomed to staying out all night."

"I suppose I'll have to get used to it." She yawns. "Gods, Kay, when was the last time you brushed this mess? You could have a whole colony living in here, for all you know."

"I've been busy."

"A lady is never too busy for a basic beauty routine," she scolds.

"Stop." I sigh. "You're starting to sound just like him."

"Like who?"

I bite my lip, unsure of what I should reveal to her.

"Ahh, yes." She reads my silence. "Your mysterious rebel. What's he like? He sounds handsome."

I laugh. "How can anyone *sound* handsome?"

"He's rich, isn't he? There is a recipe for attractiveness, if I've ever heard one." She's managed to separate my hair into three sections and is plaiting them together.

"If you think extreme seriousness and arrogance is attractive, then I'm sure you'd love him." I think of Will's squared jaw and thick brows. I suppose some people would consider him good-looking.

"And what else?" she asks.

"What do you mean?"

"Tell me more about him!"

"I don't know." I shift uncomfortably. "He's tall, he used to be a soldier. He's extremely controlling and thinks that he knows everything." I roll my eyes to the ceiling, pre-emptively annoyed at the thought of having to deal with Will's condescending attitude today.

"Sounds like a real piece of work." Lara finishes braiding my hair and ties it off, draping the end over my shoulder.

She watches me from the bed as I rise to fetch my belt. I affix it around my waist, grinning fondly at the sight of her with her brassy locks still messy from sleep.

I secure my knife and pouch in place and go to the window. "I'll see you later."

She offers me a small wave as I step outside and lift myself onto the roof. I have decided to forgo grabbing food at the market today, figuring I can eat whatever Will has lying around.

I make excellent time moving toward the centre of the City. The thought of Lara safe and secure in my bed with enough coins to keep us both fed inspires lightness in my limbs and I clear the alleyways effortlessly. In less than ten minutes, I land on the roof of Will's flat, taking a moment to stretch my arms over my head, basking in the warmth of the morning sun. I walk to the side of the building and lower myself down to the window, sticking my head inside in time to see Will cross in front of me, shirtless, rubbing his damp head with a towel.

I catch sight of his back and nearly choke on my inhale.

The taut skin is riddled with dozens of ugly, jagged scars. Some look years old and others are newer, standing out brightly from his tan. The marks stretch from his shoulders down the length of his back, disappearing into the waistband of his trousers.

“Good morning,” he greets me before I can find my voice.

“Hi,” I say, embarrassed to be caught staring.

To avoid his gaze, I slip through the window and walk to the kitchen, where I grab a slice of bread left out on the counter. I come back to the main area, my mouth full as I alternate between bites of bread and sips from a flask of water.

“Please, help yourself,” he says dryly. He reaches for a shirt draped over the arm of the couch and pulls his arms through the sleeves.

“I will, thank you.” I swallow what’s left in my mouth, sinking down into the chair opposite the couch; I stretch out my knee.

“Your hair is different today,” he says, taking me by surprise. “You look nice.”

“Oh. Thanks.” I absentmindedly grab the end of my braid and twirl it before I catch sight of my grubby fingernails; I tuck my hands at my sides. Next to Will in his clean linen shirt, I feel dirty and unkempt.

We sit in companionable silence for a few moments while I polish off the last of the bread and wash it down with the water.

“So, what’s the lesson for today?” I ask, dusting my hands free of crumbs.

“Your back-story,” he says. “Obviously, you can’t just turn up at the Palace out of the clear blue sky, so today we are going to establish your lineage.” He pokes through the pile of papers on the table, his nimble fingers searching until he extracts a folded piece of parchment. He unrolls the paper and turns it toward me.

I lean over the table and regard a series of names scribbled in old-fashioned cursive, with lines drawn to connect one name to another. There are dates written next to each name.

"It's a family tree," Will explains when my brow arches quizzically at him. "See, here we start with John Cain." He points to the name at the very top of the list, where the dates *17 A.B.* and *52 A.B.* are written.

"We only started keeping records after the Burn, everything before that was lost." His finger traces the line connecting John Cain to Margot Goode. "So, John married Margot in 43 A.B. and they had three children."

My eyes travel to the three names written below. Gradually, I can make out the growth of an expansive family. Names connecting, producing and dying. Entire lives summed up in dates of birth and death.

Will is pointing at a couple of names near the bottom right of the page. "See here, it says Justine Hunter and Martin Fellows. Those are your parents."

I squint at the cursive writing, reading the date of death as 205 A.B.—four years ago.

"They're dead?" I ask.

"Yes, and technically, so are you." His finger traces a line down to the words *Abby Fellows, b.190 A.B.*, with no date of death mentioned.

"I don't understand." I say.

"Abby Fellows died three years ago, while institutionalized," he explains. "She was orphaned and estranged from the family, but the care facility where she was living informed her one closest living relative of her passing." He gestures to the line connecting Abby's mother to the words *Shanyn Hunter b.160 A.B.—d. 207 A.B.* "Abby's aunt, my mother."

My eyes find the words *Will Cain b.185 A.B.*

"So, only your mother knew that Abby had died," I say slowly, looking up at him.

Will sits back on the couch, pulling on the sleeves of his shirt and rolling them up to his elbows. "My mother's mind was already beginning to slip at that point. My father kept her home and limited the amount of contact she had with her friends and family. As she became sicker, she became paranoid that all her thoughts and memories would be lost forever. She would write notes, obsessively. Whenever she thought of a secret or a piece of news, she would write it down immediately and pass me the scraps of paper. I must have had a whole book's worth by the time she died."

He speaks of his memories in a very matter-of-fact manner, which I find both unsettling and fascinating. I am brimming over with curiosity at the secrets Will's mother could have left, feeling enraptured by his story.

He finishes rolling up one of his sleeves and moves to the other, continuing his speech as though he were discussing a historical event rather than the passing of his mother. "After the funeral, I picked up her messages and began reading through them. One of the more interesting tidbits was that her niece, Abby, was dead. I had only very vague memories of Abby from when we were children. She and her parents moved to the Outer City and we didn't see them after that."

The Outer City is a smaller settlement just outside our City walls. It is ruled over by a snivelling lord and sports a common population that could rival our own. The uneasy sense of peace between our two cities exists largely because of the united front we must present against the savage Wastelanders. If Will's cousin, the unfortunate Abby Fellows, was a member of the Outer City's elite, then I can be sure she enjoyed a life of luxury, however brief.

"What happened to her?" I press.

"Her parents were killed during a raiders' attack and Abby was driven mad from the ordeal. She was committed to a care facility for a year and died by her own hand."

"That is so sad." I can't help but sympathize with this poor girl I never met. Even if she was a courtier, no one should have to witness the violent death of both their parents. It is no wonder that she became imbalanced.

"Sad, yes, but extremely convenient for us." Will's blasé attitude and apparent eagerness while he relates his story is worrying.

I store away this information, along with the fact that mental illness apparently runs in his family, for later analysis. This rich doctor/soldier/revolutionary having a screw loose would certainly explain a lot.

"Since no one was in contact with Abby, there will be no one questioning you when you turn up claiming to be her." He looks triumphant at the revelation. "We will simply say that you are my cousin, Abby Fellows, returned to the City." He leans back and lifts his leg so that his ankle rests on the opposite knee.

"That *is* convenient," I say, carefully. "But don't you think the King will have a problem with your mentally unstable cousin hanging about his daughter?"

"Yes, well, we will have to fudge some details on that point," he concedes. "We'll say you were away at the Outer City Academy, studying something-or-other. Abby's family was estranged from most of society; I doubt anyone knows where she was for those years after her parents died."

"I hope they don't." Internally, I admit his plan isn't half-bad. I rub my chin, thinking. "Now, I haven't been blessed with your vast knowledge of royal practices, but I am fairly certain you have to be pretty tight with the monarchy in order to waltz into the inner circle."

He grins. "Indeed, you do. I wouldn't say that myself and the King are particularly close, but my father used to be the King's chief physician. That, coupled with your natural charm and beauty, ought to be enough to get you in."

For a moment, I am stuck on his use of the phrase "charm and beauty" before my mind kicks back into gear and I realize that the disgusting man I pulled off the maid was the chief physician to the King.

"What?" Will asks.

"I didn't say anything."

"Your nose wrinkled. If this is another judgment toward me being a privileged courtier, that's fine, but you really should learn not to show so much expression. It's going to blow your cover before you get one foot through the gate."

I quickly relax my face, annoyed that I showed my distaste. Normally, I pride myself on being able to disguise my emotions.

"It's nothing. I was just wondering if we need to worry about your father seeing me traipsing around inside the Palace." I think back to Dr. Cain's pinched, furious expression when I threatened him.

"You don't need to worry about that." Will waves away my concern. "When I took over my father's role as Palace physician, I also saw to it that he was offered a cushy new opportunity in the Outer City. We won't be seeing him around."

"I hope not. I only had one encounter with him, but it was none too… pleasant." This time I manage to keep my face impassive.

"You don't need to be so gentle; I consider my father to be scum of the lowest calibre," Will says with the same callousness. "There is nothing offensive you can say about him that I haven't said to his face a thousand times."

"I'm sorry," I say, feeling awkward.

He sighs, running his hand over his head. "No, I'm sorry. I'm giving you a lot of unpleasant information about my family because I want you to have a thorough and honest back-story for your role."

"It's fine. I appreciate it." I give him a small smile.

He smiles back with the corner of his mouth. "With this messy lineage, you probably think I'm a lost cause."

"Oh, without question."

The other side of his mouth lifts up as he leans back over the table. He runs his hands over the family tree, rolling his shoulders to loosen them. "Then I shall count myself lucky that you've chosen to stay. Let's learn all these names, shall we?"

chapter 10

My stomach churns as I swing through Will's window. After a week of lessons, he has finally succumbed to my endless complaints about their tediousness and has promised that today will be a change of pace.

"Good morning." Will seems relaxed as he walks into the room, placing some salted meat and pieces of fruit on a plate for each of us.

I settle contentedly into my usual seat on the couch, accepting my breakfast when he hands it to me, being careful to chew slowly and carefully in a manner befitting a lady. Will nods his approval and lowers himself into the chair opposite, lifting his bare feet up onto the table between us.

We chew in companionable silence, each adrift in our own thoughts. I take the opportunity to study him, not for the first time noting the strong lines of his face and the pleasing darkness of his hair and brows.

"So." Will swallows the last of his food and puts his plate down on the table. "Are you ready for one of your most important lessons?"

"Definitely." I can only pray that it isn't memorizing more long lists of names.

"Don't look so nervous. I've arranged a surprise for you." A devilish half-smile tugs at his mouth.

"A surprise?" I exaggerate the wariness in my voice as I gather both of our plates and carry them to the kitchen. A knock on the door startles me and the dishes fall from my hands, striking the counter with a clatter.

"Ah, right on time!" Will crosses the room in two long strides while I edge toward the window.

In the weeks we have spent together, I have met a few of his co-conspirators in various taverns, but never once has one of Will's friends come to his flat. I was under the impression that he guards his privacy fiercely.

Will opens the door to reveal a beautiful woman nearly as tall as he is, with pin-straight black hair and wide-set features. He ushers her inside, pulling her into a warm hug as my heart thuds heavily for a beat.

The woman draws back from Will, a happy smile etched across her lovely face. "Hello, Will darling."

"Jules, thank you for coming."

I suddenly feel extremely dirty and unkempt, standing with the pair of them. She, poised in a long blue dress with a white silk scarf draped carelessly yet carefully against her tanned throat. He, the perfect gentlemen and gracious host. I tug on the hem of my worn and faded tunic as I fight to wipe the look of discomfort from my face.

"Kay, this is Jules," Will says, a bit formally while Jules extends her hand toward me.

"I am so pleased to finally meet you." Her eyes light up as I grip her palm, which is cool despite the heat outside.

"Nice to meet you, as well." I use my best courtier voice.

"Jules has kindly agreed to give us a hand today," Will explains, accepting her scarf when she hands it to him.

"Oh? That's great."

Jules chatters rapidly, "Yes, and I have to tell you that I could not be more excited. I mean, you are gorgeous." She kneels down and begins rummaging through a bag I hadn't noticed until now.

I struggle to formulate a response. "What?"

Will laughs at my discomfort and I shoot him a look.

"Your hair is so striking. It is going to compliment this dress perfectly." Jules brandishes a piece of emerald fabric and holds it up against my chest. "Yes, this is divine. Oh my gods, we are going to have so much fun!" she fairly squeals, and I find myself wincing.

"I daresay you are in extremely good hands," Will says from his vantage point, comfortably reclined against a door frame. "My sister is one of the most stylish ladies you are ever likely to meet."

"Your sister." I struggle to make sense of the situation as Jules stuffs the green garment back into her bag and turns back to me, grabbing my hand and pulling me gently toward the window ledge.

She sits me down and begins arranging strands of hair around my face. The familiarity of the contact reminds me of Lara, and my heart hammers heavily in my chest.

"Honestly, your hair is your greatest asset. We are going to work with this. I want to cut it, but don't worry, I won't be taking too much off. We just need to tidy you up and show you some style tricks," Jules twitters ceaselessly as she turns my head this way and that.

"All right." Completely out of my element, I follow her suggestions without argument.

"Will," Jules calls across the room. "Do you really need to be here for this?"

"Fortunately, no. I have some patients to tend to, today." Will straightens and grabs a vest from the hook by the door, shrugging it on over his shoulders before he takes up his satchel and medical case.

"You ladies have fun." He throws me a wink.

I stare helplessly after him while Jules fusses with my hair between her fingers.

"Bye, darling!" Jules doesn't even look over her shoulder as the door slams shut.

"Right," she says, dropping my hair and patting my knee resolutely. "First things first. Let's draw you a bath."

Some time later, my hair dries on my shoulders while I sit on the cold washroom floor. Jules has given me a silk robe to wear and I am worrying the material between my fingers while she prepares a concoction by the sink.

“What is that?” I ask, trying to peer around her.

“Wax,” she says lightly.

“Oh.” What is that meant for? Must be something to do with candles.

Jules comes to kneel down next to me, a small square of fabric held in her hand. She applies the cloth to the spot above my eyebrow and presses firmly while I flinch from an unexpected heat.

“There is one thing to remember when it comes to maintenance of oneself,” she says sombrely.

“What is that?”

All at once she rips the fabric away, tearing my skin painfully. I gasp, my hand flying to my face as surprised tears gather in my eye.

“Beauty is pain. Move your hand, please. We’re not through yet.”

I fight back the curses pooling in my mouth as she works efficiently, moving from one eyebrow to the other. After an eternity, she declares herself done and I breathe a sigh of relief.

“Oh, thank gods.” I make to stand up, my brows feeling aflame.

“No, no. Not just yet. I’m done your face, but we have to clean up some other areas.” She has busied herself again with the pot of wax.

“Like what?” I ask slowly, my eyes darting to the open door.

“Underarms, legs,” she says indifferently. “And between them.”

I clench my thighs together. “Uh uh. No way.”

She sighs as she turns to face me. I note that the piece of cloth in her hand is worryingly larger than the one she used on my eyebrows. “It’s unpleasant, I know, but we women are strong and can bear it.”

"I don't think so." I try to scoot backward, but my back is pressed against the tub. "I've experienced some pain in my time, but I will not willingly submit to this."

"Oh, don't be such a baby." Her usually chipper voice is impatient. "Look, the most prissy noble girl goes through this all the time. Are you saying that you can't handle something that those little princesses can?"

She's got me there.

"Has Will been coaching you on how to get me to go along with things?" I ask.

She giggles as she slaps the fabric down on my shin, a little too gleefully. "He may have given me a few tips. Now, stay still."

The material is ripped away suddenly and the most obscene curse falls from my mouth.

"There we are. Not so bad, is it?"

The next twenty minutes pass as the most painful of my life. The fact that rich girls go through this process willingly serves only to cement my feelings that the whole lot of them are completely mad.

"All done!" Jules' cheerful voice is suddenly the most welcome thing I have ever heard. "All that's left is to make a rug out of what we pulled." She laughs at my horrified expression, offering a hand to pull me to my feet. "I'm kidding. Did you really think I would do that?"

"You just pulled half the hair out of my body; I don't know what you're capable of." I hobble after her toward the main room.

Jules gestures for me to sit on the window ledge and turns to rummage through her bag. I run my hand up and down my leg, marvelling at the oddly pleasant sensation.

Jules approaches with a pair of fine-tipped scissors. She gathers a few strands of my hair at a time and begins snipping away, locks of red curls falling between her feet.

"Your hair really is lovely," she says sociably as I stare out the window at the people crossing below. "Does your mother have hair like this?"

"Yes, she did," I say evenly.

"Oh, I'm sorry. She's gone?"

"Yes."

"That's terrible." She tuts. "Will and I lost our mother as well."

"He told me about that. I'm sorry."

The sound of the scissors ceases abruptly. "He told you?" Surprise laces her voice.

"Yes. Why? Is that strange?"

The snipping resumes. "A little. Will doesn't usually like to talk about our family. He can be very closed off."

"No kidding."

"How did your mother die?" Her question startles me. My shoulders must have stiffened because she stops cutting again and apologizes. "Sorry, that was rude of me. Will always says that I'm too blunt."

"It's fine," I say. "She was killed."

"How awful! I can't even imagine. Were you very young when it happened?"

"I was fourteen." I abruptly change the subject. "How did your mother die?"

"She got sick. It was about… two years ago now? I was only fifteen when it happened. Will was twenty-two." She puts the scissors down and combs through my hair with her fingers, separating it into sections. "The thing of it is, I think she was glad to go. She was a gentle soul saddled with such hardships… her heart just couldn't hold out." She sighs.

"I'm so sorry," I say carefully, completely perplexed about how a courtier's life could be considered difficult. I am brimming with questions about

Will's past but am mindful of overstepping my boundaries. Luckily, Jules is happy to chatter away. I suppose there are no secrets between two people who have just shared a leg waxing.

"It was mostly my father's doing. He would bring all sorts of women home, flaunting them right in front of her. Can you imagine? And then there was the way he treated Will. My mother couldn't bear to see it." Jules sighs.

"He was unkind to Will?"

"Unkind is putting it mildly," she scoffs. "He was downright cruel. My brother has always had his own ideas. My mother would say he is spirited, but for my father, Will was a problem."

I try to imagine tall, bristly Will as a young boy. I wouldn't envy anyone the task of trying to curtail his behaviour.

"Will and my father clashed constantly," Jules continues. "I'm sure Will still bears the scars from my father's punishments. They quarrelled over Father's wishes that Will apprentice as a physician, but my brother couldn't have wanted less to do with that idea. As soon as he turned eighteen, he enlisted in the King's guard. That infuriated my father. Will knew it would."

My heart lurches in my chest, thinking of the marks littering Will's back. I never imagined that something so heinous could be inflicted by his own father. It's no wonder he's so closed off.

"Poor Will," I murmur.

"Poor Will," she agrees. "Though, that's not to say he was any angel. He was never at home, forever wandering the City with his snobby, idle friends. More than once, I caught my mother dragging him up the stairs. He would reek of booze and opium. Not a pretty sight." She shakes her head. "He straightened out after serving a year in the guard, but there were some ugly times before."

"For how long was he in the guard?" I ask.

"Around a year, I think? Yes, that's about right. I remember he switched over to the military quite abruptly and spent a further three years in the Wastelands."

As unusual as it is for a courtier to fight in the Wastelands, it is even more rare for one to willingly serve a full three years. They don't need the money the way a common soldier would, and they have the option of buying their way out of service. Will must have been extremely determined to avoid his father.

"He returned home when my mother became sick." Jules becomes more subdued. "They had a very special bond, you know. It must have been so difficult for him, taking care of her after she had spent so much time tending to him during his late-night benders. He really did everything he could to help her get better.

"It was strange, having Will home again after so long." She sighs. "He was different. I thought that perhaps something drastic had happened to him out in the Wastelands because suddenly, all his priorities had changed and he was less of a loose cannon. He and my father are on civil terms, now. Will trained in medicine during his service and just recently took over my father's job as Palace physician. My father thinks that Will is finally settling into his role, but I know better." Leaning over my shoulder, Jules talks into my ear conspiratorially. "I said to myself, this whole act with Father must be a ruse in order to keep the old man out of his business. That means that Will must be planning something big. So, when Will told me what was really going on and that he had sought you out, I wasn't the least bit surprised!" Her voice rises in triumph and I flinch.

"Right," I hear myself say. I am reeling from the boatload of information. For all the time I have spent with Will, it turns out I barely know him at all.

"I have to say, I think you are really brave for agreeing to go through with this scheme of his." Jules has finished combing my hair and is now twisting the sections around one another, pulling the locks back from my face.

"Thanks." I'm not entirely sure I should take that as a compliment. "I think you are brave for ripping the hair out of your legs on purpose."

Jules laughs and I notice that it sounds remarkably like her brother's. She loops the heavy braid over my shoulder, lashing a knot at the bottom with a thin band.

"There." She moves to stand in front of me and pulls a couple of strands loose from my braid, framing my face. "You look lovely."

I move my hands to stroke the smoothed locks as she pulls a charcoal pen out of her bag.

"We'll keep your makeup simple," she says. "I suspect you don't have a lot of experience wearing it?"

"I… no," I say honestly.

"That's fine. Kohl is simple to use and it's really all you need for those green eyes of yours. Now, close them."

I shut my eyes obediently and she draws lightly around my lash line, using her finger to smudge the colour.

"Can I look?" I ask, opening my eyes.

"Not yet! We need to find an outfit first." She goes back to her bag and draws out the swath of green fabric from earlier. "Here, put this on."

She helps me out of my robe and into the dress, guiding my arms through the lightweight material. The dress folds in layers but feels incredibly breezy. I revel in the feeling of the soft cloth brushing against my newly bare legs.

Jules stands back as I fuss with the fabric, unable to stop fidgeting.

"All right, you can look now." She grabs my hand and pulls me toward Will's bedroom, spinning me around to face a mirror leaning up against the wall. "What do you think?"

I barely hear her, so dumbfounded by the sight of a stranger staring back at me. The bright colour of the dress is striking; the quality of the material a world's difference from my patched tunics. Its long skirt pools around my feet and the straps dip into a V shape, gathering in an empire waist and complimenting my modest cleavage. My hair appears lush and healthy, draped over my shoulder in a thick braid, and the kohl lining my eyes makes me appear at once sultry and mysterious.

"I look… different," I say, finally.

Jules laughs and playfully swats at my hands as I tug on the neck of the dress, attempting to cover myself.

"You were always stunning," she says sincerely, gently tugging my shoulders back so that I stand up straight. "The clothes and makeup are just ornamentation." Her reflection shoots me a wink and then she sweeps from the room.

I allow myself to linger for a few moments longer before following her out.

I find her hovering over the low table, fussing with an unfamiliar wooden box. She winds a key hidden underneath it and the lid pops open, allowing a tinkling melody to escape.

"A music box," she explains, catching sight of my puzzled expression. "It was my mother's." She begins to sway from side to side, in tune with the music. "Have you danced before?"

"Yes, of course," I say, a bit defensively, thinking back to rowdy nights spent at the Beacon with Harry, Lara and Edmun.

"Then this should be quite easy for you to pick up."

I help Jules drag the chair and table to the side of the room. Once we've cleared some space she spreads her arms, inviting me forward.

"Here, I'll lead."

I chuckle as I step up to her, lacing my fingers with hers. She directs my free hand to her shoulder and grips my waist. "And one, two, three…"

We spin around the room in time to the music. I stumble repeatedly on the hem of my dress, each time releasing a crude curse. Jules winces when I tread on her foot.

"Sorry, sorry!" I step back, letting go of her to readjust my skirt, grimacing in frustration. I hear a key turn in the door behind me as I fuss with the folds of fabric.

"Oh, thank the gods. I don't think my poor feet could take much more abuse. Will, come over here." Jules grabs my shoulders and spins me around to face him.

His reaction causes heat to gather in my cheeks. Will remains frozen by the door, his brows raised as he takes in my appearance. I fiddle self-consciously with my braid, willing the blush away from my face.

"Well, I'll be damned." He grins, rubbing his hand over the stubble on his chin. "Kay, you look beautiful."

"Thanks." I give a small shrug and raise my chin in an effort to appear more confident than I feel.

"I'm trying to teach her to dance, but we're having some trouble." Jules picks up the music box and winds the key again, resetting the tune. "Would you mind…?"

"Certainly."

He sets his satchel down by the door and crosses the room in two long strides. Within the space of a few moments he has expertly lifted my arms into position, his palm engulfing my own while my other hand rests on his broad shoulder. I glance up at him, trying to ignore the sudden sensation of warmth at my waist.

"Kay, don't look down. Let him lead. And one, two..." Jules counts us off, clapping her hands.

I concentrate fiercely as I step in time with Will's movements, falling into a natural synchronicity. Will is firm but gentle as he guides me across the small space. I stumble once or twice, but each time he holds me securely, helping me right myself when I falter. By the time the music box's trilling melody has wound itself down, we are twirling together in perfect rhythm.

"Much better!" Jules' voice breaks through my thoughts and I drop my hand from Will's grip. I take a step back, forcing myself free of the spell woven by the music.

He blinks, watching me with a furrowed brow before he gives me a small, approving nod and turns to disappear into the kitchen. I glance at Jules but she has already moved back to the music box; she snaps the lid shut and places it back into her bag, humming a little to herself. I stand awkwardly, smoothing the nonexistent wrinkles in my expensive gown, and look up when Will returns.

"So," I say, forcing some ladylike haughtiness into my tone. "Am I finally ready? Are you going to arrange for my interview at the Palace?"

Will looks up from where he's busied himself setting plates and silverware at the rickety table. "I don't think so, Kay. You look the part, but there's still a lot I have to teach you."

Annoyance prickles my nerves. "More names and manners? Don't you trust that I have enough sense to figure it out once I get there?"

He meets my gaze head on, unwavering. "It isn't a matter of trust. The Court is a dangerous place and we're only going to get one shot at it; I want to prepare you as much as possible."

Behind me, Jules has ceased her humming and has gone quiet as a mouse.

I grit my teeth, and when I speak, my voice is low. "We shouldn't waste time."

"We shouldn't waste this opportunity." Will is infuriatingly calm. "Patience, Kay—you're making amazing progress, but we don't want to get ahead of ourselves. We'll have Jules come back a few more times to help you with your clothes and makeup, and I'll fill in the gaps about Palace customs. When it comes time for your interview, you'll ace it."

I inhale through my nose, drawing my shoulders back the way Jules taught me. I just have to last a few more days, put up with a few more tedious lessons, and then I can get back to what really matters: helping the commoners. Once I get into the Palace I'll be able to make a real difference.

Patience, Kay. Focus on the bigger picture.

"You had best change out of that dress," Will continues. "I'm going to get us all some dinner and I know how the crumbs fly when it comes to you." He nudges me lightly on his way back to the kitchen.

"Come now," I say in mock offence. "When I am dressed as a lady, I eat as a lady."

That half-grin. "You will have ample opportunity to eat as a lady once we get to the Palace. Tonight, I want to share a meal with Kay."

chapter 11

I reach my limit precisely two weeks later.

"*Enough!*" I cry, throwing the papers to the ground and stomping over to the window. I rub my face in an attempt to alleviate my pulsing headache and mounting frustration.

I can hear Will's exasperated sigh from across the room, the chair shifting under his weight.

My fingers catch in my tangled hair, which only adds to my irritation. The weeks spent cooped up in this stuffy flat, poring over old texts and being drilled on customs and protocols, have tested what little patience I possess. My brain is filled to the brim with useless gossip about insipid people and I feel that if I were to try and squeeze in one more name, one more fact, I might explode.

I draw a shaky breath, listening as Will rises from his chair and crosses the room. The thought of him being anywhere near me sends another dull throb through my brow and I seriously consider shoving him out the window. I save us both the trouble and instead step out onto the ledge, turning and pulling myself onto the roof in one smooth motion.

"Kay!"

Ignoring Will's shouts, I sink down into a seated position and dangle my legs over the side of the building. I bask in the feeling of open space and the warm sunlight on my extremities. The fresh air is invigorating after the claustrophobia of the cramped flat.

"*Kay*," he yells again, more sternly.

I lean over the edge and see his head sticking out the window, staring up at me with his lips pressed tightly together.

"What?" I ask. I remain calm, knowing it will make him furious.

"This is ridiculous. Come back inside." His voice is low, bordering on dangerous.

I lean back again and stretch my toes straight out over the street. "Actually, I think I'm fine right here. Thanks for the invitation, though."

There is silence below me and I smile, picturing him struggling to control his temper. Let him stew for a change, the arrogant twit.

"Kay." Will's voice is controlled, which only prickles my annoyance. "Please, come inside. We'll take a break and get back to this lesson later."

It infuriates me when he pulls this trick, acting like he has complete authority while I am the confused fish-out-of-water who has to lean on him for direction. Not this time.

"Sorry, I can't hear you so well," I call, lightly. "If you have anything you would like to say to me, you are more than welcome to come up and say it to my face." I fall backward and rest my shoulders against the roof, closing my eyes against the sun's glare.

Minutes pass and I assume he has gone back inside. I take slow, even breaths as I warm myself in the sunlight, savouring these precious moments of peace.

Will's nerve is absolutely astounding. The thoroughness at which he approaches our lessons is relentless and shows a complete lack of trust in me. He has no faith in my own natural abilities and doesn't put any stock in the fact that I have been successfully slipping in and out of the Court for years. These thoughts start my blood boiling again and my hands clench into fists at my sides, gathering dust from the roof between my fingers.

I start at the sound of scuffling from below me. I sit up on my elbows and listen carefully, trying to decipher the noises.

A large hand suddenly appears and grips the ledge next to my knees, followed by another. Will's scruffy head comes into view as he lifts himself over the ledge using his forearms as leverage. I can't help but let out a snort of derision when he flops awkwardly onto his stomach, then rises to his knees, revealing streaks of dirt and dust all over the front of his otherwise pristine white shirt.

For gods' sake. The man has absolutely no concept of boundaries.

"Graceful," I say, dryly.

He shoots me a look of contempt and rotates so that his long legs dangle alongside mine. I notice that his shirt has dampened between his shoulder blades and around his neck and for a moment picture the ugly scars hiding beneath the fabric. My resolve wavers. Slightly.

I refuse to be the first one to speak. I'm impressed that he managed to drag himself up here, but I won't give him the satisfaction of knowing that. From the corner of my eye I can see Will attempting to brush the dirt from his clothes, succeeding only in smearing it. I don't bother to hide my satisfaction, my smile widening when he glances up and his brow furrows further.

"Find this funny, do you?" Indignation is clear in his voice.

I shrug, refusing to look at him and instead focusing my gaze on the street below us.

"What is it? Are you not speaking to me at all, now?"

I groan. "I came up here to get *away* from you. Can't you take a hint?" My fingers are digging into the dust below me again.

"I know that you're frustrated, Kay, but we are running out of time and there is so much left to—"

"*Stop it.*" Can't he hear himself? "I've got it, Will. Really. I know all the names, the dates, the rules, the protocols, and anything that I don't know, I will just handle when the time comes. Let's get started already: we're wasting time, and Lara—" I stop myself.

"Who?" he asks.

"People are depending on me. I need to get into the Palace and begin work." I purposefully neglect to mention my plan to pilfer some shiny Palace goods while I'm there. "Every moment you spend teaching me the correct pronunciation of some disgusting exotic dish is another moment that the commoners are suffering. How can you not see that?"

I finally turn to look at him, hoping to see some trace of understanding. His grey eyes betray nothing.

"You need to trust me," I say, with all the patience I can muster. "I've trusted you. You show up out of nowhere, drag me off a wall and give me this lovely, impassioned speech about changing the world. You've asked everything of me and I've done it all. You said that we are on the same side, but you don't have any faith in me." My jaw is clenched and I rub my neck to alleviate some of the tension.

Will releases a puff of air between his teeth. I tear my eyes away from his mouth and stare back into the street, drawing my knees up to my chest.

"It isn't that I don't trust in you," he says, eventually. "I do. I've seen what you're capable of, how smart and resourceful you are. It's just…"

I wait for him to finish his thought. When he doesn't, I turn my head and look at him, placing my cheek on my knees. He is running his hand over his coarse hair, avoiding my gaze.

"You're scared," I say, matter of factly.

"That isn't it." He's quick to answer.

"You're scared that this won't work."

"It *has* to work."

I detect a note of desperation in his voice and the hair on the back of my neck prickles, despite the heat. In the weeks I've known him, Will has been nothing but calm and collected. The slight shift in mood has my instincts ringing with warning.

"There's something you're not telling me," I accuse.

A low growl sounds from his throat and I know that I've caught him.

Anger clenches at my stomach again and I fight to keep my voice low and measured. "What is it?"

Both of his hands are on his head now, a very un-Will-like gesture.

"*Will,*" I command.

"The City is closer to a full-out attack by the Wastelanders than anyone realizes." He drops his hands and finally turns to look at me fully.

Confusion must be etched across my face because he continues quickly. "This war is completely out of control. The King keeps sending our troops into the desert, but our soldiers and airships are brought down faster by the Wastelanders than we can manage. The Wasters are angry and, worse than that, they're organized."

I blink uncomprehendingly. Our war with the Wastelanders, those ungoverned tribes living roughshod in the desert, began as a battle over precious resources. In recent years, however, the battles have escalated, with more and more of our people being sent into their territory. The tactics and weapons used in the Wastelands are relatively unknown but devastating enough that few of our troops return home. I revere the Wastelanders as adept fighters but always assumed that our superior wealth and technology would win out eventually.

Perhaps I was wrong.

"Organized?" I grapple for the last word I recall him saying. "How do you know that?"

"I was there." His eyes burn into mine. "I've fought them; I've witnessed what they're capable of. I've seen the way they seek each other out and band together. It's only a matter of time before they come to our gates and finish us off."

"Why didn't you tell me?"

He shakes his head. "I should have."

"Then why didn't you?"

"I didn't know how you'd react. Bringing down the monarchy is one thing, but trying to end a war is something else entirely."

I bury my dusty hands in my hair. "What in the eternal *Burn*, Will."

"I know."

"I mean, were you planning on keeping this a secret from me and then acting surprised when they turned up at our gates?"

"No, I just didn't want to put too much on your shoulders. I didn't want to start a panic."

I want to slap him across the face.

"What is with this ridiculous, controlling complex you have?" I don't recall ever being this angry before. "You have to know everything, but everyone else must remain in the dark. You don't trust anyone but yourself. We are trying to do something incredibly dangerous, I am risking my godsforsaken *life* over here, and meanwhile you are playing your own little game, not letting anyone else in. What is wrong with you? What happened to you to make you this way?" I stare at him, my chest heaving.

The look on his face changes in an instant from shock to fury. I half-expect him to react in his usual calm manner, but instead the air prickles with electricity as he leans in toward me.

"You don't know a gods-damn *thing* about me," he hisses. "You have been nothing but self-righteous and entitled since I met you, questioning everything I say and do. *I* have trust issues? You'd better take a good, hard look at yourself."

I get to my feet and he does the same. The fact that he towers a head above me doesn't intimidate me in the slightest.

"You spoiled, selfish, *prat*." I jab my finger in his chest to emphasize each point. "You sit around, conversing with rich, idealistic thespians, hatching your grand schemes of saving us all from oppression, when you don't have a sense of what it is to suffer. You've never gone hungry, had your home taken away, had your friends shipped off to die in the Wastelands so that their family could use their pension to survive. You don't know what it is to watch everyone around you agonize over how they will live until tomorrow. I've been there. Every day, I see it."

He grabs my wrists to keep me from hitting him and I struggle in his grip.

"If you would—for just a *second*—look past the issues in your district, then you might get an idea of the real scope of this rebellion. You want change? How about you start with yourself." He holds my wrists easily as I thrash.

"Let *go*." I'm going to punch him in that stupid, unshaven jaw.

"No. You can listen for once. You think that I don't know suffering? I've seen men's faces torn from their heads. I've seen young, healthy people literally blown into pieces and scattered." I stop pulling my arms and stare at him. "I've been down there, in the desert, trying to save people for *hours* when I know they're going to die. And all for a cause none of us believe in. I've sat at state dinners, listening to the King and his followers talk casually about their latest weapons and tactics, how they plan to ship more commoners into the Wastelands, completely oblivious to the fact that they are merely placing a bandage over a fatal wound. I've kept my mouth shut, been patient, seethed, planned for *years*, waiting for just the right moment." His grip tightens. "Then I met you and I felt that finally, we had a chance."

"What is it that you want, Will? Do you want to end the war, kill the King, or abolish the sectors? You can't do it all. You're only one person."

"We're stronger together," he says. "You have the ear of the commoners, I have the ear of the soldiers. Together, we can unite everyone and build a new City, a stronger, better place."

I shake my head. "It's too much."

He draws me closer to him. "We have to try."

I can feel his heart pulsing furiously beneath his chest, every nerve tensed while his presence encompasses me. He truly believes that two people standing on a rooftop can make a difference and, for just a moment, I believe him.

chapter 12

The dust kicks and swirls around us as we stand frozen in place, Will's grip sending an unexpected heat through my entire body. His jaw clenches as he stares at me, his unsettled eyes boring into mine.

He drops my hands abruptly and steps back, a strange expression marring his dark features. Oh gods, I can't think straight. I look over my shoulder and out onto the roof of the next building, suddenly feeling the urge to distance myself. Out of habit, I calculate the speed and the amount of momentum it would take to clear the distance. The old trick clears my mind and I am able to turn back to Will, swallowing once.

"Do you still want to learn how to run?" I ask.

He seems a little taken aback by the change in subject. "Not if you're suggesting we jump that gap you're eyeing."

"I suppose that is a little advanced. What say we try something more elementary?" I stride past him, moving so that I am standing over a narrow and seldom-travelled alleyway. "How does this suit your fancy?"

He joins me at the ledge and peers down into the street. "It seems higher, suddenly."

I crack a smile, "It's best to start out at a dangerous height."

"Why is that?"

"The bigger the risk, the greater the reward."

He glances in my direction, a strange look darkening his eyes. I ignore the nervous fluttering in my stomach and instead take a few steps backward, motioning for him to do the same.

"Now, unlike princess training, there is only one lesson in running." I scuff my booted feet on the roof, getting a feel for the looseness of the sand littering the surface.

"Avoid tripping?"

"That's on you—I will not be held responsible for your giant feet. What I was going to say is that you only need to believe you've already completed the jump."

"I don't think I follow." Will shuffles in place, awkwardly copying my movements.

"If you think for even a moment that you might fall, then you almost certainly will. The best thing to do is to trick yourself into believing that you've already made it." I make a show of stretching out my arms and legs, pressing my lips together to suppress a smile when he does the same.

"Fake it 'til you make it," he mutters doubtfully.

"You've got it." I grin.

"I'm beginning to understand where you get that ridiculous self-confidence from."

"Not only my good looks. Now, pay attention. You don't need to run fast, just look at your target, visualize yourself making a beautiful leap and do what comes naturally."

"What kind of lesson is this? How about you telling me something technical, like where I should place my feet?" There is a trace of panic in his voice and I pray fervently that I am not sending this tightly wound boy to his doom.

Although, the peace might be nice.

"Sorry, young William, this is one skill that can't be learned from a book. I guess you'll just have to trust me."

I wrinkle my nose at him before I dash off toward the ledge. An instant later I leap, sailing through the air and suspending weightlessly for a few precious moments before crouching into my landing.

I straighten and dust the sand from my hands, turning back to look across the narrow gap. Will remains stock still, his face noticeably paler.

"Come on, you've made this jump hundreds of times," I call over. "Don't doubt yourself!"

His jaw sets and he takes off running. I half-expect him to falter at the last second, but his stride remains sure and strong until he jumps and sails over the alley. As he lands, I extend a hand to help him to his feet, the wide smile on my lips echoing his. There is a wildness in his eyes that I haven't seen before.

"That was fantastic!" I praise him.

The rush of adrenalin causes him to bounce in place. "I have to say, your teaching method might be a bit unusual, but it sure as hell is effective."

"Fake it 'til you make it," I tease, jogging lightly toward the next rooftop. I slow my pace just enough for Will to fall into step beside me. "Are you ready for something a little bigger?"

We stop at the next edge and peer over. I allow Will a few moments to process the slightly wider gap.

"Right. This time, keep running and we'll jump a few roofs consecutively." I walk back a couple of paces and prepare my stance.

"How do you know there won't be something too wide for us to jump across?" Nervousness dots his features.

"I'm familiar with this area."

"Familiar enough to keep me from splattering on the ground?"

"Listen, you might be the expert when it comes to royal intrigue and stuffy parlours, but the roofs are my domain." I sneak a look at him. "You make sure I'm safe from any Palace guards, and I'll keep you airborne."

I don't wait for his response, instead suddenly sprinting across the roof. Will utters a curse but dutifully takes off after me.

I plant my foot on the ledge and push out across the gap, landing lightly and immediately running again. I hear Will hit the surface behind me a few seconds later and I allow myself to relax, gradually falling into my natural rhythm.

The air feels cool against my skin as we leap together from rooftop to rooftop, no sound between us but the synchronized pounding of our feet on the dusty stone. Running has always been a solitary experience and the feeling of someone running *with* me instead of *after* me is both bizarre and strangely harmonious.

I finally draw to a stop, falling backward a step to allow space for Will to land. I push the loosened curls back up off my forehead as he straightens, his chest rising and falling from exertion.

"Fun, isn't it?" I ask.

"It's unlike anything else," he says earnestly. The man before me is completely unlike the one I left behind in the cramped flat, grimly intent as he hunched over a pile of books.

My shoulders unconsciously loosen as I release the anger from earlier, wiped away by the pure exhilaration of running.

I know Will has felt the change as well. He rolls his head back to the sky and shuts his eyes against the sun. He opens them and notices me watching him. I don't look away immediately and am rewarded with the half-grin twitching up against his cheek.

"You really have something special here, Runner," he says. "Thank you for sharing it with me."

"It was my pleasure," I tell him. "I'm just happy you were able to keep up." I incline my head over my shoulder, directing his gaze toward the view.

In the distance, an impressive structure rises up against the desert backdrop. The enormous glass spire of the Palace looms over the shorter buildings surrounding it, reflecting the dying rays of the sun.

"It does look beautiful from here," he says.

"Everything always looks better from a distance," I reply tonelessly, sinking down onto the ledge and squinting against the glare cast by the Palace.

Will sits down next to me, wiping his forehead with his wrist.

"So, do you feel ready?" he asks after a spell.

"Yes," I reply with finality.

He nods, bringing his gaze back to the view. "I'm sorry that I'm so tough on you."

I'm so taken aback by his apology that I forget to form a cheeky reply. "It's all right. You're a good teacher." I mean the words.

"So are you."

We sit in silence for a few minutes, watching the sky's ever-changing colours as the sun continues its descent. The rays dance across Will's features, softening his intense gaze and causing me to wonder what manner of boy he was before he entered the Wastelands.

Will rubs his palms on the top of his knees. "You're ready," he declares. "We shouldn't wait any longer to get you into the Palace. Anything that I neglected to teach you, well…" His gaze meets mine. "I suppose you'll just have to fake it 'til you make it."

"That's what I do best."

"Tomorrow, then," he says. "One last debrief at my flat and then we're going in."

"Sounds good to me." My heart flutters nervously in my chest. I straighten my shoulders and try to imagine what the royals are doing at this moment. Gauging the hour, I assume they are just sitting down to dinner in the Great Hall, trading gossip with the gathered nobles and eating rich mouthfuls of food off silver cutlery. My mouth waters at the thought.

"You'll have to teach me how to climb down." Will's voice cuts through my thoughts and I look over to see him peering down to the ground below, his hands gripping the ledge tightly.

"It's just like using a ladder," I muse as I decipher a safe course down to the street. "Only imagine that the rungs are windows and bricks."

"Windows and bricks," he mutters under his breath as he considers the side of the building.

"Do you know if there's any decent food around here?" I ask.

“What? Oh. There’s a tavern just over there.” He motions down the alley.

“Great.” I turn and lower myself over the ledge, my hands and feet gripping the various notches as I gradually work my way toward the street below.

I glance back up once, laughing at the sight of Will’s worried expression and white-knuckled grip on the roof’s ledge.

“Come on!” I call encouragingly. “I’m going to need you to buy supper.”

chapter 13

The following day, I sit with Will and Jules in Will's flat, my head aching from hours of regurgitating information. After nearly a month of learning customs, manners, names and history, there is nary a detail that I can't recall at the drop of a hat. As Will paces before us, I reach up a hand to touch the elaborate hairstyle I put together under Jules' supervision. Despite my complaints, I'm grateful to the Cains for all the work they've put into making sure I can pass myself off as a courtier. The skills I've learned in this shoddy flat may prove useless out on the streets, but Will has promised they'll be akin to an arsenal of weapons within the Court.

Will finally ceases his pacing, running a hand over his close-cropped hair before he sinks down into his usual place on the couch opposite. "We should go over the plan for tomorrow."

I suppress a sigh, twisting my hands nervously in my lap. "Go on, then."

"Kay, you will meet us here first thing tomorrow morning. Jules will be helping you get dressed and I have a carriage coming by to pick us up." Will transitions seamlessly from instructor to drill sergeant, his voice clipped and his gaze intense.

I nod my understanding. For once, his bossiness doesn't annoy me. Tomorrow I will be completely out of my depth and am more than willing to accept any offer of assistance.

"I have arranged an interview with the Princess' chief of staff. If she is satisfied with you—and she will be—then you will be brought straight into the ladies' quarters. I expect they will have some questions about your history and lineage." He speaks calmly, but I can sense the underlying tension. "Do you remember everything?"

"Yes." I recite confidently: "I am your cousin, Abby Fellows. After the tragic death of my parents, I spent a year living in a care facility, before moving on to study pre-Burn literature at the Outer City Academy."

"Perfect." Will nods his approval. "I have taken the liberty of having a friend forge your certification and release papers, so if anyone looks into your background, we'll have you covered."

"Good." I release a breath. "Is that everything? Any more last-minute lessons?"

"No, you're ready." His grey eyes search my face. "You have nothing to worry about. I'm going to be right there with you the entire time."

"Until they accept me," I remind him.

"I'll still be in the Palace. You can't get rid of me so easily." He sits back, raising his eyebrows. "Sorry to burst your bubble."

"You'll do wonderfully." Jules pats my leg. "The Princess' entourage is just a bunch of shallow kiss-ups, anyway. No one will suspect anything is amiss about you."

I know I couldn't be more different from those Palace nobles, but Jules sounds so certain that I find myself relaxing, ever so slightly.

After a warm dinner and several more forced recitations of tomorrow's plans, I manage to slip free of Will's apartment and run along the roofs to the depths of the Commons. My jog is slower than usual, with only the moonlight and my memory to direct me on a safe route.

I pause on the roof of the Beacon, ruffling my hair loose from its braid and smearing the leftover makeup around my eyes before I drop down onto the street and swing through the door.

The air inside the pub is thick with smoke and I have to blink to focus my vision in the dim light. No sooner have I gathered my bearings than a familiar, beefy arm is draped around my neck.

"There she is!" Harry's inebriated voice bellows in my ear.

I shove him aside playfully. "Get off, you giant oaf—you're spilling ale all over me."

"Apologies, allow me to make amends. Samus!" he shouts over his shoulder. "A draft for our Kay, please! Now, tell me where you've been, girl. My cart has been piled too high lately without your sticky fingers clawing at it."

I laugh, grabbing my tankard off the bar and taking a healthy sip. "Here and there, Harry. I'm always about. If I had known you would miss me so much, I would have made a point of robbing you blind."

"Aye, no doubt you would have, you common thief." He claps my shoulder hard enough that I sputter on my drink. "The lads are all this way. Come on!"

Harry's large figure clears an easy path, leading me to the back of the room. Our usual table is surrounded by people, Edmun and Lara among them. I release an internal sigh of relief when I find Gordy missing.

"Hey-o, boys! And my lady." Harry makes an attempt at bowing to Lara and I reach out a hand to steady him. "Looky here who I found!"

"Kay, darling! Come sit by me." Lara motions for the man next to her to move out of the way. He grumbles, reluctantly giving up his seat.

"Comrades," I say formally as Lara wraps her skinny arms around my neck and gives me a hug.

"Kay-kay! I was wondering if you would ever be gracing us with your presence again!" Edmun has his arm around a diminutive woman with garishly painted red lips.

"I figured your ugly faces could benefit from the company of at least one beauty, so I decided to stop in," I reply.

Edmun and I clank our tankards together while Edmun's girl purses her mouth and huffs.

"Speaking of ugly faces, what have you got around your eyes?" Edmun drinks his ale and stares at me. "Did you get in a tussle?"

Lara grabs my chin in her hand and tilts my head this way and that, trying to get a good look at my face.

I swat her away, saying, "It's nothing—probably just a bit of soot."

"Ah, she's been out fightin' fires," Harry teases.

"Starting them, more likely," someone else chimes in, instigating a round of laughter.

"You lot are a nosy bunch, you know that?" Lara cuts in, glaring at Edmun. "Our Kay has been out working, same as any of you. You don't need to be knowing the hows and wheres."

I give her a grateful look and she throws me a wink.

I made Lara swear that she wouldn't tell anyone what I have been up to, sparing her as many specific details as possible. Will stressed the need for extreme secrecy and for once, I agree with him.

"Well, you've missed some action." Edmun removes his arm from around his companion and leans in over the table conspiratorially.

A barmaid comes to clear the empty tankards, bringing fresh drinks and laughing with Harry when he compliments her.

"What's that?" I ask.

"The biggest story is that there was some action outside the City gates the night before last. Did you hear about it?"

"No, what happened?" I'm a bit annoyed. Usually, I am the first to know of any goings-on, but the study sessions with Will have taken a toll on my time.

"Wastelanders, apparently. They were throwing projectiles at our walls: spears and rocks. The guards chased them off but there was some damage done. Some people are calling it an attack."

"Some people?"

"Some are saying it wasn't an attack at all." Edmun leans in closer, widening his eyes. "They're saying it was a test. The Wasters are scoping us out, playing with our defences. They're trying to find a weak spot."

My blood runs cold, Will's warning about the Wastelanders attacking the City ringing in my head. I take a long sip of my tankard to buy myself some time and gather my thoughts.

"That's worrying," I say simply, trying to appear skeptical.

"Naw. Their weapons have nothing on ours, the bunch of savages. Even if they were to make it over the walls, we would disintegrate them in a second."

There is a cacophony of cheers at Edmun's words and the clanking of tankards. I force a smile and join in the revelry.

"Oh! And another piece of news." Edmun sits back again, appearing grim.

The red-mouthed girl is completely oblivious, smiling up at him and scooting closer.

"Go on then, you gossip," I encourage, glad for the change in subject.

"Gordy's been arrested."

I choke on my drink, coughing to disguise my snort of derision. "You're joking. What for?"

"Petty theft."

I immediately regret my laughter. Theft in the City can bring a grave punishment, the likes of which not even a wastrel like Gordy deserves.

"Has he been sentenced?" I ask, more seriously. Thieves from the Commons are usually given the choice of losing a hand or serving in the Wastelands.

"Not sure—no one has been able to get a word in or out of the Palace. They've got that place locked down tighter than a vault." Edmun's jovial mood has sobered and the red-lipped girl pats his arm sympathetically, simultaneously sneaking a sip from his tankard.

"What did he steal?"

"Apparently, he took a shot right in the middle of the Court, the stupid git. He went for an old lady's change purse and they nabbed him." Edmun shakes his head. "He always had more gall than sense."

"Idiot," I mutter, none too quietly.

"I feel terrible about how we razz him for pulling off weak heists. We would compare him to you, but it was only in fun, you know? I didn't mean for him to go out and try something stupid." Edmun's big hands clench into fists.

I frown. "It's not your fault, Eddy."

He nods, taking another drink, seemingly not noticing the smear of red paint left behind on the rim of his glass. "Damn fool."

"I'm sure he'll be out in no time." Lara swoops back into the conversation, her smooth voice carrying just the right sentiment, as usual. "Gordy is more slippery than any of us; they won't be able to hold him for long."

Edmun manages a smile as Harry claps him heartily on the back. "You're right about that."

"Of course I'm right! Now, who's ready for another drink?"

The night drags on, the smoke and flickering lights encroaching on us as we swap stories and jokes. I sip my beer slowly, mindful of the fact that for the first time in my life, I have to be presentable in the morning. Lara slips her arm through mine and rests her head on my shoulder, laughing as Harry regales us with a tale about one of his rich customers. The plump courtier believed the yarn Harry spun him about custard having weight-loss properties and bought out an entire supply of danishes.

I sigh as I take in my circle of friends, all of them good, hard-working people enjoying a night of simple pleasures. My mind flicks back to the image of Wastelanders pacing our perimeter and a small headache begins to throb behind my temple. I clench my jaw, finish my drink and bid my goodbyes, Lara leaning on me as we stumble out of the tavern.

It's easy to support Lara's light frame as we wind our way through the alleyways. She chatters away about the people in the bar, laughing as she makes fun of Edmun's girl. I force a smile but my heart feels heavy. I have made sure to save enough coins for Lara to be able to support herself for a few weeks, but I will have to find a way to send more money back to her if I am unable to get away from the Palace.

"I'm going to miss you, Kay," Lara says, tripping on the train of her dress.

I hold her arm while she rights herself. "I'll take every opportunity I can to slip away."

"Why would you bother with that? You will be living in the lap of luxury." She gesticulates grandly as she speaks, stumbling again and laughing as she clutches me.

I shake my head, smiling. "This isn't going to be a vacation, sweet friend. I'll mostly be trying to keep a low profile. All that courtier junk is so wasteful, anyway. Why would you need anything more than a clean bed and enough food for your belly?"

"Gods, Kay. You can be so unimaginative sometimes." Lara sighs. "I, for one, would relish the opportunity to wear beautiful dresses and eat decadent meals. I would love it if there was nothing required of me but to look pretty. I would spend every day wandering the Palace, dancing and flirting with all the handsome men."

"I am sure that you would make a wonderful noble," I tell her, "were it not for the fact that you have a brain in your head."

"Always so serious," she mock-grumbles, poking me in the cheek.

I laugh and swat her hand away. "At least one of us is," I tease.

"I'm just saying that I wouldn't be surprised if you ended up enjoying yourself, just a little."

"Doubtful, but if on the off-chance I find myself twirling across the dance floor with a handsome man, you'll be the first to know."

"Deal." She giggles, leaning her head against mine.

Our footsteps echo down the dusty alleyway, the moon and flickering streetlights casting long shadows against the crumbling buildings. Tomorrow I will be worlds away from my friends and these familiar streets. The thought turns my stomach. Despite Will's rigorous teaching and Jules' skill with makeup, I still feel about as far from a noble lady as the sand from the stars. Glossy hair and fancy dresses could not possibly disguise who I truly am: a common street urchin and thief.

Doubt tingles in the back of my mind and I have to force my worries aside. Instead, I concentrate on the next most important order of business, which is getting my friend upstairs and safely to bed.

chapter 14

I awoke before dawn and now I find myself poised and tense in Will's flat while Jules fusses with the hem of my skirt. She has dressed me in a linen toga, dyed the palest of blues and cinched at the waist with a gold belt. My hair has been combed, with a few unruly tendrils springing loose around my face, the remainder braided into a thick rope that hangs down my back. The final touch is a sweep of kohl around my eyes and a simple jewelled headpiece laid low on my head.

As Jules works, I practice drawing up my posture and reciting the names of the nobility. I haven't been this nervous since I first started breaking into courtly homes five years ago.

Losing myself briefly in the memory, I recall a modest townhouse on the fringes of the Court. I had crept in through the unlocked back door, grabbed the first item I could get my grubby hands on and scampered back out. I managed to swipe only a single serving spoon, but the heart-pumping excitement fed me more than the score ever could.

Will emerges from his bedroom, pulling on a leather vest over his shoulders. He is dressed in a white collarless shirt, which is tucked into a pair of soft trousers and rolled neatly to his elbows. His boots and vest are made of the same quality leather—strange to my eyes as I have only seen him wear scuffed and travel-worn apparel. A green kerchief is tied loosely around his neck, useful against the coarse sand blowing in the street.

As I take all this in, I almost fail to notice the biggest change of all.

"Your beard!" I exclaim.

He laughs as he rubs his jaw, "Yes, it's gone. I thought I should polish myself up a bit for your big debut."

I grin, my nervousness easing somewhat. "How considerate of you."

"You look fantastic," he says.

For the moment, I can't manage to formulate a reply.

"Jules, you're a miracle worker," he finishes.

I turn away and roll my eyes. Of course, the compliment was meant for Jules. Though I will admit, it does take a considerable amount of talent to turn a gutter rat like me into a lady to be presented at the Palace.

"I think you're all set." Jules steps back and regards me, her dark head tilted as she considers me.

I draw my shoulders back and throw her my most haughty look.

She giggles. "You've nailed it."

Will is leaning out the window, his long fingers threading the silver buttons on his vest through their holes. "The carriage is here," he announces, drawing back inside and nodding to me. "Are you ready?"

I bite my lip. "Let's go."

Jules reaches over and pulls me to her chest in a tight hug. I squeeze her back, pulling away quickly when something itches behind my eyelids. Ducking my head, I busy myself gathering my dress away from my feet.

I follow Will down the stairs and into the street. A wooden carriage drawn by a large silver gelding waits patiently by the curb. The driver is dressed smartly in a grey vest and cap, which he doffs at me while he holds open the door of the carriage and gestures us inside.

I am about to step up when I feel Will grasp my hand, supporting me as I climb aboard. He offers me a reassuring smile before disappearing around the side of the carriage. I breathe out a nervous sigh between my teeth, sitting stiffly while Will settles himself on the bench next to me.

My stomach lurches when the cart rolls forward; the movement feels unnatural.

"Are they expecting us?" I ask quietly, not wanting the driver to overhear our conversation.

"Yes," Will confirms. "We'll be meeting with Vitrola, the Princess' chief —"

"Right, chief of staff," I interrupt, remembering.

"Exactly. She conducts all the interviews for the Princess. When she deems you fit, you'll be introduced to the Princess herself."

If she deems me fit.

"Got it." I glance down, realizing that Will has taken hold of my hand and is squeezing it tightly. He seems to notice our contact in the same moment because he releases me immediately, flexing his fingers into a fist and turning to look out the window.

I watch the buildings roll past us as we are pulled along the street, the horse's hooves tapping out a steady rhythm against the sand-strewn road. We travel uphill toward the centre of the City, weaving closer and closer to the grandiose Palace situated at the peak.

The landscape begins to change as we drive deeper into the Court. The buildings here are less pockmarked and boast colourful window treatments. Brightly dyed fabrics drape the affluent people strolling past. The pace feels generally unhurried compared to the rough-and-tumble attitude of the Commons. Familiar with these streets, I am able to anticipate every turn, though it occurs to me that in a matter of minutes, I will be navigating foreign terrain.

I feel a light hand on my shoulder and turn to see Will gesturing for me to look out his window. I lean past him and peer up, my eyes widening at the sight of the Palace looming above us. I have seen the landmark every day of my life, but never so close. It boasts tall, arched walls made entirely of glass and gilded balconies circling every second storey. The ground floor is expansive while the topmost storey narrows, giving the overall impression of a glass monument reaching up to scrape against the sky. When I crane my neck, I can just make out the top balcony. How many times have I stared out toward the Palace from within my tiny attic, imagining the view offered from the City's highest point? I can scarcely believe that the great, glass doors will soon open for me.

The cart lurches to a halt and I hear the driver conversing with someone. I look back at Will, who appears unbothered.

"We're just at the gate," he explains.

There is the sound of wood creaking as an impressive gate swings open wide enough to admit us.

We pull forward again, the wheels now turning almost silently on the smooth path.

I lean out my window, unable to tear my eyes away from the sight of the flawless glass walls rising high over our heads. Will places his hand gently on my shoulder again and I fall back in my seat.

“Don’t gawk,” he whispers.

I nod wordlessly.

The carriage finally comes to rest in front of the Palace doors and the horse sighs softly. The driver comes around to Will’s side and tugs the carriage door open, standing back so that we can step out. I take Will’s hand, allowing him to help me down, using my other hand to wrangle my dress away from my feet.

Will hands the driver a handful of coins and pats him on the shoulder. The man scurries back up to his seat, leaving us standing alone in the expansive drive. Will offers me his arm and I loop my arm through his elbow, steeling myself.

Here we go.

Two guards stand stationed outside, imposing in their heavy leather armour. I can’t help but feel a bit sorry for them in this oppressive heat.

“Do you have an appointment?” the larger of the two guards asks.

“Will Cain and Abby Fellows,” Will says in a clear voice. “Here to see Vitrola.”

The guard unfurls a roll of parchment, taking his time in scanning it. After an eternity, he nods. “Welcome, Dr. Cain. Miss Fellows.”

He pushes open the door and stands aside. In the next instant, we are swept through the great mouth of the Palace and into its depths.

“Follow me.” The smaller guard speaks a bit stiffly, motioning us past the expansive foyer.

I paste a bored expression on my face as we follow him down the hall, but allow my eyes to dart around. The exterior walls are all made of glass while the interior ones are a polished stone. There are rounded archways leading to the various rooms, and multicoloured tiles decorate the walls and ceiling. Richly woven tapestries cover the furniture, boasting a level of wealth I scarcely imagined possible.

Bringing my eyes forward, I realize that the floor beneath my feet is exploding with vibrant colour. A glistening mosaic has been laid out, thousands of minuscule shingles arranged into an elaborate design that swirls down the hallway.

The guard leads us to what appears to be a waiting area, judging by the plush white couches and carefully arranged cushions. Two grand staircases rise on either side of the couches, twisting up the outer walls and disappearing into the top floors. Beyond the stairs there is a magnificent archway and two heavy, wooden doors. I strain to look into the room's depths, catching a glimpse of several dining tables. I guess that the Great Hall must lie through there.

"Please, wait here. Vitrola will be along shortly." The guard instructs curtly.

I join Will on one of the couches, adopting a rigid pose so that I don't slouch.

The guard's footsteps recede back up the entryway and I struggle not to fidget with the folds of my dress, instead glancing around at our surroundings.

"The mosaic represents the Burn. Do you see it?" Will's voice cuts through my thoughts.

I look down at the floor, frowning. "I can't see anything."

"It's difficult to make out from here," he says conversationally. "But it comes together if you look down at it from the top floor."

"I bet." I know he is just trying to distract me, but I feel as though my nerves are too frayed for friendly chit-chat.

Several minutes of tense silence pass before I hear the light tap of sandals on the steps above us.

A petite woman descends the stairs and appears at the foot of the couch, her arms laden with parchment. Her dark hair is twisted into silky ropes that protrude from under the bright headscarf she has tied around her head.

"Dr. Cain, it's good to see you." The woman gives a tight nod, a consummate professional.

"Vitrola, always a pleasure." Will stands to greet her and I follow suit, standing back as she kisses him on each cheek.

"And you must be Abby." Vitrola shifts the parchments into her left arm and extends her hand toward me. I notice that her nails have been painted a vibrant pink. "I've heard so much about you. Welcome."

"Thank you. It is a pleasure to meet you as well." I grasp her hand, conscious not to grip too tightly as I flash my most gracious smile.

"I do hope you haven't been waiting long. Things have been a touch hectic around here lately, what with the recent disturbances by the Wastelanders." Vitrola rolls her eyes as though the war serves only to complicate her day.

"Not at all, we've only just arrived," Will tells her.

"Excellent. Please, follow me. We'll have drinks in one of the drawing rooms."

We trail after her up one of the staircases to the second floor. I pause a moment to glance below, trying to make out the pattern in the mosaic on the floor. Will clears his throat and I start, hurrying to catch up.

The second-floor landing takes us to a walkway that appears to wrap around the entire outer glass wall. To my left are doors at regular intervals, some open and revealing opulent rooms, the rest shut tight. The layout of the Palace, while massive, appears to be quite straightforward. The tricky part will be remaining oriented while walking in great looping circles.

Vitrola clearly knows exactly where she is going. She turns left through a set of double doors and ushers us into a bright, white room. Several couches, chairs and tables are scattered throughout the space, turned toward each other and giving an impression of deliberate socializing.

We settle around a low table into comfortable armchairs as Vitrola puts her parchments down and begins sorting through them. A young girl appears from seemingly out of nowhere and asks if we would like anything to drink.

"I think some tea, if you don't mind," Will says.

The girl nods and looks to me.

"Water is fine, thank you," I tell her.

Vitrola shakes her head and waves the girl away, barely acknowledging her before she turns to Will and me.

"Now, then, Abby. Why don't you tell me a little about yourself?"

"I would love to." I cross my right knee over my left. "I suppose I should start by saying that I recently graduated from the Outer City Academy."

"How wonderful! What did you study?"

"Pre-Burn literature."

"Ah yes, the classics. Do you have a favourite book?"

"I…" My mind flips through the possibilities. "I love so many books, but if I had to choose a favourite, I would say *The Count of Monte Cristo*."

Will's grey eyes flash at me from the next chair, but he doesn't say anything.

"Hmm, I'm not familiar with it." Vitrola tilts her head, her glossy tendrils swaying.

"It's a wonderful story about fate and free will," I tell her. I decline to explain the overarching plot of a poor prisoner driven by vengeance and reinventing himself as a duke.

"Lovely. The Princess is an avid reader, also. I am sure she would be very keen to discuss books with you."

"I would be delighted!" I say, with what I hope sounds like a mixture of graciousness and enthusiasm.

"What did you do before studying at the Academy?" I know that she must already be aware of Abby's tragic past. The Palace would have done a thorough check on the history that Will forged for me, but Vitrola is going to force me to tell the whole story anyway.

So be it.

"Before that, I lived in a care facility. I was placed there after the death of my parents." Here, I reach for the handkerchief handed discreetly to me by Will and bring it to my eyes.

"Oh, you poor dear. I am so sorry."

Sorry, my foot, you silly gossip.

The young maid appears again, carrying a silver tray laden with our drinks. She places it on the table between us and scurries away.

I let the silence linger for a few moments as I dab at imaginary tears, waiting for Vitrola to say the question I know she is aching to ask.

"Did they die...naturally?" she words carefully.

I nearly snort with laughter and cover it up by pretending to blow my nose into the handkerchief. I don't know which is more ridiculous: that Vitrola is every bit as scandal-hungry as Will said she would be, or that she actually has the gall to ask whether two people can die of natural causes at the same time.

"No, I'm afraid it was much worse than that." I sigh, reaching for my glass of water; I take a long sip while I let Vitrola stew in her curiosity. "We lived in a gorgeous house in a good part of the Outer City." The trick to telling a convincing fib is to add a few specific details but not to overly embellish. "One day, I was out with my friend, Lara, at the market when Wastelanders attacked our walls."

"How terrible!" Vitrola gasps.

I press the handkerchief to my eyes again. "When I got back, I knew immediately what had happened. The beautiful white walls of our house were splattered with...with blood." I shudder dramatically. That ought to be enough to satiate her morbid concern. I adjust my posture, feeling a jolt of triumph as Vitrola regards me with fascination. "But that is all in the past now," I say bravely. "As the saying goes, you can't go back, you can only go forward."

"She's been so strong," Will says. "The whole family is very proud of her."

I give him a shaky smile, ever the stoic little lady.

"Clearly, you are an exceptional young woman." Vitrola sits back in her seat. "I daresay we could use someone with your education and insight."

"It would be a great honour to assist the Princess in any way," I tell her.

"Indeed, it is." Vitrola suddenly turns grave. "But being a lady-in-waiting isn't just about being a friend to the Princess. Our young ladies must conduct themselves with the utmost grace and dignity at all times."

I nod sagely. "Of course."

"If we were to accept you for this position, you would be representing the Palace. That means there will be zero tolerance for any behaviour not befitting someone of your station. You will be at the Princess' beck and call, expected to perform whatever duty she asks of you. Do you understand?"

"Perfectly."

"Well, then!" Vitrola's sober demeanour vanishes as she beams at Will and me. "I think we will get along famously."

Like a house on fire, I can't help but think.

Her small figure hovers over the table as Vitrola sorts through the parchments, efficiently selecting one, which she hands to me.

"I'll just ask you to read over this contract and sign it. It's all quite standard, but if you have any questions, let me know." Her tone suggests that she will not be entertaining any such possibility. "I'll give you a moment to read it over." She stands, straightening her dress. "Take your time!"

She sweeps from the room and I release the breath of air I hadn't realized I was holding. "All right. That wasn't so bad."

Will has taken the contract and is studying it, his brow furrowed. "I told you that you didn't have anything to worry about."

"What does the contract say?"

"Nothing unexpected. You must always look presentable, you must attend all formal Palace events, you are to limit your interaction with anyone below your station..."

I snort unattractively, ruining whatever ladylike effect I was pulling off. "That last one is charming."

"Welcome to the Palace." He withdraws a pen from the pocket of his jacket and hands both it and the contract back to me. "There's no going back now, Red."

I smile at the nickname and sign with a flourish, even adding a flamboyant heart to the signature.

Behind me, there is the sound of the door creaking open. Will and I rise quickly to our feet, turning as Vitrola steps back into the room.

This is it.

I'm in.

chapter 15

Vitrola stands rigidly, clearly anxious to get on with her day. "All set?" she asks.

I nod, resisting the urge to glance at Will. "I'm ready."

"Fabulous! Welcome aboard. You can get started right away. We can send for your things, but don't worry about bringing too many clothes—the ladies are supplied with the services of the Palace maids and dressmakers."

My head is already spinning.

"If you'll follow me, I will escort you to your room," she says.

"I have some patients to visit at the infirmary, so I will excuse myself." Will inclines his head toward us and makes to leave. He grabs my hand on the way by, giving it a reassuring squeeze.

I watch him exit, fighting to keep my confidence from wavering. Without him here, the room suddenly appears incredibly grand and I am acutely aware of just how big a fraud I am.

Fortunately, Vitrola doesn't seem to have noticed the shift. She stoops down to shuffle her papers together, gathering them to her chest, then indicates that I follow her. "This way."

I fall into step behind her as she leads me through the door, backtracking down the sloped outer hallway toward the main staircase. As we ascend I lag a little behind Vitrola, chancing a look down the third-floor hallway. I catch a glimpse of several servants hurrying between rooms, their arms laden with linens and trays. By their casual demeanour I determine that the third floor is made up of servants' quarters and closets; possibly the kitchen as well.

I follow Vitrola up to the fourth floor, craning my neck upward, distracted by the way the staircase continues to spiral up, twisting high against the glass walls and disappearing into infinity. My concentration is broken by the sound of someone politely clearing their throat. Vitrola offers me a tight smile and gestures me down the fourth-floor hallway.

This floor is bright and open, revealing a vast, open sitting area to our left, decorated in girlish hues of pink, blue and yellow. Natural light pours into the parlour from the floor above. Several girls mill about, their tinkling voices ringing through the space as they talk animatedly to one another. I pull my shoulders back and focus on Vitrola's slim figure walking determinedly in front of me; I'm suddenly self-conscious. My eyes dart sideways as we pass the parlour, feeling a heat rush to my cheeks when the ladies pause in their conversation and resume again in hushed whispers.

The parlour disappears and the hallway sweeps inward, curtaining us from the glass outer walls. Individual rooms now dot the walls on our right. We pass several of the doors before Vitrola draws to a halt. I nearly crash into her, so caught up in looking around.

"Right, then. Here we are!" She opens the door with a flourish, ushering me inside.

I step through the doorway, blinking at the sudden brightness spotting my vision. As the room swims into focus, I realize I am standing in a spacious bedroom, one solid wall being a glass window overlooking the City.

I take a couple of steps forward, spinning in place, trying to take in everything at once. There is a polished desk stocked with writing instruments, a vanity with a plush bench and a large bookcase stretching from floor to ceiling. On the opposite wall there sits a wide, cushy bed draped in what looks like the softest fabric imaginable. Bathed in the glow of the afternoon light, everything appears comfortable and welcoming.

I am daydreaming of running my fingers over the book titles and curling up on the bed when I am immediately drawn back to the present by a crushing feeling of guilt.

"This is all...for me?" I turn back to Vitrola, my stomach flipping uncomfortably as I struggle to maintain the illusion of someone accustomed to such grandeur.

Vitrola laughs lightly. "This will be your bedroom, yes. You will also be supplied with a handmaid. Sera, I think her name is. Where is that girl?"

“Right here, Miss,” a small voice pipes up from behind us. I turn to see a girl around my own age standing in the doorway, hurriedly pushing strands of pale, messy hair beneath a kerchief on her head.

“You’re late, Sera. What have I told you about focusing on your tasks?” The chipper edge to Vitrola’s voice has dropped and I narrow my eyes at her sudden coldness.

“I’m sorry, Miss.” Sera drops her gaze to the floor, scuffing the toe of her boot. “It won’t happen again.”

“See that it doesn’t.” Ignoring the girl completely, Vitrola addresses me. “Sera will be your personal maid. She can assist you in any way you need.”

“Oh. Lovely!” I force some enthusiasm into my tone.

“I’ll leave you to get settled. Remain here, and I’ll be back to introduce you to the ladies before supper.” Vitrola gives me a cursory nod before heading out the door, not breaking stride as Sera darts out of her way.

I wait until I hear her brisk footsteps retreating down the hallway before I turn and give Sera a friendly grin.

“I’m Abby,” I say, extending my hand.

She stares at my outstretched palm for a moment before taking it in a tentative grip.

“I am supposed to address you as Miss Fellows,” she tells me.

“Oh.” I scratch the back of my neck. “Is that really a hard and fast rule?”

The ghost of a smile crosses her lips. “I’m not sure. No one but the servants has ever asked me to call them by their first name.”

“I’m not much for formalities, so let’s just stick with Abby for now.” I move toward the bookshelf, my eyes skimming over the titles.

Most of the books seem to be typical princess fare—light reads about fashion and beauty—but I notice a few classics, likely slipped in as decoration.

“Would you like to change your dress for supper, Miss Abby?” Sera asks.

"Um," I stammer, glancing down at my dress. "I don't think my trunks have been brought up yet."

"Not to worry." Sera scurries across the room to a set of doors next to the bed. "You and Miss Tessa look to be about the same size. That is, until—" She catches herself before mentioning the unfortunate Miss Tessa's expanding waistline.

She flings the closet doors open and I stifle a gasp, my eyes widening at the sight of countless colours and fabrics. My fingers drop from the bookshelf and I feel my legs pulling me toward the closet. It is large enough for both Sera and I to stand in comfortably and is lined with polished wooden drawers and more gowns than I can count.

"Perhaps this?" Sera pulls down a violet shift.

I run my hand across the material, the silky texture sliding pleasantly between my fingers.

"It would go beautifully with these." She drapes the garment over her arm and pulls out a drawer beneath the racks of dresses. In it rests an assortment of jewellery, the various crystals and metals sparkling. Sera draws out a necklace of hammered silver and displays it to me, resting it against the violet colour of the dress.

It takes me a moment to remember to speak, only doing so when Sera clears her throat timidly.

"I…" I swallow, forcing an impassive expression. "That will do just fine."

My handmaid nods, tossing the garment over her shoulder and ushering me toward the vanity. "Let's get you dressed."

Half an hour later, I am pacing nervously. Sera hovers nearby, trying to make herself look busy by unnecessarily straightening the items on the desk.

"I think I'll just go out there and introduce myself," I say. "Vitrola is taking too long."

Sera looks up, alarm etched across her pale features. "She told you to wait here until she gets back."

"I'm sure there's no harm in going out to the parlour and being friendly." I glance at my reflection in the mirror. Sera has re-braided my hair and finished the end with a silver band that matches the necklace at my throat.

"You are new here, Miss Abby. Things are done in a very...particular way."

"Sera, it's just a couple of introductions—what's the harm?" I roll my eyes, pulling open the bedroom door, and step into the hallway.

I head back toward the parlour, following the sound of tittering voices. As I walk into the room I paste a smile on my face, holding my shoulders stiffly in an attempt to steady my nerves.

Roughly a dozen girls are sitting in the room, lounging on various overstuffed couches and settees.

"Hello!" I say brightly. "I'm Abby."

The girls' conversation stops abruptly as a dozen pairs of eyes turn to me.

I fight the urge to fidget with my dress as I squirm beneath the sudden rockslide of scrutiny. No one says a word in reply and the silence is maddening. Internally I curse my impatience, wishing furtively that I had heeded Sera's warning and waited in my room.

"I…" I clear my throat. "I'm the new lady-in-waiting. I am very excited to be living with you lot and serving the Princess." My cheeks are pinched with the effort to keep smiling.

"Vitrola does the introductions." One of the girls looks at me sideways. She is slightly plump, with mousy brown hair piled high on top of her head.

"That seems to be the way of it," I reply, now understanding Sera's trepidation about me coming out here on my own. "I was just sitting in my room and I figured I may as well get to meeting you all. No harm in a little politeness, is there?" I can't help but take a dig at their stony welcome and, as I suspected, not a single face shows any trace of understanding.

"We always do things a certain way." Another girl has spoken up this time. She is tall and thin and has a slightly hooked nose, her derisive tone and sharp features giving her the appearance of a hawk. "A lady should follow ceremony." One or two of the other girls nod in agreement, including Plumpy, her precarious updo wobbling atop her head.

"I see." This is not going well. Will's number one rule was to blend, and I am fairly certain that he would not approve of the circumstance I have put myself in. I wrack my mind for a solution that could somehow salvage the situation, but I cannot for the life of me figure out a way to ease the awkwardness. These girls seem bound and determined to shame me into feeling as uncomfortable as possible.

"Well, there would be no point to Vitrola introducing me now, would there?" I force some cheeriness into my voice; I'm damned if I will let these girls make me feel small. "We may as well move past it."

"What is going on out here?"

The girls' postures straighten at the voice behind me. Vitrola appears, wearing a fresh dress but still clutching her rolls of parchment.

"I was just saying hello," I explain.

There is a soft snicker from one of the couches.

"I always introduce the new recruits to the ladies. I told you that, Abby." Vitrola's brows are lowered and I bite the inside of my cheek to keep from saying something rude.

Why in the gods' names is a simple greeting so complicated?

"Yes, the ladies here have kindly reiterated that information to me."

"We do things a certain way here, Abby."

I can't believe this, I am actually being scolded.

"The next time I give you an instruction, I expect you to follow it to the letter," she says. "Is that understood?"

I clench my jaw. "Yes."

"Good." She leans to the side, looking past me and addressing the other girls. "I suppose there isn't much point to it now, but ladies, this is Abby Fellows. She comes from the Outer City and I am certain she will be a wonderful asset to our group, as well as a brilliant servant to her Royal Highness."

"Welcome, Abby." A dozen voices chime in together. Their octave is uncomfortably enthusiastic and I flinch, despite myself.

"A pleasure to meet you all," I say, tightly.

"Come then, ladies, to dinner." Vitrola marches toward the staircase, the ladies filing out after her in a perfect line.

I wait to fall into the rear of the group, my blood boiling as I fight the warning tinge of red threatening the corners of my vision.

I am pulled from my haze of loathing by the sudden weight of a curious stare. A girl is lagging behind the rest, her regal head tilted as she studies me. It isn't until I take note of her stature and the elaborate headpiece adorning her dark hair that I realize this is the person all this trouble has been over.

This is the Princess Megra.

chapter 16

The Princess is the most stunning person I have ever seen in my life.

Her hair is coal-dark and silken, rolled expertly into perfect coils and woven together in an intricate updo. She is tall, though at present I cannot tell whether my impression is due to her height or simply the way she holds herself. Her skin is the colour of rich chocolate, smooth and faultless, with fine features and full lips that are presently pursed together in either disapproval or curiosity.

I grasp the folds of my dress and curtsy deeply, using the opportunity to sweep my eyes over her costly silver gown and trim figure. Straightening, I smile graciously and force an expression of practiced reverence.

At once she looks away, brushing past me with nary a glance in my direction.

I remain stock still, stunned at her cold dismissal. I'm not sure what I was expecting when I finally laid eyes on the Princess Megra, but certainly this silent, impassive girl has left me shaken.

I maintain my distance as I follow the Princess and the rest of the ladies-in-waiting down the staircase to the first floor, my eyes stretching wide as we cross through the massive set of ornately carved double doors and into the Great Hall.

The room is massive. Tables draped in white linen are lined up on either side of the carpeted aisle running down the middle of the room. The carpet ends at a raised head table, where I suppose the King would sit. Behind the head table is an outer wall made entirely of glass and overlooking the courtyard. Common servants scurry back and forth, silently serving the chattering courtiers seated in front of their golden plates.

Vitrola escorts us to a table on the right side of the aisle and I sink down into a plush chair, situating myself with my back to the wall so that I can watch the goings-on. The Princess selects a seat on the opposite side of the table, appearing to half-listen as the ladies settle themselves around her and fill the air with high-pitched chatter.

I cast my gaze around the room, trying to work out the seating plan. Several older men sit at the table at the very front of the Hall, nearest the raised head table. They are all wearing red sashes tied with gold medals and sport grey facial hair trimmed into a variety of intricate patterns. Judging by their air of self-importance, I take it that these men are on the Board of advisors. Will refers to them simply as the Board. I recognize one man by his great bushy sideburns, nearly meeting at his chin and oiled to stick straight out. This is Chancellor Braun, the head of the Board and the King's most trusted advisor.

At a table on the other side of the aisle sits Will, his dark head bent low in conversation with his companion. He glances up at me, offering an encouraging nod from across the room. I duck my chin to study the variety of forks next to my plate, mentally reviewing the order and proper use of each one.

"Tell me, Miss Abby, do they teach much decorum at the Outer City Academy?"

I look up abruptly. Hawk Nose is sitting across from me, her dark, beady eyes protruding unattractively.

"My instructors were more concerned with information than formalities," I say, pleasantly. "I'm sorry, I didn't catch your name. Or will there be a proper ceremony for that introduction later?"

She glowers. "It's Bellany."

I immediately decide I prefer the name Hawk Nose.

"A pleasure," I say. I have made up my mind to be nice to these girls, as per Will's suggestion. Hawk Nose has another think coming if she thinks I am going to let her antagonize me into pettiness.

We are interrupted by three sharp blasts of a horn.

"His Majesty, King Francis," a herald near the entrance to the Hall suddenly announces, projecting his voice and thrusting his staff into the ground three times.

We all scramble to our feet and, finally, the King himself strides into view.

I crane my neck to get a better look, fairly brimming with curiosity. After all this time, the oppressor will have a face.

The man marching through the Hall is an impressive sight. Immediately, I can see where the Princess gets her height from: her father stands nearly seven feet tall, towering over the brawny guards who follow close behind him. He wears a silk shirt covered by a red vest and fastened with gold buttons. His facial hair is trimmed into an intricate goatee, the dark strands shot through with streaks of silver. A solid gold band sits atop his head, flashing brightly as he sweeps his gaze over the gathered crowd. When he looks in my direction, a cold shiver runs down my spine. His eyes are black, so dark they reflect no light at all.

The King marches purposefully to the front of the room. He steps up to the head table, situating his oversized figure behind his golden dinner plate before he raises his hands in front of him and addresses the room.

"Friends." His voice matches his appearance, rich and booming through the cavernous space. "The gods of fortune have blessed us with another delicious meal. My daughter and I thank you for joining us this evening. Enjoy the feast!"

I scoff to myself as I sit with the rest of the crowd among the scraping of chairs. Typical that our impassive gods would receive credit for the servants' hard work.

A bowl filled with a rich yellow soup appears in front of me. I select the widest spoon at my disposal and scoop some into my mouth, being careful to sip slowly and silently as Will taught me.

Gods help me, it is delicious.

The soup is followed by several more courses, all of them blending together in the chaos of the surrounding conversation and the pure ecstasy of savoury food. I glance around as I eat, careful to leave a small morsel left over in each dish, comparable to what the other girls have done. It pains me to see such wonderful food go to waste and I am certain I would be able to finish every last crumb on my plate, even if it kept arriving all night long.

Between the salad and dessert course, I attempt to make conversation with the girl to my right. She is small and slight, with large doe-like features and straight black hair.

"Your dress is beautiful," I tell her, meaning it. Her gown is a soft blue, perfectly complimenting her pale skin.

The girl raises her eyebrows, seemingly surprised by my comment. "Thank you," she says slowly.

"Have you been at the Palace long?" I ask, attempting to press the conversation.

She dabs her lips delicately with her napkin. "About a year."

I wait a beat for her to embellish but am met with silence.

"And do you like it here?" I ask. Come on, girl. Give me something to work with.

She folds her napkin slowly, smoothing it over her lap. "Of course. Better here than out there. There are more common beggars bumbling through the City every day." She shudders visibly.

I stiffen, pressing my lips together.

"I know." Hawk Nose sighs from across the table. "It's so disgusting. They really ought to build a wall to keep the commoners on their own side."

A couple of girls titter in agreement.

My hands clench into fists beneath the table. "Well, they really don't have a choice, do they? I mean, if the people in the Commons can't take care of the beggars, it isn't so unreasonable of them to ask for help from the Court."

Several perfectly coiffed heads glance up at me.

"Oh, please. Don't tell me you are one of *those*." Hawk Nose sneers and I feel my blood boil at the sound of her nasal voice.

"One of what?" I demand.

"Those bleeding-heart, save-the-poor-commoners type. It's so boring." Hawk Nose looks down at me over the bridge of her hooked nose.

"If you're asking whether I care about what happens to them, then you're right," I retort. The dessert course arrives and I stuff a healthy-sized forkful of pie into my mouth, chewing slowly to keep from saying anything more.

Hawk Nose sneers and opens her mouth to retort, when she's interrupted by a throaty voice further down the table.

"If you're going to care about anything, better it be other people than the latest trend in hats. Wouldn't you agree, Bellany?" The Princess speaks evenly but her gaze is piercing.

Hawk Nose visibly shrinks, self-consciously fingering the ugly grey feathers adorning her updo.

I suppress the urge to laugh as Hawk Nose snaps her trap shut and digs her fork forcefully into her dessert. Glancing up, I share the briefest of looks with the Princess, thinking for an instant that I have caught a spark in her eye before she turns back to her meal.

Dinner ends when the King rises to his feet. The rest of us stand hurriedly, our chairs scraping against the stone floor. We nod respectfully when he walks back down the centre aisle, a trail of Board members in his wake. I assume they are heading back to one of the smoking rooms to discuss matters of state and make a mental note to find a way to listen in sometime.

Princess Megra steps down first, trailing several feet behind the men. I follow Vitrola and the rest of the ladies into a neat line behind her and we walk back up the aisle toward the exit. When we pass by Will's table, he throws me a wink.

As we walk back up the stairs to the fourth floor, I can't help but wonder if I could ascend faster by scaling the outer walls. The glass appears smooth and faultless from the inside but I have noticed small ledges on each floor that could be gripped. What an interesting challenge that would be.

I am so lost in my daydream that I fail to notice when we have arrived back at the parlour. I nearly crash headfirst into Plumpy, who is directly in front of me. She gives me a strange look before she walks past me into the parlour and selects a seat. The rest of the girls are already milling about, a few setting up at a table to play cards while the rest situate themselves into various chairs surrounding the Princess, filling her ears with gossip and mindless chatter about the meal.

I wander away from the larger group and ask to join the girls playing cards. They are hesitant at first but too polite to turn me away. We play a few rounds of a game I am familiar with, betting small coin amounts at a time. I purposefully lose a couple of hands but end up pocketing a sizable win overall, already planning on sending the spoils back to Lara.

The night wears on and one by one the girls trickle out of the parlour to retire. The Princess is the first to leave; soon after, the room has completely emptied. I am more than happy to return to my luxurious room, where I greet Sera and decline her offer for a pre-bed drink. I allow her to undress me and unbraid my hair, closing my eyes at the pleasant feeling of her skilled fingers working through my locks.

By the time I climb into bed, the stresses of the day have all but dissipated. I intended to revel in the comfort of the wide mattress and silk sheets for as long as possible, but am asleep as soon as my head hits the pillow.

chapter 17

The next several days pass in a blur of brightly coloured dresses, insipid chatter and decadent feasts. I make an effort to blend in with the ladies, sitting with them in the parlour and throwing in the odd comment when they discuss the guards they are eyeing or how someone plans to style their hair. As the days pass, it becomes more and more difficult to feign interest in their shallow affairs. At the same time, as vapid as these girls are, I know that they are barely tolerant of me. I'd have to be blind not to notice the way their conversations cease whenever I walk by.

I attempt to disguise myself among the most forgettable of the group, three girls I have nicknamed Blushes, Glassy and Blinky. Blushes is a quiet girl with a habit of turning red in the face every time I address her directly, ducking her head and murmuring replies. Glassy appears distant, staring blankly with a glazed, far-off look in her eyes and Blinky, being completely uninteresting, forced me to settle on the one characteristic I was able to discern.

Shielded by these girls, I am mostly able to hide myself and avoid being conspicuously alone. I walk with them to and from meals and sit next to them in the parlour, occasionally enticing them to play a few hands of cards, which I win easily.

I have been unable to speak to the Princess alone since the first day I arrived. She is most often shadowed by Hawk Nose and Plumpy, or otherwise occupied with some business that her father has arranged. I don't want to impress myself upon her, remembering Will's instructions to concentrate on blending in and biding my time.

I ache to explore more of the Palace but am hesitant to give the ladies more fodder for gossip if I'm caught snooping. For the most part I keep to the fourth floor, leaving only for meals and the occasional walk in the courtyard when the confinement becomes too unbearable.

At supper I look for Will, my annoyance growing with each night that I find his seat empty. I expect him to send for me any day to discuss my progress and formulate our manoeuvres, but it seems that after seeing me settled, he has returned to his flat in the City and left me to fend for myself. Deprived of his dependable arrogance, I feel more alone than ever.

After a week spent at the Palace I find myself going mad from the boredom and stagnation. I pace back and forth in my room as Sera sits on the bed, darning a tear in the hem of a dress from when I trod on it the night before.

"Would you like to take a turn in the grounds, Miss Abby?" she suggests.

"I've taken enough turns," I say, not bothering to hide the curtness in my voice.

"Perhaps a novel? There are several books on the shelf that you haven't read yet."

"Pointless drivel, all of them," I declare. "I've already read everything that was written for someone with more than half a brain in their head."

Sera cringes, chewing on her bottom lip. "What of the library, then? The Palace has several more books on the seventh floor."

This stops me in my tracks. "There is a library?"

Sera nods eagerly, relieved to have stumbled on something that might interest me. "Yes, the best collection in the City. The ladies are encouraged to borrow from the library, but I don't think many of them have the inclination."

A room in the Palace full of books, and not a single lady to contend with? How is it that I am only hearing about this now?

"Thank you, Sera." I say gratefully. "I'm going to go visit it right now."

"Have a good time, Miss Abby. And keep your skirt free of your feet!"

I laugh, shaking my head as I exit the room and head toward the staircase. I pause at the landing, glancing around to see if anyone is watching. Seeing no one, I hitch up my skirt and take off up the stairs at a sprint, revelling in the feeling of exerting my legs, grown soft from the days spent indoors.

At the seventh-floor landing I stop and catch my breath. I really must find a way to get more exercise while I am stuck in here.

I adjust my loose ringlets of hair and continue walking with a renewed sense of composure, barely making it two steps before I stop and gape openly at what lies before me.

The doors to the library are open, revealing a gigantic room with a ceiling that stretches up a full two storeys, natural light pouring in from all sides and illuminating the intricately carved shelves. The bookcases are arranged in spiralling rows, reaching up into the highest alcoves of the ceiling and creating a network of passages that remind me acutely of the twisting Commons. A wide aisle leads to the middle of the room, the shelves on either side congregating around a cushy sitting area.

I walk slowly down the main aisle, swivelling my head left and right. On either side of the room is a spiral staircase leading to the second storey, and the taller shelves have narrow ladders affixed to them, which appear rickety on their rails. The couches in the centre of the room are overstuffed and shabby, appearing infinitely more welcoming than the rest of the Palace furnishings.

It is the height of the bookcases that impresses me most. After so many days trapped on the ground, I feel my muscles twitching from anticipation. The need to be high above the ground and lost among the beautiful books, to summit the highest shelf and look out across the open space, is instantly overwhelming.

I gather the folds of my dress and tie them into a secure knot just below my hip, allowing my legs to be free but still preserving my dignity in case someone happens to come by. Judging by the silence, however, I don't have much to worry about.

My skirt lashed securely, I place one hand on the ladder closest to me and scramble up it with a practiced sureness. The even rungs of the ladder are no challenge compared to the rough ledges and bricks I am accustomed to, but the thrill of the climb makes my heart feel freer than it has in days.

In no time I am at the very top of the ladder. I spin on the final rung, grip the top shelf and hoist myself onto it, letting my feet dangle high above the floor below. I revel in the height, a smile breaking out over my face as a feeling of peace washes over me. When I close my eyes I can almost feel the sandy air on my face, imagining the City stretched out in front of me, the next roof an easy leap away.

"What are you doing up there?" A voice breaks through my thoughts and I start, gripping the ledge tightly as I am brought abruptly back to the present.

"Damn," I mutter under my breath and lean forward to look below me.

Princess Megra is standing at the foot of the shelf, ethereal as always in a patterned wrap dress.

"I was just admiring the view," I say, cringing at how stupid the words sound, even as I speak them.

To my surprise, she laughs. "It looks precarious!"

I grin. "It's beautiful up here. Would you like to join me?"

She clutches a book to her chest. "I could never! I have the most awful fear of heights. Just seeing you up there is making me nervous."

"I'll come down, then," I say, turning in place and making sure my skirt is arranged decently before descending.

When I reach the ground, I notice that her knuckles have whitened from holding her book so tightly.

"I'm sorry, I didn't mean to scare you," I say gently. "I won't go up there again."

"No, no. It's fine," she says quickly, her grip loosening. "It's just that...I wish I could do that."

"Monkey up a bookshelf?"

"Yes, that, but really just...anything. Anything brave." She studies the cover of her book. "I've been treated like such a delicate flower my whole life, I'm starting to believe it myself."

"Bravery isn't climbing up a bookshelf," I tell her. "It's being scared but carrying on with it anyway."

She lifts her eyes, studying me intently.

I keep my voice low as I hold her gaze. "And as queen, you will have plenty of opportunity to be brave."

She doesn't say anything for several moments. I bite my lip, internally cursing myself. I've said too much; I've overstepped my bounds. This isn't a friend down at the pub—this is royalty. Stupid, Kay.

"You are an unusual person, Abby Fellows," she says eventually, a small smile pulling at her lips.

I laugh, relieved that the tension has been broken. "I get that a lot, your Highness."

"Oh, please, enough of that 'highness' and 'princess' ridiculousness. Just call me Meg." She gestures me over to one of the couches, where she slumps against the armrest and places the book on her lap. It is the most relaxed I have ever seen her.

"What are you reading?" I ask, sitting next to her; I unknot my skirt, frowning at the wrinkles it has left and knowing that Sera will be annoyed.

"*Pride and Prejudice*. Have you read it?"

I feel my face light up. "It's one of my absolute favourites!"

We sit for a long time, discussing Jane Austen and the vivid pictures she paints of the world before the Burn. We imagine cold, rainy weather and grassy moors, arguing passionately about Darcy.

"How can you say that? He is such a romantic!" I declare, taking the book from her and looking for the passage in which he declares his love to Elizabeth.

"Romantic? Please," Meg snorts, rolling her eyes. "He is a conceited, self-serving man who thinks of nothing but himself and what he stands to gain."

"But what about the way he searches for her sister? And pays for her wedding? What is selfish about that?"

"All to preserve the dignity of Elizabeth's family. Think about how poorly it would reflect on him if everyone knew his sister-in-law was traipsing around, making it with an unmarried soldier."

I sigh. "There must be more to it than that."

"Miss Fellows, I never would have taken you for a romantic!" she teases, snatching the book back from me.

I laugh, leaning against the couch cushions. "Romance in literature is something I can get on board with."

"Oh? Is there no one outside of the pages who strikes your fancy?"

I grab one of the cushions and press it to my face, groaning. "You're as bad as the lot of them on the fourth floor, with your talk of boys!"

She laughs, pulling the cushion off my face. "Goodness, Abby, there *is* someone, isn't there? You're as red as a sunburn!"

"It's just my hair," I say, sitting back up. Will's face flashes before my eyes and I fight to keep the blush from creeping further up my cheeks.

"Very well, keep it to yourself. I daresay, I will find out sooner or later." Meg teases.

"What about you?" I ask, changing the subject. "You may not be a romantic, but there must be someone who makes your heart flutter."

She runs a hand through her dark locks and I watch with fascination as the glossy strands fall perfectly back into place. "Oh gods, no. Though my father would love it if there were."

I sense an opportunity to gain a little information and concentrate on keeping my tone casual. "Most fathers would rather their daughters keep away from romance."

"Not my father." She sighs. "He has his mind set on marrying me off to Lord Lynal Grayson from the Outer City."

My mind reels at this revelation. The City and the Outer City are on friendly terms but have always remained completely independent of one another. Why would the King want to join forces with them, suddenly?

I immediately land on one obvious possibility: the King wants to harvest the soldiers and resources of the Outer City for use in his war with the Wastelanders. Before I can report this back to Will, however, I need to be certain.

"What is Lord Grayson like?" I ask.

"Nothing special. He is about thirty years old and completely obsessed with my father. They will shut themselves away in the study for hours, discussing matters with the Board. Don't ask me what about—they've never asked me to join them. I doubt the man has ever read a book in his life." She rolls her eyes.

If the Outer City is also interested in forming an alliance but are holding out for a wedding to Meg, then there must be something else that this Lord stands to gain through a marriage.

"It must be frustrating. I'm sure you receive a lot of suitors who are interested in the political possibilities of a royal marriage," I sympathize.

She sighs. "I can't say I blame them. The rules here are so archaic. Anyone who marries me would gain rulership over the City once my father passes, while I sit passively in the background."

And there it is.

"Well, I must say I think you win in the category of boy troubles." I shake my head.

She laughs. "And what is my prize? A lifetime of misery?"

"A slice of chocolate cake," I say, standing up; I grab her hand to hoist her to her feet. "Come on, let's see what we can scare up in the kitchen."

chapter 18

The familiar scratchiness of sand brushes against my upturned face as I step out of the carriage. I exchange a friendly smile with the driver, watching as he twitches the reins and turns the horse back toward the Palace.

As the carriage recedes into the distance, I breathe in a great lungful of air, feeling my muscles loosen and a great weight lift from my shoulders. I take in my familiar surroundings and allow the welcome sounds and smells of my beloved market to encompass me.

I long to stroll through the square and catch up with my friends, but first I have to shed these ridiculous Palace garments. Walking quickly, I make my way through the crowd toward a side alley, where I check over my shoulder to be certain no one is watching before slipping between the buildings and then ducking into a shadowed doorway.

In the sheltered area, I slide the leather satchel off my shoulder and dig through its contents, pulling out a plain, sleeveless tunic and a pair of pants. I shed my silk toga and exchange it for the less-conspicuous outfit, carefully folding the dress and placing it back in my bag.

Stepping out into the street, I look about while I tie a scarf around my neck, pulling it up to protect my face from the swirling sand. My steps are light as I head into the market, glancing upward once and squinting as I make out the sun's position, guessing that I have roughly an hour before I am due to meet Will.

My pace quickens when Harry's stall comes into view. His broad back is turned to me while he laughs with a customer, his fuzzy forearms coated in flour and gesticulating madly. I sidle up next to the cart, silent as a ghost as I reach my hand inside, my practiced fingers grasping a crusty roll. I make direct eye contact with Harry's customer as I slowly raise the bread out of the cart, laughing silently behind my scarf.

The customer's eyes widen and he, taps Harry on the arm and gestures toward me, sputtering, "Harry, you're bein' mugged!"

Harry spins around, his beefy hand coming down hard and pinning my wrist in a fluid motion that bellies his size. “Rob me, will you?” he bellows. His eyebrows shoot up in recognition. “That you, Kay?”

With my free hand, I tug the scarf down off my face. “Forgive me, Harry. Old habits, you know?”

His laugh echoes through the square, startling his confused customer. The man scurries away, shaking his head as Harry releases my wrist and pulls me into a hug. I am lifted into the air, my lungs instantly constricting against my friend’s thick chest.

“All right, you big softie. It’s nice to know that you’ve missed me,” I gasp. I shrug him off and follow him around the back of the stall, sinking down onto an upturned trough. Harry dips two tin cups into the bucket of water at his side and hands one to me, winking as he knocks my cup with his.

“So, where have you been? Haven’t heard head or tail of you in weeks. Was beginnin’ to worry that you’d done something foolish and got yourself caught.” Harry’s demeanour is as jovial as ever, but his tone contains a trace of anxiety.

I feel a stab of guilt for having left my friend in the dark. “Just been keeping a low profile—you know how it is.” I stare down at my cup, avoiding his gaze.

“Well, glad to see you’re all right, girlie. Are you back to stay for a while?”

“Unfortunately, no. My visits are going to be sporadic for a little bit, it seems.” I lean back and turn my face up to the sun, catching the warm rays on my face.

I hear Harry give a small sigh and I crack an eye open to peer at him. His posture appears as relaxed as ever as he raises his cup to his lips and speaks to me from behind it.

“Whatever it is you are getting yourself into, I hope you know what you’re doing.” He is careful to keep his voice low.

I open my other eye and regard him before subtly scanning our surroundings. The market bustles on around us, seemingly oblivious to our conversation, but with so much at stake, I don't want to take any chances. I sidle a little closer and lean back again, relaxing my shoulders.

"You don't have to worry about me. I can look after myself." I can't help the defensive note my voice takes on.

"I know you can. But I also know that you can be reckless, and I wonder if maybe this time you are tanglin' with some folks that are better left alone."

"What makes you think I'm tangling with anyone?"

Harry raises his chin, his eyes trained on something in the distance. My gaze follows his and lands on Will standing across the square. He is flipping through a bookseller's wares, trading barbs with the seller and laughing at something the man says.

"How did you know?" I ask.

"The marketplace has ears."

"We can trust him," I say, tearing my eyes away from Will and looking back at my friend.

Harry's beard twitches as the muscles in his jaw tighten. He nods, slowly. "I've seen him about. Saw him years ago, too, hangin' about the bars and dens."

"He's different now." As I say the words, I wonder if I truly believe them. After all, I had no idea who Will was until a month ago.

"He's up to something dangerous, and now he and his circle of rich lads have dragged you into it."

"No one's dragged me into anything. If I'm involved, it's because I have my own reasons." I drop my voice lower, staring angrily into my cup of water.

His voice softens. "I don't want to speak ill of anyone, but do you suppose their type would give one lick if something were to happen to you?"

"You don't know what you're talking about," I say hotly. "They're not all like that. Some of them want to help us."

"Why would any of them want to help us?"

"Because they understand how unfair it all is." I let out a deep breath and roll my shoulders back against the rough wood of the stall. How did my relaxing day at the market turn into this? "I appreciate your concern, Harry, but you need to ease up. I trust him."

"And I trust you. If you say he's square, I'll try to believe it."

We sit in silence for a while longer while Harry refills our mugs. He hands mine back, studying me.

"C'mon, don't be sore. I'm just worried about you." He nudges me playfully, causing the water to slosh over my pants.

I sigh, wiping my palms across my legs in an effort to dispel the moisture. I can't help the small smile creeping into the corner of my mouth at his good-natured ribbing. "I know. I wish there was a way to convince you that I'm fine. I know what I'm doing."

I glance up again. Will has spotted us and is making his way across the square, picking a path through the crowd.

"I know, Kay. I just wanted to remind you to look out for yourself, for once. Maybe quit taking so many chances." Harry's eyes are trained on Will as well.

I feel a small tingle going down my spine at his words, memories of Lara and her warnings reverberating through my head.

"In this case, they're necessary," I say to him just as Will arrives in front of us.

"What's necessary?" Will asks, taking my hand and pulling me to my feet.

I release his grip quickly and deliberately take a step back.

"Never mind," I say. "Will, have you met Harold? I call him Harry, because he is. Harry, this is my friend, Will."

Harry chuckles as he gets to his feet and grabs Will's hand. "Pleased to meet you, mate."

"And you as well." Will grins broadly. "Your bread is the finest in the City."

"Ah, well, that's very kind of you, but don't go complimenting me too loudly—you're likely to make the other vendors jealous." Harry easily falls back into his naturally friendly demeanour, instantly dissolving any traces of suspicion.

Will stuffs his hands into his pockets. "I hope I'm not interrupting. I'm not due to meet Kay for half an hour yet, but I spied you from across the way and thought I should come say hello."

"Not at all—your timing is fine. I've work to get back to as it is, and gods know I can't get anything done with this one distractin' me." I let out a grunt of surprise as Harry wraps me in a giant one-armed hug. "Don't be a stranger, girlie."

I use my free arm to pat his wrist. "I won't be. Nice seeing you, Harry."

"Remember what I told ya." His gruff voice tickles my ear and I wiggle out of his grasp.

I unconsciously take a step back, aligning myself with Will, who stands casually, watching the exchange.

We wave goodbye to Harry as Will gently places his hand on the small of my back and steers me out of the square. We chat idly while we walk, making trivial comments about the weather (hot and dry, as usual). Even among the distracted crowd, it is best to keep our conversation and relationship as innocent as possible.

I lead the way toward the pub, choosing an inconspicuous location far enough away from the Court and my usual common stomping grounds that we shouldn't be recognized. Will pushes open the door and steps back so I can enter first. After a moment, my eyes adjust to the darkness and I see that the establishment is mostly empty, save for a small group of men gathered by the bar. Judging from their dress and smudged faces, I guess that they just got off a shift at the mines.

Will tells me to find us a table near the back of the room and strolls up to the barkeep to get us some ale. I sit impatiently, shifting uncomfortably in my seat. It occurs to me suddenly that this is the first time in weeks we have been alone together. Despite us having spent many hours cooped up together in his tiny flat, I am at a loss as to how to behave around him. Here in this grungy bar, am I Kay, Abby, or the Runner?

My thoughts are interrupted when a mugful of ale is plopped down in front of me. I accept it gratefully and raise it to my lips, polishing off half the drink in the first sip.

Will's eyebrows are raised as I lower the mug and rub a wrist across my mouth. "Sorry, it's been a while since I've had a real drink."

He chuckles and takes a large gulp from his own tankard, purposely neglecting to wipe the foam off his upper lip and instead making a show of running his tongue across his mouth. I laugh, snorting unattractively into my cup.

I feel my shoulders loosen as the lingering traces of awkwardness dissolve. Sitting back, I revel in the comfortable silence, happy to shed the false propriety I have shouldered since arriving at the Palace.

Will gestures to the barkeep for another round and turns back to face me.

"Your beard is back," I comment.

His long fingers rub his chin. "Good or bad?"

"Good."

Two more drinks appear in front of us. I take smaller sips this time, studying him from behind my mug.

"So," I break the silence, "what is it you would like to talk about?"

We pass the next hour speaking in low tones about everything I have learned thus far at the Palace. I tell him about my growing friendship with Meg and how her father has planned to marry her off to Lord Grayson. We discuss the possible motives behind this alliance but eventually circle back to my original conclusion: the King must be planning to use the commoners from the Outer City in his war against the Wastelanders.

“What else could he possibly stand to gain from it?” Will muses. He has unbuttoned the top of his shirt and loosened his scarf. “Grayson wants the throne, that much is obvious. But what could the King want from him?”

I run a hand through my hair, pulling loose the braid Sera carefully tied for me that morning. “I think we both know what the King would consider a new source of commoners to be good for.”

Will nods gravely, his eyes steady on mine. “Whatever we do, I think we need to ensure that this rebellion begins before the Princess’s marriage takes place. I’m willing to wager that as soon as the Outer City is under control of the King, they’ll increase the draft and a new wave of soldiers will be shipped off to the Wastelands.”

“I think you’re right,” I say, sighing. “Besides that, Meg doesn’t want to marry.”

His head tilts slightly. “Meg?”

“The Princess,” I say quickly, lifting my mug and frowning at the empty bottom.

“You call her Meg?”

“Well, she asked me to, and—”

I’m cut off when the door to the pub suddenly slams open. A beam of late afternoon sunlight cuts across my vision as a pair of rowdy men enter, arguing loudly.

“Oh no,” I murmur, recognizing the voices. Of all the rotten luck...

“What is it?” Will turns in his seat to look at the door.

“Oy! Is that who I think it is?” someone calls out at us from across the room.

Still blinking spots of light out of my eyes, I can only dimly make out a pair of dark silhouettes shouldering their way toward our table.

Two chairs are dragged over as Edmun and Gordy make themselves comfortable. I shift my chair closer to Will in order to make room, my mind desperately churning through possible scenarios to explain my presence and Will.

"Kay-kay! Fancy seeing you here, and in such fine company, no less. Where have you been?" Edmun leans across the table, his usually-charming smile somewhat lopsided.

My vision finally adjusts to the weak light and I make out a trace of something hard in his eyes.

"Here and there," I reply smoothly, purposefully vague. I try to redirect the conversation. "Good to see you, Gordy. Last I heard, you were spending some time in the gaol."

Gordy makes a sound somewhere between a hack and an acknowledgement. "They canna hold me long."

"No, I didn't expect they would."

"Show them the price you paid." Edmun nudges Gordy.

Gordy drops his arm heavily onto the table and I nearly gag. The sight of a still-healing stump where his hand used to be churns my stomach and threatens to spill the ale I just ingested. From the corner of my eye, I can see Will clenching his own hands unconsciously.

"*Gods*, Gordy," I breathe. I look up to see both of them staring at me intently, waiting for my reaction. "I...I don't know what to say." Swallowing, I try to compose myself. "Didn't they give you the option to serve in the Wastelands?"

Gordy's face colours bright red. "I didn'a think that would be much better. Lose my hand or lose my life, the way I saw it. Must be easy for you to make that choice; you've never been in that stinkin' hell hole."

"I didn't mean it like that," I protest. I make to place my hand gingerly on his wrist but he pulls it away, using his remaining hand to lift a tankard to his lips.

"Forget it," he mumbles.

A moment of silence passes. I feel Will shift next to me and sense he is as on edge as I am.

"Are you two out celebrating?" I ask, by way of keeping the conversation friendly.

Edmun laughs, his elbow slipping off the table. "Celebrating? I suppose you could say that."

I catch a whiff of strong liquor on his breath and urge myself to sober up, while trying to think of an excuse to leave.

The vampirish barkeep appears once again to deposit four shots of an unidentifiable liquid onto our table.

Edmun picks his up and slams it back, his bloodshot eyes fixed on Will. "What are we celebrating, Gordy?"

"Yer last night of freedom, I suppose." Gordy's rat-like features appear even harsher than usual as he stares at me over his glass, slurping noisily.

"Ah yes, here's to the last night of revelry!" Edmun gestures at Will and I to take our drinks.

We exchange a look and pick up the glasses.

"Why is it your last night?" I ask, crinkling my nose at the smell wafting off the mysterious liquid.

"Tomorrow I ship off, don't you know? They finally called me up. It's my turn to fight for the glory of the City, to die heroically on a steaming dune out in the Wastelands." Edmun's voice is thick with bitterness and drink, his eyes never leaving Will.

I toss the drink back, buying time as I struggle not to choke with the shock.

"You're going to fight?" I say, lamely.

"That's what I said, isn't it?" Edmun's fist slams down on the table. I jump and Will places a protective hand on my arm. Stealing a glance up at him, I find his gaze locked with Edmun's, though his expression remains impassive.

"Aren't you going to introduce us to your friend, Kay-kay?" Edmun snarls. "Pretty couple you make." He spits onto the ground. "Bloody courtiers. I don't suppose you'll be fighting this damned war, will you, rich boy?"

"I've already served my time," Will says, calmly.

"Is that so? Chose not to buy your way out then, did you? Must have been nice to have the option." Edmun tears his eyes away from Will long enough to grab the untouched shot glass and down it in one gulp.

The miners near the bar have ceased their conversation and are now watching us with rapt attention.

Something flashes momentarily across Will's face. All three men have tightened their jaws and I realize I have to separate them as soon as possible. I make to stand, wobbling slightly, and cursing myself for the drinks.

"Well, this has been sufficiently awkward," I say, trying to break the tension. "But we really have to get going."

I try to kick Will under the table but miss, stumbling again. Luckily, he seems to get the message and rises to his feet.

"Ah no, no. Don't leave. We just got here." Edmun pushes back his chair and rocks on the back legs, staring up at us. His usually friendly face appears worn and my heart goes out to him. His drunken bluster is a cover for the deep-seated fear he must feel.

"I'm really sorry, Edmun." I don't know what to say.

He waves a hand dismissively. "Don't worry about it."

I feel Will tug my arm but I pull away and kneel down next to my friend, gathering his big shoulders into a hug. As he wraps his arms around me, I blink back the tears that threaten to spill, sudden memories of our childhood together with my brother overtaking me.

He pulls back first, gripping my arms and peering fixedly at my face. "I really miss him," he says bluntly. "Frye was always the brave one, not me."

"You're braver than you know," I tell him.

Unable to say anything more, I give Edmun's hand one last squeeze and allow Will to lead me out of the bar. The sun has sunk lower in the sky and the alley is bathed in a hazy orange light, illuminating the stone buildings and stretching their shadows into eerie proportions.

"Are you all right?" Will asks.

We are leaning against a wall in the alleyway; my arms are wrapped tightly around myself despite the warm air.

"I'm fine," I say, pinching the bridge of my nose. As I draw a shaky breath, my emotions gradually recede back under control.

"Who was he talking about, back there?" Will asks. "Who's Frye?"

I open my eyes to see him watching me intently.

"My brother," I say simply. Saying the words causes a hollow thud to reverberate through my chest.

"Is he..." Will trails off.

"He's dead," I confirm. I step to the side, avoiding Will's outstretched hand reaching for my shoulder.

He drops his arm back down. "The war?"

"Yes," I say, keeping my eyes trained on his. "More than five years, now."

Will doesn't say anything, his face impassive but for the trace of sympathy in his eyes. "I'm sorry."

I turn away, unwilling to let the old feelings grab hold of me again. "Don't be sorry, just help me finish this damnable war and this damnable monarchy."

chapter 19

"Abby? Hello? Earth to Abby?"

I blink rapidly, the words on the page swimming back into focus as a voice cuts through my thoughts. Meg is sitting across from me, waving her hand in front of my face; a look of amusement crosses her fine features.

"Yes, sorry. Did you say something?" With some difficulty, I force myself to concentrate on the Princess. We are in the library, sitting together on one of the overstuffed couches, books lying open across our respective laps. We are of the same mind that the pressures and drudgery of Palace life are best left to the shallow-minded and we have fallen into the habit of sneaking off together to share the always-abandoned seventh floor.

"Welcome back. Where did you go? I know you can't be too wrapped up in that book—I've read it before and it is exceptionally dull." Meg arches an eyebrow at me, her tone teasing but her eyes concerned.

"Oh, I just completely lost my focus, I suppose. I must be tired." I shut the book and stretch my arms, giving an exaggerated yawn to reinforce my point. When I open my eyes again, I see her expression hasn't changed.

"All right," she says. Her tone is unconvinced but for now she seems unwilling to push the point. She closes her own book and re-crosses her long legs.

The afternoon sun washes over us, warming my shoulders and making even the cavernous room feel cozy. The overall effect makes me drowsy and threatens to pull me back into my thoughts of the previous day. I look toward the library's expansive windows, watching as one of our airships floats lazily across the sky, destined for the Wastelands.

I wonder if Edmun is aboard. My stomach flips just thinking about how scared he must be, an unwieldy weapon clenched in a hand better suited to a blacksmith's artistry. I turn and regard Meg, reclining comfortably on the couch next to me. Does she realize the impact her father's will has upon my friends' lives?

"I have to say, I am not looking forward to next week's ball at all." She sighs, completely unaware of the anger percolating just below my surface.

I swallow the burning feeling in my chest and force myself to remember my role. "It can't be so bad," I say, with some difficulty. "There will be the usual feasting and shallow conversations, yes, but at least this time we will get to wear our best dresses and dance."

She laughs lightly, one hand absentmindedly playing with the end of her braided hair.

Can her concerns really be so trivial? As much as I have come to enjoy Meg's company, her quick wit and conversation being a welcome respite, at times it is hard to keep at bay my frustration toward her. In these moments, I take a deep breath, reminding myself that her ignorance is not her own fault. What else can I expect from someone who has lived their entire life behind Palace walls?

There is a mystery to this girl, an untold side to her that I do not yet understand. Here is a person who devours books, yet seems reluctant to bring up her own thoughts about City policies. Someone who laments being pushed aside by her father, but seems disinclined to consider ruling in his stead.

I turn this idea over in my mind as I watch her undo and re-plait her hair. It would be dangerous for someone within the Palace to voice an opinion that contradicts the King's, and what reason have I given Meg to trust me? For as much as she seems to prefer my company over her other cronies, we haven't really shared true confidences. I decide to prod, just a little, to see what I can find.

"I've been thinking, lately," I begin.

"Don't hurt yourself," Meg cuts in, nudging my leg with her toe.

I swat her away. "Thanks for your concern, Princess. No, I've been thinking of *Pride and Prejudice*."

"Oh, Mr. Darcy." She fans herself exaggeratedly. "Your literary crush."

"Do you think a love like that could ever happen?" I ask.

"What do you mean?"

"You know, a love between classes." I shift on the couch, drawing my leg up and turning to face her.

"Hmm." She tilts her head thoughtfully. "They do say that great love defies all obstacles."

"How about a courtier and a commoner? Could they ever be together, or are they too different?"

Her head suddenly swivels toward me, brown eyes unblinking. She doesn't say anything for a long moment and I begin to regret my tactics.

"A courtier and a commoner," she says, considering. "Yes, I think they could potentially fall in love. Real love."

My heart is thudding heavily in my chest as I press forward. "Could it ever really work, though? Isn't one better than the other?"

"Better? Better how?" She would appear the picture of innocence if it weren't for the sharp look in her eyes.

I chew my lip, thinking. Easy, Kay, these are dangerous waters.

I tread carefully. "Some people think that because we are the descendants of the original survivors, we are more deserving of our advantages."

"Is that what you think?" Her straightforwardness takes no prisoners.

Hedging my bets, I show my cards. "No."

She nods slowly, thoughtfully, her clear gaze remaining trained on me.

"Me neither," she confirms, lifting her lips into a small smile.

I release the breath I didn't realize I was holding, returning her grin.

"It's such a taboo subject, isn't it?" Meg continues. "I mean, no one will even speak about the Commons around my father's table, unless they're discussing the war or taxes. You'd think they'd have more respect for the people who perform the work that fuels their city." She shakes her head.

"That's terrible." I don't have to feign my disgust.

"You're not wrong."

We are silent for a moment while Meg picks at a bit of her fingernail, an unfamiliar gesture. She seems a little anxious for me to continue the discussion.

"What would you do differently?" I ask.

At once she hops off the couch, striding across the room to shut the heavy library doors. She hurries back and leans in closer to me, a high colour in her cheeks.

"Everyone should receive the same education," she says in a low voice. "That is the key. We need to support the people who want to build and refine their skills, not the ones who waste their time loafing about. Imagine how much the City could accomplish if we rewarded great minds and innovation."

I sit silently, staring, completely taken aback at the turn of events.

"That's...beautiful," I manage eventually. "You've given this some thought."

Her smile broadens, "And when I say everyone, I mean everyone. This division of genders and generations is so archaic, it kills me to think of how much brilliance we are wasting by holding on to the past." Meg sits back, her eyes so dark they are almost black. A vibrant energy has settled over the Princess, making her appear at once older and wiser than her years.

I blink, jolted into regarding this girl in a whole new light. Who would have guessed that this silent, stewing princess was harbouring such radical ideas?

"Have you told your father any of this?" I ask.

A line appears in her forehead.

"I've tried," she says bitterly. "He stops listening as soon as I start in about my thoughts. He won't hear a word about change. All he cares about is fuelling his precious war."

She sighs, her fingers returning to twirl the ends of her hair. “He thinks the old ways are still the best ways. He’ll hang on to every word those ancient Board men spew into his ears. They aren’t trying to improve the City and the lives of the people in it; the only thing any of them are interested in is how to make themselves richer. When I say anything that contradicts the status quo, he gets angry and sends me away. It’s like talking to a brick wall.”

“That doesn’t surprise me.” I think of the nightly meals in the Hall and the way the Board members clamber over one another in their starched jackets, desperate to gain the attention of the King. I don’t envy Meg having to spend an extended period of time with any of them.

“Even when it comes to our methods of punishment, my father refuses to listen to reason,” Meg continues. “I mean, chopping off people’s hands? Doesn’t that seem a tad barbaric?”

I flex my right hand, remembering the gory stump at the end of Gordy’s arm. “Sometimes desperate people have to make desperate decisions.”

“Exactly. When you create a society where people are born into poverty, what else can you expect but crime? And then that mass arrest, yesterday. The punishment for those poor people is entirely excessive.”

My head snaps up from my furled hand. “What happened?”

“You didn’t hear? There was a riot in the market—some protest over the cost of the latest water shipment.” Meg shakes her head, twisting and worrying the strands at the end of her braid. “The guards arrested nearly thirty commoners and are holding them in the gaol indefinitely.”

My palms pinch where my nails dig into them. “What’s going to happen to them?”

“I’m not sure.” Meg shrugs sadly. “I suspect the men will soon be sent off to the Wastelands, but the gods only know what will become of the women.”

My jaw clenches, a red haze overtaking my vision. Nearly thirty people, sitting and waiting for an undeserving fate. I have heard the rumours of the gaol and its putrid conditions. The Commons are awash with whispers about people being forgotten and left to rot beneath the Palace, their only company the screams from the torture chamber. Those fortunate enough to return from the gaol's depths forever carry a haunted look in their eye and a silence bred from experiencing the unspeakable.

As I watch Meg, who sits back in a huff, an idea slowly begins to take seed in my mind.

With a small push in the right direction, Meg could be persuaded to represent the rebellion. Her intentions are honourable; all she lacks is support.

Perhaps we don't need to completely dispel the monarchy. Maybe all we need to do is clear the way for the next in line.

The library door creaks open, startling us both. My handmaid, Sera, pokes her head inside, a regretful look on her small face. She scurries toward us, her quick footsteps tapping against the wooden floor.

"I am so sorry to interrupt you, your Highness, my lady. Vitrola is asking to speak with her Highness."

Meg turns back to me and rolls her eyes, dutifully rising and making her way toward the door as Sera scurries aside and bows her head respectfully.

"Thank you, Sera. Abby, I'll speak with you later."

"Goodbye, your Highness." I speak formally for Sera's benefit as Meg swishes through the door, her long dress disappearing down the hall in a soft cloud.

I sigh and place my book down on the couch, sitting forward and rubbing my temple as though I could massage the typhoon of thoughts into alignment.

"Do you need anything from me, Miss Abby?" Sera's voice breaks in.

"No, I'm—" I straighten, suddenly struck by a thought. "Actually, there is something you could do for me." I pat the spot on the couch next to me, recently vacated by Meg.

Sera comes closer, hovering near the arm of the couch but not sitting.

"What can I help you with?" she asks.

"I was wondering if there were any schematics of the Palace," I inquire. "It's such a fascinating layout—I would be interested to see the design." I keep an easy level of enthusiasm in my voice.

Sera is silent for a moment, her hands twisting over her apron.

"Well," she says slowly, "there are maps we use to train the new servants, but I'm not sure we're supposed to bring them out of the kitchen. I could ask the head housekeeper."

"Oh, I am sure there is no reason to bother her," I say, waving my hand in the air. "I wouldn't want to get you in trouble—I just thought maybe if it was a simple thing, you could procure it for me, but don't go out of your way." Never underestimate the ways in which kindness can be used as a weapon.

"It's no trouble!" she says quickly. "I'm sure it's fine if I borrow one for you. If they show the maps to the staff, then you are certainly well within your rights to see them. I'll bring a copy to your room in just a few minutes."

I cringe a little at her self-deprecating comments but thank her, placing a grateful hand on her shoulder before she scurries away. I walk back to my room slowly, my stomach churning as the new information continually swirls through my mind. I rub my forehead again, seeking to alleviate the pressure of the headache forming between my eyes.

No sooner have I arrived in my room and carelessly tossed my earrings onto the desk than Sera returns, slightly breathless and clutching a rolled-up piece of parchment.

"Here you are, miss," she says, her face flushed.

"Thank you, Sera. You are too sweet." I withdraw a coin from my pocket, pressing it into her hand as she murmurs her appreciation.

"Will there be anything else, Miss Abby?"

"No, thank you. I think I'll just go to bed early tonight." I am itching to comb through the map but wish to do so in private.

Sera nods and begins to take her leave. She pauses at the door and looks back at me, colouring slightly. "Miss, if you could refrain from telling..."

I nod and wave her through the door. "Of course. If anyone sees this map, I'll tell them I got it myself. Don't worry about it."

She gives me a small smile and leaves, closing the door softly behind her.

Finally alone, I clear the desk with a hurried sweep of my arm. Carefully, I unfurl the map and stretch it over the surface of the desk, rotating it until I have the proper orientation.

I locate my room and the ladies' parlour almost immediately and begin tracing a path down to the main floor toward the Great Hall. Finding it, I continue pulling my finger to the very bottom of the map and East of the Palace, then tap my finger on the building I was searching for.

The gaol.

From the schematics, I gather that the prison houses three main chambers. The main area is made up of two cells of general population, likely separated into male and female. Past that are the isolation cells; the far chamber is, ominously enough, not labelled. I wonder if this is the rumoured torture chamber, and a chill runs down my spine

As I pore over the map, I feel the blood coursing through my veins and a familiar thrill run down my spine. This is it. Finally, I have found a way to use my newfound position within the Palace to help my people and at the same time extract some much-deserved retribution against the crown. A voice that sounds suspiciously like Will's warns me to forget this scheme, but a second, stronger voice—fuelled by the plight of Edmun and the rest of my friends—urges me onward.

The schematics show only one route to enter or leave the prison. The main entrance is directly beside the guards' barracks, to the east of the courtyard.

As far as I can tell, moving several people out of their cells and transporting them back into the City without being detected presents a few minor problems.

First, how to get in and out of the guardhouse without the guards raising alarm? I would have to count the number of men stationed around the gaol at any given time and take stock of their shifts. If I can accomplish that, I should be able to find a window of time when someone wouldn't be immediately missed if they were to become indisposed.

Second, I would have to procure the keys for the door to the gaol and the door to the general-population chamber.

Finally, the trickiest element would be transporting people away from the Palace and back to the Commons. How to sneak several people past the countless guards and nobles milling about the Palace grounds? Could I hide them, somehow?

I chew on my lip, thinking. Scanning the room absently, I find myself fixated on the open doors of the closet. Of course: I am already an expert at obscuring a commoner among a sea of courtiers. I don't need a hiding place, just enough costumes.

Hide them in plain sight.

The goddess of luck must be pleased, since she's seen fit to provide me with the ideal opportunity that will see the Palace teeming with extra people. A few more snuck into their midst would scarcely be noticed.

The ball.

That's it. I can take advantage of the party being held at the Palace in one week's time. If I could organize a way to get down to the gaol and extract the prisoners, then I could sneak them out of the Palace under the guise of guests returning home. The Palace and courtyard will be full of people: the perfect disguise.

The throbbing in my head begins to ease as I locate some paper and a pen from the scattered pile on the floor. I painstakingly copy out the schematic by hand as accurately as I can so that Sera can return the original map to the servant's quarters immediately.

The clarity that comes with tracing the map onto my sheet of paper helps me focus my thoughts and gradually piece together the logistics of my riskiest scheme yet. I am going to pull off a jailbreak right under the noses of the City's richest and most powerful.

chapter 20

By the time I have finished tracing the map and memorizing key passages, the sun has long since set and I find myself shivering from the cool night air.

I grab a blanket off the bed, wrapping it around myself as I cross the room to the open window. I welcome the fresh breeze against my face, smoothing my forehead where it has been tight with tension since I began formulating a plan to release the commoners held in the Palace gaol.

Over the last several hours, I have managed to piece together an idea that, if executed seamlessly, should implement the perfect cover for a couple dozen people walking out of their prison cells and straight through the front gate of the Palace.

I pull the blanket tightly over my shoulders as I look up toward the night sky, my eyes reflexively picking through the familiar patterns etched by the stars. Out of habit I orient myself relative to my old childhood home using a technique my father taught me.

My thoughts drift back to the nights spent with my parents and my brother, all crammed into the tiny flat we shared. I remember my father taking my brother and I up to the roof to get a respite from the cramped space.

"See that right there?" His large hand encircles my own as he points my finger up toward a line of bright stars. "That is the Fireline. It was formed after the Burn, when the ashes of our old civilization floated up into the sky. Notice how it begins at the horizon and trails upward? It is forever guiding you toward the North. If you can find the Fireline, you can always find your way home."

My eyes are wide as I fight to take in the million twinkling points above us. My father's grip tightens around me, warm and secure.

"I want you to remember that, my sweet Kay. This world can sometimes seem very big, but you are never lost so long as you can find your stars."

I nod reverently while our joined hands trace the distant mass of silver highlighting the night sky. Leaning back against my father's warm, solid form, I know I am safe and loved as he hugs me close.

Here, in my plush Palace bedroom high above the City, I can almost smell the warm scent of clay on his favourite linen shirt, remnants of a day's work in the mines. I shut my eyes tight, fighting to preserve the memory as my tired mind slowly releases it back to the stars above. I open my eyes and start to pull the window shut before changing my mind and leaving it open to the fragrant night air.

As I crawl into bed, I turn the next steps over in my mind once more; with only one week left until the ball, I will have to work quickly. First, I will have to watch the guards, noting their schedules and shift changes. Next, I will figure out a way to get down to the gaol so that I will know the various impediments between the commoners and the Palace gate. While I'm down there I will take stock of the number of prisoners, both male and female, so I know how many outfits I'll have to arrange for. Finally, I will have to organize several carriages for transporting people out of the Palace during what is sure to be one of the busiest nights of the year.

It couldn't be more simple.

Sighing, I flip over in my bed and punch my pillow into submission before flopping back down again. With so many pieces to contend with, I can't help but think back to Harry and Lara's warnings about my habit of taking unnecessary risks.

I weigh the concerns of my friends against the leaden guilt that has plagued me since I began flitting around in beautiful clothes, sleeping in a comfortable bed and stuffing myself with food every day. The weeks spent pretending to be a courtier have yielded no results; I had hoped that by now, Will would have made some progress toward his rebellion but he seems content to take his precious time.

The truth is that while I have several reasons for wanting to help the people sitting in those mouldy cells belowground, one all-encompassing fact is that I need to feel like myself again. I need to remember who I am and prove that I haven't completely turned my back on the commoners.

My father's words echo in my head as sleep finally takes me:

You are never lost so long as you can find your stars.

After only a few hours of dream-filled rest, I allow Sera to dress me, then stumble out of my room into the hallway. I join the throng of ladies emerging from their own rooms, their hair carefully set and clothes less creased than my own.

I fall into step with Blushes, Glassy and Blinky, allowing their inane chit-chat to flow over me as we trod the now-familiar route down to the Great Hall for breakfast. When we arrive, I all but collapse into my usual chair and take a long sip from the steaming, caffeinated drink placed before me.

Chairs scrape roughly against the stone floor and we all rise to greet Meg and her father. Today, the King wears a wine-coloured jacket cuffed with gold filigree while Meg trails several steps behind, looking as elegant as ever in a floating crimson gown. I catch her eye as she walks by our table and she sticks her tongue out at me. I snort, coughing into my napkin while a couple of the ladies shoot me looks of disapproval.

After we sit down to our breakfast, I glance over at Will's table. He appears a bit haggard this morning as well, with a couple of days' worth of stubble covering his cheeks and faint shadows bordering his eyes. He looks up just as I realize my gaze has lingered a bit too long and I bring my attention immediately to my plate, shovelling several large forkfuls of eggs into my mouth as though nothing has ever been so important.

While sketching out the Palace schematics last night, I briefly considered confiding in Will. There is no doubt that the jailbreak would be infinitely easier to pull off with his help, but I ultimately decided to keep him in the dark. For one, I couldn't imagine a scenario in which careful, single-minded Will would approve of such a risk. No, it is best that I protect him from any knowledge of my goings-on, in case something goes wrong.

Or in case he tries to stop me.

I keep my eyes downcast for the entirety of the meal. The ladies' conversation feels even more mundane than usual and I struggle to keep an expression of feigned interest on my face. When we are finally excused, I watch as the half-finished plates are cleared and our leftovers are whisked away, the sight of all that wasted food readying me to enact the first step in my plan.

We file back upstairs and I rush to grab a cloak and book before stopping by the parlour and remarking to Blinky that I am going into the garden to read. Blinky's eyelids flutter uncomprehendingly while the rest of the ladies pull out embroidery and go about their usual routine of ignoring me entirely.

Finally free of the stifling, perfumed atmosphere, I hurry down the stairs and out to the courtyard. I pull the cloak up over my head and force myself to walk leisurely through the yard and out the east exit, toward the barracks.

Over the courtyard wall, I spy the low building that houses the off-duty guards. The barracks are dark and discreet, nestled securely against the much more formidable gaol. The darkened prison is pocked with small, narrow slits for windows and is completely unadorned save for the heavy wooden door that bars it. Though it seems small and sits low to the ground, I know from studying the schematics that the level below sprawls expansively beneath the earth.

I stroll over to the far end of the yard and sink down onto a bench. I flip open my book, seemingly oblivious to the world around me. In reality, I am watching the surrounding area and taking careful note of anyone entering or leaving the barracks or the gaol.

The afternoon drags on and I take care to change my position from time to time, always keeping a sharp eye on the comings and goings of any man wearing a guard's uniform. As the sun performs its arc across the sky, I begin to regret not bringing along any food or water, but I am unwilling to leave my perch for a moment and miss a crucial detail in the routine of the guardsmen.

Eventually, the hour grows late and I hear the tread of horses' hooves and the rumbling of carriages, signalling the arrival of the evening's dinner guests. A distant, tinkling laughter and a general stirring reminds me that it is time to make myself seen again, and I reluctantly rise to my feet, rubbing my sore backside. I head back through the courtyard and up to my room, only half paying attention to my surroundings as the guards' schedule solidifies in my mind's eye.

I stand passively while Sera re-dresses me for the evening meal, forcing idle chit-chat with her as I mentally catalogue what I learned and file away the information. A warm, pleasant feeling flows through my limbs, filling me with the familiar buzzing of a plot being raised against our suppressors. *This* is the feeling I have anticipated for the entirety of the time that I have been here. For too long I have loafed about in inaction, every day struggling with the frustration of following someone else's scheme, of spending day after day participating in the most mundane of activities while Will and his conspirators bide their time.

I am taking this matter into my own hands and doing what I do best. Today was a good day; I took a small, but crucial, step toward learning the everyday goings-on of the Palace guards, and tomorrow I shall do the same. Soon, I will have enough information to figure out a safe moment to slip into the barracks, steal a uniform and enter the gaol. Within the week, I will be seeing the prisoners and their conditions for myself.

"Ready, miss?" There is a note of impatience in Sera's tone and I realize she has been repeating herself while I have been wrapped up in my own thoughts.

I roll my shoulders back, tilting my head at my reflection in the mirror, noting the high colour in my cheeks and the mischievous glint in my eye.

"Yes, I'm ready," I tell her.

chapter 21

I sit huddled on the roof of the guards' barracks, watching the moon as it silently rises ever higher in the sky. My eyes trace the Fireline and I instinctively orient myself while I wait patiently for the guards' next shift change. The Palace residents have all long since retired to bed and the footpath below me is silent, but at any moment, I should be able to pick up on the heavy shuffle of the last guard emerging from the barracks to begin his night of work.

The dark clothes I lifted from the laundry help me melt into the shadows. I relax, focusing on keeping my heartbeat slow and steady.

As I wait, it occurs to me how strange it was not to run into anyone during the silent journey from my bedroom to the gaol. Assuredly, the courtiers must feel safe behind the faultless walls of their Palace. They sleep soundly, certain that any threat of Wastelanders would be first felt by the unfortunates at the outer edges of the City.

Finally, the man I was waiting for emerges from the building below me. From my position I see him adjust the sword at his waist before he strolls off toward the gaol, whistling a low tune. I stay perched on the roof, listening for any sounds of someone awake and rustling about inside the barracks. Hearing nothing, I assume that all the men are tucked securely into bed and snoring contentedly.

This is the moment. I roll over the edge of the roof and lower myself toward the window, swinging forward and landing silently on the floor inside. Finding myself between two narrow beds, I drop down onto my stomach between them, slowing my heartbeat so I can make out the individual sounds from the beds around me. I lie stone still, concentrating and counting the number of distinct snores. I repeat the count one more time, just to be certain, before I rise slowly to my feet, assured that every off-duty guardsman is accounted for and dead asleep.

With my breaths shallow and my footsteps light, I ease my way over to the footlocker at the end of one of the beds. I grasp the lid of the wooden chest and lift it, my heart leaping into my throat at the sound of the groaning wood. The man in the bed in front of me snorts loudly and I freeze, the lid of the footlocker only half-raised. The man shifts his position and expels wind before sighing and sinking back into his steady symphony of snores.

I wrinkle my nose, raising the lid further and pulling out one of his neatly folded uniforms. Taking stock of a pair of boots, a tunic and pants, I gather the items into a bundle and gently place his sword and belt on top. I tie the assortment quickly and securely before closing the lid and then tiptoe back toward the window, chucking the items out onto the ground below.

I heave myself through the window, my landing muffled as I land on the bundle of stolen clothes. I grin to myself, pulling the items on over my own dark outfit and hoping that the extra layer will help to fill out the uniform. After pulling the boots on, I tie a dark scarf around the lower half of my face, tucking my braided hair down the neck of the tunic and smoothing away any wayward strands. Finally, I pull on the heavy leather breastplate and cinch the belt and sword around my waist, grunting when it slips down my hips. I wrestle with the belt for a moment before impatiently tying the length of leather around my waist in a crude knot.

I pull the hood up over my head and cross the short distance from the barracks to the gaol. I was lucky in that the guard I had relieved of his clothes appears to be on the smaller side, but the boots shift around uncomfortably against my feet and rub blisters onto the back of my heels. I ignore the discomfort and continue onward, adopting the kind of swagger I have seen the guards use; I pull open the thick wooden door of the gaol and stride inside.

A low, flickering torchlight laps against my face and I slow my pace to take stock of my surroundings. The entrance is occupied by a single older man sitting behind a wooden desk in front of an ominous gated door. He glances up lazily at my approach, his expression blank.

“Heading down?” he asks.

I nod and he stands up, rattling his keys, and unlocks the heavy door behind him. I sidle past him and head down the stairs, the sound of my footsteps echoing off the low rocks around me as I descend.

I can scarcely believe how smoothly everything is going. I move slowly and purposefully down the stairs, wanting to give myself ample time to allow my eyes to adjust to the darkness.

The air feels dry and heavy, made cold by the oppressive stone walls surrounding me. I am warmed by my heavy breastplate, at the same time feeling a stab of sympathy for anyone made to stay down here without such luxuries. I can hear the low murmur of voices coming from below, interrupted intermittently by wracking coughs. Besides that, it is ominously quiet.

I reach the bottom of the stairs and walk down a low-ceilinged hallway, my mental map laying out the ground before me. I know that the general-population prisoners will be split between two cells located at the far end of the hallway, but I am uncertain of how many guards will be down here and where they will loiter. The aim of tonight's scouting mission will be to familiarize myself with the area and the guards' placement so I can plot an escape route.

The voices grow louder as I reach the end of the tunnel. Here, the space opens up and the torches dotting the wall cast an eerie glow, throwing menacing shadows across the narrow tunnel. Directly in front of me are two heavy wooden doors, which I know to be the locked entrances to the men and women's cells. Following the sound of talking, I turn my head and spy two guards sitting at a small wooden table shoved against the far wall.

One of the men looks up at me and raises a hand in greeting. I nod and make my way over to them, wrinkling my nose at the smell permeating from their corner, worse than the unwashed bodies behind the cell doors.

The source of the stench appears to be coming from the tin cask on the table between the guards. The smaller of the two takes healthy drags from it; cheap whisky dribbles down his chin.

"Evenin'," the larger man greets me. His partner sets the cask down and grunts out his own acknowledgement.

"Evenin'," I say, speaking from my chest and lowering my voice by several octaves. I rest my hand casually on the hilt of my sword and widen my stance, believing myself to be taller and broader than I am.

The cask is offered to me and I shake my head, gesturing at the darkened corridor ahead.

"Rounds," I grunt. When impersonating a different gender, I find it best to keep to low light and limit my words as much as possible.

The glassy eyes of the larger guard seem free of suspicion. He turns away from me, suddenly distracted by an itchy armpit. His associate appears even less interested; he slumps forward in his seat, crashing his head onto the surface of the table.

I turn and walk into the gloom, careful to pass near the cell doors. Allowing my eyes to rove over the brass locks, I note that they appear to be secured with a single, heavy latch. I make a mental note to check the guards for the keys on my way out.

Rounding a corner, I find myself in a narrow, darker tunnel illuminated by the occasional torch; several others are burned out and long forgotten.

The solid wooden doors of the isolation cells begin to dot the walls to my left and right but I keep my eyes straight ahead, ears pricked for the sound of unwanted company. The silence begins to feel claustrophobic as I move deeper and deeper into the depths of the gaol. The isolation corridor appears completely unpopulated and I don't spy a single guard as the tunnel curves further. I round another corner and make my way toward the very back of the prison.

My heartbeat and footsteps reverberate loudly as I am plunged ever deeper into the darkness and encroaching silence.

Eventually, the hallway widens once again and I stop in my tracks to regard the final chamber, listening for the sounds of any remaining guards. Hearing nothing, I step forward, surveying the imposing doors of the final rooms.

I have no doubt that these are the doors to the torture chambers. Each is made of a solid piece of wood and sits snugly in the cold stone frames, silent and strong, guarding the secrets of the atrocities hidden behind.

I shiver beneath my layers of clothing, though whether it is from fear or anger, I can't be sure. My gaze travels down the hall toward the dead end and my breath catches in my throat when I notice the very last door standing open on its hinges.

I should turn back. I have established that there are only two guards stationed out front and none further along; I don't stand to gain anything by looking into that room.

But my feet are already moving forward and my hand has reached up to grab a torch off the wall. I brace myself against the door frame and hold the torch in front of me, illuminating my path as I step inside.

At first, there is nothing. My eyes gradually adjust to the darkness as I sweep the torch in front of me, expecting at any moment to see an instrument of unspeakable torture or some other garish scene, but all I can make out is a single wooden pole, centred in the space and standing harmless. An inconspicuous fireplace lies beyond, the coals long burned out and turned to ash.

I circle the pole, looking around at the walls and floor. Nothing jumps out at me and my breathing gradually returns to normal. I am making my way back toward the exit when the torchlight reveals several objects hanging on the wall near the door and I stop dead in my tracks.

I gasp, stumbling back a step.

Whips. Dozens of them.

Arranged by a careful hand, they cover the facade of the chamber. Some are long and forked with cruel leather tongues swaying in the draft; others are short and biting, nothing more than a brutal wooden switch. My chest constricts as I take in the sight, scarcely able to believe the sheer size of such a macabre collection. I choke on a gag as I notice the oily stains soaking the ends of various straps, mementoes of a job done.

It is then that I remember the pole standing in the middle of the room.

I turn around slowly, holding the torch up higher and bringing my eyes to the top of the wooden pole, understanding now that I see the iron manacles dangling impassively from a hook near the top of the pole.

"There you are."

I nearly drop the torch as I whip back toward the door, forgetting momentarily that I am wearing a disguise. The darkened form of the larger guard stands in the archway, his features shadowed and impossible to make out in the flickering torchlight.

"I..." I clear my throat and try again. "I was just looking around. Quite the display over here." I nearly retch again as I say the words.

The guard chuckles and moves into the room, positioning himself so he is looking up at the wall of torture.

"It's somethin', ain't it? You can tell that our Inquisitor takes a lot of pride in what he does." He snorts and yaks a ball of spit onto the floor.

"Right." I have no desire to linger and dwell on any questions about the mysterious Inquisitor or any sick pleasure he might get from tearing open the backs of his victims. I want to get out of this room, finish my scouting and return aboveground as soon as humanly possible.

"We should be gettin' back," I say, moving into the hallway and waiting for the man to fall into step behind me.

We make our way wordlessly down the tunnel back toward general population. I pick up the sound of jangling metal behind me and surmise that this man does indeed hold the keys to the men and women's cells.

When we reach the front of the prison, I halt in front of one of the two large doors barring the prisoners.

"Last thing to check," I say, holding out my hand for the keys.

The man makes no move to reach for his belt and instead eyes me, scratching at his armpit again.

"We don't usually bother with that," he says. "C'mon, I'll get you a drink."

"I was told to be thorough." My voice is even as I leave my palm out expectantly. The image of the whips flashes before my eyes again and I have to concentrate to keep my hand from shaking.

I am met with a glassy stare, though now his eyebrows are furrowed and he appears more alert.

"Who told you to do that?" he asks.

"Lieutenant Griss," I say smoothly, drawing from the back-story I fact-checked and rehearsed.

Without another word, the guard unclips the keys from his belt; he tosses them over to me and stumbles back toward his companion at the wooden table. He collapses ungracefully into his seat and takes another dram from the cask.

I turn to the first door and study the keys in my hand, trying to make a quick assessment so that I don't appear to be fumbling with the correct combination. I draw out a large brass key that seems to be made of the same material as the lock and slip it through the hole; I turn once firmly and breathe an internal sigh of relief when the latch lifts. After glancing once more toward the table, where both guards appear fully engrossed in scratching and snoring, I push the door open and slip inside.

The room is illuminated only by a small barred window near the roof, which allows a weak trickle of moonlight to filter in. Through the gloom I can make out roughly a dozen bodies huddled against the walls. Scanning the dank cell, I feel my heart break at the sight of the men curled around themselves, some coughing feebly. As my gaze lingers near the far end of the room, I am arrested suddenly by a pair of eyes staring intently at me from beneath lowered brows.

I pick a path across the room, careful not to disturb any of the sleeping prisoners. Reaching the man, I lower myself into a crouch in front of him, noting that he doesn't flinch or move away when I get close.

Now that my face is level with his, I am struck by how bright his eyes are, striking against his dark, matted hair and grubby features. He appears to be about Will's age, but it's difficult to be certain with all the grime coating his face.

I reach up and tug down my scarf. His brows shoot up in surprise and his eyes widen.

"I don't have much time, so I'll make this quick." I keep my voice as soft as possible. "What is your name?"

"Marc," he whispers in a scratchy voice.

"Marc. I am going to get you all out of here, but I need your help. Will you help me?"

"Yes."

"Brave man," I say, shooting him a small smile. I reach into the pocket of my uniform and pull out a folded piece of paper. I grab hold of Marc's hand and press the parchment into his palm, curling his fingers around it. "I will be back in four days. In the meantime, I need you to read these instructions and get everyone ready. Can you do that?"

"Yes." He swallows and then coughs. "Yes, I can do that."

I make to stand when his hand shoots out and grabs my wrist. His grip is surprisingly strong.

"Are you her?" he asks softly.

I grin and gently pull my arm away, tugging the scarf back over my face.

"Four days," I tell him.

I ease back toward the door, catching one last glimpse of Marc studying the slip of paper in his hands as I pull the door closed and lock it again.

Glancing back at the guards, I see they have both passed out, the smaller one practically beneath the table. I shake my head as I move to the door of the women's cell. With any luck, these two bozos will be the ones on the midnight shift the night of the ball.

The lock barring the women's cell clicks open and I prepare to repeat my routine, feeling more eager than ever to return aboveground. There is still much to take care of in order to be ready for my return in four days.

Four days.

chapter 22

I am jerked awake the next morning when someone grips my shoulder and shakes me roughly.

My eyes shoot open and I instinctively slap the hand away. I roll across the mattress and onto the floor, landing in a defensive position between the bed and the wall. A second later I gather my bearings, adjusting to my plush and now-familiar bedroom. I stand up slowly and find Sera standing on the other side of the bed, her offended hand clutched to her chest as she stares at me incredulously.

"Rough night, miss?" she asks, pointedly.

"Oh gods, Sera, I am so sorry," I say, pushing my tangled hair from my face.

She rolls her eyes and begins stripping the sheets off my bed, pulling them into a pile on the floor.

"What time is it?" I ask, rubbing my eyes as I walk over to the balcony, blinking sleepily in the bright sunlight.

"Past breakfast," Sera answers from behind me. "Most of the ladies are already gathered in the parlour."

I groan. "Why didn't you wake me? I'm starving."

"I figured you would be. I took the liberty of scrounging up some food from the kitchen."

I turn around and smile delightedly, crossing over to the silver bowl of strawberries on my desk.

"You're a saint." I tell her, stuffing a berry into my mouth. "Now I feel particularly bad about slapping you."

I offer her the bowl and she takes a couple of berries before turning back to the laundry. I wander into the closet and absentmindedly flip through the hanging dresses as I turn over in my mind the events of the previous night.

"Uhh, miss?"

"What is it?"

I step back into the bedroom. One glance at Sera and I gasp audibly, sucking the partially chewed fruit back into my throat. My handmaid is holding up a guard's uniform.

I cough, pounding my chest as I fight for breath. I feel rather than see Sera rush across the room. She grabs me by the shoulders and steers me firmly back toward the bed, where she sits down next to me and rubs my back as my lungs gradually clear.

"Those clothes..." I begin, then choke on another cough in my struggle to explain. "They aren't mine."

To my surprise, Sera starts laughing. I stare open-mouthed as my sullen, timid handmaid doubles over, clutching her stomach and laughing so hard I think she might begin choking as well.

"Not yours," she says eventually, wiping tears from the corner of her eyes. "No, Miss Abby. I didn't gather they were yours." She begins giggling again at my shocked expression.

"Not to worry." She pats my knee playfully. "You aren't the first lady to have a guard visit her quarters and I daresay you won't be the last."

"Right," I breathe, fighting to keep from wrinkling my nose at the thought of sharing my bed with one of the King's dimwitted lackeys. "You won't say anything, then?"

"Of course not." Sera winks and rises from the bed; she stoops to gather the offending garments and attempts to hide them among the rest of her gathered laundry,

"Wait!" I reach out a hand, grabbing her wrist.

She stops what she is doing and eyes me curiously.

"Could you... leave those here?" I ask, feeling a blush creep up my throat. "You know, just in case he, uh... comes back."

Impressively, though visibly struggling, Sera manages to keep her face perfectly straight. "Certainly, miss," she acquiesces smoothly, the consummate professional. “I will just put them somewhere a little... more discreet.”

She begins folding the uniform with such a droll expression that I can’t help but burst into my own fit of laughter, revelling in the wonderful feeling of last night’s stressful events lifting from my shoulders.

We are both still giggling by the time I pull on a dress and Sera finishes folding the tunic. She places it neatly under the bed where it joins the breastplate and boots I had already managed to stash away.

With the basket of laundry balanced expertly on one hip, she strides over to the door and places her hand on the knob.

“Oh, and Miss Abby.” She turns back to face me. “I might suggest that you not wear the white dress today.” She throws me a coquettish wink before disappearing into the hall and closing the door, leaving me standing with my mouth agape.

I grab a half-finished book from my nightstand and head to the parlour. Having spent the last few days skulking around the Palace, today I think it wise to make myself seen.

When I arrive in the parlour I find the ladies draped in various states of recline across the couches and cushions, some fussing with needlework while others make no pretense at busying themselves at all, content to simply sit and gossip.

Not a single person glances in my direction when I walk across the tiled floor, a pleasant smile plastered on my face. I find a plush chair at the back of the room near the window and settle myself into it, pulling my legs up to tuck against the armrest comfortably. The ladies’ voices fade into a distant hum as I allow myself to become absorbed in the book Meg lent me. Since my visit to the prison, I am decidedly confident, and it feels wonderful to lose myself in the story of a fictional character.

I become so engrossed that I fail to notice how much time has gone by until someone lays a hand gently on my shoulder. I jump, jolted abruptly into the present for the second time in one day.

"Sorry to disturb." Meg laughs at my wide-eyed reaction. "I take it you are enjoying the book, then?"

"Yes, immensely." I press my thumb down to hold my place as I slap the book shut.

"Glad to hear it. I was just heading to the garden and I wanted to see if you'd fancy a walk?"

I open my mouth to reply when a nasally voice pipes up from behind Meg, "Are you going outside? I was just thinking about taking a turn myself. I would love to join you, your Highness."

Hawk Nose has sauntered over to us, a simperingly sweet smile covering her pointed face. With her sharp nose and over-the-top, plumage-type hairstyle, I can't help but feel she looks even more like an overgrown bird than usual.

"I am certain that you were, Bellany, but perhaps you could join us another time." Meg gives Hawk Nose a cursory nod before manoeuvring her slim shoulders past the girl, pulling the gathered yellow train of her dress behind her.

I keep my head lowered to hide a smirk as I drop my book onto the chair and follow Meg out of the parlour, feeling the heat of Hawk Nose's glare burning into the back of my neck.

Out in the garden, Meg slips her arm through mine and tilts her head up to catch the rays of the afternoon sun. We stroll together down the cobblestone path, talking amiably about the book and the upcoming ball as we take in the sight of flowers and ferns exploding all around us, an unending wall of colour as the foliage spills across the yard.

"I feel as though I haven't seen you in ages," Meg says lightly as we wander. "Listening to the insipid chatter of the ladies without you there was beginning to wear on me."

"You know, I've realized recently that if you listen carefully to their talk, you can pick up on some real pearls of wisdom," I reply, dodging her questions.

"Is that so?"

"Oh yes. Why, just the other day, someone observed that she could lose weight by eating less dessert, so she split her tart into four slices instead of eight before scarfing down the entire thing."

"My goodness, that is industrious!" Meg laughs.

"Quite brilliant, I thought," I agree, pausing to smell a blossom.

"So, where have you been?" The Princess is maddeningly persistent.

I straighten, pasting a casual expression on my face as I pluck the flower and twirl it in my fingers. "Nowhere terribly interesting. I needed a break from the parlour, so I've been exploring the grounds a bit."

"Exploring" meaning I've been lurking about the various corridors, tracking the guards' movements and schedules.

"You've just been wandering the Palace?" One perfectly arched brow is raised in question.

"Uninterestingly, yes. I know it isn't really delicate behaviour befitting a lady." Rolling my eyes at this, I see Meg give a slight smile. "But I find myself feeling so confined here, sometimes. It helps to be able to get outside and stretch my legs."

"I suppose I can't fault you for that." She sighs. "I know the feeling."

I tuck the flower into my braid and slip my arm through Meg's again. "My poor princess," I tease lightly, falling back into step with her. "I'm sorry for leaving you alone with the ladies. I'll tell you what, why don't you and I go on our own little adventure? We may not be permitted to go into the City, but I have found a couple interesting areas inside our humble Palace."

"I think that is a marvellous idea." Meg seems satisfied.

"Perhaps you could show me some hidden treasures?" I suggest. "I am sure that the secrets filling your head could fill a book."

She giggles mischievously. "I may know a thing or two. Rumour has it that our original King, Traynor, installed a hidden escape tunnel when the Palace was first constructed. Perhaps we could find it."

"Perhaps we can." I wink.

We fall into a companionable silence. As we stroll, I find myself turning over a possibility in my mind, and not for the first time. I imagine what the City would be like if it were ruled over by someone caring, someone with vision and an eye for equality.

I glance over at Meg, studying her. She carries herself with a certain haughtiness that belies the strength lying dormant beneath her surface. Beneath her poised princess façade, there is a kind heart and a fierce determination just aching to be set free.

Meg might just possess the heart of a queen.

We turn at the sound of heavy footsteps. Will, tan under the bright afternoon sunlight, is crossing the garden with his long stride and making his way toward us.

"Good afternoon, your Highness; Lady Abby." He inclines his head respectfully as he draws up, flashing his most charming smile. "Please forgive the interruption. I was just doing a bit of gardening when I heard you talking."

"Not at all, Dr. Cain. I didn't know you had a green thumb," Meg remarks prettily.

"I don't, unfortunately." Will pats his forehead with the scarf loosely circling his neck.

I instantly notice the smudges of dirt staining his shirt and hands. His rumpled appearance is a far cry from the polished doctor I've become accustomed to seeing around Court, and more in tune with the rebel pacing about his musty flat.

"The Palace gardeners are kind enough to grow some medicinal plants for me and I get the pleasure of digging them up." His eyes move over to me, conveying something. He wants to talk.

"How interesting! Can you show us some of your plants?" Meg asks.

"Certainly." Will swings his leather satchel out from under his shoulder and reaches inside. "These are used for relieving headaches. When you chew on the leaves, they get gummy and release a nasty-tasting juice.

Pretty foul, but effective." He hands a leaf to Meg and digs back into his bag. "These, right here, are used for sedation."

My eyes snap over to the gnarled bit of mushroom in his hand.

"If you were to grind this up into a powder and drink it, you'd be put right to sleep," he explains.

I take the mushroom from him and examine it, memorizing the look of the fungus.

"Your Highness!" Vitrola's shrill voice cuts across the garden and I clench my shoulders involuntarily.

"Drat. It appears I'm needed for something." Meg sighs. "Thank you for the lesson, Dr. Cain. And Abby, thank you for the respite."

The Princess turns and walks down the path back to the Palace. Standing by the door I can see Vitrola, her expression strained and her hands clutching her ever-present supply of parchments. The Princess' chief of staff is so tightly wound I fear that if she were to relax, she would collapse straight to the floor.

"Would you care to help me prepare these medicines, cousin?" Will asks pleasantly.

"I'd love to," I reply, falling into step beside him and smoothly pocketing the mushroom.

He leads me to a side door, holding it open and then moving beside me as we walk companionably down the hallway. I hang back ever so slightly, letting Will think he is leading me to a new part of the Palace. In truth, I memorized this route a long time ago.

I can't resist a peek inside the infirmary when we walk by. I catch a glimpse of polished stone floors and crisp sheets, white-clad medical assistants going about their duties. When we reach the end of the hallway, Will unlocks a narrow, wooden door and ushers me inside.

His office is one of the inner rooms and has no windows, lit only by a single lantern. Will strikes a match, moving to light the remaining lanterns, bit by bit bringing the room into focus. My attention is captured by the expansive shelves lining one of the walls and I wander over, picking up the occasional item and examining it before placing it back down.

Despite the lack of sunlight, the room is warm and comforting. Glass bottles on a shelf on one side of the room catch the firelight; books line the wall opposite. There is a heavy wooden desk next to the door and a single examination table covered with a sterile, white cloth.

The air is spicy with medicinal fragrances and something else: a whiff of Will's old flat in the City. Immediately, I feel more comfortable here than I have anywhere else in the Palace.

"Make yourself at home," Will says, shaking out the match as he watches me sort through the various medicine bottles.

"Don't mind if I do," I say, replacing the glass jar I was turning over in my hands and moving across the room to look at the bookshelf.

"How is the research going?"

For a moment, I think he is referring to the book I am flipping through, before I remember Meg.

"Very well," I reply; I replace the book and take another.

"It looks as though you and the Princess are becoming close."

I look up at him. He is standing over his desk, sorting the leaves and mushrooms into neat piles.

"She prefers my company to any of the ladies. I think she trusts me." I put the book back and walk over to Will's desk, where I sink into the worn leather chair opposite.

"Good work." He looks up from the messy desk. "I mean it."

"Thanks," I say.

"I heard your talk about exploring the Palace."

"Spying on a spy?" I quirk an eyebrow at him. "Yes, I'm going to see if Meg will show me some of the Palace's secret passageways. Those should prove useful."

"I was referring to you wandering around on your own." Will stops poking through the plants and stares directly at me.

For a moment I think he's onto me and I have to bite down hard on my tongue to keep from confessing my scheme. I pause, swallowing once, and when I speak again, my voice is smooth and even.

"Just performing my due diligence, captain." I allow the barest trace of sarcasm to seep into my tone. "I managed to get my hands on some Palace schematics and I've been looking around, familiarizing myself with the layout."

"I see," he says slowly. He seems to be turning the idea over in his mind. "That was good thinking, but you should have spoken to me about it first."

For a moment I am too shocked to say anything. When I do speak, my voice is tight. "I might have done so, if I could get an appointment."

"What is that supposed to mean?"

"It means that you're never around, Will. You leave me to play 'pretty pretty princess' for days at a time—without a word of where you're going or what you're plotting—and expect me to just sit back and cool my heels. I'm forever left waiting until you're good and ready to show up."

His dark brows lower in warning. "I can't be here all the time. There is a lot of organization that I need to take part in. Believe it or not, there is more going on here than just your 'princess' game."

"I have no doubt that you do a great deal of organizing," I say, darkly. "What I'm not convinced of is that you can actually *act* upon these grand plans."

"What were you expecting? That everything would happen overnight? This isn't one of your practical jokes that we're trying to pull off. A little more thought has to go into it."

"Why did you bring me here, exactly? If you thought all I was good for was practical jokes, if you think what I do is so pointless, then why did you drag me into this?" Heat courses through my entire body and I feel myself practically vibrate with rage. This courtier has kept me idle for weeks upon weeks, and then somehow in the span of a couple minutes has managed to inspire abject fury. Realizing that he has the power to affect me in such a way just makes me angrier.

"Keep your voice down," Will mutters between clenched teeth. His hands have curled into fists on the desk and the knuckles have turned bone white.

"Relax, Will. These doors are six inches thick and completely soundproof. There is nothing in this wing except for the infirmary, and the guard assigned to patrol this area won't pass by for another fifteen to twenty minutes. You see, while you have been twiddling your thumbs, hemming and hawing with your rich friends, I have been studying the goings-on." I cross my arms and lean back in the chair.

He shuts his eyes tightly, visibly drawing a breath.

"Look," he says, with distinct effort. As though *I* am the difficult person. "This type of behaviour is not conducive to what we are trying to accomplish."

"I agree—your behaviour has been completely unacceptable."

"Gods *damn* it." I jump as he knocks his fists on the solid top of the desk. "Could you just for a moment stop talking and *listen*?"

I narrow my eyes at him but stay silent.

"You are seriously the most difficult person I have ever met. You know that?" He brings one hand up to squeeze the bridge of his nose.

"If you're going to start in on the personal attacks, I don't see why I should have to sit silently while you run amok over my character."

"That's enough." His voice is sharp and I once again clench my jaw shut, tapping my foot in aggravation.

"What I was going to say was that *despite* all that, I really do admire your skills and I really do want your help." His hand moves from his nose to run over his shorn head.

I sit as patiently as I can and glare at him. He has inadvertently rubbed dirt across his forehead and stained his linen shirt. I fight the urge to smirk with the satisfaction of seeing careful, composed Will so exasperated.

"That said, I think that you should respect my tactics. You understand what it's like out *there*." He inclines his head toward the door. "But I understand what it's like in *here*. We have to be slow and careful in order to get this right."

I stay silent, waiting for him to continue.

"Is that it?" I ask. "May I say something now?"

"I think we still have another ten minutes until the guard comes by, so you may as well," he says tiredly.

"Closer to fifteen minutes. It didn't take you as long to subtly insult me as you think it did." I re-cross my legs and lean forward in my seat. "I am not confident in your ability to pull this off." With a wave of anger still simmering beneath my surface, I aim to hit him where it hurts. "You remain here comfortably day after day, puttering around in your garden or milling about in the City, while I sit in that stuffy parlour bored out of my *mind*. I ask you, what is that accomplishing? You wanted my help and I'm giving it the best way I know how. I'm the one taking the risk. You're a courtier, Will—you have a safety net. I don't."

"I'm not going to let anything happen to you."

I shake my head. "You don't get it; that's not the point. I don't care about the risk. What I care about is making sure that this has all been for something."

His eyes burn into mine. "It will be."

"When?" I ask. "Because I've been here for nearly a month, and in that time I've seen nothing change. My friends are still getting shipped off to a war that we have no part in. Commoners are still being oppressed and persecuted. Every day we get closer to this marriage and the certainty that thousands of people will be sent into the Wastelands. Will, we are running out of time."

"I know that." He rubs his head again. "I'm working on it."

"Let me help." I search his face carefully. "I can get myself anywhere in this Palace without being seen. I can find out anything you need to know."

He shakes his head. “It’s too dangerous. I know it’s difficult, but I really need you to remain with the ladies. If anyone notices you snooping about, then this really will all have been for nothing.”

This isn’t going anywhere. I don’t know how I could have expected anything more from him. His arrogance and control issues really know no bounds.

“You still don’t trust me,” I say, glowering at him across the heavy desk.

“There’s just too much at stake.” He meets my gaze and holds it. “I’m not trying to hold you back. I’m trying to warn you.”

“Warn me about what?”

“That you aren’t as inconspicuous as you think.” He leans across the table, shoulders drawn up in either anger or aggravation. “Someone has seen you.”

My retort catches in my throat. “Who?”

“He was in my office the other day, inquiring about his only daughter’s new best friend.” Will sinks into his chair, appearing worn out.

“The King?” The fight ebbs from my body.

“Apparently, you’ve made an impression.” He looks up at me. “I don’t want you to take this the wrong way.”

“What do you mean?” I press. “What did you tell him?”

“I told him that you and the Princess have a shared interest in scholarly pursuits and how pleased you were to have a friend you could discuss books with.” He pauses and regards me as I take in this new information. “I tried to downplay you as somewhat less effervescent.”

I snort, feeling both mollified and flattered. “Thanks, I suppose.”

He ignores my remark and peers at me intently. “Do you understand what I’m saying? You’re pretty and you’re clever, Red. People are bound to notice you.” He is careful not to use my real name within these walls. “You need to be careful. It is imperative that you not draw any more unnecessary attention to yourself. Do you think you can handle that?”

I bite the inside of my cheek as I take in this new information, feeling my anger recede as the unfamiliar flicker of anxiety creeps up from the pit of my stomach. The King has been here, asking after me. Up until now, I truly felt like I was operating without notice, and for the moment I can't think of anything to say. The world has shifted and I need time to process and sort through the change in events.

"I can handle it," I hear myself say eventually; my voice is cold. "Thanks for looking out for me." I look around the office, toward the shelves and the desk, anywhere but at Will's face. My fists clench at my sides and I know that if I were to meet his gaze, I wouldn't be able to trust my mouth. "Was there anything else?"

"How are you holding up?" His words startle me and I look up before I can stop myself. The corners of his grey eyes crinkle in concern beneath thick brows.

The question is so unexpected that I have to blink a few times in order to refocus my thoughts.

"I'm fine," I say slowly.

He nods. "Because you know, you could tell me if you were feeling a bit overwhelmed. You don't have to have it completely together all of the time." He speaks carefully, a small smile playing at the edge of his lips.

I groan, rubbing a hand over my face. "Gods, Will. You can be the teacher, the rebel, the scolding mother or the friend, but you can't be all of them. Please, just pick a role and stay there, because the constant shifts are exhausting."

He laughs and the sound echoes off the windowless walls. "My apologies. Maybe I'm a complicated person."

"'Complicated' is putting it mildly. I can never tell if you're angry or pleased with me; it seems to switch from one moment to the next." I am suddenly incredibly tired. This comfortable room and Will's heady presence, combined with the sobering shaking up, have left me completely bewildered.

“I suppose I’m both.” He leans back in his chair and fiddles with one of his sleeves, untucking it and rolling the material up his forearm, revealing one of his jagged scars. “Your methods may make me insane, but I can’t deny that overall you’ve made amazing progress with the Princess.” His mouth turns grim, his gaze steely. “Just be careful.”

chapter 23

The day of the ball has finally arrived and the Palace is a flurry of activity.

I walk down the third-floor hallway, keeping my head lowered as I dodge the servants streaming past. The Palace maids and stewards seem preoccupied with their chores and no one pays me any notice as I make my fourth trip back from the laundry room, a sack laden with stolen dresses and tunics flung over my shoulder.

Pushing back a lock of hair that has escaped my maid's kerchief, I skip lightly down the narrow set of servants' stairs. I tread the familiar path down to the east exit and toward the gaol, feeling a line of sweat trickle down the back of my neck. I push through the exit and hurry along the side of the courtyard, sticking to the crowds of servants and guards. Heading for the alley behind the gaol, I check once over my shoulder before ducking into the shadowed passage in behind. Prying open the lid of an ale barrel, I dump the sack of clothes inside. The barrel is mostly dried out, but unfortunately there is nothing I can do for the smell of soured drink. I shut the lid and secure it, thinking that it may help to cover the odour of the soon-to-be-released prisoners.

I slip out of the alley and back into the throng of people, glancing up to check the position of the sun. I estimate that we are only a couple of hours from when the first of the guests are expected, giving me a small window of time to get ready. The other ladies have been primping since the early morning, locked away on the fourth floor with their handmaids helping to style their hair and prepare their outfits. Sera protested only a little when I sent her on an errand, but she understood well enough that I have no interest in wasting hours on styling. As soon as she left, I donned my maid's disguise and began stealing back and forth from the laundry.

I re-enter the Palace through the servants' door and make my way back up to the fourth floor, ducking my chin and striding quickly back toward my room. I feel a headache coming on at the sound of a dozen high-pitched voices. Girls in various states of undress, sporting elaborate, precarious-looking hairstyles, cross back and forth through the hallway, exclaiming over one another and laughing gaily.

I arrive at my room and slip inside; closing the door behind me, I lean back against it. I feel my heart thudding heavily in my chest and concentrate on relaxing, drawing deep, calming breaths as I try to clear my thoughts.

There is a tapping of knuckles directly behind my head and my eyes fly open.

"Miss Abby?" Sera's voice calls through the door.

"Just a moment!" I say. I strip off my maid's uniform as quickly as I can, dropping the articles to the ground and stuffing them under my bed.

"We really need to start getting you ready," she insists.

I look around desperately for something to cover myself with and grab a sheet off the bed, wrapping it hurriedly around my torso.

"You can come in!" I call.

As the door knob turns, I catch a glimpse of myself in the mirror. I snatch the white kerchief off of my head and drop it to the ground, kicking it behind me as Sera opens the door, her arms laden with swaths of coral fabric.

"Are you just getting out of bed?" she exclaims as she takes in my appearance.

I must look a sight, a blush creeping up my cheeks and my hair standing out at all angles.

"I took a nap," I say, arranging the bottom of my bedsheet around the discarded kerchief. "I wanted to be refreshed."

Sera *tsks* under her breath, leaves the coral bundle draped over a chair and makes a beeline for my washroom. A moment later I hear water running and she re-emerges, gesturing for me to get into the bath.

I drop the sheet and obediently get into the tub, grinning a little at the stubborn set of Sera's chin as she arranges my soaps in an efficient line along the edge of the bath.

"I am perfectly capable of doing this myself, you know," I tell her.

"With all due respect, miss, we are running very far behind schedule and I think it best that I take it from here."

I barely have enough time to shut my eyes before she squirts soap over my scalp, gathers my hair into her hands and starts rubbing vigorously.

"Whatever happened to my meek little handmaiden?" I ask, shivering when a bucket of cold water is thrown over me.

"Your impertinence must have rubbed off on her," Sera replies; she hands me a cloth, indicating that I should finish up.

I scrub and rinse again, accepting a towel from Sera as I step out of the bath. She hustles me over to the vanity and presses gently on my shoulders until I am seated. I allow her to arrange me as needed and take the opportunity to think through my plan for the millionth time as she begins to pat my hair dry.

By midnight the King and his guests will be deeply entrenched in their wine and ale, leaving them suitably occupied and providing me with the ideal opportunity to disappear. I will enter the gaol dressed in my soldier's garb, slip Will's dried mushroom into the guards' drink and wait for them to doze off. Then, with Marc's help, we can pass the stolen clothes to the prisoners and escort them out a few at a time, leading them from the gaol, across the courtyard, into the Palace, through the front door and into the waiting carriages. I have paid off a carriage-master with enough coins to silence his questions about driving Palace guests into the Commons, and in return he has promised to have four carriages ready for me at half-hour intervals. I will recognize the carriages by the green flags displayed at their front.

Sera finishes towelling my hair and begins to separate the curls, twisting them in her fingers and draping the tendrils over my shoulders to finish drying. She turns my face toward her and applies dashes of kohl and lip stain with a practiced hand.

I close my eyes and try to relax as she moves back to my hair, relishing the feeling of her nimble fingers massaging my scalp. My thoughts drift to Meg and how she must also be getting ready at this very moment, likely dreading this ball as much as I am. The King has arranged for Lord Lynal Grayson to attend tonight and I know that the Princess is apprehensive about seeing him. Meg once confessed to me that it's the pretense of propriety for the sake of appearances that she hates more than anything. I had to bite my tongue to keep from saying that I knew exactly what she meant.

My eyes open when Sera taps my shoulder. She pulls me away from the mirror and stands me up in the centre of the room before moving to fetch the pink dress. I obediently put the towel aside and step into the skirt she has held out.

Sera flitters around me, adjusting the folds of the dress here and there before darting over to the closet and rummaging through the drawers of jewellery.

"Nothing too heavy, please," I call over.

I think I hear a small grunt of annoyance but my handmaid emerges almost immediately, her selection made.

She slips a coiled bracelet over my wrist and pushes it up to my forearm. I turn my arm over to admire the design as she clips on my earrings. If I wasn't so determined to hate these unnecessary adornments, I might enjoy the beautiful, unique craftsmanship.

Finally finished, Sera takes a step back. She regards me as I stand uncomfortably before her, fiddling with my bracelet. She arranges a few pieces of hair around my face and nods with satisfaction, the tight line that pierces her brow finally disappearing.

"Well? Do I meet your approval?" I ask impatiently.

"See for yourself." She steps aside and gestures toward the full-length mirror. I walk over to the glass and my eyebrows rise in surprise.

The dress is something I never would have chosen for myself, but I have to admit that it is absolutely gorgeous. Light and airy, it sports a dramatic neckline that cuts deeply between my modest breasts before gathering at my natural waist and seeming to float down my thighs to my feet. Sera has gathered my hair into an elaborate, twisting rope that coils over my shoulder, spilling a few strategic strands. Slender gold earrings reach nearly to my shoulders and offset the bright colour of the dress and the red of my hair. My lashes have been outlined in kohl and a light dusting of gold, their green colour jumping out dramatically from my wide-eyed stare.

“Pleased, are you, miss?” Sera’s voice cuts through my thoughts.

I spin in place, unable to keep the smile from my face. “I love it. Thank you, Sera. You’ve outdone yourself.”

“You look absolutely beautiful, Abby. If I do say so myself.”

I smile wider at her forgetting to address me formally. Sera moves to open the door and ushers me through, arranging the drape of my skirt behind me before I join the train of ladies headed for the stairwell.

I keep my chin up as I glance around at the girls. We chatter excitedly, taking in each other’s appearance and dashing off compliments, laughing as we grip arms companionably.

Vitrola is waiting for us at the top of the landing, her rolls of parchment clutched in a death grip as she walks among us, adjusting a strand of hair here, a dress there. She looks lovely in a long, royal-blue gown, unfortunately obscured by the unsightly papers.

“Right then, ladies, you all look gorgeous,” she finally calls out, standing back to give us a last once-over.

The girls shift nervously around me and I force an eager smile.

“Before we head down, I want to stress that, yes, this is a party, but I do expect you all to be on your best behaviour. Remember, a true lady always conducts herself in a manner befitting the Princess. Keep that in mind and have fun!” Vitrola stands to the side and ushers us down the stairs, gesticulating grandly.

In pairs of two we descend the staircase. I can hear the swelling of music and the excited chatter of guests; feeling my heart begin to beat harder. Our feet tread lightly in perfect unison against the plush crimson carpet laid out especially for the occasion.

“Her Royal Highness Princess Megra’s ladies-in-waiting!” The herald’s voice booms out over the din and I keep my eyes trained straight ahead, gripping Blinky’s arm to keep from tripping on the long folds of my dress.

I have never seen the main hallway so flush with people. Bright colours reeking of wealth and indulgence flash from every corner of the expansive space as the guests move among each other like peacocks. Men and women, all dressed in their finest, mill about the room, walking in and out of the Great Hall beyond the staircase and dancing in the open area directly in front. White-gloved servants carry trays of food and drink through the crowd.

I feel a clench in my stomach at the display of excess. Pristine white linen, bunches of flowers and tall candles in gold candlesticks decorate the space. With a single, cursory glance I spy enough jewellery to supply the entire market with a year’s worth of food. As we walk through the crowd, my fingers twitch with the urge to pocket a few pieces.

A tray of wine floats by and I grab a glass, sipping carefully as I join a circle of ladies, keeping one ear on their chatter while I covertly scan the room.

I find Will almost immediately. He is standing on the other side of the dance floor, wearing a tight expression as he converses with a Board member. As soon as I spot him, his piercing gaze flicks up to meet mine, arresting me entirely. I tear my eyes away and turn back toward the ladies, struggling to grasp their conversation.

A moment later there is the lightest graze on my elbow and I turn to see a familiar, tall figure striding past me, heading for the far end of the dance floor near the musicians.

I murmur something about more wine and slip away. I catch up with Will as he lounges against a wall, sipping a drink and looking out at the couples on the dance floor. I take my time walking toward him, using the opportunity to study his appearance. He is wearing a formal leather vest over his familiar linen shirt, buttoned high with a kerchief tucked in at his throat. His boots appear new and shine without the familiar telltale scuffs. He looks good.

"Cousin," he says at my approach, extending his drink and tapping our glasses together.

I take a sip. "I must say that you are looking unusually dashing this evening, young William." I notice that his chin is freshly shaved and feel a strange tug at my chest.

"And you look...incredible."

I raise an eyebrow at him. "I know."

He chuckles, angling himself so that his arm brushes mine, directing my gaze across the room.

"Do you see that man there? With the gold jacket?" He speaks from behind his glass, leaning his head closer to me so that our words are covered by the riotous music playing behind us.

"The one by the table? Yes, I see him."

"That's Lynal Grayson. He's the Lord from the Outer City, the one our king intends to marry to the Princess."

I squint toward the man, noting an arrogant posture and the obnoxious way he projects his voice over the men and ladies gathered around him.

"Notice all the medals on his breast? I bet the King is positively salivating over Grayson's army." Will's voice takes on a note of derision, and I nod.

"Without a doubt, I can imagine that a man such as him would derive a lot of pleasure from having such a large army," I observe.

"It isn't just the having. With a force that size, the King will finally be able to launch an all-out attack against the Wastelanders," Will confirms, glancing over his shoulder. "The scale of this war could take on a whole new meaning."

He is interrupted by the sound of the herald tapping his staff on the ground. The chatter dies down as everyone turns to face the staircase.

"Ladies and gentlemen," the herald's voice booms out across the space, "her Royal Highness, the Princess Megra."

Along with everyone else, my eyes flick to the top of the staircase. Meg's voluminous silver gown positively sparkles under the lantern light and an ethereal smile lights up her face as she waves graciously. Only I know how much she must hate this.

"Nice dress," Will remarks under his breath.

I feel an unwelcome stab of jealousy and nod, watching as Meg reaches the bottom of the stairs. She steps to the side, situating herself between the two sets of staircases and clasping her hands delicately together.

The herald taps his staff on the ground again. "And now, please raise your glasses to your host, your king and your protector. Presenting his Royal Eminence, King Francis."

Trumpets sound as the King approaches the top of the stairs, blinding in the layers of jewels he has draped over his trademark crimson jacket. I raise my glass along with the rest of the guests and loudly declare my allegiance, feeling my heart twist sickeningly in my chest as I do so.

The King and Megra link arms and begin to make their way through the room as the chatter picks up again.

"We better go mingle." Will nods imperceptibly toward Grayson. "See what you can find out."

He steps away before I have a moment to reply. I take another small sip of my wine before discarding the half-full glass and then making my way back into the crowd. Gods willing, the next few hours will pass quickly.

I wander over to a banquet table near Grayson and look over the variety of wonderful-smelling dishes. I sample a biscuit topped with heavy cream and strawberries off a gold plate, popping it into my mouth and closing my eyes to savour the heavenly taste. When this whole mess is over, I swear that the only thing I will miss is the food.

"Delicious, is it?" A voice speaks close to my ear and I jump, forcibly swallowing the remainder of the biscuit.

"I am so sorry, are you quite all right?"

"I'm fine, thank—" I pat my throat, turn and freeze when I recognize the insipid lout staring down at me. "You."

A blindingly white smile creases Lord Lynal Grayson's face. His wavy hair is the colour of a peach and has been combed back and up, moulded into place artfully. His brows are darker, offsetting light brown eyes. If I didn't know that he intended to send thousands of people to their deaths, I might think him handsome.

"You startled me." I say.

"My apologies, I have a habit of catching people off guard." Grayson extends his arm past me, hovering for a beat near my shoulder before he picks up a biscuit and samples it. "Divine."

He chews thoughtfully, his gaze raking over my figure and making my skin crawl. "You know, I don't believe I have seen you before." His accent is refined with a trace of superiority.

"I'm new to the Palace. I only arrived last month."

"And how are you finding it?" He leans casually against the wall next to me, examining his wine as he swirls it in his glass. I am impressed by his ability to appear so attentive and so disinterested at once. "Are the specimens to your liking?"

I drum a finger thoughtfully against my lip. "They're not quite what I expected."

"How so?"

"For one thing, they're a lot more forward than I'd consider gentlemanly."

He laughs, but his caramel eyes show no trace of merriment. "You're a straightforward little thing, aren't you?"

"So I've been told." I accept the drink he lifts from a passing tray and offers to me. "And what about you? You strike me as the kind of person who enjoys all facets of Palace events."

"Some parts more than others." He looks over my head and I turn to follow his gaze, spying Meg and her father talking to a gaudily dressed woman.

"Ah, the Princess," I say conspiratorially. "Are you a romantic?"

He laughs again. "I suppose you could say that. I do have a great interest in the Princess and her affairs."

"The Princess has a great many admirers." I watch him over the top of my glass as I sip delicately. "Why should she choose you over another?"

Grayson looks at me closely. "Do you know her?"

"I'm one of her ladies-in-waiting."

"In that case, I assume you are in her confidence and I will tell you exactly why her marrying me would be a wise decision." He leans in close and I catch the scent of old tobacco mixed with wine on his breath. He taps one of the shiny medals decorating his chest. "I command an army three times larger than her father's. I hold the outcome of his little Wastelander problem right in the palm of my hand. If she and I were to be wed, this city would be powerful enough to take anything it wanted."

I wait impassively as he finishes his drink in one gulp and grabs another.

"Are you a soldier?" I ask.

"I'm a lord," he sneers, peering into his glass.

"Yes, I gathered that." I nod toward the medals. "But are you a soldier as well? Do you fight?"

"Fight?" he scoffs. "No, I don't fight. I have commoners to do that for me."

I open my mouth to speak again and then feel Meg's familiar hold on my arm.

"Your Majesties." I curtsy low to Meg and the King while Grayson offers up a cursory nod. He grabs Meg's hand and raises it to his lips before she pulls her arm back, giving him a tight smile.

"Lord Grayson, I am so pleased that you could attend our little event." The King cuts an imposing figure, with his great height and booming voice.

Will's warning rings in my head and I keep my head ducked low, looking to slip away at the earliest possible opportunity.

"It is always my pleasure to come to the City, my King, especially when it is for a party as splendid as this."

As the men speak, Meg shoots me a look, her eyebrows raised. I feel the urge to roll my eyes behind Grayson's back but somehow manage keep a placid expression.

As if on cue, the King turns back toward us. "Megra, isn't this your scholarly friend?"

"Yes, Father." Meg's voice is smooth and polished. "This is Abby Fellows."

"Abby, I have heard a great deal about you." The King's tone suggests that he has heard more about me than Meg has related.

"Your Majesty, it is truly an honour to make your acquaintance. This ball is fabulous—my compliments especially on the strawberry biscuits." I clamp my mouth shut, realizing that I have said too much all at once. A tight, angry ball of anxiety wells up within me, clouding my judgment. I can feel the weight of the King's, Grayson's and Meg's stares upon me as my cheeks begin to pinch with the stress of smiling.

"Thank you, they're my personal favourite as well." The King takes a biscuit for himself and I relax slightly. "My daughter tells me that you have been great company to her, which I should thank you for. She has always found her ladies to be a bit...what was the word you used, my dear?"

"Vacuous," Meg answers.

"Yes, well, nevertheless, I am relieved that you have been able to provide some stimulating conversation for Megra. Her ideas have always been rather...imaginative."

I sense that I am balancing on the fine edge of a very dangerous conversation.

"The Princess has been very gracious in making me feel welcome at the Palace," I say.

The King's eyebrows lower.

"Excuse me, gentlemen, but I must go powder my nose. Abby, will you join me?" Meg breaks in, slipping her arm smoothly through mine.

"Certainly, Princess. Your Majesty, it was a pleasure to speak with you. And you as well, sir." I remember at the last instant that I am not supposed to know Grayson's name and allow myself to be led away by Meg, my knees fairly shaking in my relief to be done with the conversation.

Meg leads me through the Great Hall and out into the courtyard. The cool night air feels marvellous against my skin and eases my heartbeat back into its usual rhythm.

"So, was that him?" I ask once we are a safe distance from any potential gossips.

"The bag of hot air wearing the shiny medals? Yes, that was Lynal Grayson." She sighs. "What did you think of him?"

"He is..." I struggle to find the right words. "Confident, to say the least."

She releases an exasperated breath through her nose. "That is kind of you. I'd say that he is one of the most stuck-up, intolerant people to ever have graced the earth. And do you know what the worst part is? He is completely transparent. Everyone, including my father, knows exactly what Lynal's motives are but they still insist that we carry on with this...*sham* of a courtship." A high colour has risen to Meg's cheeks. "When my father looks at Lynal, all he sees is his giant army of commoners; he doesn't care that he is handing the reins of the City over to a spoiled, selfish prat."

"Can't you just refuse him?" I ask.

She laughs bitterly. "I have *been* refusing him. Father insists that I must think of the City and not just myself. He has told me that if I don't marry Lynal, he will have to overtake the Outer City by force. You know what that means: more fighting."

"My gods," I say, mostly to myself.

"It is so completely horrible, Abby. What am I supposed to do? I despise Lynal and I shudder to think of him occupying the throne, but regardless of what I say or do, there is going to be a war. I can't do anything to stop it."

We walk slowly now, our heads bent closely together as Meg's voice breaks.

I squeeze her arm, unsure of what to say. From here I can see the guards outside the east wall, making their first shift change. Soon, everyone will be at their designated posts and I will be free to slip in behind the gaol and change into my guard's outfit.

The time for risk-taking will come. For now, I remain still and let Meg lean into me; I rub her shoulder as she cries her silent tears.

chapter 24

Nearing midnight, the party is in full swing. I make my way across the dance floor toward the staircase, shouldering past two chubby ladies and purposefully treading on the toes of an older gentlemen. No one seems to be feeling any pain or taking any notice of me. I arrive at the staircase and stand on the second step, sipping delicately at my drink as I survey the room. The crowd swells between the foyer and the Great Hall and all royal-blooded parties seem suitably occupied. I scan the room one more time, feeling a twinge of nervousness when I fail to locate Will. His absence hopefully means that he won't be disrupting the jailbreak, but I would have liked to reassure myself with one last glimpse of him. Nothing for it: it's now or never.

I step down off the staircase and into the hallway that runs alongside the Great Hall, placing my drink on a side table and holding up my skirts as I quicken my steps. The crowd has thinned here and I tread silently down the path before slipping through the servants' east door, emerging just outside the courtyard on the side nearest the gaol.

As I predicted, no one is about. The last shift change has ensured that the guards are all at their designated stations. This route should be clear long enough for me to make four trips between the gaol and the courtyard without being noticed.

After glancing once more over my shoulder, I slip into the alleyway behind the gaol and retrieve my guard's uniform from the ale barrel. I hitch up my skirts and pull the guard's trousers and tunic on over my dress, tucking away the bright fabric before I reach for the armoured breastplate and belt. I kick off my sandals and stick my feet into the boots, then affix the sword to my belt. Finally, I secure my hair back beneath the hood and pull the dark scarf up over my face.

I inspect the pouch at my waist. Inside are a flask filled with spirit and mixed with the dried mushroom I borrowed from Will, some strips of leather thong and spare handkerchiefs. Satisfied, I stick my head out of the alleyway, checking that the coast is clear before I take a deep breath and stride purposefully to the gaol's front entrance.

Pushing open the heavy front door, I exchange a cursory nod with the gate guard. He barely glances at me before rising to his feet with a groan and reaching for the keys at his waist.

“The party showin’ any signs of slowin’ down?” he asks conversationally as I move toward the open gate.

“No sir, it’ll be going on ’til dawn at least,” I reply.

I pass him, then spin in place, grip the hilt of my sword and whip it free of the scabbard. The poor man barely gets a chance to register what’s happened before I pummel him on the back of the head and his unconscious form crashes to the ground.

There is no turning back now.

I retrieve two pieces of thong and a handkerchief from my pouch; quickly I bind the man’s hands and feet before gagging him tightly. I lift his shoulders and drag him so that he is hidden behind the desk. Hopefully, I will have time to get back up here and retrieve him before he wakes up. For now I will just have to pray that no one comes in and notices a passed-out, trussed-up gate guard.

Grabbing the keys from where they fell, I descend the stairs as quickly as I dare without my footsteps raising an alarm. I slow my pace near the bottom, recalling the way sound echoes in the dank space.

I turn right at the end of the hall, aiming for the table where my two favourite bozos have already begun helpfully drinking themselves into a stupor. The sour scent of bad whisky hits my nostrils and, as I draw up next to their table.

“Ah remember you.” The larger man cracks one eye open as he regards me.

“Mind if I join?” I ask.

He lifts his glass and I sink down into the third chair, taking care to keep my face out of the lantern light. Bozo number two sits across from me, already slouched forward and half-asleep. He utters a healthy snort as I settle myself.

Bozo one makes to pour me a glass of whisky, but I shake my head. "Brought my own." I retrieve the flask from the pouch at my waist and brandish it toward him. "It's good stuff, too. Wanna try?"

"Let me see it." He takes the flask from me and studies it. "What's this?"

"Moonshine," I grunt. "Hard to get, can't find it anywhere." I lean back in my chair, rocking on the back legs. "I got a source, though."

"Huh."

I watch with satisfaction as he tilts the drink down his throat.

I nudge Bozo two with my boot. "How about you, buddy?"

Bozo one wipes his mouth with his sleeve. "He's half in the bag already—leave him be."

"Oh come on, now. It's a party, ain't it?" I take the flask back and wave it under the nose of the half-conscious guard. The harsh odour wakes him with a start and he snatches it from my hand, drinking greedily.

"Busy night?" I ask, by way of distracting the men from noticing that I haven't taken a sip for myself. I don't know how long it will take for the mushroom to take effect and I am acutely aware that the gate guard upstairs could awake at any moment.

"What? No. Yes, I mean. What...uh." Bozo one is blinking in confusion, staring into the dram of whisky in his glass. "What was that drink again?"

"Moonshine," I reply. "Good, ain't it?"

"S'rong." He shakes his head. "Strong."

Bozo two suddenly pitches forward, crumpling into a heap over the table and beginning to snore mightily.

The larger man regards his companion, his eyes beginning to lose focus. "What's wrong with 'im?"

Wordlessly, I stand and whack his head with the hilt of my sword, watching with satisfaction as he keels over next to his partner.

The time for stealth is over. I dash to the cells and unlock the door, throwing it open. Marc is already waiting for me, eyes bright, ready to go.

"Everyone out, now. Stand to the side, I need to clear this cell." I pull down my scarf and usher everyone through the door. "You and you," I point at two strong-looking men, "put those two into the cell." I indicate the guards slouched over the table. "Marc, get someone to help you carry down the guard from upstairs. I'm going to get the clothes. Here." I toss the keys to a gangly youth. "Unlock the women's cell. I'll be right back. Under no circumstances is anyone to leave, understand?"

A few people nod and I turn to run back down the passage, Marc and another man following close to my heels.

We take the stairs two at a time and arrive back in the entryway. Marc and the other man grab the leaden gate guard and begin to drag him down the stairs while I move briskly to the exit, peering outside.

The way remains dark and empty. Seeing no one about, I scurry to the alley behind the gaol and open the ale barrel. I retrieve the stashed clothes and bundle them into a sack, checking once more that no one is watching before I rush back inside, pulling the heavy load behind me.

I close the front door and heave the sack back toward the unlocked gate, making slow progress until a couple of people run up to help me. The commoners are mercifully quiet when we arrive back in general population; Marc clearly did an excellent job briefing them on the plan. Someone has already pumped water into a barrel and the men and women are taking turns splashing their hands and faces to remove the grime.

I thank the people who helped me with the sack of clothes and tug it open; pulling out the tunics and dresses, I distribute them to the crowd.

"Marc, are all of the guards put away?" I call out over the grasping hands.

He materializes next to me. "They're in the cell and the door is locked."

"Perfect. I can take six of you up now—who's ready to go?"

I shed my guard's uniform, leaving it in a pile on the floor. My lightweight pink dress feels hopelessly inadequate after the heavy armour. Instantly missing the comforting weight of a sword at my waist, I register a twinge of doubt as I look around at the scattered commoners struggling into their wrinkled formalwear.

“We’re ready.” A soft, raspy voice speaks near my elbow and I turn to see two women, one wearing a loose, violet toga and the other a pale yellow shift. Both garments fit awkwardly on the women’s malnourished frames and there are still traces of grime around their hairlines.

I pull a washcloth out of the water bucket and hurriedly wipe their faces, doling out pieces of leather thong so they can pull their hair back. The leftover dirt and greasy hair can’t be helped but I’m banking on no one looking too closely.

Another woman and three men join my first group and I give them all a cursory inspection, ever mindful of the passage of time and the waiting carriage. Now that everything’s said and done and I can take a step back to admire my work, I have to admit that my brilliant crew looks astoundingly like a gang of commoners escaping from prison. Albeit, a gang of commoners in very fine clothing.

“All right, everyone, listen up.” I do my best to speak clearly and calmly, eliminating any traces of misgiving from my voice. “I’m going to escort you out six at a time. The rest of you, wait here and clean yourselves up as best you can. Once we’re outside, the rules are to stick together, look happy and speak to no one. Any questions?”

I look around at the men and women. A few eyes blink fearfully, but for the most part I am met with grim determination.

“You’re all going to be fine—there’s nothing to worry about.” I force a smile, anxious to get moving. “Let’s go home.” I turn to the first group. “You’re up.”

Together, we hurry down the hallway and up the stairs. I put a finger to my lips and leave the group to wait in the guards’ room while I crack open the front door and sweep my gaze over the darkened path. Seeing no one, I beckon the commoners through the exit one at a time and walk briskly to the courtyard, checking once or twice over my shoulder to make sure no one is lagging behind. Just before we enter the yard I pull one of the men and one of the women up beside me.

I speak nonsense to my companions as I direct them along the fringes of the crowd, continually darting my eyes between my company and the route in front of us, taking great care not to engage any of the Palace guests.

We reach the inner hallway without incident. It's more crowded indoors but I keep my charges to the far wall and aim for the foyer near the Palace's front entrance. We have just about reached it when I hear a commotion behind me.

"Hey, watch it!" An older lady has spilled her drink and is clutching at the hem of her layered blue dress, staring daggers at one of the common women.

I rush back a few steps and insert myself between them.

"That's it, Jani, you're cut off." I grip the common woman's elbow and steer her away, shooting an apologetic look over my shoulder.

The older lady huffs and turns back to her companions, complaining loudly but seemingly uninterested in stirring up any trouble.

I can feel the woman trembling as I pull her away and I give her arm a reassuring squeeze. We finally reach the foyer and cross to the very front of the Palace.

There are a couple of bored-looking guards standing on either side of the front door. I offer up a silent prayer to the gods that neither will recognize the prisoners as we hurry by them. The first carriage is already waiting, the green flag flapping prominently from the open door. As the carriage driver climbs down, I usher the prisoners one by one into the seats, loudly wishing them safe travels, all the while half-expecting one of the guards to shout after us.

The driver helps me load the last of my charges into the carriage and doffs his cap at me. He moves to climb back into his seat and a hand appears through the back window, grasping my wrist tightly.

"Thank you," the woman says, her eyes moist. "I will never forget what you have done for us."

I nod wordlessly, stepping back as the carriage starts and rumbles down the driveway. I wait until they have been waved through the main gate before I release my breath, allowing myself the briefest of moments to compose my nerves before I square my shoulders and turn to walk briskly back through the party.

The two subsequent trips between the gaol and the carriages are blessedly uneventful. I lead the third group of commoners through the party and usher them into the open door of the second-to-last carriage, making a mental note to seek out the brilliant carriage-master so I can tip him handsomely. After pushing the door closed, I pause to make sure my charges pass safely through the gate before I head back to the gaol to retrieve the last of the prisoners, rubbing my aching neck in an effort to relieve some of the tension.

Marc and the remaining five commoners are waiting for me when I get back, clean-faced and dressed in the rumpled formalwear.

"One of them woke up." Marc nods toward the men's cell.

I lean past him, noting the sound of an angry guard rustling around inside, raving and spewing curses.

"It doesn't matter. We're almost done." I keep my voice low, disguising my gender as best I can against the conscious guard as I motion for the group to follow me.

Once outside, I pull the heavy gaol door shut for the last time. We cross quickly to the courtyard, hugging the wall as we join the party, Marc and the rest of the commoners sticking close. With the staircase in sight and the ballroom just past it, I am aiming my charges toward the front entrance when a gold-clad arm suddenly darts out of the crowd and comes to rest on the wall in front of my nose.

I leap back, narrowly avoiding crashing into Marc. I ignore the instinct to glance over my shoulder and force myself to remain stock still, waiting as Grayson steps out of the throng and positions himself directly in my path.

"Well, well, well. Where have you been?" Grayson isn't much taller than me but still manages to peer downward as he sips his drink.

I notice that he is slightly unsteady on his feet and I fight to keep my eyes on his face, willing him to keep looking at me and not the scruffy group at my back.

"Drinking, dancing, the usual," I say, casually. We are mere steps from the front hall and freedom, but with each passing moment the chances of someone noticing the escaping prisoners increases.

"I can't say I've seen much drinking nor dancing from you tonight." Grayson tilts his head and sneers, revealing the pointed ends of his teeth. "It seems to me that you've been spending the majority of your time running back and forth."

My heart hammers heavily in my chest. Grayson isn't overly large, but in this crowded space he blocks my path. I could dodge him easily if I were alone but getting past him with my company intact will be next to impossible.

"Tell me about it." I sigh, twirling the end of my braid flirtatiously. "I've had some business to attend to for the Princess. A lady's duty never ends!" I attempt a laugh but my throat has gone bone dry. "I'm actually in the middle of a chore right now, so if you'll excuse me, I'll be right back to finish this conversation."

I angle myself to manoeuvre past him but he sidesteps and claps his clammy hand down on my shoulder, shoving me back against the wall. From the corner of my eye, I see Marc move toward us; he stops in his tracks when I give the barest shake of my head.

"I'm a powerful man, you know," Grayson slurs into my ear.

I feel the sour notes of his breath on my neck and suppress a shudder.

My every fibre rings with warning and the urge for flight. I clench my fists at my side, furiously trying to think of a way out. My addled mind refuses to clear as Grayson's hand slips around my waist and panic begins to work its way up my throat.

"Forgive my interruption, Lynal." A familiar voice sounds from over Grayson's shoulder and I nearly collapse from relief, my eyes seeking Will's.

"Don't concern yourself with this, doctor. The lady and I are having a conversation." Grayson's clawed hand digs into my side and I wince.

"It looks to be a little more than a conversation to me." A dangerous shadow crosses Will's face. "I strongly suggest that you give her some space and fetch yourself another drink." I notice how he looms over Grayson's aristocratic frame and feel the lord's grip on me loosen.

"I don't see how it's any of your business," Grayson grumbles, still uncomfortably close to my ear. "I saw her first."

"You have forgotten your manners, my lord. Excuse yourself, now, and you can preserve some small measure of gentlemanlike behaviour." Will appears calm but I can hear the thinly veiled note of loathing in his voice.

After what seems like an eternity, Grayson finally releases me, stepping back and purposefully taking a long, defiant gulp from his wine glass before he slams the empty cup down on a table and shrinks back into the crowd.

I straighten my spine to quell my shaking and push myself away from the wall, shooting Marc a small reassuring smile before I turn back to Will.

"Cousin, if you could assist me, it is of the utmost importance that I escort my guests to their carriage." I stare hard at Will, keeping my tone deliberate and measured.

Will looks behind me at the commoners. Something indistinguishable flickers across his dark eyes and my heart skips a beat, waiting. After a moment he gives a tight nod and leads us toward the front entrance, his frame carving an easy path.

I tug Marc along, following Will through the front hallway. My gaze continually flicks from side to side and I hurry to scamper ahead, guiding the group toward the main entrance and past the door guards. Like a merciful beacon sent by the gods themselves, I find the last carriage sitting patiently in the drive. I covertly pass the driver a handful of stolen coins, whispering my thanks before I hurry to escort Marc and the others to their seats.

Will shoves the carriage door shut and I step up to hold Marc's hand through the window. "You were wonderful," I tell him, sincerely.

"Thank you." His voice is hoarse. "I hope I get the chance to return the favour, someday." It's the most I've heard him speak in the relatively short period of time I've known him.

I nod, leaning forward to kiss him on the cheek. "Stay safe."

His hand is jerked from mine as the carriage rolls forward. I stand back, resigned as I watch them rumble down the drive.

When the carriage disappears through the gate, I sag, feeling the last bit of tension finally lift from my shoulders. Will's grip on my elbow offers a strange kind of strength and I find myself leaning against him.

"Come on." His voice is soft in my ear, sending a shiver down my spine. "Let's go for a run."

chapter 25

I let Will lead me to a waiting carriage, his warm hand encircling mine as I step inside. While he goes to speak with the driver, I sigh and let my head tilt back against the plush leather of the seat, suddenly so tired I can hardly keep my eyes open.

A small smile tugs at my lips. The stress, planning and risk was all worth it; the escape was a success. It will be hours still before someone discovers the guards left locked in the cell, and by then the commoners will be long gone. For the first time since I arrived at the Palace, I feel as though I have accomplished something. I feel like myself again.

I am jolted from my stupor when Will opens the door and climbs in next to me. He doesn't say anything and I don't ask where we are going as the carriage rumbles down the drive and through the gate. I stare out the window at the gilded Palace receding into the distance, marvelling at the way the lanterns illuminate the glass walls so starkly against the dark night sky.

As we roll down the empty streets, there is no sound but the tap of the horse's feet against the stone and Will's own soft breathing. The cool night air floating in through the carriage windows is pleasant on my face, rousing me and making me more aware of Will's presence. He hasn't said a word about the jailbreak and I can't be sure yet that he isn't completely furious.

Finally, the carriage draws to a stop. I don't worry about propriety this far from the Court and open the door myself, stepping out into the street. Clutching my skirts in my hand, I look about at our surroundings, confusion and happiness welling up within me.

"The market?" I ask as Will's shoulder brushes mine. Behind us, I can hear the carriage driver snap his reins and the horse begin its methodical plod back up the road.

"I figured this was as good a place to start as any." Will nods to the building closest to us. "Could you teach me how to climb?"

I grin, grabbing his hand and pulling him into the alleyway. In the tight space, I feel his breath on my neck, familiar and warm.

He stands back as I stoop and begin gathering my skirts. I pull the long fabric above my knees and between my legs, rolling and twisting the leftover material so that it is wrapped around my waist and tucked into secure folds. I look back up to see Will regarding me, a quizzical look on his face.

“What?” I ask.

“Been working on that, have you?” There is a note of amusement in his tone.

“I like to be prepared.”

“I should have known you would find a way to run in a dress.” He steps closer, peering up at the wall while he unbuttons his starched vest, sliding it down off his arms before he loosens his collar. “So, how do we accomplish this, exactly?”

I am momentarily distracted and have to blink myself back into focus, following his gaze up the wall. “Same principle as when we climbed down. Look for window ledges and bricks that you can use as a step or a grip, and watch out for anything loose. You don’t want to kick a brick down onto some unfortunate person on the street or, worse,” I raise my eyebrow at him, “wake the tenant.”

He has loosened his kerchief and broadened his stance, now standing in serious concentration. His eyes crisscross the facade of the building while his brow furrows in deep thought. I kick off my sandals, tossing them in a pile with Will’s discarded vest before I jump up to grab a ledge and pull myself up the side of the building a bit at a time.

The thudding in my chest increases with the exhilaration of rediscovering my first love while my eyes pick out the familiar patterns, revealing my route. My polished nails chip on the brick as I pull myself up and over the roof edge, ignoring the muscles protesting from disuse.

I look down to see Will following a similar route up the building, moving more slowly than I was but ascending at a steady pace. I step back as he heaves himself up to the top and offer a hand to pull him to his feet.

“Dr. Cain, you’re a natural,” I tell him.

He smiles that half-grin at me, grey eyes twinkling in the moonlight. "Ready to run?"

My heart fairly soars as we turn together and dash for the next building, leaping simultaneously over the edge and landing in identical crouches. I feel my body relaxing into the motions as we run; it propels me easily across the roofs and lifts me high into the air during every jump, bending into a coiled spring to catch me when I land.

We run wordlessly, matching our stride breath for breath. I fly atop the buildings, my footsteps perfectly in sync with Will's, both of us knowing intuitively where we are headed. Together, we leap across city streets, our path lit only by the light of the moon and stars.

The gaps beneath our feet grow narrower and after a time I slow and stop, feeling rather than seeing Will draw up next to me. I stand and look straight out over the ledge, taking in the familiar sight as I saw it for weeks from the room below. The roof of Will's flat appears the same, yet entirely different from the first time we stood in this spot together.

Will's shoulders move up and down in tune with his breath, laboured from his run and echoing my own. His skin smells acutely of sandalwood and glistens with a light dusting of perspiration.

"Are you angry with me?" I ask.

His breathing gradually slows into its usual calm rhythm.

"No," he answers. "I'm not sure exactly why...but I'm not."

I smile, a little sadly. "You should be furious."

"I know that I should be. I asked you to be careful and the next thing I know, you're waltzing prisoners straight through a Palace ball." He shakes his head. "Have you any idea how mad that is?"

I chew on my bottom lip, watching him. Historically, this is the moment where we find ourselves screaming at each other, but Will doesn't appear angry. There is no telltale bunching in his shoulders, crinkling in his brow. He stands impassive, a look of bewilderment crossing his dark features.

"You took a huge risk, doing that." He runs a hand over the back of his neck. "You could have jeopardized everything."

"But I didn't."

"But you didn't," he agrees. Looking over at me, he says, "It's difficult to be angry, when I'm so impressed."

I am thankful that the moonlight hides the blush staining my cheeks. "I wanted to tell you. I could have used your help."

"I know why you kept me out of it." He releases a breath of air between his teeth. "I would have tried to stop you."

"Yes." The wind whips strands of hair around my face and I shove them back impatiently. "I had to do it, Will. I couldn't just leave them there. Not when I could do something."

"I know."

"I've tried to be patient, I really have, but I feel so useless in that parlour."

"I know."

"I needed to feel like myself again."

He closes the distance between us with one smooth stride. "I know."

I shake my head, frustrated. "How can you, when I don't understand myself?"

"Because I see you. You're a lot of things, Red. Brash, reckless, impatient…" His grey eyes burn into mine. "And brave with too much heart for your own good. It's why I sought you out in the first place—it's why I wanted your help."

I stare up at him, waiting.

"I've put so much time and effort toward beginning this rebellion that I think I've lost sight of where it ends." He seems to stumble on his words but sets his jaw and stays his course. "I convinced myself that with enough preparation, we would be able to launch a flawless attack, but every step just seems to lead to more obstacles. Maybe there is no such thing as the perfect plan. Maybe we need to have a go at it, take a chance." He rubs the scruff on his head, something he does when he's trying to work through a problem. "I don't want to leave any room for misstep." Searching my face. "Do you know how it is, to feel like you have only one opportunity to get things right?"

"What's the matter with having only one chance?" I ask. "All the more reason to put everything you have into it."

He stares at me, his expression unreadable.

I press on, speaking slowly. "When you jump, you cannot fear the fall."

He blinks once and his brow clears. He looks at me as though he is finally seeing his long-sought-after solution. The cool breeze tickles the exposed skin on my back and my flesh rises in goosebumps.

"Well?" I ask, when I can no longer stand the silence. "Have you finally decided to trust me?"

"I could ask you the same thing." A dimple creases his cheek. "Am I going to be consulted the next time you organize a jailbreak?"

"Yes. As long as you don't try to stop me."

"I don't think I could stand a chance." He moves closer and tugs gently on the end of my braid. "You'll be bringing down the monarchy, with or without my help."

I shake my head. "I don't have a hope of it without you. You were right about me being small-time, Will. Anyone could see that there was something rotten with this city, but you're actually finding a way to fix it." I swallow, my throat suddenly dry. "There couldn't be a rebellion without you."

He doesn't say anything for a very long time. I wait, for once not feeling the usual restlessness, instead content to simply watch the way the moonlight paints dappled patterns across his features.

"What was that you said about jumping, Kay?" His voice is low, rough.

"Don't be afraid of the fall."

He draws me to him, cupping my face with his hand and pressing his lips to mine. I let my arms snake their way around his back and hold him tightly, revelling in the sensation of our heartbeats thudding against one another.

His frame dwarfs mine, suffocating and liberating all at once. I grasp the folds of his shirt, needing to feel him against me, needing the contact of skin against skin.

"Kay," he whispers against my mouth.

But I don't want to talk. I reach up, tugging him closer, silencing our questions. I feel his hands against the small of my back, warming the skin there and sending a bolt of heat coursing through my entire body.

He rests his forehead against mine as we draw apart. Our breaths are ragged, passed from one to the other.

Finally, Will breaks the silence. "Can I ask you something?"

"Sure."

"What compels you to do it?"

I look up at him, confused. "To do what?"

He raises his brows. "To risk yourself this way. Why do you do it? I know that you want to help your friends, but the way you put yourself on the line for them..." His thumb brushes my cheek as he studies me. "Frankly...it's foolhardy. It makes me think that you aren't looking out for yourself."

I blink a couple times, momentarily taken aback.

I open my mouth to answer him, then close it again, thinking. His question is familiar, an echo of both Harry and Lara's concerns, but the sense of déjà vu I am experiencing goes back further than that.

For perhaps the first time in my life, I don't have any words.

"I once asked my father that same question," I hear myself say, eventually. "I couldn't comprehend why it wasn't enough that we would miss him if he was hurt or killed. He told me that he risked himself because the reward was greater than what his life was worth." I shrug. "I didn't really know what he meant at the time."

The great aching pit of loss opens up inside me, but this time I give in to the memory instead of pushing it away. "I think I understand now. The reward is a great city, and that is worth so much more to me than anything else."

I take a deep, shuddering breath and look up at the sky, reflexively tracing the patterns in the stars and orienting myself toward my childhood home. "My father believed in a City that took care of everyone, regardless of their lot in life. He was the bravest, most selfless person I have ever known. I want to finish what he started. I want him to be proud of me."

I shut my eyes, expecting the usual bout of grief, surprised when I feel an incredible lightness instead. Speaking of my family for the first time since I lost them fills me with a sense of pride for who they were, rather than anger for how they died.

I tilt my head to look up at Will. He is watching me intently, his expression unreadable.

A heat rises to my cheeks and I bite my lip. "Does that make any sense?" I ask.

His small smile echoes my own. "I don't know if I will ever fully understand you, Red, but I feel as though I'm getting closer."

And he kisses me again. I feel his half-grin under my lips and my heart gives an agonizing lurch. Oh, gods. I'm in trouble.

"I'm in trouble," he murmurs.

I don't say anything in response, not trusting myself to speak. I don't want to think about what this is, I just want to have it.

"I'm ready to do this," he says, finally. "I don't want to wait any longer."

"Is that a proposition?" I ask. "Because your manners could use some work."

He laughs, smoothing the strands of hair away from my face. "I was referring to the rebellion."

"Oh, *that,*" I tease. "Good, because I have an idea."

"Come on, then. We shouldn't speak out here."

He steps back, keeping hold of my hand as he tugs me toward the ledge of the roof. Together, we climb over the edge and swing in through the window of his flat. Will busies himself lighting the lanterns while I perch impatiently on the couch, watching his movements anxiously.

He shakes out the match and disappears into the kitchen, returning a moment later with a flask of water. I take it from him when he offers it, shifting to make room on the couch. He remains on his feet, pacing back and forth in front of me.

"Sit, will you? You're making me nervous."

"I received some worrying news tonight." He rubs his fingers tiredly over his eyes. "The King intends to marry Grayson and the Princess at the earliest opportunity."

"We can delay that. She hasn't accepted him yet." I tilt the flask and take a drink.

"The King accepted Grayson for her. They are to be married in two weeks."

The water catches in my throat, seizing my breath.

Will continues to pace and doesn't look up, talking seemingly to himself. "Once they're married, the King is going to hold another, larger draft for both the City and the Outer City. He wants to send at least a thousand men into the Wastelands, but the draft isn't going to stop until he has eradicated the desert of every single Waster."

I drag my wrist over my chin to wipe away the droplets of water.

"They'll be slaughtered," I say, gravely. "Even if they do eventually wipe out the Wastelanders, the battles will be made up of untrained labourers against mercenaries." I shake my head. "We won't stand a chance."

Will finally ceases his relentless pacing and turns to look directly at me. "Which is why we need to usurp the throne now. Before anyone gets shipped out."

"If we manage to pull this off," I say, slowly. "What happens afterward?"

He wrinkles his brow. "What do you mean?"

"I mean, how do you intend the City to be ruled, if not by the King?"

"It won't be ruled—that's the whole point!" Will looks incredulous. "We will govern ourselves, everyone, together. I thought that's what you wanted?"

"No, that isn't what I want, and trust me, that isn't what you want, either." I think of my father, of his warnings. "Think about it, Will. There is a war at our borders, and without one person to unite us, we won't stand a chance. We will have turned the City into a place of chaos and anarchy."

"What are you saying?"

"I'm saying that we don't need the King, but that Meg would make a remarkable queen."

His eyes widen in surprise. "A queen?"

"She understands us, Will," I say, hurriedly. "At first I had written her off as another spoiled courtier, but she really cares. She has these amazing ideas about opportunity and equality and education…" As I speak, the idea begins to crystallize in my mind. I look up at Will, trying to gauge his reaction. "Just imagine the possibilities if we could draw her to our cause. She's a leader, someone the people will naturally follow. She just needs us to support her."

He walks back over to the couch and sinks down next to me, his expression thoughtful.

"Do you really think that is what the people want?" he asks, eventually.

"What the people want is someone who cares about them." I angle myself so I am looking directly at him, our knees nearly touching. "If we eliminate the King, the Board and Grayson, there will be no one to speak up against

Meg and her right to rule. I think we need to give the monarchy a chance to make things right."

He nods, slowly. "All right."

I blink. "Really?"

"Yes. I trust you." His eyes have taken on that low, smouldering light.

I lean closer, tracing the small imprint in his cheek.

"So, are we really doing this?" I ask, quietly.

In answer, he pulls me toward him. I close my eyes, feeling strong arms envelop me as I fall.

chapter 26

The moon has waned but the small slivers of leftover light filter in between the bedroom curtains. A cool breeze wafts through the open window and tickles my bare shoulders. I am propped up on one elbow in Will's bed, my fingers rhythmically stroking the scars on his back.

"Your father gave you these." It isn't a question. In the dim light, I feel rather than see the raised welts covering every part of his back from neck to hips.

He lifts his head and repositions himself so he is looking up at me. "I was a difficult kid."

"I have no doubt."

He chuckles softly as he brushes my lips with his thumb.

I wait a beat before pressing further. "What happened?" I want to hear his story in his words.

He sighs, not saying anything for a moment, his eyes searching mine. "Do you really want to hear the sad tale of a spoiled courtier?"

"I have all night."

The corner of his mouth twitches slightly, but not up into the grin that I know so well. I see his brow furrow and feel a tug in my chest as I register his nerves.

I place my hand over his, resting them both against my cheek. "What is it?" I whisper.

"I don't want you to think less of me," he says plainly.

I respond by turning my head and kissing his palm, revelling in its warmth against my face as I wait. I know he will speak when he is ready.

Will sighs and arranges himself so that he is looking up at the ceiling. I lie down next to him, cushioned between his arm and torso.

"My father raised me to be the best courtier I could be," he begins, matter of factly. "He wanted me to understand wholeheartedly that there was *us* and then there was *them*. Our ancestors were among the first to arrive in the City and we were therefore better, smarter, and more deserving of our station. Commoners were less fortunate underlings meant to serve us."

I can hear the bitterness in his voice and force myself to bite my tongue and listen patiently.

"On some level, I knew it was wrong, but I was punished whenever I raised a question."

At this, he pauses meaningfully and I feel a painful lurch. I lightly touch a particularly gruesome scar peeking around his ribcage. He gives a slight inhale at the contact but remains perfectly still.

"He beat you?"

"After a while, the lesson began to sink in."

He rolls his eyes to the ceiling and folds his arms under his head, waiting as I settle myself against his shoulder. From this position, I can hear his heart beating steadily.

"We lived in a big house filled with servants." I lift my head from its reclined position to see him looking at me. "I'm sure you can imagine the way my father treated them."

I wrinkle my nose at the memory of pulling Will's father off the maid.

"I was such a selfish prick then, Kay. I would never hurt anyone; I wasn't as bad as that, but I really believed I was better than the commoners. I was a bully. I demanded that they serve me hand and foot, and when my orders weren't met, I berated them." He runs a hand over his face.

I furrow my brow, trying to imagine passionate, determined Will as a spoiled brat. Try as I might, I can't conjure up the image.

"So, what happened?" I ask.

"I became an ugly, bitter person. My father and I began to argue more frequently and the beatings became worse. It got to a point where we were fighting every day. The idea of being anywhere near my father filled me with such revulsion that I would make excuses to be out of the house whenever I could. I hung around the bars and opium dens, loafing about with my friends and leaving my mother and sister to deal with my father on their own. Eventually, home became so unbearable that I signed up for a term in the King's guard just so I could get away."

I nod, knowing all too well the need to run from something.

"Serving in the guard gave me an outlet for all my pent-up anger. For a year I worked patrolling the streets, pushing people around and generally getting off on a false sense of power. The things I had to do, Kay." He shakes his head, clenching his jaw at some secret memory. "You would be ashamed of me."

"I wouldn't," I tell him. "You didn't know any better."

"I knew it was wrong," he insists. "But I found a way to justify it, saying I was acting on behalf of the King, following his orders. It was easy at first, but then…" He sucks in a breath, holding it for several beats before he releases it slowly. "Once I was away from my father, I was finally able to think for myself. I resigned from the guard and enrolled instead as a soldier. I spent the next three years training as a medic and fighting in the Wastelands."

He shifts and wraps an arm around me. I snuggle in closer, melting into the cocoon of his body.

"That's where everything changed. Out there, commoners and courtiers fought side by side. There was nothing to distinguish anyone; at the core, we were just terrified people fighting a war no one understood. I forged friendships with people I never would have given the time of day to back in the City. The medical training I resisted for so long let me help them. Finally, I felt as though I had a purpose."

He doesn't say anything for a long time. I shiver, though whether it from the cool air filtering in through the open window or Will's story, I can't be sure. I am just wondering whether he has drifted off to sleep when he speaks again.

"The friends I lost were some of the bravest, most honest people I have ever known. In the Wastelands it didn't matter if you were rich or poor; you died just the same." His arm tightens around me. "That was when I realized what I had to fight for."

The tone his voice takes on when he is speaking of our cause returns, familiar in its ferocity.

"I suppose that's it," he says. His hand moves slowly up and down my side, causing goosebumps to rise on the bare flesh. "I returned home when my mother got sick. I helped her as best I could and kept my father off my back by following him into his medical practice. In the meantime, I met with rebels and helped gather support for the cause."

He tilts his head toward me and I look up to meet him. His grey eyes shine in the gathering light as the sun gradually works its way over the horizon.

"Then I met you," he says, huskily.

My eyes drift closed as his lips meet mine. I savour his warmth, my heart so full I feel as though it could burst. My throat constricts at the unending wave building up within me, so unlike anything I have felt before.

I shift on top of him, drinking him in, wanting, needing to heal every scar with my kisses. He wraps his arms around my back and pulls me closer, as though he could absorb me through his skin.

"You are a good person, Will." I draw back so he has to look at me directly. "I can see it in you. Everything you're doing here, now—it's more than enough to make up for whatever's happened in the past."

That familiar half-smile gets my heart racing again. "I've never told anyone about my scars before."

I quirk an eyebrow and sit up, pushing his shoulder aside so that I am looking at his back again. "You aren't going to be able to scare me off with these little things." I kiss one of the ridges, smiling to myself when I elicit a soft groan from him. "Nope." I move my lips down to another scar. "Not so scary."

He rolls over and lifts me up in one smooth motion, holding me on top of him. "I don't think there's anything that scares you," he murmurs against my neck.

I give in to his kisses, giving my hips a tempting little twirl.

He grunts and flips me off him. I slam down onto the pillows and he looms over me, pinioning my hands above my head.

"Look at that," I say. "It's like how we first met."

"Enough of your teasing, Runner." His voice is rough. "We need to get you back to the Palace."

"This is enough of a Palace for me."

"I could keep you here all day." He uses his free hand to stroke my midsection and I wriggle in his grasp. "But it's almost daylight and soon someone will notice you're gone."

I sigh as he releases me, watching as he rolls off the bed and pulls on his clothes. His scarred back disappears beneath his white shirt and he chuckles at my pouting. "Here." He tosses the wrinkled pink dress to me and I catch it reluctantly. "Don't tempt me any more than you already are."

Once we are both dressed, he leads me down the stairs and onto the street; he takes my hand as we walk through the silent morning alleyways. We reach the main road and he sticks out one hand to signal an approaching carriage, still holding me with the other.

"Wait," I say, suddenly remembering. "My shoes, your vest. We left them in the alley."

He shrugs. "I guess we will have to consider them lost to the cause."

The carriage pulls up and I let him help me into the seat. He shuts the door and remains on the road, leaning through the open window.

"You aren't coming?" I ask.

He shakes his head. "I'm needed here. If you recall, there's been a slight change in plans and I need to relay it to our friends. I trust you can sneak into your bed without anyone noticing?"

"Piece of cake." At the mention of bed, my eyelids grow heavy. I realize that I haven't slept in over a day.

"I'll be in touch with you soon. Stay safe." He leans in through the window and kisses me, holding my hot cheeks between his hands.

I am released all too soon, sinking back against the leather seat as the carriage pulls away and Will's figure retreats into the distance. I take advantage of the ride's rhythmic swaying, managing to steal a few precious minutes of sleep while the events of the night swirl together in my brain to create vivid and confusing dreams. I awake again with a start when the carriage turns through the main gate of the Palace and drives around to the back door.

I thank the driver but he waves away my offer of payment, saying it's already been taken care of. I remain in the drive, waiting until the carriage has pulled away before I dart through one of the servant's entrances and silently up towards the fourth floor.

The sun cuts cruelly through my vision as I claw my way to consciousness. I force my eyelids open slowly while I fight to adapt to the sunlight streaming full force through the glass wall of my bedroom.

I hug a pillow to my chest and sigh at the memory of last night. I breathe in the scent of the clean linen, thinking of Will in his cramped flat, with his sheets rumpled and smelling of me. Sighing, I roll over and squeeze the pillow tighter, curling my legs up from where they lie tangled in the blankets. My heart constricts at the image of my fingers splayed over his scarred back, his breath warming my neck as he pulls me more urgently against him.

I am cozy and comfortable in my oversized bed surrounded by opulence, but at this moment I want nothing more than to wake up next to him in the dingy flat. To look into those grey eyes while he wraps me in his arms.

Gradually, I become aware of the sounds of the Palace coming alive outside my door. By the height of the sun, I guess it is nearly afternoon, but I'd wager that most people will still be sleeping off the debauchery of the ball.

I am considering rolling over and trying to catch a few more minutes of sleep, when my door opens and Sera sweeps into the room. She transfers the tray she is balancing on her hip to her hands and skillfully pushes the door closed with her heel. I ease myself up onto my elbows, still clutching my pillow as I watch her place the tray down on the desk.

"Good morning." I yawn, turning my head and resting my cheek on the pillow.

"Morning? It's past noon, Miss Abby. Did you sleep well?" Sera comes and perches on the edge of the bed.

I notice that the skin under her eyes is shadowed and I nudge her with my foot. "Well enough, and what about you? Did you have a fun night?" I tease.

A colour rises in her cheeks and I suspect I'm not the only one whose lips still tingle.

"Sera, you wench! Did you get up to anything untoward?" I scold.

She lightly slaps my prodding foot away. "A lady doesn't speak of such things." Her voice is stern but her eyes twinkle and I laugh.

"I'm glad you were able to enjoy yourself," I say fondly.

"It appears that you did as well." Sera rises from the mattress and heads to the washroom. A moment later, I hear water splashing into my washbasin and she reappears.

I sigh and force myself out of bed, padding to the washroom, where I wash my face, taking care to rub around my eyes and remove any leftover traces of kohl. I pat my face dry with a towel and head back into the bedroom, smiling gratefully at Sera as she helps me shrug on a light robe before I take a seat in front of the platter she brought in. My stomach grumbles noisily as the scent of breakfast hits my nostrils.

I devour the food, suddenly ravenous, while Sera lifts the hair from my neck and begins to patiently comb through the tangles. From my seat, I stare out of the window, munching thoughtfully on my fruit.

"How is the rest of the Palace faring today?" I ask conversationally.

Sera snorts. "Poorly, I daresay. Most are still abed and those who are up and about appear the worse for wear. It's been quite a treat for us servants, actually."

I laugh, tossing a strawberry into the air and catching it. "For all their airs and graces, they were certainly a rowdy bunch last night."

"The King is in a right temper. If I were you, I would steer clear of him today."

I freeze, another strawberry halfway to my mouth. "What do you mean?"

"Well, you didn't hear it from me, but apparently two dozen prisoners escaped from the gaol last night."

I bite down on the berry, chewing slowly and deliberately. "You don't say. How did that happen?"

"No one knows. The guards were found locked in a cell this morning and not a prisoner was in sight. They don't know where they went or how they got out, but the King is as furious as I've ever seen him, ranting and raving at his Board members and the captain of the guards." Sera finishes combing my hair and gathers it in a loose knot at the nape of my neck, pinning it in place. "Lieutenant Griss thinks someone broke in to free the prisoners. He has sent his guards out to scour the grounds looking for the perpetrator. Fat lot of good it will do, if you ask me. Whoever it was will be long gone by now."

"Long gone," I echo, licking the last traces of strawberry from my swollen lips.

chapter 27

I dress in one of my most comfortable tunics, a pale green linen shift belted loosely with a gold cord. After snatching a book from my desk, I pad quietly to the staircase, making my way up to the seventh floor.

The hallway is quieter than usual. A few servants shuffle about as they perform their duties, talking in hushed tones so as not to disturb the patrons sleeping behind their thick wooden doors. Likely, most will be nursing a severe headache today.

The door to the library stands open. I slip inside, smiling to myself when I spot a familiar, dark head peeking up at me from the centre of the room.

I slide down onto the pile of cushions Meg has tossed onto the floor. She doesn't appear to have lost much sleep, which doesn't surprise me, as I have never known her to have so much as a hair out of place.

"You look well," I comment, arranging my skirt around my legs and then settling back against the pillows.

"So do you." She tilts her head at me.

I feel my face warm under her gaze and flip open my novel.

"Wait a moment." She scoots closer and playfully pokes my cheek. "What happened to you last night?"

I jerk my head away, feigning indifference and pretending to become engrossed in my book. "I don't know what you're talking about."

"Oh, please." She snatches the book from my hand, making a show of holding it just out of my reach. "Do you think I didn't notice how you completely disappeared?"

I make a half-hearted attempt at grabbing my book back. "I didn't disappear."

"You most certainly did." She tosses the book behind her and leans back, her brown eyes scrutinizing me.

I feel myself squirming under her cool gaze and self-consciously touch my lips, cursing myself immediately when her face lights up with understanding.

“There’s a boy, isn’t there?” she asks, laughing with glee at my cheeks reddening in response. “I knew it. Who is he?”

“No one you know,” I say, quickly. “He’s an old friend from the Outer City. He turned up at the ball last night—one thing led to another and...” The lie comes quickly and I gain a little more time by trailing off.

Meg tosses a pillow at me and I catch it instinctively. “Miss Fellows, I had no idea. I wish you had introduced me!”

“It happened quickly,” I say, shrugging and allowing myself a cheeky grin.

“So, what’s he like?” Sitting cross-legged on the cushions, her chin in her hands, Meg seems younger. Her familiar mannerisms and conspiratorial nature are far removed from the cool, stoic princess I met just a few weeks earlier.

“He’s kind,” I tell her vaguely. “Smart. Really driven.”

“Handsome?”

“Yes, handsome.” Will’s grey eyes and stubbled jaw fill my mind as I relax into the conversation. I find myself smiling at the memory and have to keep from hugging myself.

“You must really like him. Your whole face has lit up!”

I pause, catching myself partway between a lie and a truth. “He’s special,” I affirm neutrally.

“He sounds wonderful.” Meg sighs, her clear face open and truly glad for me.

I feel a stab of guilt for lying to her, but push the ugly feeling deep down inside before I can consider the web of lies I have spun.

I bite my lip as I busy myself rearranging the cushions, buying myself some time and averting my gaze from hers. A surprisingly large part of myself longs to toss all pretenses aside and relax into a genuine friendship.

I wish I could flop down next to Meg and relate every detail about Will and our night together, to give in to the fact that my heart is fairly bursting with the joy and confusion of everything.

The other, guilt-ridden part of me struggles with the weight of my dishonesty. Liking and trusting Meg was never a part of the plan, and I can't forget that I still have to sway her toward our cause and convince her to abandon her family so that she can lead the City. How incredibly simple.

With a considerable amount of effort, I manage to shift gears and slide back into my courtly persona.

"And how was the rest of your night?" I ask, lacing my voice with genuine sympathy.

She sighs, her exuberance dimming. "As well as could be expected. I was able to avoid Lynal for the majority of it; he managed to get himself completely inebriated, which worked to my advantage."

I suppress a shudder, remembering Grayson's cold, clammy hands pinning me to the wall.

"I suppose that's positive," I say. "Has your father made any more mention of an engagement?"

She gives me a strange look and shakes her head. "Your mystery man really must have kept your attention. Father made a formal announcement last night."

I stare at her wide-eyed, questioning.

"The whole Court knows we're engaged now." Her earlier girlishness has disappeared and she now appears weary, dejected. "The engagement party is to be held in a few days."

"Oh, Meg. I am so sorry." I scoot closer and let her slump tiredly against me, leaning my head on top of hers.

"It's the story of my life, isn't it?" she says. "I will forever be a pawn in my father's games."

"You're worth so much more than that," I tell her.

She groans and lifts her head from my shoulder. "I've had it, Abby—I really have."

"What do you mean?"

"This 'dutiful princess' business. Being traded away like a sack of flour. Father says that if I don't marry Lynal, he will declare war on the Outer City. If I *do* marry him, we'll just end up sending more people to die in the Wastelands. How can those be the only options?" Her eyes are dry and her long fingers clench into fists. "Why should *he* get to make all the decisions?"

I know that this is a key moment, and I speak carefully, treading softly. "You should be ruler, not him." I want to encourage her, not force her or scare her away.

She doesn't say anything for a long moment and I fear that I have pressed too far.

"Do you really think so?" She looks at me earnestly, her bright eyes serious.

"I do," I reply with complete honesty. "I do, Meg. You want to help everyone, not just the courtiers. You could be the queen this city needs." I clutch her hands. "Is that something you want?"

Her cool fingers grasp mine. "Yes. More than anything in the world." Her brow furrows, her dark eyebrows coming together. "But how could that ever be?"

I chew on my bottom lip, studying her. "Your father and his supporters would have to be removed."

"Removed?"

"If they weren't standing in the way, the people would look to a new leader. Someone strong who wants what's best for everyone, not just the rich."

"But why would they think that person is me? What cause does the City have to support me? "

She has a point.

"What you need is an endorsement," I say, thoughtfully. "From someone the commoners trust."

"The Runner."

Her words catch me completely off guard and I nearly topple of my perch on the cushion, only the clutch of her hands keeping me upright.

I peer at her face, expecting an accusing glare, but am instead met with a far-off gaze. "That's who I need," she says.

"You know of the Runner?" I keep my voice low.

"Of course—who doesn't? The long-arm of the Commons." She leans in toward me, conspiratorially. "You know, I'll bet it was her who helped those prisoners escape last night."

I blink, trying to make sense of how to proceed. I wasn't aware that my reputation had stretched all the way to the Palace; I'd imagined I was insignificant enough to stay under their radar. It appears my latest stunt has just made me a subject of the King's interest and the target of his entire royal guard. The ground I am treading just became infinitely more toxic.

"It's just a shame that I have no chance of reaching out to her. No one has a clue who she is." Meg releases my hands, sighing. "I suppose it's just as well. Even if I could talk to her for a few minutes and convince her to favour me, to what end would that be? I couldn't very well ask my father to kindly step down."

I nod, thoughtfully. Of course, Meg doesn't have a violent bone in her body. Even if her father wasn't a cruel dictator, there would be no conceivable way that she would wish him harm.

Unfortunately, the reality of the situation is that the King will relinquish his throne only if it were pried from his cold, dead hands. There is no shortage of people who would relish the opportunity to end his reign in as bloody a manner as possible, and should a rebellion form, few would be satisfied with his merely stepping aside.

"There may be a way," I say, slowly. I look into her honest gaze as the truth threatens to spill forth.

I could do it. I could tell her everything. That I am the Runner, that I was merely pretending to be a lady in order to get close to her, that I believe in her and that together we can bring this city to a place of equality and face down the Wastelanders, united.

A warning hums through me. She would be furious. More than furious—she would be hurt, mortified. This girl was closed off, untrusting, and slowly she opened herself up to me. I prodded details from her of her personal life, encouraged her to tell me the secrets of her family, let her pour her heart out to me and cry on my shoulder. What she thinks is a close friendship is all built on a lie and a plot to destroy her and her family. If I told her who I really was she would never forgive me. At this moment more than ever, on the cusp of rebellion, I need her strong and focused.

"What is it?" she asks.

I place a finger to my lips before rising to my feet and doing a quick survey of the library, checking behind the shelves and around corners. When I'm certain that we're completely alone, I go to the doors and push them closed, wincing at the creak of the hinges echoing down the cavernous hall.

I pad back to Meg and sink onto my knees. She eyes me questioningly but doesn't say anything, waiting patiently.

"I know someone in the Commons," I tell her, in a low voice. "I daren't say who, but it's someone who can get a message to the Runner. I could get word to her, maybe pass her a letter?"

She blinks once, quickly. "Really?"

"If you truly want this, Meg, I can help you make it happen."

"But what about my father?"

I bite my lip at this, unsure of how to respond.

"Perhaps your father can be encouraged to step aside," I say, slowly. "Once he sees how the commoners far outweigh his guards, he may reconsider his position. Together, we could pose enough of a threat that your father may choose not to go up against us." *Unlikely*, I think to myself. However, the matter of removing the King is Will's domain.

Meg doesn't say anything for a long moment, her eyes searching my face. I don't have to pretend to look as earnest as possible.

"What you do have to consider," I continue gently, "is that if you decide to go through with this, there will be no turning back. You will be declared an enemy of the crown. You won't be under your father's control anymore, but neither his protection."

Meg rises to her feet and paces in front of me. The late afternoon sun filters in through the library windows, illuminating her white dress and lighting her like a beacon. I cannot tear my eyes away from her regal figure as she circles the floor, her brow furrowed in concentration.

"I have to try," she says, eventually. She draws herself up to her full, impressive height and crosses her arms in front of herself, her mouth set in a grim line of determination. "If I don't stand up to my father now, in a few weeks he'll send countless people into the Wastelands to be slaughtered in droves. I cannot in good conscience consider my own safety above thousands of other people."

I feel tears prick my eyelashes and blink to clear them. "Spoken like a true queen."

I stand and join her at the window. From the seventh floor, we are granted an impressive view of the City, the twisting streets stretching from the gates of the Palace all the way down to the stone wall that bars us from the desert Wasteland beyond. I slip my arm around Meg's waist and hug her to my side.

"I'll write a letter," she affirms. "And I'll need you to be the contact between myself and the Runner. Dear friend, I'll be putting you in a dangerous position—are you certain that you want to risk yourself?"

I grin. The risk to myself is already far greater than she could ever know. "Absolutely. You have my complete support. I will do anything you ask of me."

"Thank you, for everything. I mean it." She wraps a slim arm around my shoulder. "You're the only one I trust."

The familiar weight of guilt threatens me and I forcefully push it aside, instead focusing on the ray of hope I feel as we look out over the City together.

chapter 28

I step out of the carriage and flip a coin to the driver, waiting for him to drive away before I set off down the street toward Will's flat, the satchel Meg gave me clutched tightly against my shoulder.

After yesterday's chat in the library, Meg and I devised a scenario to get me out of the Palace with a letter addressed to the Runner. This morning Meg sought me out me in the parlour and handed over the satchel, loudly requesting that I drive into the market to pick up some items for her. I supplemented our treasonous contraband with some comfortable items of clothing, along with a small purse of coins that I had managed to squirrel away for Lara. It has been weeks since I have seen my best friend and I whistle a little to myself in anticipation.

I walk the few blocks to the flat, sticking to the main streets and keeping my pace to a slow amble. Dressed in my Palace garb, I give no reason for anyone to suspect that I am anything but a respectable lady out for a day of shopping.

When I reach Will's building, I glance up the outer wall. For a moment I contemplate hitching up my skirt and shimmying up to his window, but instead opt for the more ladylike option and enter through the front door.

My heart is beating heavily in my chest as I ascend the stairs. I rap lightly on the door to his flat, smiling when it swings open.

A small yelp escapes my lips as his arm wraps around my waist and he pulls me inside, swinging me around and capturing me in a kiss while the door slams shut behind us. I place my hands behind his head and pull him closer, opening my mouth to his.

A low murmur sounds from his throat and he lifts me from my feet, carrying me over to the couch. I love that he isn't too gentle and respond with a hungry nip to his neck.

"Gods, I've missed you," he says between kisses.

I sigh happily and pull his shirt over his head, running my hands up and down his scarred back.

Within moments my dress is gone and we are pulling at each other as though we will never get another chance. I arch my back against him, every part of me crying out to bring him closer and closer, feeling that I will never get enough of this ridiculous man who can make me feel things I never knew existed.

When we've both had our fill, I hold him against me, listening as our synchronized breathing gradually slows.

"Well, hello to you as well," I say. He covers my laughing mouth with another kiss and I playfully push him off me. "I have things I need to do today. I didn't come here just for you."

"Liar," he accuses.

I climb out from underneath him and reach for Meg's satchel, seeking out the spare clothes I have brought with me and pulling them on. He watches me from the couch, raising an eyebrow suggestively and patting the seat next to him.

I laugh and toss him his trousers. "I feel as though you aren't taking this seriously," I tease.

He sighs dramatically, reaching for his clothes, his eyes never leaving me. "You're beautiful," he says.

I glance down at my street-rat outfit of loose, patched pants and a cropped top. "You're mad," I accuse, my attention diverted by his open shirt and chiselled stomach.

"No argument there." He stands up and makes a show of stretching his arms.

I dig through my bag for the letter, carefully averting my eyes from his physique. Gods, he's distracting.

"I have news," I say, brandishing the letter at him.

"What's that?"

"It's a letter from Meg."

"To who?"

"To me. Well, not to me, exactly. To the Runner."

"Why would the Princess give you a letter for the Runner?"

"Because she thinks I know someone who can deliver it to her. She wants the support of the commoners and needs the Runner to endorse her. She wants to be queen."

His brow wrinkles in confusion. "You're going to have to catch me up."

I explain as best I can the newest developments, trying with some effort to cover all of the details and not get ahead of myself in my excitement. When I'm done, I hand him the letter, standing up and pacing the room while he reads silently.

"Well?" I demand, when I can no longer stand to wait.

He holds one finger up in response and I return to pacing; eventually, I stop at the window and pull myself up onto the ledge, leaving my legs to dangle inside the room. I tap my heels against the wall restlessly, staring at his dark head bent over the paper.

Just when I think I will go mad with impatience, he finally puts the paper down on the table, leans back and looks at me thoughtfully.

I raise my eyebrows. "So?"

"This does change things." He scratches at his chin as he thinks.

"She wants to be a part of this," I point out. "I thought you would be pleased."

"I *am* pleased, but I'm trying to work out where we go from here." He drops his hands, but the pinched line between his brows remains. "Now we have another element to contend with. We need to get the Princess out of the Palace before we launch an attack. Not only that, but we have to get this letter out to the masses, rally support for her and, at the same time, keep her intentions totally hidden from the Court."

"Sounds simple enough," I say, sarcastically. "What's the problem?"

"What do you plan on doing with this?" he asks, gesturing to the letter.

"I was going to gather some friends and take Meg's letter down to the Beacon," I reply. "Say my piece, let the word spread organically." I glance out the window. "In fact, it's starting to get late. Put your boots on—we should get moving."

"Slow down, Kay. You're not thinking this through." Will folds up the letter. "You can't just rush down there with this. What we have here is a very dangerous letter. This is high treason. We have to tread carefully."

"Did you know that the wedding date is already set? There's going to be an engagement party in less than a week. Time is not on our side, Will. If we don't act soon, it will be too late: Meg will marry Grayson and we'll be in the middle of a whole new war." I chew on the inside of my cheek to keep the frustration from rising in my voice.

"I realize that, but before you go running up and down the streets, waving your banner, let's just take a moment and think about this." Will taps the folded piece of paper on his knee. One corner of his mouth tilts up as he regards me.

"What?" I ask, irritably.

"You're very pretty when you're mad at me."

I roll my eyes. "Be serious," I scold him.

"If we're going to come out of the woodwork, we're going to do it the right way." He speaks assertively, the consummate soldier. "Let's gather my friends and your friends, *discreetly* tell them to spread the word and come down to the Beacon at a set time, tonight. Once everyone is gathered together, you can make a nice, rousing speech, maybe read the Princess' letter and tell them what we want to do." He slaps the paper across his palm definitively.

"And what is it that we want to do, exactly?" I snatch the letter back from his hands and stuff it securely into my satchel. "I think it's time we discuss that."

"Yes, I think we should." Without the paper to fiddle with, Will compensates by bouncing his leg up and down.

"How are you going to remove the King and the Board?"

"I don't think you'll like it."

"Spit it out, Will. I think I already have enough of an idea."

His expression turns grim. "We're going to take the Palace by force. We'll organize an army, give them weapons, gain entry to the Palace and fight our way to the King and his advisors. Anyone who opposes us, we kill." His normally clear eyes have darkened and the corners of his mouth twitch down. "My friends are all trained soldiers, we're ready and willing to fight, but our numbers are not enough without the support of the Commons."

I nod tightly, contemplating his words.

I'm not surprised. I was told of this fight five years ago, when my father first began gathering support for his own rebellion. He tried his best to shield me from the realities of bloodshed, but I always found a way to listen in on his talks with his co-conspirators. I recall hushed conversations and sharpened pickaxes, dark preparations brought to an abrupt halt at the sound of Palace guards banging down the door to our flat. It was on the night that he died—the night of the fire—that I made a vow to pierce the King with my father's own dagger.

That was before. Now, I find myself hesitating. The weeks spent living behind Palace walls have given my enemy a face. The world won't be any worse off without King Francis, but what of the rest of them? The courtiers might be largely selfish and insipid, but does that make them worthy of murder?

I recall yesterday's image of Meg in the library, when she stood tall and regal and spoke of her hopes for the City's future. It was then that I knew for certain I would follow her anywhere. The effect she had on me was immediate, and I wonder if her impact will be enough to cause the King's supporters to lay down their arms and defer to her peacefully. With Meg at our helm, there is a chance that this can all be resolved with minimal bloodshed.

"What are you thinking?" Will's voice cuts through the fog and I glance up, watching as he rises and comes to sit on the ledge beside me. "I feel as though I've lost you."

"I'm not lost." On the contrary, I'm more certain of this rebellion and my place in it than I've ever been before. There is going to be a battle, true, but if I can convince Meg to lead us and the commoners to follow, then I will have achieved what my father could only dream of.

I study Will. This man has fought before, has held a sword and struck people down. The actions he's taken have made him strong, but have also robbed him of a piece of himself. Can I make the same leap?

Suddenly weary, I let my head drop to his shoulder. His broad arms wrap around me, holding tightly.

As if reading my thoughts, Will speaks quietly. "I wish it didn't have to be this way, Kay—I really do. War is coming. It will be out there," he nods his head out the window, indicating the Wastelands, "or it will be in here. At least we have a say over what happens within our walls."

"I'm not scared to fight," I say, lifting my head to look at him fully.

That half-grin. "You're not scared of anything."

"I wouldn't say that. I'm not so keen on giving that rousing speech you mentioned. Maybe you should be the one to talk to the crowd tonight."

He chuckles, pulling me against him. When he speaks, I feel the reverberation in his chest. "It has to be you, Runner. Don't underestimate yourself; your name is one of the greatest weapons in our arsenal, and now the time has come to wield it."

I groan, shoving him back. "This is a mistake. I don't know what I'm doing."

"Then fake it 'til you make it." He tugs lightly on the end of my braid. "You've made it this far."

I sigh, looking back out the window toward the Wastelands. "My father would roll over in his grave if he could see us now," I say, speaking mostly to myself.

There is a silence before Will breaks through my thoughts. "What happened to your father?"

I shake my head, bringing myself back to the present. "Never mind." I hop down off the ledge, crossing the room and pulling on my boots. "Are you coming?"

"Where to?"

"My place. I need to talk to Lara and start rounding up our friends."

He shakes his head. "We'll cover more ground if you spread the word in your neck of the woods and I spread it in mine. I'll meet you at the Beacon tonight. Nine o'clock?"

I finish lacing up my boots and straighten, adjusting my satchel across my shoulders as I come back over to him.

"Deal." I place both hands on his cheeks and kiss him, then laugh as he pulls me off my feet.

"Nine o'clock." I shoot him a smile before I duck through the window and heave myself onto the roof, immediately turning and leaping across the alleyways, heading back toward my old attic.

I swing through my window and land soundlessly on the floor of the flat, smiling to myself from the exhilaration of the run. My limbs feel light, tired but alive and buzzing with the thrill of soaring across the rooftops.

Across the room, someone gasps and there is the sound of an object hitting the floor.

"Sorry! I didn't mean to—"

I'm cut off as Lara rushes over and wraps her arms around my neck. I hug her back, frowning at her noticeably slimmer frame.

"Kay, darling, I'm so glad you're here." Lara's voice is raspy but her grip is strong as she draws back, holding me at arm's length. "You look wonderful."

"Thanks, so do you." Lying is coming to me a lot easier these days. "You're thinner—have you been eating?"

"Oh yes, when I can. Been so busy, you know." Lara speaks quickly, almost frantically.

I allow her to lead me to the bed. We sink down onto the cushions and sit cross-legged, facing each other, a ritual we've repeated countless times over the years.

"I brought you something," I say, breaking the silence. I reach into my satchel and pull out the change purse, handing it over to her.

"Thank you." She accepts the money but barely glances at it, instead transferring it from hand to hand absentmindedly as if testing the weight.

"Have you been receiving the rest of the money I've sent?" I ask.

"Yes, yes, I have." She places the purse gently on the bed next to her, as if it were made of glass. "I feel as though I haven't seen you in ages! What's the Palace like? Tell me everything."

Her question causes an unexpected spark of annoyance to rise in my chest. All my guilt about living in plush splendour while my friends toil away on the streets at once comes rushing back. Lara stares at me with wide, eager eyes, waiting.

"It's...beautiful," I say, carefully. "It's what you would expect. Fancy. Frivolous. Stacked to the brim with excess." I trail off, unsure of how to continue.

"What are your clothes like? Have you been dancing? Are the men handsome?" Lara's expression has softened and taken on a dreamlike quality.

It takes me several moments to formulate a response. "What is it that you suppose I'm doing there?" I ask, the ugly feeling of guilt turning to anger.

"I'm not lounging about on cushions and getting fat, if that's what you're thinking."

She appears stunned, blinking at me. "I didn't say anything like that."

"You're obviously much more interested in some shallow affairs than the rebellion. If you want to know the truth, it's that those people are more murderous behind gilded doors than they are on our streets." I snap my mouth shut, biting down hard on my tongue.

"Gods' sake, Kay. I get it, all right? You're extremely brave. We're all very impressed." Lara rolls her eyes, scoops up the change purse and stalks over to the small desk. She tilts the coins out onto the surface and makes a show of counting them.

My mouth drops open. "What is your problem?"

"What is *my* problem? I haven't seen you in weeks and then you drop in here—unannounced— and immediately begin a row with me."

"I didn't come here to row, I just wanted to check up on you."

"Well, thank goodness for that. Gods know that if I didn't have you to look after me, I'd be out begging for coin." The sarcasm drips from her voice like acid.

"More like spreading your legs for it." I regret the words instantly but am incapable of stopping myself.

She gasps and hurls a coin at me. It misses by a mile and hits the wall, dropping heavily behind the bed. "How *dare* you," she growls.

I backtrack hurriedly: "I'm sorry, I shouldn't have said that."

"You've always had this hero complex, you know. Your whole family did."

I open my mouth to protest but she raises her voice, speaking over me.

"You think you have to save everyone, protect everyone. Well, guess what, Kay. Not everyone wants your help." She swipes angrily at her eyes.

I take a deep breath, burying my hands in my hair. "Lara, I—"

"If you must know, I asked about the Palace because yes, frankly, it does sound a lot better than this shithole. Is it really so crazy that I might want to indulge in some nice things, for once in my life? Maybe I would like to have my hair done so prettily, and wear nice clothes. I don't have to feel bad about wanting that." She crosses her arms, a high colour rising to her bronzed cheeks.

"Those pretty things aren't free, Lara. You of all people should know there is a reason that only the courtiers get to enjoy them: it's because the rest of us suffer for it."

"But that's just the way it is, isn't it? It has always been this way: us and them. And yes, it's sad that some of us were born into the Commons, but why shouldn't we imagine what things would be like if the gods had favoured us, instead? What's wrong with that?"

"What's *wrong* with that?" I ask, staring at her incredulously. "You know, that is exactly the attitude of someone who's given up. That's the attitude that accepts an unfair lot in life and doesn't want to change it."

"Maybe I'm tired of fighting, Kay."

"Don't say that." I reach into my satchel and brandish Meg's letter at her. "Do you know what I have here? This is a pledge from the Princess Megra. She wants us to support her in overturning the King. She wants to lead us into a new future. Imagine it, Lara—the division of commoners and courtiers will be a thing of the past, everyone will have a fair chance." I can hear the desperation in my voice, but I have to make her see.

Lara is silent, watching me. Her bright-eyed dreaminess from earlier has been replaced by a world-weary exhaustion.

"It's a lovely idea," she says, eventually.

"It's more than an idea, Lara. It's *really* happening. Tonight, at the Beacon, we are going to raise our army. We're going to get organized, and when the time is right, we are going to march on the Palace, take down the King and put Meg up in his place. This is *real*."

"Do you realize how mad you sound?" Her pale eyes search my face, disbelieving. "We aren't soldiers. The soldiers are up there." She thrusts her hand toward the window, pointing at the glass Palace in the distance. "*They're* the ones with training, with swords. We're just a bunch of miners. What do you expect? That Harry would bash them over the heads with his rolls of bread?" She laughs, bitterly. "Be real, Kay. This is farfetched, even for you."

I shake my head, unfolding the letter with trembling hands. "No, we can do this."

Her hand comes down on top of mine, cool on my hot skin. "Kay, please." She lifts my chin and forces my eyes into hers. "Come home. If you go through with this, they'll kill you."

I hiccup, taken aback. "We have to try," is all I can manage.

She doesn't say anything but keeps my eyes arrested with hers.

"Edmun is dead," she says.

I wrench my chin from her grasp. "What?"

She nods, slowly. "We received word just a few days ago. He was struck down in the Wastelands."

I take a step back. "No."

Her tears flow freely down her cheeks. "What do you think now? Edmun was our friend, they stuck a sword in his hand and now he's gone forever. Do you still want the rest of us to fight?"

My head falls into my hands, my fingers entangling in my hair. I picture Edmun's smoke-blackened, smiling face. The way his eyes lit up when he teased me. When I last saw him, he was a broken man, doomed and terrified. The fact that his worst fear has come to fruition causes scratchy tears to gather behind my eyelids and I have to struggle to get myself back under control.

"All the more reason," I say, after a time.

"Excuse me?" She's incredulous.

I look up. "If we don't do this, the draft will only worsen. They'll just keep sending more and more of us into the Wastelands. Don't you get it, Lara? We don't *matter* to them."

"At least we have a chance of surviving the Wastelands. What you're suggesting is suicide." Her voice has grown shrill.

Suddenly, the room feels incredibly small and suffocating.

"I have to go," I hear myself say.

My vision blurs as I stand and adjust my satchel with trembling hands. I brush by her, crossing to the window and swinging my legs out. I look back once more to see Lara staring at me, eyes glistening. She appears incredibly frail and vulnerable and I feel a shameful pit of guilt clawing up my throat at leaving her. Ashamed, I turn away.

"The Beacon, nine o'clock tonight." I rotate and allow myself to dangle partway out the window, my feet finding purchase on a familiar protruding rock. "I hope you'll be there."

Without waiting for a response, I release the ledge and climb down to the street.

chapter 29

The dust flies up around me when I land, scratching and choking. I pull my scarf up over my face and walk blindly, my thoughts wrapped up in what has just transpired.

Edmun is dead. I brush angrily at my eyes, shoving away the feeling of loss and blaming the surging sand for the moisture clouding my vision. These last few weeks have wreaked havoc on my world, the ground below my feet no longer solid. For the first time in many weeks, I crave my old, simple life tucked away in the attic, scoring small-time purses and annoying the Palace guards.

As I stumble toward the market, someone suddenly emerges from a side street and places their hand on my shoulder. I let out a gasp of surprise and turn instinctively, slamming my elbow up into my attacker's chin.

"Gods *damn it*," a familiar voice shouts in pain.

My eyes widen and I straighten out of my fighting stance, cautiously regarding the tall figure hunched over in front of me.

"Marc?" I ask.

"Who did you think it was?" He straightens, rubbing his chin.

"I'm so sorry! You snuck up on me." I incline my head to examine his jaw, wincing when I see that the skin has already started to redden. "I really got you good, huh?"

"I'd hate to see what you'd do to someone you really had a problem with." He offers me a small grin of forgiveness. "Since I owe you a favour, I supposed I could give you a free pass on this one."

"I appreciate it. I really am sorry—I didn't even recognize you."

It's true: Marc looks entirely different from the man I found in the gaol. His dark hair is actually a sandy blond, light and flying about his head in the dusty wind. Clean of grime and freshly shaved, his olive skin is clear, with a light dusting of freckles across his nose.

"I suppose I wasn't really looking my best when you last saw me." He chuckles. "It's a wonder what some sunshine and a hundred baths will do for a body."

"So you're doing well?" I ask, studying him closely.

"Better than well. Every day I'm free of that place, I thank my lucky stars." One hand moves to push the hair back from his face.

"I'm glad to hear it."

"What are you doing out here?" he asks.

At the question, I start, brought abruptly back to the present and the fight with Lara.

Something must have shown on my face because Marc frowns and his brows knit together in concern. "Whatever it is, it can't be good. How about I buy you some lunch and you can catch me up?"

"Oh," I say, surprised at the offer. "That's really kind of you, but I don't want to be a bother. You were probably on your way somewhere..."

"It's fine. I don't have to be anywhere important. After everything you've done for me, getting you a meal would be the least I can do." He inclines his head down the street, indicating that I follow him.

"All right," I agree. I don't really feel up to being by myself and besides, Marc could prove to be a valuable asset in Will's rebellion. "Let's go."

He leads me to a small shop and purchases us two portions of smoked meat and ale, waving off my offer of payment. We take our meals to a table in the corner and settle in, chewing and drinking in companionable silence.

"So." Marc has polished off his food and is hunched conspiratorially over the small table. "What's going on?"

I pause, unsure of how to begin. I nearly spill the details of what transpired between myself and Lara but, instead I swallow what's left of my lunch and lean in toward him. "We're starting a rebellion," I say, bluntly.

To my delight, a slow, impish grin spreads over Marc's face. "Finally," he says.

I snort with laughter, unable to stop myself. “That’s the best response I could ask for.” Take that, Lara.

“How are we going about it?” he asks.

I could hug him for his use of the word “we.”

“For now, I need to spread the word that there’s going to be a meeting tonight at the Beacon. We’ll give all the details then.” I widen my eyes in question: “Can you help me gather people to come?”

“Absolutely,” he says assertively. He drains his ale and looks about the shop. “In fact, I can do you one better. I’ve got a little cousin who runs like the wind and positively worships you. I’ll find her and I guarantee that she’ll spread the word like wildfire.”

“Commoners only,” I tell him. “Just the ones you trust. My friend, Will, is gathering the dependable courtiers; we don’t want the wrong people getting wind of this.”

“Will. He’s the tall one who helped you at the ball, right?”

“That’s right.”

“Hmm.” He looks thoughtful, regarding me. “You know, I can’t put my finger on it, but I swear I know him from somewhere.”

“Really? It’s possible. He fought in the Wastelands—maybe you know him from there.” I finish my drink and make to stand. “Are you coming?”

“Right behind you, captain.”

He mock-salutes and I laugh, my earlier anxiety dissolving at his enthusiasm. Marc’s eagerness is more in line with what I expected from the commoners. Together, we’ll round up plenty of dissatisfied people and I’ll show Lara that she is entirely wrong. People *do* care, they want change, and they are willing to fight for it.

With Marc’s help, the word spreads quickly. He introduces me to his cousin, Ruby, a spunky little twelve-year-old who fairly shakes at the knees when I offer her my hand.

"Like I said, she's a big fan," Marc teases and she hits his arm playfully, a blush rising to her cheeks.

"Marc here tells me you're a hell of a runner," I say kindly, in an effort to alleviate the poor girl's embarrassment.

She thrusts back her scrawny shoulders. "I can run to the Palace and back in just twenty minutes," she boasts.

"Wow," I say, widening my eyes. "You must have some killer speed."

"Sure do! People give me money to run their letters and messages to their friends. I save a lot of it. Soon, I'll have enough for a brand-new pair of boots." She thrusts out one of her legs dramatically, indicating an old, patched boot worn nearly through.

"I'll tell you what," I say, unclipping my purse from my waist and tipping a few coins into my palm. "I'd like to tender your services. I'll give you what I have here," I place the coins in her hand, smiling at her bewildered stare, "if you can deliver some messages for me."

Marc offers me a scrap of parchment and we hurriedly scribble down the names of as many people we can think of, as well as where to find them. I fold the paper and hand it to Ruby, solemnly, as though it is made of something precious.

"Find these people. Tell them that the Runner will be at the Beacon tonight at nine o'clock and if they want change, they had best come." It feels a bit absurd to use my alter ego as an incentive, but Will insisted it was the best way to drum up interest. "Tell them to bring anyone they trust."

Ruby glances at the paper and tucks it into her pocket. She nods seriously. "You can count on me."

"I have no doubt. Now, get going."

She takes off at a run, leaving Marc and I chuckling to ourselves.

"She's a little spitfire," I say, approvingly.

"She's something," he agrees. "She'll give us a good head start, but we should be rounding up as many people as possible. Want to head to the market?"

"Sure."

As we walk toward the main square, we fall into an easy chatter, with me explaining the details of Will's plot and Meg's potential for leadership. Marc listens intently, throwing out a question here and there.

"So you've really been living in the Palace this whole time." He shakes his head in wonderment. "Unbelievable."

"Some days I can scarcely believe it myself," I admit. "I feel ridiculous wearing fancy dresses and being served, like I'm obviously a big fat imposter. At any moment, I expect someone to open their eyes and point at me, screaming."

He chuckles softly, shaking his head. "You've got a lot of nerve, I'll give you that. You managed to pass yourself off as a guard, as well. Incredible."

I blush a little at his flattery, shrugging. "I find that hiding in plain sight is often one of the safest places to be. People rarely look at what's right under their noses."

"You've got that right," Marc agrees, staring off into the distance.

I follow his line of vision, tracing his gaze over our heads to where the Court rises above us and, past that, the Palace. Its glass walls glint in the afternoon sun, momentarily blinding me.

"I can't believe it's really happening," he says quietly, almost to himself.

I look back at him, my eyebrows raised in question.

"After all these years, ignoring us and soaking up the fruits of our labour, they're finally going to have to answer for their crimes," he continues.

I notice his hands balling into fists at his sides and touch him gently on the shoulder. He fingers unfurl as he visibly relaxes.

"I'm glad you're in this with us," I tell him, honestly. "Thank you."

"I'm honoured to be on the side of the Runner."

We reach the market and disperse into the crowd. I traverse the swarm, pulling the occasional sleeve and whispering into ears. My heartbeat thrums as we work our way through the throng; it thuds louder as the various murmurs gradually rise in crescendo.

Finally, I arrive at Harry's cart. After I've managed to disentangle myself from his enthusiastic hug, I tell him about the plan to meet. His usually jovial eyes darken and he nods grimly.

"I'd expected this was comin' when you started spendin' time with that rich boy." He dusts his flour-encrusted hands on his apron.

"Say you'll be there, Harry. We really need you."

"Of course I'll be there. And I'll shut down early to see if I can round up the other bakers." He pulls me to him again, wrapping me in a one-armed hug.

Abruptly caught with my face pressed against his dusty smock, I cough in surprise. "Thank you," I manage.

"Ain't a thing, Kay. Edmun would be all over this. We'll fight in his memory."

I choke again, this time less on the flour of his apron, and push myself away from him. "For Edmun."

Marc appears at my elbow and nods to Harry in greeting. "I trust I'll be seeing you tonight?"

"Absolutely," Harry answers.

My heart swells at the look of solidarity passing between my two friends, one new and one old. If we can get enough strangers willing to come together and fight, we might actually have a chance of raising an army.

It is nearing nine o'clock, and in the gathering darkness I almost trip over a small figure darting out of a side alleyway and straight into my path.

"Ruby!" Marc steadies her, hands on her shoulders. "Watch your speed—you're going to run someone over."

Ruby nods, her chest hitching as she struggles to catch her breath. "I've... done it," she manages, beaming proudly. "Everyone on the list."

"That's incredible! Great job," I tell her.

"I've just come from the Beacon." She bounces energetically from foot to foot. "You won't believe it: it's filled to the brim."

"Really?" I exchange a look with Marc, my chest constricting uncomfortably.

Ruby nods. "You'd better get down there."

"Thanks, Ruby. You'd make an excellent Runner."

She beams at me as Marc and I quicken our pace, the tavern coming into view when we round the bend.

Ruby wasn't kidding. The light from inside is almost completely obscured by the sheer number of bodies pressed against the windows. I hiccup and Marc slaps my back.

"Nothing to be nervous about," he says. "You're going to do great."

I nod wordlessly and let my legs carry me forward, my eyes darting around as I search the crowd gathered outside for a familiar face.

"There you are." Will's voice sounds from beside me just as I reach the door of the pub.

I breathe a sigh of relief and turn to him, some of my nervousness dissolving at the touch of his hand on the small of my back.

"I'm so glad you're here," I tell him.

"I wasn't going to let you go in there by yourself," he assures me. Looking over my shoulder, he thrusts out a hand toward Marc, who I'd nearly forgotten was still standing with me. "Hey, mate."

"Sorry. Will, this is Marc. Marc, Will." The men shake hands and I notice Marc's brow furrow. "Will, Marc was one of the people you helped me escort from the gaol."

"Glad to see you on the outside." Will quirks a friendly grin.

"Glad to be out," Marc responds, his eyebrows drawing further together. "Have we met before?"

"Not that I can recall. Maybe I just have one of those faces." Will turns away and back toward me. "Are you ready to go in?"

"Yes," I lie. Suddenly remembering something, I open my satchel and thrust my hand inside. I don't immediately find what I'm looking for, my fingers sifting through the contents. "Uh oh."

"What is it?" Will asks.

My fingers scrabble around in the bag. "Oh, shit. Oh no."

I kneel down and dump the contents of my satchel onto the sandy ground, sorting through the pile desperately. "The letter—it's gone."

"The Princess' letter?" Will crouches next to me, helping me search. "When did you have it last?"

"I don't know!" I bury my hands in my hair. "It could be anywhere—it could have fallen out when I was in the market." I let out a cry of frustration. "It isn't here."

"You don't need it." Will puts his hands on my shoulders and forces me to look at him.

"Will, if that letter were to fall into the wrong hands..." Images of the torture chambers flash through my mind and I feel suddenly nauseous.

"Then we'll deal with it. One problem at a time—you taught me that, didn't you? Forget the letter for now and focus on what you have to do next. Keep going."

“I need Meg’s words.” I glance back at the tavern behind me, the many voices inside mixing together to create an ugly buzzing in my ears. “She’s a leader, not me. I can’t do this alone.”

“You’re not on your own. Look at this.” Will pulls me to my feet and spins me so that I am looking straight in the door of the pub. “All these people, they came here for *you*. They want to listen to what *you* have to say. Just tell them the truth and they’ll follow.”

“I’m not who they think I am.” Kay, Abby, the Runner.

“Do you remember what you told me once?” Will’s breath is hot in my ear, sending shivers down my spine. “Visualize that you’ve already made the jump, then leap. You can’t miss.”

I take a shaky breath, swallowing the bile that threatens to rise in my throat. Marc hands me my satchel and I accept it numbly. “Okay.”

Before I have a chance to change my mind, I step forward and push open the doors of the tavern.

chapter 30

Inside, the atmosphere sparks with tension and low murmurs of conversation sound from all sides. The tables are crowded with men and women packed tightly together, and where chairs are scarce, people have taken to standing in the pathways and against the walls. Some are even perched on the bar top, while Samus works feverishly around them to hand out mugs of ale.

I pull my spine up as straight as I can, squaring my shoulders and using them as leverage to clear a route toward the front of the room. I feel Will close behind me, his solid presence propelling me forward as I fight to ignore the hush that follows our progress.

Near the head of the tavern I spy Harry, his broad frame taking up the space of two men. I smile at him, relieved to see a friendly face among the skeptics. Wordlessly, he hands me a drink, which I accept gratefully, wrinkling my nose at the sour taste. The burning sensation in my throat helps to calm my nerves, somewhat.

Harry and Will help me clear a table and I step up to stand on top of it. Scanning the room, my legs quake slightly, for a brief moment having the clarity of mind to be amused that I'm nervous while standing a mere three feet above the ground.

From this vantage point, I can tell there is a clear divide down the centre of the room. One side of the bar looks to be mostly courtiers, a few of whom I recognize as Will's friends. They shift positions uncomfortably, clearly feeling out of place in the dingy setting. To the other side of the room and in greater proportion are the commoners, their faces hard and scuffed from a day of work.

Both groups shoot glances at their counterparts and mutter to their companions. Several pairs of eyes are trained on me, their expression questioning.

I swallow, scanning the room once more; my heart sinks when I fail to find Lara.

"Friends," I begin, my voice hoarse.

A few more people look up and I feel Will nudge my calf. I clear my throat and try again.

“Friends!” I say, louder this time.

The conversations die out as people turn one by one to look at me.

I lock my knees and imagine I am standing high above the City, about to make an exhilarating leap to the next roof.

“Many of you know me,” I begin.

Someone lets out a whoop and there is a scattering of laughter.

I relax, somewhat. “I am one of you,” I tell them. “I grew up here, my father worked alongside you in the quarry, my mother sewed your clothes and my brother served with you in the Wastelands. Your struggles are my struggles. Two hundred and nine years is too long to labour under a system that favours the rich and spits on the poor. I say the time has come to rise up, to usher in a new era!”

There are a few more whoops this time, but I notice the courtiers shooting sidelong glances at one another uncomfortably.

“People raised in the Commons are no different, no better or worse than anyone from the Court. We don’t want power or gold, all we want is to be treated fairly.” I look pointedly at Will’s friends. “The courtiers here tonight are not our enemies; they are our friends and our supporters. I, for one, welcome them and commend them for their bravery.”

Reluctant murmurs of agreement are followed by laughter when Harry gives one of the courtiers a too-enthusiastic slap on the back, causing the man to sputter and choke on his drink.

I wait for the din to die down before continuing. “So the question is, what are we going to do about it?”

“Spit it out, Runner!” a voice calls from the back.

“Rebellion!” I shout, to a cacophony of hollers from the crowd. “Courtiers and commoners, united together and fighting side by side, not in the Wastelands for a scrap of desert, but right here at home for our freedom!”

This time the cheers rise together in a roar, with mugs and fists pounding heavily on the table tops. I glance down at Will, who shoots me an encouraging smile.

"Death to the monarchy!" someone shouts out and the chant is picked up with enthusiasm.

Shit. This isn't the reaction I was hoping for. "Death is not the answer!" I try to yell over the unruly crowd, but my voice gets lost in the chaos.

"Friends, please!" I try again, feeling a well of panic build up inside of me.

The table rattles beneath my feet as Will climbs up next to me. He raises his fingers to his lips and blows a whistle so shrill I have to cover my ears.

The voices recede and I speak quickly before I lose them again. "We march on the Palace for equality, not for revenge! If we slaughter without thought, then we are no better than the King. This is our opportunity to lay the groundwork for a new, better city, a place where every citizen is given the same opportunities and freedom of choice! I ask you to take up swords and cut out the disease, not the cure! The Princess Megra wants us to have what I have just spoken of—all we need do is make room for her on the throne!"

"The Princess is poison, just like the rest of them!" someone shouts out and I gasp as a heavy mug is hurled at the courtiers. It explodes against the wall, sending ale showering over their' fine clothes.

"The time for these old prejudices is over!" My shot glass is still clenched in my fist and I throw it across the room, scoring a direct hit with the perpetrator's forehead. I draw myself up to my full height as the room rings with laughter, and I take advantage of having recaptured their attention. "It is no longer us and them!" I yell, pointedly. "We are united! We are one! There will come a day when we are led by a fair and just queen! Join us!"

I'm losing them. I can hear some cheers while others chatter angrily; questions and shouts of protest fly across the room.

"What has the monarchy done for us? Why should we trust her?"

"Yer a bloody courtier sympathizer!"

"No more royals!"

I look at Will. He stands next to me on the table, hands balled into fists at his sides.

"Easy," I whisper under my breath.

"The monarchy is not our enemy!" His voice rings out, louder than mine. Gradually, the conversation dies down. "The enemy is here, inside of you! The enemy is your anger, your resentment, your prejudices. I agree that you've been treated unjustly, but this is your chance to make things right. Trust me when I say that the Runner is your most passionate advocate. Time and time again she has risked her life for this cause, and now she stands before you with an answer! Listen to what she has to say!"

"What do you know of it, rich boy?" a woman shouts, garnering barks of agreement.

"Anyone who doubts the Runner has no place in this rebellion and has no right to their place in the new order!" Marc has materialized out of the crowd from near the bar. His hair flops onto his forehead and he pushes it back impatiently. "She risked her life to save mine, and I would be willing to wager that there are few in this room who haven't been assisted by her in some way." There are a few reluctant grumbles and I feel my cheeks reddening. "Shame on any of you who would doubt her. If the Runner says the Princess should be queen, then I will draw my sword and fight for her place on the throne!"

I catch sight of several people making their way to the bar toward Marc and for a moment I stiffen, sure that they mean to hurt him. A woman leads the group and steps up next to him. She is tall and thin but her voice is strong.

"If it weren't for the Runner, we would still be rotting in the Palace gaol!" she cries out, and I relax when I recognize her as one of the commoners from the ball. "She is our hero and our hope!"

I swallow, tears pricking my vision at the woman's words.

"She delayed my brother's draft!" Harry's booming voice reverberates through the entire room. "I will follow the Runner!"

"My children would have starved if it weren't for her generosity! I follow the Runner!" another woman calls out.

Bit by bit, the sounds of assent drown out the naysayers. In some region of my mind, I know I am meant to speak, but the words are completely lost. My chest and throat are constricted so tightly that I can barely breathe. It takes every reserve of control I have to keep from staggering from my perch atop the table.

"My friends!" I finally manage, my voice breaking. "You know me. You knew my father, my brother, my mother. You know that they dreamed of this day, that they died for it. Know now that with every fibre of my being, I will fight for a city free of oppression. I have found a way, and I have found the person to lead us! Now, who is with me?"

Someone hands me a stein and I thrust it into the air, feeling my heart swell as dozens of tankards rise in unison.

"To the Queen!" I yell, my voice strong and sure.

"To the Queen!" The voices unite in such a crescendo that I am nearly knocked over. Together as one, we toast uncertainty and hope.

Several hours later, the bar has started to empty and my mind is spinning from a heady combination of the speech, the upcoming rebellion, the drink and frustration.

I hold my head in my hand and look at the piece of parchment in front of me. Will has marked a small tick for every person who has agreed to arm themselves and march with us to the Palace when the time is right. Despite the enthusiasm earlier, the number of marks on the page is depressingly low.

"I'm sorry, I really am." A burly man with a shaven head is sitting at the table across from us, twisting his handkerchief in his thick hands. "It's just that I have three little ones at home. If something were to happen to me, what would become of them?"

I sigh, exchanging a look with Will. "I understand, Marty. I've met your children. I don't want to take you away from them, but wouldn't they be proud of their papa for fighting for a better future for them?"

Marty runs a hand over his scalp. "I just can't take the risk. I'm sorry." He pats my hand apologetically as he stands. "Good luck."

As Marty shuffles away, I lift my tankard to my mouth and grimace when I find it empty. Next to me, Will sighs and shoves his chair back from the table.

"So," I say, casting a sideways glance at him.

"I guess that's everyone." He frowns at the parchment laid before us.

"A little underwhelming, is it not?" I ask.

He doesn't say anything, his eyes never leaving the paper.

"I just don't understand." I clench my fists. "They all want change, but no one is willing to fight for it."

"They're scared," he replies evenly.

"They *should* be scared." I slam my empty mug onto the table, causing Will to jump and a few of the stragglers to look up at us. "If we don't act soon, this Wasteland war will take away the last of our choices and there won't be enough of us *left* to stand up to the King."

"You aren't telling me anything I don't know." He sounds distracted.

I look up and follow his gaze to where Marc stands at the opposite end of the room, talking with a small group.

"He says he knows you," I say.

Will murmurs non-committally, "I'll get you a fresh drink."

I make to hand him my tankard, but he has already risen and is shouldering his way toward the bar. Exasperated, I put my empty mug down again and rest my aching head on my folded arms.

Why would they all come tonight? Why would they sing my praises and toast Meg if they weren't committed to this cause? It seems it is one thing to get everyone riled up and feeling self-righteous, but quite another to put a weapon in their hands and point them toward the Palace. At this rate, we'll be slaughtered before we even reach the front gate.

I lift my head. Marc has joined Will at the bar and they are talking to one another, their voices too low for me to hear. Marc's eyebrows are furrowed and Will's shoulders seem stooped forward defensively.

My vision blurs as another bout of nausea threatens me. I groan and shut my eyes, suddenly overcome with tiredness.

Eventually, I feel the chair next to me shift as Will's weight is lowered into it again.

"What was all that about?" I murmur into the folds of my arms.

"Nothing—just chatting. I think we had better get you back to the Palace, don't you?"

"No." I raise my head to look at him. "I already sent a message ahead to Vitrola. I told her that I'm staying with a friend in the City tonight."

"Is that what I am? A friend?"

"Who said I was talking about you?"

He stands and lifts me under the shoulders. I lean against him gratefully, breathing in his scent.

"It better be me," he grunts as we weave our way toward the door. "I'm not sure who else would put up with you."

As we pass the bar, I catch Marc's eye. His mouth is pressed into a tight line, but he nods cordially. Will pushes open the door of the tavern and we step out into the cool night air.

The walk to Will's flat helps to sober me up and I begin to feel less melancholic and more angry.

"Honestly, I don't know why we bother," I grumble. "What's the point, really? They won't lift a finger to help themselves."

"Most of them are just concerned about their families," Will replies. "There are people who are already receiving a pension from their sons, brothers and fathers dying in the Wastelands. If they throw that away, it's like their loved one died for nothing."

"Why are you standing up for them?" I ask, incredulously. "This whole thing was *your* idea."

He shrugs. "I guess I just understand their hesitation. We can't expect everyone to be as crazy as you."

"Maybe it's because I don't have a family." I scuff the toe of my boot on the dusty ground. "If you don't have anyone depending on you, then you don't have anything to lose."

Will stops abruptly. He grabs my shoulders and turns me roughly to face him.

"What?" I demand angrily, stumbling on the uneven ground.

I can only barely make out his features in the dim lamplight of the street. He arrests my eyes with his before placing his warm hands on my cheeks and kissing me soundly.

"*I* depend on you," he says, matter of factly. "If you were to be gone, it would matter. It would matter more than I can say. Do you understand that?"

I blink rapidly, my mouth suddenly dry.

"Don't you ever say that you have nothing to lose. I know I don't have any say over your mad stunts, but know that when you fall. I feel the impact. If you hurt, I hurt. Get it?"

I nod, wordlessly.

“Good.” He takes my hand in his and we walk the rest of the way home in silence.

chapter 31

My arms are wrapped around Will's shoulders as I hold him against me, my mouth pressed to his throat's pulse. He murmurs into my ear and I shut my eyes tightly, crying out and feeling myself soar.

I'm not sure how much time has passed before I feel him stirring next to me. He brushes the damp strands of hair away from my forehead and wraps an arm around my waist, pulling me against him. I curl my legs and turn to him, burying my head into his chest. I nearly drift off as he gently runs his hands up and down my back, the warmth of him at my front and the coolness from the open window behind me.

"Tell me about your family," he says after a spell, his voice muffled by my hair.

I groan, nestling more securely against him. "Let's not talk about that."

"I want to know everything about you."

"Not that." The drink has nearly worked its way through my system and now I buzz from the sensation of Will. I fight to hold on to the high, but the mention of my family has it slowly evaporating.

"You never talk about them."

"There isn't anything to say. They're dead."

"What happened?"

I groan, pushing away from him and sitting up straight. Will, his grey eyes serious, watches me as I pull the covers around myself.

"Why don't you want to tell me?"

I feel my face growing warm and fight to keep my breathing even. "It's just not something I like to discuss."

He raises himself up onto one elbow and regards me. I look away, fiddling absently with a loose thread in the bed sheet.

After a moment, one of his large hands comes down on mine, ceasing my fidgeting. "Kay."

I bite my lip. "If I tell you, you have to make a promise to me."

"What is it?"

"That nothing will change afterwards."

That half-grin. "That's ridiculous."

"Will."

"Kay." His brows lower sternly and I feel my heart softening. "Knowing you better won't change anything. After all the shit I've done, there's nothing you can say that will scare me off."

I stall a moment longer, tracing patterns on the bedspread before I draw a deep, shaky breath. "All right."

He pats the space in front of him on the bed and I lower myself so that I am lying with my back to him. He curls around me, his arm under my chin. I reach for his outstretched hand and play with his fingers, marvelling at how comparatively small my hand looks.

"Tell me." His voice is low in my ear.

"I was fourteen." I speak robotically, feeling as though I am outside of my body, watching us lying in the bed from a place high above. It is easier to speak when I imagine that I am narrating the story of a stranger. "My father, mother and I lived together in a tiny apartment. Frye—that's my brother—was lost in the Wastelands a few months previous. My father was never the same after Frye died. I don't think he wanted revenge—I think he wanted to create a change."

My father worked long hours in the quarry, but at night he would meet other commoners in our kitchen or down at the Beacon, speaking in low voices about revolution. At one point, it felt as though there was a very real possibility that we would rise up and take a stand against all the injustices wrought upon us by the King and the Court.

I recall coming down to the kitchen late one night to find a single lamp burning and my father sitting at our tiny table with his friends, their heads bent closely together as they spoke in hushed tones. I stomped into the room and slammed my hands down between them.

"I know what you're planning," I declared with all the fierceness I could muster. "And I want to help."

His friends chuckled at my outburst but my father remained perfectly still, regarding me without a word for several moments. I bit my tongue, maintaining eye contact with him and drawing myself up as tall as I could.

In telling the story, I can see clearly my father's lined, tired eyes and his dark beard, speckled with grey. His hands were large and there was constantly a line of dirt under the trimmed nails from his days spent at the quarry.

Eventually, a weary smile crept up his lips; wordlessly, he pushed one of the kitchen chairs back, inviting me to join them. I remember how mature I felt, sitting with him and the other rebels while they discussed revolution. To me, they were the bravest people in the entire world. I never for a moment thought their dream would end the way it did.

The night they came for us, I was awoken from a sound sleep by my mother frantically shaking my shoulder.

"Kay, wake up," she whispered.

I cracked my eyes open, blinking in an effort to adjust to the darkness. "What is it?" I asked, wincing as she grabbed me by my upper arm and pulled me from my cot. Her auburn hair was mussed from sleep and she'd thrown a patched shawl haphazardly around her shoulders.

"Get under the bed," she urged desperately.

I heard the front door of our flat being forced open, then several booted feet marching into our home.

"Who's there?" I asked her, fearfully.

Her eyes were wide. My father's voice sounded from the hall, calm and measured.

"Under the bed. Now!"

My mother pushed me to the floor and I scrambled beneath the cot, willing myself to be as small and flat as possible. I held my breath as my bedroom door flew open.

From my vantage point under the cot, I could see my mother's feet. "What do you want?" she demanded.

"This household has been charged with conspiracy and treason. Captain Harmen has ordered you all to gather in the main room." The voice from my doorway was that of a stranger and presumably a King's guard, from the looks of his shiny boots. "Where is your daughter?"

"She isn't here. She's staying with a friend." My mother's voice was strong and unwavering, not missing a beat.

The shiny black boots stepped up next to her scuffed slippers. I watched them drag her away, protesting.

Once they had left, I heard muffled voices from the other room. I slowed my breathing as much as possible and strained my ears to try and pick up what was being said.

My father's deep voice rang out: "I'm telling you, you've made a mistake. My family is innocent; it's me you want. I will go to the Palace quietly, if you leave them be."

I clenched my hands into fists and shook with fear.

"We aren't here to arrest you. Your punishment is to be carried out immediately."

"Please, you don't have to do this." My mother's strong voice had broken.

What was happening out there?

I heard metal grating against leather.

"No!" a voice yelled out, and then my mother uttered a single, blood-curdling scream.

I clawed my way out from under the bed and ran to my father's room, where I yanked open the door of his bedside table and with trembling fingers grappled for the dagger hidden within.

There was another scream, followed by a hideous gurgling. I nearly tripped over my own feet from a combination of adrenalin and fear as I tore down the hall back to the main room.

The floor was bathed in crimson. I stopped in my tracks, my addled brain fighting to make sense of the scene. Several guards stood on either side of the room while my mother sprawled out on the floor, blood staining her clothes, unmoving. My father was on his knees, facing me, the captain's sword held to his neck. His eyes widened when he saw me, frozen in the doorway with the dagger clenched in my shaking hand.

"*Run.*" My father managed a single word before the captain sliced the sword cleanly across his throat. Blood gushed from the wound in a fountain, drenching the front of his tunic and cushioning his fall as he slumped face first down onto the floor.

My body became incredibly light and my vision spotted. The shadow of a stranger moved toward me and I swiped blindly in their direction, vaguely aware of some resistance against my dagger as a disembodied voice cried out in pain. I drew my eyes up slowly to see the man—little more than a boy—pull back, clutching his arm where it was spotted with blood.

"Get her," my parents' murderer ordered.

The guards began to close in on me, swords drawn. As if in slow motion, I felt myself reach out toward a table near the doorway. I knocked an oil lantern off it and watched with fascination as the fire began to spread.

The books scattering the floor in piles ignited, the flames hungrily devouring them. The guards drew back, their arms over their mouths to block out the smoke. Through the haze, I could just make out the man who had killed my parents: his shiny captain's badge and the sunken lines of his face seared into my memory.

Run.

I gave the still forms littering the floor of my home one last glance before I turned and darted back down the hallway.

Bootsteps pounded the floor behind me as I tore toward the window of my parents' bedroom. I leaped onto the bed and aimed for the dark, star-spotted night sky. In the next instant, I was airborne, completely weightless and free.

All too soon, the ground rose up beneath me and my legs crumpled as I landed, shocked by the sudden impact. Pain shot up my left leg and sparked an inferno in my knee. I pulled my leg to my chest, only in that moment realizing I was still clutching my father's dagger.

I raised my eyes to the storey I had fallen from. A single figure stood in the window, staring down at me, silhouetted by the flames roaring behind. At the sight of the guard, my heart hardened and broke, my loss suddenly and monumentally apparent.

He would pay for what he had done. That night, the King and Captain Harmen made an enemy of the wrong girl.

I somehow managed to drag myself to my feet and limp away—away from the burning flat, the King's guard and what was once my family. I took nothing with me but my father's dagger and a searing hatred in my heart.

I unlace my hand from Will's and lie stone still, feeling his heartbeat against my spine. For a long moment, we exist like that, both completely aware of the other's presence but absorbed in our own worlds.

After an eternity, I feel his arms tighten around me, drawing me closer. His body sends an excruciating heat through my middle, spreading down to my toes and the tips of my hair. I allow him to hold me as the first tears I have cried in five years trickle down my cheeks and soak his pillow.

chapter 32

I awake with the sun warming my face. Blinking, I stretch out my arms and roll over, expecting to find Will lying next to me, but when I reach out my arm I touch only cool, empty sheets.

Sitting up, I hold the blanket against myself and look around the room. Will is nowhere to be seen and the clothes he tossed over the chair the night before have disappeared. I hear a noise from the hall and swing my legs out of the bed.

I pull on the dress I was wearing when I arrived yesterday and pad down the hall, one hand working to untangle the knots in my hair.

"Will?" I call, poking my head around the door frame.

He is standing barefoot, his shirt buttoned partway and tucked into a pair of soft, suede trousers. He is reaching into the cupboard and glances up when I come into view.

"Good morning." I smile.

"Hey." He gestures to a plate set out on the counter next to him. "I have some breakfast for you right there."

"Thanks." I pick up the plate and move over to the couch. "Are you going to join me?"

"I already ate."

"Oh." I nibble on the food, watching him as he moves about, loading items into his medical kit and satchel. "Are we in a hurry to get back?"

"I don't think you should stay away from the ladies for too long. It will look suspicious."

"Right." I furrow my brow as I watch his hectic movements. "Are you all right?"

"Fine." He straightens and looks at me, a strange expression pulling at his handsome face. "Are you packed?"

I nod, swallowing the last of my breakfast. "I'll just go get my things."

I head back to his bedroom, stopping off at the lavatory to wash before gathering my effects and throwing them into my satchel. I take a moment to sift once more through the bag's contents in search of Meg's letter. Nothing.

Frowning, I toss the bag onto the unmade bed and move to the mirror, braiding my hair loosely. I smudge a little kohl around my eyes and bite my lips to colour them, standing back to admire the effect. Much better.

Will is already waiting by the door when I approach. He doesn't say a word, but I can feel him watching me intently while I pull on my sandals. A self-conscious blush rises to my cheeks under his scrutiny.

"Ready?" he asks as I straighten.

I nod, hitching my bag up onto my shoulder.

We walk down the stairs and into the street, where Will flags down a carriage. He takes my satchel and places it inside before helping me step up, then closes the door firmly and walks around the other side of the cart while I get myself situated.

Everything about his company feels off. The silence, the underlying sense of urgency. I fiddle with the folds of my dress while he settles in next to me.

As we roll through the streets toward the Palace, a dip in the road throws me to the side and against him. His hands reach out to catch me instinctively, lingering longer than necessary on my bare arms.

"Sorry," he says, drawing away and turning to look out the window.

What is he apologizing for?

After what feels like ages of prolonged silence, we finally arrive at the gates. Will instructs the driver to pull around to the back entrance. We draw to a stop and I snatch up my satchel and open the door myself, eschewing decorum. I start walking toward the Palace, not bothering to wait while Will pays the driver.

I keep my eyes straight ahead, ignoring the hurried footsteps behind me; I stumble when he grabs my wrist.

“What?” I snap, pulling free.

Will stands awkwardly, shifting his weight from foot to foot. “I have to catch up on some work in the surgery, so I’ll find you in a couple of days,” he says, eventually.

I roll my eyes, turning away. “Fine.”

His hand circles my arm again. “Kay,” he says softly.

I look up, shocked at his use of my real name on Palace grounds. He glances to the side and then pulls me behind a pillar.

“What is it?” I ask, keeping my voice low.

He responds by pressing me back against the pillar and kissing me. I shut my eyes and snake my arms around him, feeling my heart quicken despite myself. His beard tickles my cheeks as he pulls back, keeping his forehead pressed against mine.

“I’ll miss you,” he says.

“Me too,” I breathe.

He releases me and walks toward the door, relinquishing my hand at the last instant. I am left walking a few steps behind him, staring at his back and wondering what in the eternal Burn just happened.

After dropping my bag in my room, I make my way to the parlour to put in some face time with the ladies.

Blushes, Glassy and Blinky are sitting around a white linen-draped table, eating miniature cakes and playing cards. Blushes catches sight of me first and waves me over, a high colour rising to her cheeks when I pull a chair up next to them.

We play a couple of hands and I am just reaching for a pink frosting-covered treat when a familiar, pointed shadow looms over the table.

“And where exactly have *you* been?” Hawk Nose peers down at me, her nostrils flaring obnoxiously. She speaks just loudly enough to give the other ladies cause to swivel their heads in our direction.

“In town,” I say. I stuff the pink cake into my mouth, allowing the frosting to smear unattractively. I lick it off my lips slowly as I regard her. “I think the more important question is, where exactly have *you* been?”

She looks taken aback. “What are you talking about? I was here.”

“Really? Well, I didn’t see you.”

Her nostrils flare even wider. “You didn’t see me because you were out cavorting. Don’t try and be strange. “

“Me, strange? You’re the one who was unaccounted for yesterday.”

“I was *here* yesterday. Everyone saw me—ask them!”

“I wouldn’t trust these ladies enough to ask. Sketchy lot, all of them. You know, I didn’t see any of them yesterday.”

Someone lets out a giggle, covered by a dainty cough.

Hawk Nose’s hands slam down on the table in front of me, causing the cards to jump and Blinky to let out a small shriek of surprise. “You’re not fooling anyone,” she accuses, shrilly.

I lick the rest of the frosting from my fingertips, my eyebrow arched in question.

“You think just because you are some kind of special friend of the Princess, you have the right to go around shirking your duties and screwing some john in town.”

"What duties?" I ask, laughing. "Attending dinners and milling about, getting fat on cake? Perhaps you haven't noticed, but there aren't a lot of demands placed on us."

Hawk Nose bares her sharp little teeth, staring down at me over the bridge of her hooked nose. "I, for one, am not fooled, and I'm telling you now: the game is up."

I look at her calmly, fascinated by the pulsing vein standing out against her pale forehead. "I'm really sorry that the Princess didn't ask you to run an errand for her, Bellany. I know how important that is to you."

The vein pops out further. "Stop trying to change the subject." If her jaw were clenched any tighter, she'd crack her dental work.

"I'm fairly certain we are talking about the same thing—you clearly have a problem with me being a confidante of the Princess. Just some friendly advice: perhaps if you conducted yourself with just a little more friendliness and a lot less suspicion, she would be more inclined to spend time with you." It's almost too easy.

She points one shaking, perfectly manicured finger at me. Glassy pushes herself back from the table, the scrape of the chair against the floor reverberating in the otherwise silent room.

"I. Don't. Trust. You." Hawk Nose has never looked more like her nickname than she does now, with her talons poised and her nostrils flared large enough to swallow me whole.

I shrug, picking up my cards again. "I don't really care what you think."

"What's going on here?" Meg has appeared in her usual silent fashion and now stands with her hands on her hips, glaring at us.

"Your Highness," Hawk Nose gasps.

I could laugh out loud at the absolute perfection of this moment, with her red faced and flustered, slipping when she whirls away from me and attempts to curtsy in the same movement.

"Bellany." Meg's tone is cool, reserved. "Is there a problem?"

"It's her, your Highness." Hawk Nose straightens and glares at me. "She was gone all day yesterday."

"Abby was sent on an errand by myself, personally," Meg replies. "You could have spoken to myself or Vitrola if you were so concerned about her whereabouts."

"It's not only that!" Hawk Nose protests. "She is always sneaking around. I am worried about how her behaviour reflects on all of us, you see."

Meg's eyes narrow. "I would suggest strongly that you exercise caution when making these kinds of accusations. It is not your job to interrogate your fellow ladies, Bellany. I assure you—I am more than capable of managing a group of silly girls."

I duck my head so that I don't catch Meg's eye and burst out laughing.

"Now, if you are so eager for something to do, there is a load of hemming my handmaid could use some assistance with." Meg smoothly gestures Hawk Nose's dismissal from the room.

"Hemming? Your Highness, I don't know how..." Clearly horrified, Hawk Nose stumbles on her words, glancing about for help while the other ladies deliberately avoid her eye.

"Well, I think now would be an ideal time to learn. You could benefit from having at least one useful skill."

I practically shiver from Meg's cool tone, almost feeling sorry for Hawk Nose. Almost.

Hawk Nose slowly gathers her skirts, thrusting her nose into the air in an attempt to salvage a shred of her remaining dignity. As she shuffles away, she shoots me a look of utter contempt, to which I respond with a quick wink.

Meg doesn't even turn around as the girl skulks from the room. "All right, then. Now, if we could all move on with our day. Abby, I believe you have some items you retrieved for me from town?"

"Yes, your Highness." I slide out of my seat and duck a quick curtsy, following her across the parlour and toward my bedroom while the remaining ladies return urgently to their gossip.

Once we are safely ensconced, I shut the door tightly, joining Meg where she sits primly on my neatly made bed.

"Well? How did it go?" she asks, eagerly.

"Very well," I tell her. "I was able to hand off your letter, then I loitered around for the rest of the night, waiting to see if I could hear of any interest for your cause."

"Did you meet her? The Runner?"

"No," I say, too quickly. "I told you, I only know her indirectly."

"Right, right." She seems disappointed, but recovers. "Of course. So, did you learn anything?"

"I know that she is going to support you."

It is impossible to keep from smiling at the look of pure joy that overcomes Meg's porcelain features. I laugh as she throws her arms around my neck.

"That is wonderful!" she says, attempting to keep her voice low, lest someone be listening in the hallway. "Are you certain?"

"Completely," I say. "From what I hear, she is attempting to gather more supporters for you."

"Oh, Abby, thank you so much." Meg's eyes glisten as she holds her hands to her cheeks. "It means so much to me that you did this."

I bite my lip, feeling uncomfortable with her gratitude. Would she feel the same if she knew that I was really the Runner? "It's nothing," I manage, eventually. "I'm happy to help you."

"So." She rubs her hands together, leaning toward me. "What happens next?"

"I'm going to be the point of contact between the Runner and yourself," I tell her. "But for now, you should prepare to leave the Palace. Soon it will no longer be safe for you here."

Meg nods gravely. "Yes, I expected as much."

Some of the colour has drained from her face. I know she is thinking about the repercussions of abandoning her father, and my initial instinct is to make sure she is all right. I harden my heart and push down the urge to be a sympathetic friend in this moment, giving over to the more important task of ensuring that she will stay focused and leave when the time calls for it. I swallow my concerns and stay the course.

"They'll keep you somewhere safe and you'll be redeposited on the throne when the way has been cleared." I choose my words carefully, the back of my mind awash with images of weapons and bloodshed. Before she can dwell too much, I grab her hands and force her to look at me. "It's in the works, Meg. There is no going back now. There is a bright future ahead, after all." I say encouragingly, coaxing a small smile from her.

"You're right." She draws a shaky breath and sits up taller. "This is the way forward. A queen is not afraid of her decisions."

"That's it," I tell her. "Don't lose sight of why you made this choice. You saw something wrong in your kingdom and you are going to make it right. That is why you are the true queen."

"Thank you, Abby." Some of the life has returned to her cheeks and she squeezes my hands tightly. "I swear, I don't know what I would do without you. You are the only one who really believes in me."

"Not anymore," I tell her, seriously. "There are a lot of people out there who support you."

I gesture out my windowed wall, following her gaze as she turns to look out at the polished Court and derelict Commons, fanning our perimeter.

When Meg speaks again, her voice is strong, steady, not betraying a trace of the anxiety she must feel. "I won't let them down," she promises.

chapter 33

I am finishing up my meal in the Hall the next day when I see them. Members of the Board, sitting atop their usual benches at the front of the Hall with their bald spots plainly visible as they lean across the table and talk anxiously among themselves.

I watch them thoughtfully, dabbing my mouth with a napkin. Most mornings, many of the Board members are absent from breakfast, but today they are all gathered together. This immediately gives me cause to think something is up. They appear unusually tense and hurried and I surmise they will be meeting in the Boardroom on the second floor after the meal.

One by one, the ladies fold their napkins and rise from the table, trickling back toward the parlour or out to wander the courtyard. I take my time, scraping the sauce from my plate with a bit of toast as I spy on the men from the corner of my eye.

Will sits behind the Board's table, closer to them than I am. I shift my focus momentarily to regard his scruffy head bent over his plate as he eats.

Defiance blooms in my chest. He hasn't made eye contact with me once during yesterday's meals or this morning's breakfast, and has been conspicuously absent immediately afterward. He's purposefully trying to avoid me.

I chew carefully, willing him to look up. By now, all the ladies except for myself and Blinky have left. Blinky chatters away happily, completely oblivious to the fact that I haven't heard a word she's said.

Finally, Will looks up and is suddenly staring right at me. I almost drop my toast in surprise but recover my wits well enough to nob subtly at the Board's table.

His dark brows lower as he looks to the old men, watching them carefully. I can practically see the cogs in his brain working while he takes in the scene. After a few moments, he inclines his head toward the courtyard.

"How interesting," I say, balling up my napkin and tossing it onto the plate.

"I know, isn't it? And I could swear that I had already eaten it!" Blinky laughs, not missing a beat.

"I'm going to take a turn in the grounds." I rise and straighten my skirt.

"If you want some company..."

Her voice trails off as I step away from the table and make my way toward the exit.

I wander slowly down the garden path, seemingly admiring the way the light from the open roof streams in around me. I keep a slow pace and, after a moment, Will appears beside me.

"Cousin," he says, falling into step.

"Good morning," I greet him.

As we walk, I am painfully aware of the space between our arms. We used to walk so that we could graze each other lightly, but now the distance between us is obvious and deliberate.

We stroll toward the end of the yard, where there are fewer people. In the back of my mind I recall that no guard is scheduled to walk by this area for another twenty minutes but am careful to keep my voice low, just in case.

"Well, what do you make of it?" I ask.

"They are definitely worked up about something," Will replies. His voice is quiet but he keeps his expression neutral while he looks around. Anyone watching from a distance would think there is nothing untoward occurring but a friendly chat between cousins.

"Do you think there could have been another Wastelander attack?" I ask.

"I'm not sure, but whatever it is, it can't be good for us."

"What makes you say that?"

He takes one more glance about the yard before shifting his gaze back to me. "I heard one mention something about a spy."

My heart thuds loudly and I swallow, my mouth suddenly dry. “We have to find out what it is they’re talking about.”

He nods, slowly. “Do you know a way to listen in to that meeting?”

I bite my lip, amused despite the seriousness of the situation. “Will Cain, correct me if I’m wrong, but it sounds as though you are condoning something risky.”

A dimple pocks his cheek and for a moment I forget about the strange distance between us. “I suppose I am.”

“Lucky for you, you’ve come to the right girl.” I start walking again, looping around the back of the courtyard and returning to the hall.

Together, we walk unhurriedly along the tiled floor, him nodding to the occasional courtesan as we stroll. Once we reach one of the entrances to the servants’ stairs I slow my pace, glancing around to make sure we are alone before I grip his wrist and pull him up the stairs.

The servants’ passageways are low and narrow, lined with a rough stone that is in stark contrast to the gleaming tiles of the main quarters. The route I have chosen wraps along the east side of the inner Palace—an area few servants occupy, as it leads in the opposite direction of the kitchen and the laundry room.

The stairs twist up toward the second floor and I keep one hand on the wall to stabilize myself in the small space. I can hear Will breathing steadily behind me.

The passageway widens once we reach the top of the spiral staircase. I turn right and walk down the hall, in my mind’s eye counting off the doors that we pass until we reach one in particular.

“Where in the eternal Burn are we?” Will whispers.

I shush him and press my ear against the door, listening for the sound of several heavy chairs scraping against the floor while their occupants situate themselves.

It sounds as though the meeting hasn’t started yet. I pull back and take a couple of steps away from the door, gesturing at Will to come closer.

"Each of these doors is the servants' entrance to a room on this floor," I explain, quietly. "This is the door to the Boardroom. If we stay very quiet, we should be able to hear the entirety of the proceedings from back here."

He shakes his head slowly, regarding me. "You really are something else."

"Stick around," I tell him. "You might learn something."

We move back to the door and lean in, listening intently to the murmuring voices from behind.

Someone speaks up, quieting the last of the chatter: "This meeting of the Board is now called to order."

There is the sound of a particularly phlegmy cough and I wrinkle my nose in disgust.

"Gentlemen, being that you are all well aware of why we are here today, I will get straight to the point." The first man expresses himself with an air of authority and I guess that the speaker is Chancellor Braun, the King's chief advisor.

"We have reason to believe that the commoners are organizing a revolt, once again." Braun's words set off a flurry of hushed whispers.

I raise my eyebrows at Will. His jaw is clenched as he listens carefully.

"How do you know this?" someone calls out.

"Our sources in the Commons have relayed rumours that the Runner is attempting to gather supporters." Braun's voice is deliberate and controlled, as though he were speaking of nothing more serious than an incoming dust storm.

"Are these rumours substantiated?"

"Not yet. At this moment, we don't have confirmation that she has managed to organize anything, but obviously we must take any threat against his Majesty or the throne very seriously."

There is a murmur of agreement and someone calls out, "Hear, hear!"

"I will now open the floor to your suggestions." A gavel bangs against a tabletop and I picture the Board members raising their hands to volunteer their solutions.

"Senator Field," Braun says.

A nasally voice pipes up, "We could hold a larger draft. Pierce their numbers and leave no one behind to form a rebel army."

I ball my hands into fists at my sides, my fingernails digging into my palms.

"Very good. Anyone else? Senator Healy."

"I propose a curfew. Any citizen caught out after dark or suspected of conspiring in groups would be arrested."

There is the sound of a heavy door swinging open and I jump back instinctively, so on edge that for a moment I forget I am concealed in a separate hallway. Will glances up at my reaction, his eyes concerned.

"Your Majesty," Braun says.

I hear several chairs pushed back hurriedly as the Board members scramble to their feet.

"Chancellor. Forgive the interruption, but I felt it necessary to partake in this meeting."

At the sound of the King's booming voice, my palms grow slick. I hold my breath and press my ear back against the door, my brow furrowed in concentration.

"Of course, your Majesty."

"I understand that you are discussing methods for handling our latest Runner situation. If you would all take a seat, I will offer up my idea."

From the commanding tone of his voice, I know this will be less a suggestion than an order.

The chairs scrape against the floor again as the men seat themselves. There is a pause and I strain to pick up any small sound from the room.

"This so-called Runner has been a thorn in my side for too many years now. She steals from my people and mocks my power from within my own gates, tampering with my cavalry and releasing my prisoners. She undermines my position and I cannot have the commoners looking up to her, thinking that her behaviour exempts her from the full weight of my justice."

There is a fearsome banging as heavy fists connect with the table and I flinch, jostling Will. He places a hand on the small of my back and leaves it there.

"I want her taken off the streets. Immediately. Every available guard is to be dispatched into the Commons with the sole mission of tracking her down and bringing her to me so she can be made an example of. I give full permission to use any methods that my men deem necessary, so long as she is found and captured."

No one says anything. Next to me, I can't even hear Will breathe.

"Is that understood, Chancellor?"

"Perfectly, your Majesty. A most attractive solution, I must say. I will personally pass along your order to Lieutenant Griss."

"Very good. And, Braun?"

"Yes, your Majesty?"

"Do not fail me. If I don't have her, I will have to give someone else over to my Inquisitor. Harmen is expecting a new guest."

At the mention of Harmen, the breath rushes from my body. Once a captain, now the head Inquisitor to the King. My parents' murderer still lives.

"Yes, your Majesty." Braun's voice is strained.

"That is all."

I step away from the door at the sound of the Board members concluding their meeting. A dull throb has formed between my eyes, clouding my thoughts.

"Can you take us to my surgery?" Will whispers softly in my ear.

I nod wordlessly, turning on my heel and blindly leading the way back. Our footsteps are quiet in the narrow passageway as I lead him back down the stairwell and along the first floor toward his office.

Once we are safely ensconced Will closes the door, locking it before he turns to look at me, his expression worried.

"It's fine," I tell him, my voice sounding hollow in my ears. I take a deep breath and try again. "It's nothing I can't handle."

He nods, looking as though he wants to move toward me but remaining firmly rooted in place.

I run a hand through my hair, my fingers snagging in my updo and springing my locks loose. My mind is working furiously in an effort to sort through what I have just heard.

"We have to get Meg out of here," I say, eventually. "They already know that the Runner is trying to start a rebellion—it is only a matter of time until they find out there is support for Meg to be queen."

"I can take her to my sister's," Will says. "They seem to be focused on the Commons; no one should suspect that the Princess would hide in the Court."

"Good, good." I'm pacing back and forth, suddenly feeling extremely confined despite the spaciousness of Will's office.

"The trouble is where to put you," he ponders, almost to himself.

"I'm staying here," I say, not looking up.

"No, you're not."

"If I leave with Meg, they'll put two and two together and realize who the Runner is. Plus, you heard them: they're going to be looking for me out there." I shrug my shoulders, pausing in my pacing to look at him. "The Palace is the safest place for me right now."

Will looks astonished, his dark brows raised nearly to his hairline. "You can't stay here."

"Why not? It will be helpful to have someone on the inside. I can lift the gate and open the doors for you when the time comes, continue feeding intelligence, incapacitate the guards, whatever you need."

"It's madness," he says. "These people want to kill you."

"I don't think they ever said 'kill,' specifically," I correct him in a low voice.

"Something worse, then."

"Use your head. Will. We're so close, do you really want to throw away everything we've done up to now?"

He draws a shaky breath. "I honestly can't tell if you're being incredibly brave or incredibly stupid."

I shrug grimly. "Maybe a little bit of both."

He runs a hand back and forth over his stubbled hair. "I don't think I can let you do this."

"I don't think you have much of a choice," I say, with resignation. "You said it yourself—you can't stop me when I get a crazy idea." I take a step toward him, tilting my head. "It's nice of you to worry about me, though."

He glances behind him toward the door, as though searching for an escape.

I bite down on my tongue, feeling my shoulders tense in frustration. "We still have fifteen minutes until a guard passes through here."

"Oh, good," he says. His eyes dart back to me. "You should get back to the parlour—the Princess will be wondering where you've gone. How about we touch base tomorrow night at the engagement party?"

"What's with you?" I demand.

"What do you mean?"

"You've been avoiding me ever since I told you what happened to my family." Saying it aloud bolsters my confidence and I cross my arms as I stare him down.

"No, I haven't," he insists, unconvincingly.

"Yes, you have. Did you think I wouldn't notice? Look, I didn't *want* to tell you, but you *begged* me to. I knew you couldn't handle it and now something's changed." I bite my lip, fighting the angry blush that rises to my cheeks. "So what is it, Will? Do you feel sorry for me? Are you afraid of me? Do you think I'm unstable? Spill it and let's have an honest conversation, for once."

His face softens. "Kay," he says quietly.

I hold firm, refusing to take my eyes from his.

"So, what's the reason?" I ask again, waiting.

"I..." He rubs his fingers against his temple as though he could soothe an ache behind it.

"Say it, Will."

"I can't," he says eventually, looking away.

I feel a lump rise in my throat as I wait for him to say something else, the lump growing larger with each passing second.

"You don't have to hide anything from me," I tell him. "We've come a long way, you and I."

He makes a low sound of frustration and raises his eyes to mine. My heart thuds heavily at his tortured expression, confusion and fear lacing through me.

"I don't want to hurt you," he says, his voice strangled.

"Then tell me what's going on." I take a deep breath and force the words. "Can you be with me, or not?"

An eternity passes before he shakes his head, ever so imperceptibly.

Something wrenches inside me, twisting my stomach. This room is too small. This *Palace* is too small. I need to get out. I need to be away from him.

“Fine. That’s all I needed to know.” Blinking rapidly, I stride past him, my hand groping for the key in the door before I open it and step back out into the hall, slamming the door closed behind me.

chapter 34

I walk quickly back toward my room, my head lowered while my feet chart the familiar path. I am so wrapped up in my own thoughts that I fail to notice the King and his entourage until we nearly collide at the bottom of one of the main staircases.

I stumble back at his approach; he's large and imposing as he descends the stairs toward me, flanked by his personal guards. My mouth goes dry and I sweep a curtsy, keeping my eyes trained on the floor and hoping that if I duck low enough, he might pass me by.

No such luck.

"It's Lady Abby, is it not?" The voice that just minutes ago ordered my arrest now speaks to me directly.

I swallow, attempting to coat my parched throat and stand up straight, clasping my sweaty hands together in front of me.

"Your Majesty," I say. "You are looking well." Hatching murder plots becomes him.

He is dressed in his signature crimson, the gold buttons affixed to his vest polished to a fine sheen. As I look up at his cold, black eyes, so unlike Meg's, a blinding fury causes my vision to spot and extinguishes my lingering fear. The King stands impassively, stroking his immaculate silver beard as he regards me.

"I'm glad I ran into you," he says. "I have a favour to ask."

"Certainly," I begin, but he has already turned to dismiss his guards.

The men melt away and stand at a safe distance, their gloved hands loosely gripping the hilts of their swords. I bite down a sneer and turn to give the King my most charming smile, wiping my palms on the folds of my dress.

"Walk with me."

He marches down the last of the stairs and turns briskly toward the courtyard. I have to scurry to keep up with his long strides.

"You've been a good friend to my daughter," the King remarks as we walk into the afternoon sunlight.

"She has been a good friend to me," I tell him, choosing my words carefully.

"As you may be aware, she is engaged to Lord Grayson. I am most pleased with the match. At long last, we can unite the City and the Outer City."

"I was informed. The ladies are all looking forward to the engagement party tomorrow night."

"Then I am sure you know that my daughter is reluctant to form the union." He stops in his tracks and turns to me, his fearsome gaze full of challenge.

I stay an arm's length away, waiting, keeping my face impassive.

A few moments pass. He is waiting for me to say something.

I speak haltingly, "Young women are prone to romance."

His grey brows furrow. "A princess is not afforded the luxury of romance. Megra has a duty, and she must realize that."

I nod slowly, not sure what he is driving at.

"My daughter is confused. I have tried to set her on the right path, but she is too much like her mother: strong-willed and stubborn. I do not wish to force her down the aisle—I would prefer that she marry Grayson of her own volition." The King watches me and I force myself to maintain eye contact, ignoring the burning feeling of disgust welling up inside me. "Do you understand what I am saying to you?"

"You want me to talk to the Princess about marrying Grayson." The words taste bitter on my tongue.

"No, I want you to *convince* her to marry Grayson, without any fuss." His tone suggests that this is not up for discussion.

"As you say, your Majesty, the Princess is strong-willed. I cannot change her heart." The King may have the power to place a warrant on my head, but he is truly mad if he thinks he can control Meg's feelings.

He is silent for several seconds, studying me, before he turns and continues deeper into the courtyard. I reluctantly trail after him, watching as he bends and plucks a flower from the path, holding it to his nose and breathing in its scent.

"Do you know who your duty is to, Lady Abby?" He keeps his eyes on the flower, twisting the delicate stem in his meaty fingers.

"To the Princess," I say.

"*Wrong*." His face has grown hard and the flower bends in his hand.

He swivels his head to look at me and I take an involuntary step back.

"Your duty is to *me*. Every citizen of this city is under *my* rule. Without me, the City would fall and crumble into dust."

The head of the flower pops off with a flick of his thumb, floating to the ground and landing at my feet. Something about those pathetic petals stirs an uncontrollable rage within me and suddenly, I am feeling everything.

The cruelty of the King. The cowardice of Will. The suffering of my people. The courage of Meg.

"The City would still stand without you," I hear myself say. Any trace of anxiety I once felt at my proximity to the King has vanished. I thrust my chin up at him, no longer caring what this pitiful man can do to me. "Not everyone is ruled by fear and intimidation."

His expression darkens, his eyes flashing with a barely constrained fury. I stand my ground, glaring at him as I gesture to the rest of the flowers growing around us.

"You can pluck the head off one flower, but do you see how the rest still flourish? They don't need your permission to grow; they don't grow for you, for me, for anyone."

"Stupid girl," he hisses. "You wish to make an enemy of your King?"

"I don't wish to make an enemy of anyone, but as I have already stated, my duty is to my Princess. Whatever she chooses, I will support her."

My arm flies out instinctively to block the incoming blow. My eyes widen in disbelief when my forearm collides with the King's, the back of his hand mere inches from my cheek.

For a fleeting moment, he looks as shocked as I do. His arm lowers and his face clouds over with suspicion. I gulp and take a step back. I should have let him strike me. What lady would possess the reflexes to block such an attack?

"If you will excuse me, your Majesty," I say quietly, "I must be getting back to the parlour."

He says nothing as I turn and walk back across the courtyard, increasing my speed as the force of his glare burns into my retreating back.

Why couldn't I have controlled my temper? Why couldn't I have just blindly agreed to the King's request? Internally, I curse Will for fighting with me right after we overheard the order for my arrest. As if the stress of the entire situation wasn't bad enough, I had to go and complicate matters further by falling for a rich rebel with hopeless trust issues.

My hands clench and unclench at my sides. All of our grand plans are collapsing around me, and I can't even keep it together long enough to have a civil conversation with the one man who has the power to eliminate us all. The window to rescue Meg and raise an army keeps shrinking and my presence isn't helping matters.

Suddenly, staying behind in the Palace doesn't seem like such a good idea after all.

The next morning, I toss and turn in my bed, flipping my pillow over and lying back down on the cool linen. I barely managed to sleep a wink all night and the sun is already streaming in through my window.

Groaning, I roll onto my stomach and bury my face into the bedclothes. Thoughts of Will keep me awake and my chest aches with a heaviness I haven't felt since the night of the fire.

I need to face him. After spying on the Board meeting and my subsequent mouthing off to the King, it is of the utmost importance that Meg and I get out of the Palace as soon as possible. I hate to admit it, but we need Will's help.

In the back of my mind, I feel a twinge of fear over the manhunt underway for the Runner. The King said to use any means of interrogation necessary; have Lieutenant Griss and his guards managed to track down my friends? Is Harry all right? Is Lara?

I finally give up on sleep, throwing my pillow across the room in frustration. I sit up, rubbing my fingers against my temple while I try to quiet the pounding in my head.

Sighing, I slide out of bed. After padding over to the washroom, I splash some water on my face and slip on a lightweight dress that falls just above my ankles. I sit down at the vanity and attempt to braid my hair, noting the bruised colour beneath my eyes. The engagement party for Meg and Grayson is tonight and I already know Vitrola will scold me for my appearance.

I slip from my bedroom and make my way up to the library, determined to steal a few hours of peace before I have to see Will and the King at the party. When I arrive at the seventh floor I expect to find Meg waiting for me, her nose buried in her latest novel, but the room stands empty, abandoned but for the shelves stretching high into the alcoves of the ceiling. Walking among them, I feel small and unimportant.

I sigh to myself as I settle into the cushions of the familiar couch. Total anonymity is exactly what I need today, knowing that half the King's guard is out scouring the streets for me.

Looking in all the wrong places.

As I read, I become absorbed in the story, my worries gradually ebbed away by the plight of a fictional heroine. I don't realize that I have fallen asleep until I am jolted back to the present by Sera, who has the sense to jump back when I lash out instinctively.

“Gods, Sera.” I rub my eyes forcefully with my hands.

“I knew I’d find you here. Come on now, Miss Abby. The party is starting in a few hours, and we need to start getting you ready.” She picks up my book from where I dropped it and tucks it under her arm, gesturing for me to come with her.

“Right, the party,” I say, reluctantly rising to my feet and trailing after her back down to the fourth floor.

Less rushed than she was before the ball, Sera is gentle as she washes and dries my hair, even taking the time to paint my nails a deep red.

I hold up my fingers to admire the glossy sheen as she carefully arranges my locks into an elaborate twisting rope and drapes the heavy mass over my shoulder. She flits around me like a bird, placing a pin here and there. When she has finished, she sets a thin gold band on top of my head, positioning it so that it sits across my brow.

“Lovely,” she says finally, satisfied.

Together, we select an emerald dress and I slip it on. The skirt is made up of what looks like dozens of layers, all floating on top of one another and flying into the air with every motion I make. The neckline is modest but the back is open and a high slit runs up the side of the skirt so that my leg pokes through when I walk.

I briefly wonder what Will would think of the dress and then shake my head to refocus my thoughts, closing my eyes patiently while Sera applies a layer of kohl.

“Well?” I say, opening my eyes.

“You look perfect.”

We both turn at the sound of someone knocking on the door. Sera strides over to open it and admits a timid-looking housemaid.

"Pardon me, miss, but the Princess requests your presence in her chambers." The girl dips a curtsy while keeping her eyes lowered.

"Very well." I thank Sera before I stand and follow the girl toward Meg's room at the very end of the hall. The door swings open and I am admitted, stepping over the threshold while the maid ducks her head and slips away, shutting the door silently behind her.

Meg sits at her bureau, her charcoal-black hair brushed to a silken sheen and arranged in an intricate updo. Wearing an ivory gown and with her lips painted scarlet, she looks absolutely beautiful.

"What's wrong?" I ask.

"I need to get out of here." In one graceful movement, she stands and begins pacing the length of her expansive chamber, the train of her gown sweeping behind her as she turns.

"It won't be much longer now," I promise.

"How much longer, exactly?"

"Soon."

"I can't take much more of this, Abby. Really, I can't." She looks down at her hands and I notice them shaking.

"What happened?" I ask her.

She sighs, clasping and unclasping her long fingers in an attempt to alleviate the tremors. "My father spoke with me yesterday afternoon."

"Ah." I move to sit on the bed, careful not to wrinkle my dress as I perch. "What did he say?" He must have sent for her soon after the conversation we shared in the courtyard.

"I really think he may have gone mad. If I don't put on a pleasant face tonight, if I don't follow through with this wedding, then he's going to have me punished." She shudders. "The things he said, Abby—they were absolutely horrible."

"What did he say?"

"He threatened to give his guards free range over my bedchamber; told me I would be cast out into the Wastelands. I knew he always despised me, but I am still his daughter. How can he treat me this way?" Her voice breaks as she speaks and I feel my heart twist painfully in my chest.

I clench my hands into fists at my side. Maybe the King really is starting to lose grip of his mind. Perhaps he senses that his power over us is slipping and these threats are a desperate bid to regain control.

"You have to move forward," I tell her. "Play the part of the compliant princess for just one more night. Soon we will be far away from here and none of this will matter anymore."

"Can't we leave tonight?" she begs.

I don't think I've ever heard her plead before; she is usually so calm and collected.

I stand and walk over to her, reaching up to place my hands on either side of her face and forcing her eyes into mine. She is half a head taller than me and I have to tilt my chin to look at her, but I manage it.

"Listen to me, Meg. You can do this. It's a show, that's all. All those people out there? They're just an audience. They don't control you. Grayson doesn't control you. Your father doesn't control you. You are stronger than all of them."

Her brown eyes are warm where her father's are cold. "I'm scared."

"I'm right here with you." I lower my hands and lace her cool fingers with mine. "I won't let anything happen to you." I take a deep breath. "You can trust me."

She nods slowly, squaring her shoulders and squeezing my hands with hers. "All right," she says, her voice still shaking. She breathes deeply and tries again, steadier this time. "Let's go put on a show."

Once again, the Hall is swarming with people. I shoulder my way between two old men, my eyes scanning the room as I look for the dessert display. I am just about to reach for a tiny cake with yellow frosting when a familiar figure steps up next to me.

"Care to dance?" Will asks.

I curse my traitorous heart for thudding so loudly in my chest. He is dressed immaculately, in soft suede pants and a white linen shirt under a vest, his best handkerchief—a vibrant green—knotted about his throat. He has trimmed his beard and hair recently and smells of sandalwood.

"I'm a bit busy at the moment," I say, tearing my eyes away from him and looking back toward the yellow cake.

He calls my bluff and grabs my hand, pulling me onto the dance floor, knowing I won't make a scene.

His warm hand encircles my back, tugging me close while we spin in a slow circle. My blood boils beneath my skin at the contact and I concentrate on glancing about the room at the other couples, at the decor, at my neglected cake. Anywhere but at Will.

"What did you do?" He speaks in a low voice, close to my ear.

My head snaps over to stare at him. "What did *I* do? You're the one who —"

His grip tightens in warning. "I meant, what did you do to the King? He's been staring daggers at you all night."

I allow my gaze to casually sweep the room, resting for an instant on the King sitting atop his ornate throne at the front of the Hall. Tonight, he is wearing a champagne-coloured vest and is surrounded by Board members, all with similar pinched expressions on their faces and whispering among themselves.

The King is staring directly at me, his fingers drumming on the arm of his chair. I quickly look away and back at Will, pretending not to have seen.

We dance away from the King and toward the opposite end of the room, Will's hand warming my bare back.

Once we are a safe distance away, he speaks again. "Well?"

I offer an inconsequential shrug. "We had a small disagreement."

"When did you even have cause to speak with him?"

I feel an irrational jolt of annoyance at the question. "Right after I left the surgery yesterday. He pulled me aside and told me to convince Meg to marry Grayson."

His eyebrows rise. "And what did you tell him?"

"In so many words, no."

I think I may have seen his lips twitch in amusement but it happened so quickly that I can't be certain.

"I don't suppose it occurred to you to simply go along with him, being that we are down to mere days before we leave?"

"You can't really blame me for not being entirely rational. I was a bit upset at the time."

I feel him tense.

"I need to talk to you," he says, his words barely audible.

"We're talking now."

"I mean, when all this is over."

"It doesn't matter." I tear my eyes away from him and spot Meg dancing past us, escorted by Grayson. She sees me looking and rolls her eyes. I watch as Grayson leads her toward the stairs and tugs her reluctantly upward.

"It *does* matter," Will is insisting.

"I don't want to talk about it," I say through clenched teeth. I can't stay here and listen to him rationalize why we can't be together. Gods damn him if he thinks I will give him my blessing to behave like an insufferable twat.

Even if the insufferable twat is an incredible dancer.

We twirl in silence as the song comes to a close. I allow myself a moment to shut my eyes and breathe in the scent of sandalwood, basking in the memories of being tangled up in his cool sheets.

"Enough," I say, whether to myself or to him, I can't be certain. I pull away, his hand slipping from my back. Without his touch, my exposed skin feels suddenly cold. I draw a shaky breath and chance a look back into his eyes, feeling my heart ache at what is reflected there.

"Come find me when we can talk about moving Meg," I tell him.

Before he can say anything more I turn away, grabbing a glass of wine from a passing tray and then fading into the crowd.

I situate myself against a wall, sipping my wine and watching the party. I risk another look toward the King, relaxing slightly when I see he is no longer watching me. Instead, his crowned head is bent to listen to a guard whispering in his ear.

I start as a hand grabs hold of my wrist.

"Sera?"

My handmaid is white as a ghost, her eyes wide and screaming. "Miss, please, you must come with me. Immediately."

I nod and put down my drink, following her from the room. I expect her to stop in one of the quieter areas of the first floor, but instead she leads me to the main staircase and hurries up the steps. I hold my layered skirt above my feet and follow wordlessly. We bypass the offices on the second floor and disembark at the servants' quarters on the third. A couple of footmen, their arms laden with delicious-looking trays of food, give us a strange look as we pass by, but Sera ignores them, ushering me into the laundry room.

I bite down my questions, waiting as she checks the hall and then shuts the door behind us.

"What is it?" I ask, finally.

"They're coming for you. You have to leave. Now."

chapter 35

I blink, uncomprehending.

"Did you hear me?" Sera steps forward, her eyes searching my face urgently. "They know you're the Runner. They know that Princess Megra is a traitor. The guards are coming for both of you *right now*. You have to take the Princess and get out, while you still have a chance."

I shake my head, desperately trying to sort through the wave of information.

"I…" Gradually, everything begins to sink in. I stare at Sera, at her pale face pinched tightly. "How do you know who I am?"

"I figured it out the day they discovered the prisoners escaped. They said someone disguised as a guard helped them and I remembered the uniform I found in your room."

"So you knew? This whole time?"

She shrugs. "It made sense. You didn't behave like the rest of the ladies, and you were kind to the servants." A small smile plays on her lips. "You are exactly the kind of person I always hoped she would be."

I run my hand through my hair, willing my mind back to the task at hand. "And you say the King knows?"

"Someone turned you in. I don't know all of the details, but the word is the King was told that you and the Princess are planning to run away and start a rebellion against him. He has ordered your arrest."

Meg. I have to find her. Get her out.

"Find Dr. Cain," I tell Sera, thinking fast. "As quickly and quietly as you can. Tell him I have to move Meg out now and he must bring a carriage to the west entrance. Immediately, before they put the Palace on lockdown."

"What about you?"

"Tell him not to wait for me. I'm going to find my own way out."

She nods, moving with her trademark briskness to the door. I follow her and together we peer left and right down the hallway. A few servants scurry back and forth, but there is no sign yet of any guards.

Sera slips out first, heading back to the main stairs. I turn in the opposite direction, toward the servants' passage.

"Sera." I grab her hand just before she leaves. "Thank you."

She smiles, broader than I've ever seen. "Anytime, Miss."

We drop hands and turn to run in separate directions. I take the servants' stairs up to the next floor, pausing momentarily in the stairwell to kick off my sandals. I hitch up the layers of my dress and glance both ways down the fourth-floor hallway.

Finding it abandoned and hearing no warning sound of armour clinking in the distance, I slip out into the hall, creeping toward Meg's room.

The door is locked tightly. I try the handle a few times, then press my ear to the wood, frowning when I hear nothing from within.

She isn't here. I know I saw Grayson pull her up the stairs… so, where would they go? I bite down hard on my lip and think.

Meg wouldn't wish to go anywhere too private with him. Knowing her, I'd guess she would want to be somewhere spacious—somewhere she could be found if needed.

The library.

I tear down the hallway, slipping back into the servants' staircase just as the sound of several heavy footsteps reaches the fourth-floor landing behind me.

My breath echoes in my ears as I run up the spiralling staircase to the seventh floor, emerging from behind a bookshelf when I reach the library. It is only when I begin weaving my way through the crowded aisles that I start to doubt my plan. What if Meg isn't here? What if she's returned to the Hall? I may already be too late.

"Lynal, enough. I'm going back to the party."

I have never been so happy to hear a voice in my life. Rounding the corner, I see Meg and Grayson on the couch, him leaning over her with a hand on her thigh, her looking at me with a mixture of relief and surprise.

"Meg. Thank the gods." I race straight past them to the main doors, cursing as I stumble on the long layers of my dress.

"Abby? Where did you come from?"

"We are leaving. Now." I push the doors to the main entrance closed. Thinking quickly, I spot a heavy desk off to the side and run behind it, shoving it toward the door.

Meg appears at my side instantly, helping me bar the entrance.

"What's happening?" she asks.

"Your father knows everything. There's no time to explain—we have to get you out of here."

"How? We just blocked the only way out."

"Um, pardon me?"

We glance up. Grayson is standing in front of the couch, staring at us with utter contempt.

"One moment—I need to take care of this," I say to Meg, reaching for the heavy clay vase set on top of the desk. I test the weight in my hand and stalk calmly across the floor toward Grayson.

"Whoa, there. What do you think you're doing?" His eyes are wide with fear and his weak chin begins to tremble. "Put that down."

"I'm sorry about this." I maintain my even stride, watching him carefully.

Meg lets out a shriek as Grayson suddenly darts across the room, sprinting for the exit. I snatch a pillow off the couch and toss it along the floor, aiming for his path and smirking with a grim sense of satisfaction when his shiny boot comes down on top of the soft fabric.

Immediately, his leg slips out from under him and he careens backward, falling hard and landing in an inelegant heap. By the time he raises his head, I have come to a sliding stop directly next to him. He manages only a single cowardly yelp before I bring the vase down across the back of his skull, rendering him unconscious with one fell swoop.

I support his head as his neck slumps to the side. The vase clatters to the ground and I rise to my feet, raising my chin to look back up at Meg. She stands rooted to the spot, her hands clenched at her mouth.

"What in the eternal Burn was *that*." She lowers her arms slowly as she stares at Grayson's limp form, her eyes stretched into giant saucers.

"We can't have him telling the guards where you've gone."

"But...how were you able to do that?" she asks in a thin voice. She looks from Grayson and back up at me. "Who are you?"

"Meg, you know me." I take a step toward her. She flinches at my approach and I feel a stab of guilt.

"Is your name really Abby?"

I stop in my tracks.

"Please, Meg, I'm begging you. We can't do this now. We have to go." I reach tentatively for her arm, but she jerks away.

"Tell me." Her perfectly arched brows are drawn together as if she is in pain.

"My name is Kay," I tell her. "I'm the Runner."

Her mouth opens, then closes. "I don't understand."

"I can explain it all to you later, I promise. Right now, I just need you to trust me." I look over my shoulder, thinking I have heard the sound of approaching footsteps.

She is shaking her head. "I can't trust you. I don't even know you."

"I'm sorry I lied to you, Meg, but I swear I never betrayed you. Everything that we planned, the support of the Commons, that's all real. I know it is, because I was there. I talked to them. They want *you* for their queen and I'm going to help make it happen."

She takes a step backward. “You pretended to be my friend.”

“It started out that way, but I swear everything is different, now.” I speak hurriedly, my stomach turning somersaults as I struggle with the weight of my guilt and the loss of time. “I wanted to tell you the truth so many times, but I couldn’t. I thought that you wouldn’t leave the Palace if you knew who I really was; I thought you’d be too angry to trust me.” I can hear the desperation in my voice and swallow. I just have to focus on getting Meg down to Will, whatever it takes.

There is the now-unmistakable sound of heavy footsteps filing down the hall just outside the library. We both jump as someone pounds a fist against the door.

“This way,” I hiss, lifting my skirts again and weaving my way back through the bookcases toward the servant’s entrance.

Behind us, the door is straining against the desk. Men’s voices shout incomprehensibly.

“Through here,” I tell her, gesturing down the darkened passage. “Take the stairs to the first floor. Turn left and go down the hall, the sixth door on your right is the exit. Will is waiting for you, he’ll take you somewhere safe.”

“Will?”

“Dr. Cain,” I correct myself.

I usher her through the door, drawing back when she stiffens at my touch. She glances into the stairwell and back up at me, her beautiful face drawn in an expression of utter hurt.

My chest constricts painfully. “I know I don’t deserve it, Meg, but please, I really need you to believe me.”

“What about you?”

The pounding on the door has grown louder and I hear the heavy desk move on the floor.

“I’m going to distract them. Don’t worry about me—I’ll see you soon.”

She nods. "Be careful."

Her cool hand squeezes mine once, not a hint of a tremor between us. I watch her gown slip around the corner before I take off back toward the front of the library, holding my skirt in my hands and forcefully tearing the fabric as I run.

The main door is partially ajar and I see one leather-gloved hand slip through the gap, followed by a broad shoulder. Someone grunts, straining against the barrier.

I leap over Grayson's prone form, skidding to a stop in front of the bookcase nearest the door and scrambling up it, forgoing the ladder and instead heaving myself up the shelves one at a time.

There is the mighty sound of wood scraping against wood and the desk is finally pushed back far enough for the guards to file into the library one by one.

"We know you're in here!" the man in front shouts authoritatively, brandishing his sword. "What the—?" A piece of emerald green fabric floats lazily in front of his face and he bats it away, looking about in confusion.

More strips of green fabric cascade down over the men, swirling through the air in a vibrant display against the ornate backdrop of books. I tear the layers of my skirt into strips, tossing the pieces gaily so that they fall from every direction, delighting in the guards' confused reactions.

"Hey! I see you up there!" The first man points up at me, directing the attention of the others.

"Good evening, gentlemen!" I call. I am sitting comfortably on top of the bookcase, kicking my legs where they dangle over the edge. I look down triumphantly at the shower of emerald fabric, grinning when one man daintily plucks a piece from the shoulder of his comrade.

"You are under arrest by order of the King. I demand that you surrender and come down at once." I recognize the man as Lieutenant Griss, captain of the King's guards.

"Oh, dear." I sigh, slumping forward to place my chin in my hand, tilting my head at the captain reluctantly. "I'm flattered that you went to all this trouble, but I'm afraid I will have to respectfully decline the invitation. However, you are more than welcome to come up here and join me instead."

"Enough of your games, Runner. Surrender or we will have to use force."

"I'm not sure why you suppose I would do that, Lieutenant. You see, I have the advantage of being all the way up here." I gesture at the height of the bookcase, my eyes stretched wide.

Griss nods to the guards. "Get her."

Having anticipated this, I wait before I rise to my feet, watching while two of the guards move to the ladder of the bookcase I am sitting on. They ascend clumsily, making it about halfway up before I jump, nimble in my new, shorter skirt. As I leap, I push my legs back as hard as I can, kicking the shelf backward.

Every one of my muscles is poised as I land. I grit my teeth, clutching the top of the next shelf tightly, the bookcase wobbling precariously beneath my feet. I glance back at the platform I just jumped from, watching as it slowly tilts backward, the weight of the two unfortunate guards inadvertently pulling it over.

The trapped men shout out in alarm as the bookcase topples and collides with the case standing behind it, emitting an ear-shattering crash. As I hoped, the circular layout of the library has allowed for the perfect domino effect.

And one hell of a distraction.

Guards shout from below as they scramble over one another to get away from the falling bookcases. I train my eyes on the path of still-standing shelves lined up in front of me and leap across them one by one, gradually making my way toward the ever-growing pile of destroyed furniture and, past that, the open door of the library.

The room has exploded into utter chaos, books and splintered wood flying in all directions, a veritable symphony of shouts and crashing furniture. I am in my element, leaping from one bookcase to the next, my every instinct primed and honed for this very moment. I can see from the corner of my eye the eradicated shelves circling past the door, heading straight for me.

I manage to get airborne at the same instant that the bookcase I am standing on is hit. Bracing for an awkward landing, I come down unsteadily on a slanted surface, using the scattered books as a slide while I eye my next target.

"Over there!" someone, presumably Griss, hollers.

I shut my senses to everything and focus on staying upright, leaping over the top of the next case and repeating my sliding technique down its front, picking my way over to the exit.

I am vaguely aware of the men scrambling toward me as I near the end of the last bookcase. I grin to myself, knowing they are too late. In one smooth motion, I shoot straight up and vault seamlessly over the desk, sliding across its polished surface and twisting my body so that I slip sideways through the open door.

Once free of the library, I have to ignore the inclination to disappear back into the servants' passage. Instead, I turn to the main stairwell and run up the steps, slowing my pace just enough so that the guards will see where I've gone.

I have to keep them chasing me. I have to give Meg and Will time to escape.

The staircase reverberates beneath me as more and more guards fall into pursuit, tracking me past the eighth floor and up to the ninth, straight into the King's personal quarters.

The topmost room opens directly into a spacious parlour and office. Having never been up here, I rely on what I can recall of the schematics I studied, and tear across the opulent parlour toward the balcony doors.

I take no small amount of pleasure in pulling over pieces of furniture as I run. Expensive wooden and precious metal–laden items scatter the ground behind me, tripping Griss and his men and buying me a few precious seconds.

Finally reaching the balcony, I dart through the opening and slam the door shut behind me; groping for a lock, I curse when I find none. I make my way along the circular terrace, searching desperately for another way back into the King's room.

Somewhere in the recesses of my memory, I recall that the Palace has four wraparound balconies, one for every other floor. Unfortunately for me, it appears that the King's private walkout was designed with only one entrance. Having always admired the great, glass spire from my perch inside my tiny attic flat, I can't help but regret not being able to enjoy the view. The wind whips at my ruined dress and tangled hair as my eyes dart between the two sets of guards closing in on either side of me.

"It's over, Runner." Griss appears out of breath as he approaches, his sword raised in warning. "This is the end of the line."

I raise my hands. Slowly.

"What's wrong?" he sneers. "Don't you have a plan?"

"I was never much for plans," I admit. "I prefer to improvise."

Planting my hands on the ledge behind me, I smoothly vault myself up and over.

The next balcony is a full two storeys below me and I brace for the rough landing, angling my body so that I don't hit the ledge.

I land with such force that my teeth rattle in my skull. I attempt to crouch and tuck into a roll in the last instant, but end up crashing inelegantly into the wall of the seventh floor.

I unfurl myself gingerly, limbs protesting as I fight to clear my head and think of the next move.

I can hear the angry shouts from two floors above. I glance up, spotting Griss leaning over the balcony, his face twisted into an expression of utter fury. He yells orders to his men, who promptly disperse and disappear back inside.

There isn't much time before they make it back to the library. I have to keep moving.

I rise to my feet and peer over the ledge toward the fifth-floor balcony. A warning itch of pain shoots up my knee as I regard the two-storey height and I grit my teeth, raising my gaze to look out across the Palace yard. From this vantage point, I can see the roof of the gaol and the stables to either side, the courtyard directly in front of me and, beyond that, the Palace gates. My eyes dart across the surfaces below, desperately trying to find a safe path out of the Palace. The gaol is across the yard and sits two storeys above the ground; it's possible that I could leap from the Palace's third-floor balcony and across to the roof of the gaol, but first I have to find a way to descend four levels.

The glass outer walls of the Palace are faultless, effectively eliminating the option of climbing down the facade. A slight reverberation below my feet tells me I have just lost my opportunity to take the stairs. The guards are already back in the library.

Stifling a sigh, I climb over the balcony wall and lower myself so I am dangling above the ground, the muscles in my sore arms straining as I give myself as much slack as possible in preparation for the next drop.

I look up again. Through the clear glass ledge, I can see the guards rounding the catwalk, heading straight for me. With some effort, I release one of my hands and give them a crude gesture, winking before I let go with my other hand and drop out of sight, once again.

This time, my landing is a touch more graceful. I am able to anticipate the force of the impact and the texture of the surface. I ignore the tenderness in my knee, hobbling slightly as I head inside, intent on taking the stairs this time.

I shove open the balcony doors and round the altar situated at the front of the room, my bare feet padding on the carpeted aisle. A few scattered nobles are praying while kneeling on the plush cushions arranged on either side of the aisle. I disregard the heads bobbing up in confusion and sprint toward the servants' staircase at the very back of the room.

"What is she *wearing*?" someone mutters to their neighbour as I run past. I imagine how I must appear: a barefooted girl materializing on a balcony and tearing through a chapel in a torn emerald dress.

Once inside the servants' passage, my knee begins to throb again. I briefly consider taking the stairs all the way down to the first floor but ultimately decide against it. It's likely that Griss already has his guards barring the main front and back entrances. On top of that, the first floor will be filled with party guests, and I don't want to risk any bystanders getting caught in the crossfire.

I'm going to have to jump.

I pause on the third floor, catching my breath. I remain inside the servants' entrance, my back pressed against the stone wall as I listen for the sounds of traffic. Straining, I can make out the footsteps of servants moving back and forth. Past that, nearest the main stairs and the balcony doors, there is a distinctly heavy tread. I grimace, recognizing the unmistakable sound of armoured men walking in formation.

The first floor is not an option. If I have any chance of getting out of here, it will be from this balcony. That means my only exit is straight past an unknown number of guards.

I delay a few moments longer, praying fervently that the footsteps will recede up or down the stairs, but the gods must have been offended by my behaviour in the chapel. The guards remain firmly in place, waiting.

"Here goes nothing," I murmur. I take a deep breath and twist around the corner, tearing into the hallway.

My bare feet slap against the tiled floor as I run, narrowly avoiding the maids and stewards who step smoothly aside with practiced grace. Rounding the curved hallway, I can make out the dark silhouettes of the guards shuffling near the landing.

"*There!*" someone shouts.

I grit my teeth and urge myself to run faster, my sore muscles screaming and my knee protesting. I force myself to focus on the balcony doors coming into view, actively pushing away the nagging warning that says I won't have enough time to get to balcony before the guards head me off.

"What are you doing? Get out of the way!" a man shouts angrily.

I chance a glance in their direction. A crowd of servants have gathered in front of my pursuers, creating a human barrier between us.

The guards push and shove, bodily forcing the servants back and fighting their way toward me. It's too late—I've already been given all the time I need. I unleash a final burst of speed and propel myself through the balcony doors, hurtling over the ledge and throwing myself into the clear night sky.

My heart ceases to beat as I fall, tumbling through the air at full velocity toward the roof of the gaol.

Miraculously, I manage to hit feet first but the force of the landing causes my legs to collapse. I tuck into a roll instinctively, desperately trying to cover my head. The rough stone scrapes and tears at my skin and clothes as my body skids across the roof.

My back slams full force into the raised ledge of the gaol and I finally, mercifully, come to a stop. The world is dark and I feel nothing, no pain in any part of my body, as I nearly give myself over to a beautiful, inky blackness.

Not yet.

With difficulty, I pry my eyes open, blinking up at the Fireline swimming into view above me.

You're still alive.

You need to get off the roof.

Groaning, I roll over onto my hands and knees.

Get up.

I try to push myself up, crying out as a stabbing pain causes me to collapse back onto all fours.

Get up.

Somewhere in the distance I can hear people shouting.

Get up. They're coming.

I push myself up again, gritting my teeth as I stumble into a shaky standing position, keeping most of the weight on my right leg.

Now, run.

I take a shuddering step forward, then another, planting my foot on top of the ledge and looking down. It's just two more storeys. That's nothing.

Every bone in my battered body cries out in protest as I stoop and gingerly lower myself over the edge, digging my fingers into the rough stone before I release and drop straight down.

My leg crumples beneath me as I land. I stagger against the wall, biting back a scream. Shutting my eyes tight, I take deep, shuddering breaths. I have managed to make it to the ground; now I just have to get through the gate and down to the City before I'm home free.

One problem at a time.

I turn and lean my head back against the gaol wall, trying with great effort to gauge how far away the voices are. My head swims as I fight protestations from a million different pain points.

Doubtless, they will have closed the main gate by now. If I can't go through, I will have to go over. I study the smooth, impassive wall in front of me. It is only a few yards off, but I will have to cross open ground in order to reach it.

I just have to move twenty feet and climb up one measly wall.

On a bum leg.

I push off the side of the gaol and limp as quickly as I can toward the barricade, sweat pouring down my face and clouding my vision.

Fifteen feet. Ten. Five.

Just as I reach the wall, someone calls out, "Over here!"

Gods. I look up. The wall is made of large slabs of stone and there appears to be a few gaps in the brickwork, though they are far shallower than what I'm used to. Nothing for it. I grip what I can manage and begin inching my way up the face of the wall a single brick at a time.

As I climb I am acutely aware of the stampede of men running toward me, Griss at their head, their swords drawn and glinting in the moonlight.

I reach up and my fingers slip free of the wall. My heart seizes as I hold on with my other hand, pressing my face against the rock and curling my toes, desperately gripping the stone with everything I have left. I regain my hold and glance upward. I am nearly at the top; a few feet more and they won't be able to reach me.

It sounds as though Griss is directly below me, but I don't want to chance looking down. Instead, I grope for the very top of the wall, something pulling and cracking painfully in my ribcage as I pull myself up, my tired legs limp and useless.

There is a wisp of air beneath my foot just as I bring it on top of the wall. Griss took a swipe at me, missing by mere inches.

With barely anything left in my reserves, I fairly roll over the top of the wall and down onto the ground on the other side, another shot of pain in my left knee causing spots to blink across my vision.

I did it. I'm out.

Taking advantage of the darkness, knowing I have only minutes before the guards change course and come through the gate after me, I drag myself upright. I focus what little remaining strength I have left on reaching the flickering lamplight of the City buildings and the familiarity of its darkened alleyways.

Step by painful step, I push myself forward, limping toward home.

chapter 36

I arrive at my attic in a haze of pain and exhaustion. The journey from the Palace, through the Court and into the depths of the Commons took infinitely longer than usual. I stuck to the shadows and back alleys as much as I could, feeling exposed on the ground. More than once I glanced up the side of a building and yearned to make my way home over my rooftops, the ever-present throb in my knee keeping me from them.

My eyes are barely open by the time I reach my dilapidated home. I make my way up the stairs to my room, distantly aware of my landlady clutching a robe around her wiry frame and caterwauling at my appearance.

When I reach the door of my flat, I raise my hand and knock lightly, resting my forehead on the wood frame.

I slump forward as the door opens a crack, my weary body finally succumbing to everything it has been through. I hear Lara exclaim as I fall into her, nestling against her neck and breathing in the familiar scent of home.

"Oh my gods, Kay." She slings my arm around her neck and helps me to the bed, laying me down gently and swinging my legs so that I'm laid out flat.

I give an involuntary yelp when she moves my knee and she jumps back in shock.

"Where does it hurt?" she asks, frantically.

"Most places," I groan, curling up into a ball on the bed. I gesture toward a trunk pushed against the wall. "Could you get me something to wear? I need to get out of this dress."

"Is that what you call it?" She rises obediently and scurries over to the trunk, sifting through its contents. "I'll get you something comfortable to sleep in."

"No, not sleep." I grimace and push myself up into a sitting position, rotating my left leg gingerly and studying it. "I need to go down to the Beacon."

"Are you kidding me? You look as though you've been run over by a carriage."

I crack a smile, immediately regretting it when I feel a bruise pull at the side of my face. "You're not far from the truth." I nod at the shirt and pants she holds in her hand. "That right there will do."

She helps me pull the destroyed green dress over my head, *tsk*-ing over the state of it, muttering about wastefulness.

I ignore her and reach for the pants. I begin pulling them on, then flinch as Lara gasps, "Oh, Kay."

I follow her gaze, glancing down at my body. She was right when she said I look as though I was run over. Large, ugly bruises tinged with shades of purple and red cover my torso, one particularly nasty-looking contusion wrapping around my ribcage. That explains what I felt crack down there.

"It's not as bad as it looks," I say, absently. Together, we manage to get the pants and shirt on, effectively covering the worst of my damage.

I tear a long strip of fabric off what remains of the green dress, stretching it out and wrapping it tightly around my knee. I'll have to get some more of that medicine from Will.

I reach my hand up and Lara reluctantly helps me to my feet, watching with a tense wariness as I test the weight on my leg and hobble over to the washbasin.

"Are you going to tell me what happened?" she asks.

I splash the water on my face and arms, scrubbing as best I can around the cuts in an effort to remove the bulk of the gravel I picked up from the gaol's roof.

"It's a long story. Boring, mostly. I promise I'll tell you all about it when I get back."

I pat my face dry with a towel and move to pull on a spare pair of boots, tucking my trusty dagger down inside. The boots are a size too small, but there's nothing for it at the moment. Once I find Will and make certain

Meg is safe, I'll have to find a new place for Lara and I to hide out. It isn't safe to stay here.

"I really think you should be resting," Lara says as she watches me, twisting her hands anxiously.

"Trust me, I'll be dead to the world, nestled in bed as soon as I finish this." I say. I glance back at my friend as I pull open the door, but Lara's gaze has already diverted over to the once-beautiful dress crumbled into rags on the bed.

I say nothing as I slip back into the hallway, leaving her to it.

Feeling slightly refreshed, I walk to the Beacon as quickly as I can while keeping a wary eye out for any guards. Luckily, at this late hour and so deep in the Commons, I come across no one halfway respectable-looking.

The pub is darkened, occupied by a handful of miners. A few low-burning lamps hold dominion over the scattered tables. I look for Will, feeling a pinch of anxiety when I fail to catch sight of him.

I spy Marc over by the bar. His eyes widen in shock beneath his mop of blond hair but he stands and hurries toward me, gripping my arm and escorting me firmly over to a darkened table in the corner.

Neither of us looks up as Samus drops off a pint, turning back to the bar before we can pay.

Marc glances around while I drink greedily, closing my eyes at the sensation of the cool liquid coating my dry throat.

"You shouldn't be here," he says when I lower my mug. "They're looking for you."

"I know." I wipe my arm over my upper lip.

"Don't take this the wrong way, but you look terrible. What happened?"

"Have you seen Will?" I ask, ignoring his question.

He stares at me, considering. "Tonight? No."

"I need to stay here until he shows up."

"I see." Marc remains silent as I take another sip of my drink.

I hear the door swing open and glance up, frowning.

"How well do you know him?" Marc asks.

I swivel back to the table, taken aback by the question. "Will? Pretty well, I guess. Why?"

"I don't think you do." He reaches across the table and grabs hold of my hand.

I look down in surprise but don't move.

"What are you talking about?"

"I have to tell you something, Kay. I shouldn't have kept this from you, but I was hoping that Will would speak up first."

"Tell me what?"

Marc sighs, pushing his hair back from his forehead. "I figured out how Will I know each other. I served with him in the guard. He isn't who you think he is."

I shake my head, drawing my hand away from his. "I already know that he worked for the King. He regrets his time as a guard, as I'm sure you do."

"Did he tell you what they made us do?"

I rub my forehead as I fight a wave of exhaustion, thinking. "He said that you arrested people, bullied them. Commoners, mostly. Like I said, he isn't proud of it."

"It's worse than that."

I slam my hand down on the table with more force than I intended, frustration and tiredness getting the better of me. "Whatever it is, Marc, I don't care. We all make mistakes; what's in the past is past." I take a deep breath, wincing at Marc's sympathetic expression. I take up my tankard again. "I'm sorry. It's been a long night and I've had enough gossip and intrigue to last a lifetime."

"We were there. Will and I. The night of the fire."

I freeze, ale halfway to my lips. "What?"

"I couldn't place where I'd seen you before. It wasn't until you made your speech at the tavern and I had a chance to speak with Will that everything finally fell into place. We were all in the flat that night, and you were the skinny little red-headed girl."

The stein slips from my hand. Beer fizzes over the surface of the table, but neither of us makes a move to clean it.

I can't say anything. I can't be certain if I am thinking, if I'm breathing, as Marc continues to talk, his words pounding over me like a heavy dust storm.

"We were just kids, both of us. We were serving our first year in the guard when our troop was called to shake down a rebellion leader. I honestly thought it was going to be a typical arrest." He speaks quickly, as if that will soften the blow. "It wasn't until we got there and Captain Harmen ordered us to herd all of the family members into the front room that I had any idea of what was really going on."

Hiding under the bed, watching the shiny boots of the guard as my mother is dragged away.

"I am so, so sorry, Kay. It wasn't right to keep this from you."

The heat of the fire. The blood pooling on the floor. Falling from the open window. Looking up to see someone watching me from inside my old home.

Will was there.

Will killed them.

"Look, you've obviously been through a lot tonight. Do you need somewhere to stay?" Marc reaches for my hand again and I snatch it away, holding it against my chest as if burned. I stare at him incredulously, watching as his bright eyes recover from a look of hurt to dart at something over my shoulder.

I turn slowly in my seat, following his gaze.

Will, his handkerchief loosened and his vest unbuttoned, spots us and starts picking his way over to our table.

I stare at him as he draws closer, a faint hum filling my ears.

"Kay, thank the gods you're here." His expression is one of relief, then confusion as he takes in my face. "What is it?"

His gaze flickers to Marc sitting across from me. Slowly, realization dawns over his handsome features.

"Kay." His voice is strangled. "Can we go somewhere and talk privately? Please?"

"You were there," I hear myself say, the humming in my ears increasing to a high-pitched wail.

"I was going to tell you. Please, come with me. Let's not talk about this here—I can explain." Tentatively, he reaches out a hand to me.

I flinch back. "You *knew*." The voice coming from me is not my own, originating from somewhere deep and dark and dead.

"I am so sorry, I am so incredibly sorry. I wanted to tell you, but how..." He swallows. "How could I tell you something like that?"

I don't say anything. I fixate on the ale pooling off the edge of the table and falling in steady drips down onto the floor.

"Is Meg safe?" I ask, finally.

No one says anything. I wait patiently, counting the droplets.

"Yes, she's safe."

"Good." I push back from the table, my chair scraping loudly against the stone floor. I keep my eyes averted and shoulder my way past him.

"Kay, wait."

I ignore him, slipping between the last of the tables and the stragglers before pushing blindly through the door.

I have turned down the narrow alleyway next to the pub when Will's hand encircles my arm, spinning me around to face him. It is then that something within me shatters completely, fractured and irreplaceable.

"Why didn't you tell me?" I ask, quietly.

"I wanted to. I was going to."

"How could you keep something like this from me? Didn't you realize that I would find out eventually? What was your plan then?"

"I didn't have one."

"Come on, Will," I scoff. "You always have a plan."

He flinches at my tone. "Not this time. I have never spoken about that night to anyone. I never expected to see Marc again, and I certainly never thought I would see you again."

"Had you done your job correctly, you never would have." I wrench my arm from his grasp and stagger when he grips me again, his eyes burning into mine.

"How can you say that? You must understand how much I hate myself for following those orders." His expression is twisted in anguish, his voice shaking.

"You hating yourself isn't going to bring my family back," I cry, shoving him away from me.

We stand across from each other on either side of the darkened alleyway, breathing heavily. Despite the pain tearing at my insides, I can't help but remember how we stood in similar positions only a few months past, when he pulled me from a wall and demanded that I join his rebellion.

He rubs his hand across his short hair, looking at me helplessly. "I'm so sorry, Kay."

I stand impassively, regarding him as I feel the fight draining from my body. "When you realized I was there that night, why didn't you just come out and say it?"

He takes a long time in answering, ever-careful. "Because I thought that if you knew what I had done, you would lose your focus. I didn't think that telling you right away was worth risking the rebellion. I needed you." A muscle twitches near his jaw. "I still need you."

I stare at him, the words that have always come so easily now lost. Realization dawns slowly as I recognize the steely defiance in his eyes.

"Right," I say, finally. "Right. The rebellion."

"This is bigger than you and me, Kay. One step at a time, remember? You've already got the Princess free of the Palace, you've uncovered the King's plot, you've managed to save yourself. Now we just need to turn the people toward our cause and launch an attack. We can make things right." Will speaks quickly and moves closer. "I know I made a mistake, but I was a different person back then. I swear, I would never do anything to hurt you."

"But you did hurt me," I say softly. Shaking my head, I take a step back, stiffening when I hit the wall behind me. "You promised that nothing would change."

"Nothing has to change. I can make it up to you. Please, let's go back to my flat. We can talk." He brings a trembling hand up to my face, his thumb brushing my cheek.

I stay perfectly still, blinking my dry eyes up at him. After a moment I pull his hand away, keeping hold of it as I roll up his sleeve. There, illuminated by the flickering lamplight is the scar: a long, jagged ridge cut by a girl in a burning flat. I know without looking that his other arm has a fresher marking, a scar made by the Runner.

"I can't do this," I say, hollowly. My eyes skip over his features, familiar and unfamiliar all at once. "From now on, this is about the rebellion. Nothing more. Never again."

I push past him, ignoring the feeling of his fingers trailing down my arm.

Shaking on my bad leg, I stop after a few steps and turn to look back. Will's shoulders are slumped in defeat as he watches me, his face partially obscured by the shadows.

"I loved you, you know." I feel surprisingly little as I say the words, just an acute sense of finality to anything we may have once been to each other.

"I know."

I stare at him for a second longer, willing my heart to harden before I tear my eyes from his and shuffle back down the alley.

chapter 37

My steps are heavy as I trudge up the stairs to my flat for the second time in one night. When I push open the door, I find Lara curled up on the bed, her back to me. I sink down onto the cushions beside her, slumping forward with my head in my hands.

I feel the bed shift as she sits up, her thin arms snaking around me and drawing me back against her. I turn into the crook of her neck and finally let the weight of everything cascade off me. At last, I allow myself to feel every bump, cut and bruise, inside and out.

I am not sure how long we sit like that, our arms wrapped around each other, before I pull back, rubbing my eyes with my hand.

"What happened?" she asks softly, smoothing the strands of hair away from my face.

"He lied," I say, my voice scratchy. I shake my head, fighting to sort through my hazy thoughts. "No, I suppose he never actually lied. He just… withheld some truth."

"Who?"

"He was there, the night of the fire. The night they killed my parents."

Lara gasps, drawing back from me. "That courtier you've been plotting with?"

I blink slowly, my eyes heavy with exhaustion. "It turns out you were right. We can't trust them."

"Oh my gods." Her face crumples. "Kay, I'm so sorry."

I fall back onto the bed, hugging my knees to my chest. "I miss them so much."

"I know you do, sweet. I miss them too."

"I let everyone down. Meg especially." I think of the hurt expression on my friend's face when I told her who I really was. Her heartbreak is an echo of the leaden feeling pulling at my own chest.

Lara doesn't say anything. The bed shifts beneath me as she moves about, pulling off my boots and arranging the blanket over my shoulders.

My eyes drift shut as warm lips brush my forehead, Lara's tenderness reminding me of my mother. Another wave of hurt washes over me and I burrow my head deeper into the scratchy bedclothes, so unlike Will's cool sheets.

"Sleep now." The voice is a million miles away.

And finally, I do.

My sleep is deep and dreamless. I crawl slowly through a thick, suffocating mist, dragging my weary body toward consciousness. Before I even manage to pry open an eye, I am aware of every cut and bruise dotting my body, all enthusiastic to welcome me back into the world of the living.

Someone places their hand on my back and shakes me roughly. I groan, swatting them away. There is the sound of metal scraping against a scabbard and my eyes fly open, searching wildly.

Lieutenant Griss stands over my bed, his sword drawn and held inches away from my throat.

"Good morning," he says, drawing his lips back into a sneer and revealing two rows of perfectly shiny, white teeth.

I bolt upright, my back slamming against the wall behind me. No fewer than six guards have crowded into my attic, their broad shoulders filling the small space. My eyes dart automatically to the open window. One oversized guard has already firmly planted himself there, his arms crossed, smirking as though he can tell exactly what I'm thinking. Another guard stands barring the door, and still a third is with Lara in the corner. She stares at me with wide, terrified eyes, her thin form hunched and shaking.

There's no way out. I feel a lump of panic rise in my throat as I slowly bring my gaze back to Griss and his sword.

"I think you may well and truly be out of luck this time, Runner."

His accent is refined, but the intention behind his words sends shivers down my spine. Every one of my sore muscles is tensed and I keep my eyes locked on Griss', nearly vibrating with fury as I stare daggers at him.

"You can rot in the eternal Burn," I spit. "I'm not scared of a king's lapdog."

Griss' eyes narrow and he jerks the sword forward an inch, nicking my cheek. From across the room, I hear Lara gasp.

"If it were up to me, I would slice your pretty face off right here." His voice is low, menacing. "So trust me when I say you should be extremely grateful that I am tasked only with escorting you back to the Palace."

"I'm sure it's easy to make threats when you're surrounded by your lackeys," I mock, swiping my hand across my cut cheek and smearing the blood. "Why not hand me a sword and make this a fair fight?"

"Enough." Griss straightens and gestures for Lara. Someone drags her forward and Griss grabs her arm roughly, holding her tight and pressing his sword against her neck.

Red spots my vision, clouding my thoughts and hardening my heart. How dare he. How dare these men come into my home, pull me from the sweet release of unconsciousness and threaten the only family I have left?

Lieutenant Griss has made a grave error in judgment by tangling with the Runner.

I cast my gaze down, eyes searching as my hands ball into fists on the bedspread. Will's instructions echo in my head. *Patience.*

"Give me my shoes," I say, my voice low, dangerous. "I won't go to the Palace barefoot."

The guard nearest me kicks my boots over and I take my time in pulling them on. My hand slips down inside the worn leather and closes around the dagger hidden within.

“Ready, Runner?” Griss’ tone is mocking; he believes he’s already won.

“Not quite yet.” The colour red presses itself in further, thudding into my mind and drowning Will’s lessons. All I can see is Lara’s tear-streaked face and Griss’ sneer. My father mouthing the word, “*Run*.”

I release a guttural cry, throwing myself at the lieutenant. Taken aback, he stumbles, his hold on Lara loosening as I slam into him. We crash to the ground, Lara shrieking and darting away. Before any of the guards can react, I have Griss pinned, the point of my dagger held against his cheek.

“Hold!” Griss chokes, ordering his men back.

I trap his shoulders beneath my knees, pushing the dagger further and releasing a bright droplet of blood.

The cloud of red is all encompassing, binding and freeing all at once. I am dimly aware of the deadly circle of swords levelled at me but my rage blinds me to all but Griss’ fearful, wide-eyed stare and the ease with which I could turn them dim, forever.

“Don’t be a fool, Runner.” Griss’ voice is raspy. “Try to run and a dozen men will arrest you the moment your feet hit the ground. Take to the roofs and I kill your friend. You don’t have any options.”

“You’re wrong,” I growl. “I could kill you.”

He swallows, skin turning ashen beneath my blade.

“Kay, please.” A voice cuts through the fog.

I blink, Griss’ face blurring while my hand wavers, ever so slightly.

“Kay,” Lara calls out to me again. “This isn’t you.”

It could be. It would be so easy. One quick movement and all of Griss’ cruelty would be wiped away. His death wouldn’t undo any of the injustices inflicted upon us, but it would be a start.

The familiar weight of Lara's hand rests on my shoulder, easing me away from the cloud and back to the cramped and guard-filled attic. I shut my eyes, letting my dagger fall to the ground and slumping forward.

I am immediately seized, yanked to my feet while Griss scrambles out from under me.

I grunt, choking back a cry of pain as my bruised arms are forced behind me. From the corner of my eye, I can see a second guard approaching us, a length of rope in his hands.

"Forgive me for not wanting to take any chances, Runner. You haven't proven yourself trustworthy." Griss stands back, rubbing his neck and watching the scene from a safe distance.

"There's a lot of that going around." I wince as my wrists are bound behind my back.

"Nice work, gentlemen. And lady." Griss nods to Lara.

I try to catch her eye but Lara isn't looking toward me. I watch in confusion as she reaches cautiously for Griss' arm, getting his attention.

"I think there is another matter?" she asks him, tentatively.

I wrinkle my brow as the knots around my wrists are tightened and someone clasps my arm firmly.

"Of course." Absently, Griss unties the pouch at his waist and draws out a rolled piece of parchment, handing it to her.

"Lara?" My gaze darts back and forth between my friend and the lieutenant. "What's going on?"

"Your friend is one clever little lady." Griss speaks for her, clearly enjoying himself. "She cut herself a tidy little deal in exchange for your capture."

"Lara?" My knees buckle, staying upright only because of the guard's hold on my upper arm.

Lara has unrolled the parchment and is staring at it, her eyes wide. "So, it's official?" she asks Griss, ignoring me.

"It's official. Bid goodbye to the Commons, missy. The King has arranged a fine house for you in the Court." Griss' needle-like gaze is trained on me as he gleefully awaits my reaction.

Gradually, the pieces begin to fall into place. Meg's missing letter. Sera's warning.

"It was you? You turned us in?" I struggle against the guard, feeling sick. "Lara, how *could* you?"

She finally turns to look at me, rolling up the parchment and tucking it delicately into her bodice. "I'm sorry, Kay. I just couldn't go on like this anymore."

I shake my head, uncomprehending. "It won't change anything, you know," I hear myself say. "The money, the house, the dresses."

"Why shouldn't it?" She stalks toward me and jabs a finger in my chest, scoring a direct hit with a bruise. "What, do you suppose you're good enough for the Court but I'm not?"

"What are you—"

"You left me here to rot!" she shrieks, her blue eyes wide and wild. "You pat me on the head and shove money in my hands, treat me as though coins are all it takes to placate me, your poor-little-prostitute project." She shakes her head, her expression one of utter disgust. "I never wanted your charity, Kay. I wanted your love."

I stare at her, disbelieving. She shudders and pokes me again.

"I lost *everything* when I lost your brother, do you realize that? I'm not like you, I can't run from my problems the way you can. The things I had to do in order to survive..." She trails off, appearing adrift for a moment before her eyes flash with anger again. "Meanwhile, you flew about on those stupid roofs, consorting with courtiers, forgetting all about me."

"How can you say that? I did *everything* for you. I risked my *life* for you!"

"Oh please, you didn't do it for me. You did it for yourself. For the glory. For that ridiculous hero complex your father left you with."

I blink, still not completely registering the situation. When I speak, my voice is shaking. "You've made a huge mistake."

"I don't think so." She pats her bodice. "This is the world we live in, Kay. You have to look out for yourself, because no one else is going to give a damn. That's what I've done."

"You're a coward. You have no idea what you've done," I seethe, digging in my heels as Griss signals us from the room.

Lara doesn't reply. I catch one last glimpse of her as I am hauled through the door, her brassy head bent over the unrolled parchment and a small smile tugging at her lips.

I stumble on the stairs, biting my lip to keep from crying out as my bad leg bangs against the steps.

"Take it easy, will you?" I yell at the oaf holding me.

He says nothing, pushing me onward and out into a waiting carriage bedecked with the King's insignia.

A small crowd has gathered to watch the proceedings, peering out at the street from the shadows of their doorways. Several guards stand around on horseback, eyeing the curious commoners warily. I almost feel flattered at the number of armed men sent to arrest me.

I keep my head down as they haul me toward the carriage, avoiding the sympathetic looks of my neighbours. I can feel the disappointment radiating off them and my shoulders hunch, mortified that I have been brought to this state, trussed and freighted away like a common thief.

Which I suppose I am.

The drive back to the Palace—jostled in the back seat between two guards—is depressingly short compared to the long, painful trip I took getting away from it. As we drive, I make a point of staring out the window as much as possible, drinking in the familiar sights. Even the run-down Commons buildings appear beautiful, bathed in the white light of the afternoon sun, their dappled exteriors baking warmly. I fight the rising sense of anxiety as I come to the realization that this may be one of the last times I am outdoors, the last time I look upon these streets. I concentrate on my breathing and try not to think about how furious the King will be, about the deep, mouldy gaol and the dark chambers hidden at the far end of it.

One step at a time.

A shudder runs through me as we rumble under the threshold of the Palace gate, its great wooden doors swinging open ominously. How many times have I ridden up this path, dressed in finery and waiting to be escorted to a plush bedchamber? Then, the Palace seemed a mighty and beautiful thing, an architectural testament. Now, as we roll ever closer to its gaping maw, I find no beauty, only an ugly sense of foreboding.

I expected to drive around to the gaol entrance, but instead the carriage halts directly in front of the Palace doors. I am hauled out, a guard gripping either of my arms as the rest of the men dismount and arrange themselves around us. Griss stands in front, his shoulders drawn back and his chin raised proudly. Disgust churns my stomach at seeing the sick sense of satisfaction he clearly derives from my capture.

They yank me forward and I have to fight to keep my bad leg from twisting beneath me. The front doors swing open and we parade through, the soldiers' heavy footsteps echoing obnoxiously in the tiled hallway. I stumble once and the man on my left hauls me roughly upward, barely adjusting his pace. We march down the foyer and past the staircases, advancing on the Great Hall.

The grand room is still configured for the engagement party. The tables are pushed back against the walls and a wide aisle sweeps from the doors all the way down to the King's gilded throne. A low murmuring fills my ears as I am dragged past what looks to be every noble in the City. Finely dressed men and women are lined up against all sides of the room, pointing at me and whispering among themselves. I feel a heat creep up my cheeks and focus on putting one foot in front of the other without falling.

We break formation near the front of the room. Griss bows and steps to the side, gesturing dramatically as I am shoved forward onto my knees in front of the throne. I grunt and grit my teeth when my bad knee collides with the unforgiving stone floor.

"Your Majesty, may I present to you the Runner."

I raise my head, peering upwards. The King is leaning forward in his great gold throne, his jewellery-laden fingers clasping the arms of the chair. I watch as a gleeful sneer creeps up his face, and I know that he has been waiting for this moment for a very long time.

chapter 38

A shiver runs down my spine. I blame it on the cold floor I am forced to kneel upon. I thrust up my chin and stare the King directly in the eye, twisting my wrists behind my back to test my bonds. The rope bites into my still-bruised skin and I flinch, cursing myself for showing my discomfort in front of the courtiers.

"Welcome back." The King speaks louder than necessary, his deep voice projecting across the cavernous space. His meaty hands move to stroke his beard and he leans closer, his lip curling. "I have anticipated a formal meeting between us for quite some time now."

"Whatever do you mean, Sire? We've already met." I roll my shoulders back. "I've enjoyed the fruits of your hospitality for several weeks." Tilting my head, I raise my eyebrows at him in mock surprise. "How embarrassing that someone as wise as yourself could fail to notice my presence."

Someone cuffs the back of my head and I wince, shutting my eyes tight as my sore muscles spasm in reaction.

The King raises a lazy hand, calling off his lieutenant. The hatred is clear behind his dark eyes as he glares down at me from atop his throne.

"I would strongly advise that you watch your tongue, Runner." He fairly spits out the nickname. "Your position is not a favourable one."

"Neither is yours," I reply.

Something dangerous crosses his face. The King leans back in his seat, sweeping his gaze over the gathered courtiers. My knee throbs angrily from my uncomfortable kneeling position and I shift, causing Griss to reach for the hilt of his sword in warning.

I wait for the King to speak, bracing myself for the inevitable question.

"Where is she?" His voice is low but still manages to carry to the back of the Hall, eliciting murmurs and a restless shuffling from the crowd.

I hold his gaze, remaining silent as I stare at him in challenge. From the corner of my eye I can see Griss unsheathe his sword and level it at my neck. My gaze flickers down the silvery point and back to the King, taking note of the flushed hue his face has taken.

"Forgive my ignorance, Majesty. Have you misplaced someone?" I ask, allowing the fake concern to drip into my voice. Despite my predicament, there is something marvellously freeing about dropping all pretences. I might be inches from death, but at least I am no longer pretending to be someone I'm not.

The end of Griss' sword presses against the soft flesh at the side of my neck but I don't waver, knowing they won't kill me. Not yet.

"Insolent gutter filth. How dare you defy your *King*." The mask begins to crack as the King's face turns to thunder. His hands clench into tight fists, the knuckles blazing white.

"You are no king of mine." Fury courses through me. "I owe you nothing, do you hear me? I told you once: you can't control us with fear. Change is coming. Your reign is over. I suggest that you step down now and save yourself a good deal of time and trouble."

There is the mighty sound of metal slamming against wood as his jewelled knuckles connect with the arms of throne, eliciting more than one startled gasp from the crowd. Even Griss jumps and I manage to avoid being stabbed only by jerking my head away at the last instant.

The spacious Hall is dead silent as the King slowly stands, straightening to his full, impressive height. I twist in my bonds again while he steps down toward me, clenching and unclenching his fists.

I shut my eyes as the back of his hand connects with my face, feeling my lip split open from the force of the blow.

A high-pitched ringing fills my ears and I struggle to keep from falling over. I shake my head to clear it, glaring up at the King as he leers over me, his teeth bared. I wrinkle my nose at him in disgust, then lean forward and spit an impressive gob of blood onto his beautiful, shiny boots.

An inhuman cry of rage tears from his throat and in the next instant I am keeled over on the floor, drawing my knees up to my chest and retching from the painful kick directly to my gut. I am vaguely aware of the King shouting angrily as I am hauled up, a hand gripping each of my forearms as I'm dragged backward out of the Hall.

I kick against the guards holding me, an icy panic taking hold as they march me out a side entrance and toward the gaol. I twist my head back and forth wildly, watching the scenery rush by me, much too fast. We cross the yard and past the barracks, entering the gaol. When the gate guard admits us, I notice a yellow bruise still colouring his temple. He shoots me a hate-filled grimace as he rattles his ring of heavy keys, then unlocks the door to the stairs.

Darkness coats us as we descend, the sun long forgotten. My protestations turn feeble and my feet drag against the worn stone steps. When we reach the bottom of the stairs, my head jerks over to the table pushed against the far wall. The two guards I incapacitated the night of the ball stand next to it, barely visible in the flickering torchlight. The men wear identical looks of satisfaction, clearly revelling in my arrest.

Griss leads us past the large front cells and I dig my heels in harder, feeling half crazed at the prospect of moving toward the rooms hidden at the very back of the prison. The hands gripping my arms dig in tightly, forcing me onward.

I nearly shake with relief when we stop in front of an isolation cell; the prospect of containment in a dark, dingy room seems like a small measure of consolation compared to the torture chambers. The rope binding my wrists is cut and I am shoved forward into the gaping hole; I fall to my hands and knees as my rubbery legs give out.

I keep my head down, breathing in the dry, musty air and listening to the sound of the door behind me swinging shut and the heavy bolt locking securely.

"Sleep tight," someone mocks to a cacophony of low chuckles.

I wait until their footsteps have receded before I drag myself upright, holding my hands out to the wall for balance.

Now that I'm finally alone, the adrenalin slowly ebbs from my body and I once again become aware of the various injuries crying out from my broken body. If my rib wasn't cracked before, the King's boot most certainly completed the job. I wince as I straighten, my fingers scraping the cold stone wall. Gingerly, I trace the perimeter of the cell, walking along the wall and returning to the door within a dismally small number of steps.

My eyes gradually adjust to the darkness and I am able to take in my surroundings. The only source of light stems from a distant torch flickering weakly through the barred window of the door. My cell has no bed, only four solid walls and a rusty bucket—I shudder at the thought of using it.

I lower myself into a far corner, holding an arm around my sore ribs and drawing my legs to my chest. I pick at the grungy bit of emerald fabric I wrapped around my bad knee, marvelling distantly how something so beautiful can be ruined so irreparably.

I strain my ears but hear nothing: no cough of fellow prisoners or shuffling steps of the guards. I wrap my arms around my legs and lower my forehead onto my knees, choking on the threat of tears.

Lara. How could she? I blink forcefully, willing the sadness away and replacing it with the icy grasp of rage. Since I was a child, I have looked up to her, always so glamorous on the arm of my brother. How many times have we shared confidences, talked long into the night about everything under the sun, held and supported one another? It was her door that I knocked on five years ago, reeking of soot and clutching my father's bloodstained dagger. We all grieved when news of my brother came from the Wastelands, but only Lara truly understood the hole left in lieu of Frye's life.

I took advantage of her kindness, believing it to be as solid and dependable as the great wall surrounding our city. I curse myself for thinking that I could save her; that I could save anyone.

You did it for yourself. For the glory.

The mouldy walls of my cell appear to press in closer. Every fibre of my being aches for flight and I bury my head in my hands, willing my thoughts away from the reality of the locked door, the low ceiling and the miles of earth over my head.

Run.

I can't.

Run.

I *can't*.

The old darkness creeps in. I feel the damp chill worm its way around my heart, shielding and confining me, readying me for what's to come.

chapter 39

I am unsure of how many hours have passed. Perhaps it's already been a day; perhaps it's been two.

I remain curled on my side on the floor facing the door, occupying myself with drifting intermittently in and out of consciousness. There is nothing for my eyes to focus on but the small point of light coming through the barred window. I lie with my cheek pressed against stone, staring at the weak flicker.

My stomach growls angrily, jerking me back to the present. I shift, groaning as the blood rushes back into my hip, awareness returning to my body. I settle back into an equally uncomfortable position, pushing away my discomfort and returning to the festering darkness within.

This is it. This is where it is all going to end. How stupid was I to think that I could go up against the King, to think that I could succeed where my father had failed? Who am I to have such an ego? What right did I have to believe that the City could ever be anything but a cruel, hierarchical system? Everyone warned me that the risk was too great, but I didn't listen. My only accomplishment is making a complete and utter fool of myself and, in the process, risking the life of a true friend.

Meg is out there, somewhere, alone and scared. She put her faith in me and I lied to her. I am a senseless fraud, the same as Lara or Will.

Will.

My eyes screw closed tightly. I don't know why I should even care about shedding a tear, here about as far from the rest of the world as anyone could be. I suppose old habits die hard.

He was everything. I was so blinded by my belief in his rebellion—in him—that I shouldn't be surprised to discover where my recklessness has led. Against my better judgment, I trusted a courtier, allowed myself to be persuaded by a pair of pretty grey eyes. I let down my guard and gave myself over to him completely, opening myself up in ways that I had never dared with anyone else.

The guards who stormed our home five years ago were once faceless drones, soulless incantations of the King's will. Now, when I shut my eyes all I can see is Will's handsome face, anguished but unflinching.

Over and over I berate myself for my stupidity and short-sightedness while the hours or days pass overhead. I approach Will's betrayal from every possible angle, the hurt turning unbearable each time I recall the feeling of his arms wrapped around me or his heartbeat pressing into my back as we slept. The pain sustains me and helps to keep me from grasping onto that one nagging impossibility.

Maybe he's coming for me.

He isn't. It's been made crystal clear to me that his focus will always remain on his rebellion. Locked away in this dank corner of the eternal Burn, I'm of no further use, and so he'll have resolved himself to press forward. I find some comfort in knowing that he's keeping Meg safe and vow to do the same, though I am sure that my small efforts will make no difference in the grand scheme. After all, even if by some crazy miracle we managed to start an uprising, somewhere down the line the need for power would corrupt and the ugliness of humanity would overrule. The world is made up of people stepping over the weak as they claw for greater riches.

I'm no better than any of them. I pretended to be someone I wasn't, manipulating one of the only people to offer me a genuine friendship. Meg was willing to abandon everything she had ever known to follow me into a madcap rebellion, casting aside a world of riches and privilege for the life of a traitor. As far as I can tell, the Princess is the only person in this whole, sordid mess who showed real courage.

The torch outside my door continues to spew a weak light. I watch the dappled patterns as I turn these thoughts over and over in my mind, unable to distract myself with anything except my own misery. I think about shouting for some food and water but dismiss it; there are worse fates than starving to death. I sit back against the wall and re-tie the grimy bandage on my knee, securing it as tightly as I can with shaking fingers.

I loll my head against the impassive stone behind me, allowing my eyes to drift closed, waiting for the next wave of unconsciousness to overtake me.

The tread of heavy footsteps outside the door jerks me to attention. I crack one eye open and adopt a look of measured disdain while my muscles contract in panic. As horrible as this dank cell is, I am not such a fool to think that anything better is awaiting me outside.

A key turns in the lock and the heavy door swings open, creaking on its hinges. A guard's broad shoulders fill the doorway before he takes a step toward me, reaches out and grips my arm to yank me to my feet. A second guard remains in the hallway, watching warily.

"Wait—" I protest, wincing as I am dragged through the hallway and deeper into the gloom. I try to dig my heels into the floor when I realize where we are heading, jerking my arm violently in the guard's grip.

The second man wordlessly grabs my other arm and helps to pull me toward the chambers, cuffing me in the back of the head when I spout obscenities and try to kick him.

A combination of dizziness and fear almost causes me to pass out and I stop thrashing, my feet dragging inelegantly on the rough stone floor as we draw closer and closer to the darkest corner of the gaol. To my dread, we enter the room that I explored only a few weeks previous.

"Listen, you're making a mistake," I say, fighting to catch the eye of one of the guards.

He avoids my eyeline, forcing my wrist above my head and into one of the manacles at the top of the pole in the centre of the room. The iron is cold and bites into my skin.

"You don't have to do this." I swallow in an effort to keep the terror from my voice. "The King is just using you to do his dirty work, but you can make your own choice—you can see there is a better way."

My pleas fall on deaf ears as my other arm is raised and shackled into place. I clench my hands into fists and breathe deep, shuddering breaths, looking over my shoulder at the guards moving to stand on either side of the doorway. They remain still and stone faced, waiting.

"Shit." I pull at the manacles binding my wrists, grimacing when the flesh tears anew.

"This is wrong," I say, trying in vain to get one of the men to look at me, to acknowledge me. "Don't you see it's only blind chance that you were born to the Court? In another life, you could have been a commoner, and then it might have been one of you up here instead of me."

The younger man glances at his companion uneasily.

I feel a small spark of hope and keep pushing. "I'm no different from you; this is going to hurt me as much as it would hurt you or anyone you love. Blind obedience is the only thing keeping the King on the throne; it's the only thing allowing him to condemn people this way, but you can change all that." I cough, my throat completely dried up. "Help me."

"There is an awful lot of conversation in here." A shadow materializes in the door frame and I freeze, my eyes wide as they struggle to adjust to the darkness.

His silhouette looms larger as he makes his way into the room. I watch as he moves to the wall and strikes a match, lighting the torch below the macabre display.

The light flares up, coating the dark brick and illuminating the whips. A bout of nausea turns my empty stomach and I nearly gag, swallowing hard and forcing my eyes to the Inquisitor, trying unsuccessfully to avoid looking at the wall behind him.

He looks the same as he did five years ago. Older, with harder eyes and thinner hair, but the same murderous intent written clearly across his plain features.

"I have heard a great deal about you," Harmen says conversationally. He moves around the pole so he is standing in front of me; he crosses his arms and tucks them into the folds of his jacket. He tilts his head, adjusting his spectacles with one hand as he regards me. "You are not what I expected."

My skin crawls under his scrutiny. "Sorry to disappoint you."

"Disappointed? Dear me, no. I am impressed, actually. I assumed that the infamous Runner would be someone older, with more experience. You must be very clever to have forged such a reputation at so young an age. And a woman, no less!" His smile widens, stretching unnaturally tight across his face. "I flatter myself in thinking that I had a hand in your success."

I flinch, my breath coming in short gasps.

"You didn't think I remembered you, did you? How could I forget." Harmen circles me, his movements reminding me of a buzzard. "That hair, that defiance. Not much has changed since we last crossed paths."

"You killed my family," I say, my voice low.

"Your family was naught but a bunch of traitors," he retorts. "I'm not surprised to see you've chosen the same path."

I stiffen and tug unconsciously again at the manacles. My every sense strains to be as far away from this man as possible.

"You would be surprised at the things I know about you, Kay." I flinch again at his use of my name. "Down here, there are no secrets between us. You will find that I can be a great friend to you."

Harmen reaches one hand up and I draw back, but he is only reaching to remove his spectacles, plucking them daintily off his nose and rubbing them with a lace handkerchief.

"You're unusually quiet." He looks up. "Could you be a bit nervous? What about all that chatter from a moment ago, that blasphemous talk about your King?"

"He isn't my King," I mutter.

"Well, we'll just see about that, won't we?" He finishes polishing his glasses and deposits them in the pocket of his jacket. "Oh, but I'm getting ahead of myself. Let's not start off on the wrong foot; it seems unfair that I know so much about you and you don't know me, doesn't it?"

He seems to be waiting for a response, his cruel smile unwavering. I stare at him stonily, refusing to play his games.

He doesn't seem the least bit bothered by my silence. "My circumstances have changed since we were last acquainted. I am now employed by our

King for the most noble task of extracting information from traitors. It is a profession I am proud to have excelled at."

"Is that all?" I ask.

"I beg your pardon?"

"Not to be rude, but you sound terribly boring. Haven't you any hobbies? Friends? Perhaps you have a woman kept in your bed, wallowing in self-loathing?" I force myself to keep my eyes locked with his, glaring at him in challenge.

Something dangerous flickers across his face. "I can see we are going to be very good friends, you and I."

Harmen moves back toward the whips and takes off his jacket, folding it carefully and placing it on the table.

"I like to begin my session with a new client by asking them a question simply and reasonably. I find that a lot of trouble can be avoided by a polite conversation. You are clearly a smart girl, so look around." He gestures to the display on the wall. "Resisting my techniques will only keep you here for longer. You may be interested to know that I have ways of keeping you alive for however much time it takes to retrieve the information I require. That said, I don't have to hurt you if you tell me what I want to know, right now."

He makes a show of rolling up his sleeves, revealing forearms surprisingly muscled for someone of such average stature.

"So this is your chance, Kay." He pauses a beat, watching me. "Where is the Princess Megra?"

I swallow in an attempt to soothe my parched throat. Harmen leans casually against the table, framed perfectly by the mosaic of torture behind him.

I tear my gaze down from the wall and force it back to him, adjusting my hands in the manacles. "I don't know."

He nods, slowly. "Very well, then." Turning, he regards the whips, his fingers dancing across the options as he carefully makes his selection. I adjust my stance, planting my feet as best I can. I want to turn away, knowing that I don't need to see which one he chooses, but I am incapable of looking anywhere else.

Finally, his hand comes to rest on a relatively tame wooden switch. My back burns as sweat drips down my spine, coating the underside of my shirt. Harmen nods to the guards and one of them moves toward me, efficiently rolling up the back of my tunic.

I take a deep breath, rotating my wrists so that my hands grip the chains of the manacles. I stare hard at the pole in front of me, concentrating on a specific knot in the wood.

There is the sound of shuffling feet over my shoulder but Harmen takes his precious time in readying himself. In the meantime, I am coiled as tight as a spring, feeling as though I could pass out from the stress of anticipation.

All at once, there is a lick of pain shooting up my back unlike anything I have ever felt. A split second later, the sound of the whip slices through the air, deafening my senses. There is an almighty crack and my knees buckle, fire dancing across my spine and pouring into every thought, every breath, every last nerve ending my battered body has left.

I gasp and pull myself upright, heaving on the chains. I have barely managed to gather my bearings when the next strike comes, retracing the same path as the first. I bite down a scream as the fire burns anew, the fresh pain joining the still-smouldering coals of the first hit, effectively obliterating every scrap of light.

Two more strikes arrive in quick succession and I remain standing only by the unforgiving hold of the manacles. From the recesses of my mind I realize that Harmen has spoken and I fight to focus, pain and shock rendering any clear thought impossible.

"That was just a taste. Now I will ask you again, as nicely as I can: Where is the Princess?"

Something warm and sticky trickles down my back. Every shaky breath I draw tugs and tears at the gaping cuts.

My chin is cupped by heinously gentle fingers as Harmen forces my eyes into his. "Where is she?" he asks, so softly that he may have said nothing at all.

I stare into muddy brown eyes, for one crystalline moment wanting nothing more than to tell him what he wants to know and return to the beautiful abandonment of my cell.

"I don't know," a voice that is not my own replies wearily, and I brace myself for another round.

chapter 40

Over and over I awake curled up on the cold floor of my cell, with only a vague recollection of being dragged back toward it and flung inside.

There is a merciful instant before I become fully aware of my surroundings, when I am able to imagine myself somewhere else, back on the roofs of the City. The sun bakes my skin, warming me while I look across the vast network of stone buildings and desert, the horizon stretching to a finite point at the furthest reaches of my vision.

I struggle to hold onto the memory as my body contracts in agony. This last interrogation was particularly monstrous, and I lost count of Harmen's strikes long before I passed out. By the way my tunic sticks stubbornly to my back, I can wager that the last of my unmarked skin has been decimated.

It is with great difficulty that I manage to pull myself into a seated position, leaning forward so I don't brush up against the rough stone behind me. I collapse over my knees and draw great, shallow breaths, the effort of adjusting my position making me fully aware of the remainder of my wounds and rendering me exhausted. I shut my eyes tightly, willing myself back into unconsciousness and away from the chorus of malicious whispers encroaching from all sides.

Each day passes the same, any semblance of wakefulness peppered by endless questions and more pain. Sometimes I awake in my cell, sometimes shackled to the pole. Even the interrogation has become predictable: where is Meg, who am I working with, what have I planned. Any satisfaction I get out of remaining silent is abolished with each fresh lick.

Nothing ever changes, but I long ago stopped expecting it to.

My fitful sleep is disturbed all too soon by the sound of my cell door being unlocked. Torchlight blazes across my vision and I blink at the invasive brightness, waiting.

The now-familiar silhouette of Harmen swims into view. The Inquisitor takes a step toward me, a tray balanced delicately in his hands. I eye him suspiciously as the platter is placed before me. The greasy smell of food hits my nostrils and causes my stomach to growl hungrily.

Someone has left a small stool near the door and I watch as Harmen lowers himself onto it, sweeping away the long tails of his jacket. He gives a slight nod and the door swings closed, leaving us alone. He studies me, not saying anything, his legs crossed elegantly as though he is making himself comfortable in a Palace lounge.

“Don’t wait on my account,” he says, lightly. “You must be hungry.”

My hand darts out, grabbing hold of the bowl and scooping up large mouthfuls of stew with my fingers. Harmen sits and waits as I scarf greedily, not bothering to examine what it is that I am eating. It could be rat, for all I care. When I’ve finished, I tilt the bowl up and lick it clean, finally lowering it and rubbing my mouth with my wrist, wincing at the skin torn by my bindings.

“Better?” he asks.

My response is a hurled bowl, which he dodges easily. I’d have no problem braining him if I were in better form.

Harmen makes a low *tsk* in his throat as he shakes his head, seemingly disappointed. “I see there is still some work we can do.”

I shrug, keeping my eyes trained on his. “I have the time.”

“Indeed, you do.” The creepy smile returns to his face, stretched tightly over his jaw. “How is your back today?”

“You seem unusually concerned about me.”

“On the contrary—I am always interested in the well-being of my clients. I prefer them to be in the best possible health so that our sessions may continue for as long as necessary.” He remains perfectly still save for one long finger drumming against his knee.

“How considerate,” I say, dryly.

“That said, I do happen to have a personal interest in you, Kay. Usually, an interrogation does not drag on quite the way yours has.”

"I must be special."

"In a way, you are." He ignores my sarcasm and leans forward, forearms on his thighs. "I will admit that I find you incredibly fascinating. What drives a person such as yourself to so fiercely protect a princess of the royal house? Do you suppose that if your positions were reversed, she would lift a finger to help you?"

A flush of anger creeps up my neck. "You wouldn't know anything about it."

"I thought by now we had established that there is very little I don't know."

I shudder, snippets of memory returning. There is Harmen hissing a bloody narrative, telling and retelling me how I failed to protect my family. There is Will's name, demands that I reveal his and Meg's whereabouts. There is the sting of the whip in between accusations.

Shaking my head, I force myself to focus back on Harmen, blinking. "I'm sorry, were you saying something?"

His grin widens. "I was wondering why you would put yourself through such an ordeal for someone who has clearly abandoned you."

It's a fair question. Why should I prolong my execution when we have already failed in overthrowing the King? What am I holding on to? Under the maniacal gaze of Harmen and encompassed in the cloak of my shattered body, I struggle to find the reason.

"I am flattered that you are taking such a vested interest in me," I say, tiredly. "And I'll say it again only because you are so woefully forgetful: Mind your own bloody business."

"Such a shame." Harmen shakes his head, sighing. "You were born to the wrong side, Kay. Were you born to the Court, you might have been very happy. You would have lived a long life, and all that cleverness would not have gone to waste."

"That is the difference between us, Harmen. You think a person is made better by circumstance and handouts."

"And you believe otherwise?" His voice has taken on a conversational tone, his head tilted to one side as he listens intently.

"I have been both a courtier and a commoner, which I think makes me the foremost expert on the subject." I straighten my leg, stretching the left knee. "Good and evil, courage and cowardice, right and wrong: Court or Commons makes no difference. One is as bad as the other."

"Are you always so certain of everything?"

"Yes."

"I thought so." Harmen sits up, one finger tapping his lips. "But I wonder if you have ever considered that our system—while flawed—is still the best chance we have for survival?"

"You will have a very hard time convincing me that condemning thousands of people to war and servitude is good for anyone."

"You're a smart girl, Kay. Think about it. The gods granted your monarchy the sacred—some would say impossible—task of keeping our society alive beneath a sun that burned us nearly to the point of extinction." He leans closer. "Survival is not about the individual. It is about the group. These are desperate times, and the fact that you or anyone from the Commons has survived is a testament to the wisdom of your King."

I stare at him, unblinking.

He re-crosses his legs and continues, "You could argue that your people are the most important members of the City; the true backbone of our society. Without their sacrifice, we couldn't construct our homes, harvest our food or protect our wall. A courtier may lead a more comfortable existence, but it is the commoner who will build the new world."

"Walls and wars," I say bitterly. "That's all this city will ever be remembered for. We're surviving, perhaps, but that is a world of difference from living." I shake my head, speaking mostly to myself. "Your system assumes that we should naturally be at odds with one another. Commoners against courtiers, all of us against the Wastelanders. We haven't been given the chance to try and work together."

He chuckles softly, in an almost fatherly way. My skin rises in goosebumps at the sound.

"After everything you have been through, you still think people have the capacity to get along? My dear Kay, you have already learned a very important lesson." He pauses, scrutinizing me. "People only care about themselves. Give them freedom of choice and they will destroy everything."

"You don't know that."

"Trust me, I do. I have studied the history books. One head, one voice speaking for everyone: that is the only way to have order. That is the only method for ensuring that we continue to survive."

"There are other ways."

"You've seen it for yourself. Wasn't it your friend who orchestrated your arrest?"

My heart lurches. At this moment, Lara is likely comfortably ensconced in her plush new flat, dressing up in expensive clothes. The price of my freedom.

I open my mouth to say something, then close it again.

"Lara was Frye's lover, wasn't she? You must have been close."

At the mention of my brother, my throat swells shut, choking me. Harmen's unnaturally tight smile stretches wide as he scrutinizes my reaction.

"From what I gather, you were stealing from the Palace for the sake of some half-baked plot to save her and the rest of those common nobodies. That's quite a risk to take, isn't it? You put yourself directly in front of the King so that you could help a friend, and how does she repay you?"

The greasy food turns over in my stomach

"Enough," I manage, my voice barely audible.

"…By turning you over to the guards at the first opportunity. She saw her chance and she took it. Let me ask you: does this seem like someone capable of governing themselves?" His eyes flash menacingly in the dim light, betraying his casual demeanour.

Another bout of nausea sends me clawing toward the bucket. I heave into it, muscles contracting painfully over and over until there is nothing left in my stomach. I am vaguely aware of Harmen crouching over me, holding my hair away from my face.

Lacking the strength to slap him away, I slump back against the wall, grimacing as the movement sends agonizing spasms streaming down my back. I sigh heavily, my eyes glazed and staring at the ceiling.

"Where is she, Kay?"

I have just enough left in my reserves to kick my leg out at the bucket. There is a satisfying clatter and a pool of watery vomit gathers beneath the Inquisitor's shoes.

Harmen stands abruptly, knocking the stool backward and releasing a stream of curses. I smirk, feeling a bruise pull at my cheek as I watch his demeanour turn from composure to abject fury.

"Very well." When he speaks, his voice is low, danger percolating just below his surface. "I can see there will be no rationalizing with you."

"What took you so long."

"You've disappointed me, Kay, but I fear it isn't my disappointment that should concern you. The King is calling for a halt to your interrogation." There is a scraping of wood against stone as Harmen repositions his stool away from the mess.

I remain silent, counting the blocks in the low ceiling for the thousandth time.

"This, of course, means you will be receiving your punishment."

I almost laugh aloud at the suggestion. Punishment? What have I been doing down here all this time?

"You have been charged with kidnapping, among a host of other felonies." Harmen's tone is grave, imploring.

"I daren't ask when the trial will be."

He doesn't respond to that, instead clenching his jaw tightly in disapproval. "The King has declared his daughter to be his most precious treasure—"

I actually do manage to snort out loud at that.

"—and as such, your punishment shall be that of a thief, to the highest extent," he continues, his tone scolding.

"I imagine that is a sight worse than chopping off my hands." I examine my wrists, rubbed raw and spotted with dried blood.

"You are to be executed tomorrow by beheading."

I glance up, catching the maniacal glint in Harmen's eye as he waits for my reaction. It isn't difficult to keep my face devoid of any emotion.

"This is your last chance, Kay. This isn't a game anymore." He leans forward, resting his elbows on his knees while he curls and uncurls his fists.

I unconsciously shift away.

"You are going to die tomorrow. All of your stubbornness and so-called-bravery will count for nothing." Spittle flies free of his lips. "Tell me what I want to know. Tell me and I can save you."

I remain very still, watching him. I take stock of the sheen of perspiration dotting his forehead and the way his starched collar sits slightly askew. Glancing down at his hands, I recall the way they furled around the worn leather whips, his callused palms a sharp contrast to his otherwise pristine appearance.

The cell echoes with Harmen's laboured breathing and reeks of sick. I feel the walls press in closer, the rough stone scratching and tearing at my broken flesh. Everything is too close, too cloying. The time spent here has robbed me of everything I once loved—the feeling of sun on my face, the whisper of wind against my skin. Harmen is right: there is nothing left.

Finally, I drag my eyes up to meet the Inquisitor's, forcing as much strength into my voice as I can.

"I will meet you in the eternal Burn," I spit.

Harmen's face crumples, his grief as unsettling as his smile. "I don't understand." His voice breaks as he withdraws his handkerchief and dabs spastically at his brow. "They always tell me. Why won't you tell me?"

One question I wish I could answer.

"So be it." He fusses with the handkerchief, folding and refolding it before he straightens his glasses and smoothes his hair. "Your execution will be held tomorrow in the courtyard. Your death will be a demonstration of the might and justice of King Francis and—I think—a very fitting end to the legend of the infamous Runner."

Harmen studies me for a moment longer before rising to his feet and closing the short distance between us. I flinch as he kneels down in front of me. With surprisingly gentle fingers, he brushes a matted strand of hair from my eyes, his touch causing my blood to curdle and my empty stomach to heave. When he speaks, I can hardly hear him over the rushing in my ears.

"It was me who suggested that you be executed out of doors. I thought you might enjoy the sunlight during your last moments. It is one kindness I can grant you." He tucks the strand of hair behind my ear. "I'm going to miss you, Kay."

Cursing my weakness, I can only remain frozen, my mouth clamped shut defiantly as Harmen steps back. When the cell door swings open, he is briefly illuminated, the damp torchlight giving me a glimpse of what it is to be condemned. In the instant before I am returned to my darkness, I see an old man, broken and already forgotten.

chapter 41

I pass what I can only assume is the night in restless fits of wakefulness, unable to find a comfortable position on the floor. Giving up on sleep, I force myself to my feet and test my strength, pacing back and forth and stretching my near-useless limbs. The skin on my back pulls and chafes with each movement, but I grit my teeth and force myself to breathe through the pain, working until I can move from wall to wall without showing any discomfort.

I rattle the iron bars on the door, then lean my forehead against them. How different would things have turned out if the rebellion had been a success? Would Meg have made a good queen? Would the districts have united? Would there have still been injustice, war, famine? The wasted possibilities cycle over and over, throbbing behind my temple. I rub the ache and cross back to the opposite end of the small cell, gingerly easing myself down into a seated position. Inevitably, my mind turns to Will.

Isolation is relentlessly unforgiving. All this time spent alone with my thoughts has driven me madder than Harmen's questioning ever could. Now, with nothing ahead of me but death and nothing behind me but darkness, I have finally been forced to see through my own veil of stubbornness. I've spent the last five years dreaming of vengeance, flitting about the rooftops in a vain bid to exist outside of the monarchy. I've robbed people, invaded their homes, taken advantage of them, betrayed their trust. I've hurt people in order to fuel my own, selfish agenda. Yes, I've been hurt, but I could never consider myself innocent.

I think I now understand why Will couldn't tell me about his part in my parents' deaths.

We are both victims of a hopeless goal, single-minded to a fault. What I did to Meg was really no different from what Will did to me. Considering how much it pained me to come clean to the Princess after so many weeks of wrestling with guilt, I can only imagine what Will must have gone through.

Try as I might, I can't rectify the guard in my parents' smouldering flat with the person I came to love. Will and the murderous guard are two entirely different people. One is a boy, abused and angry. The other is a fighter, his every move planned and precise. The only thing connecting the two is a rebellious nature. Will has changed, I am certain of that.

I'm also certain that no one has a hope of capturing his heart, not so long as he has a cause to aim for. It's hard to fault him for that, as he was never anything but upfront about his plans. It would be foolish of me to think I could ever matter more to him than an opportunity to change the world, not when I am unsure of what I would do if our situations were reversed. In moments of complete hopelessness, I may have imagined him bursting through that door to rescue me, but now those fancies have all but faded away.

My past mistakes rain down upon me as I wait to hear the sound of footsteps echoing through the tunnel. When they finally come for me, I am tense but controlled.

A key turns noisily in the cell door and it swings open. Lieutenant Griss strides purposefully into the cell, a satisfied sneer curling the corners of his cruel mouth. He signals and two guards step around him. I allow the men to hoist me to my feet and pull my hands behind my back; with some effort, I try to keep my spine straight and refrain from flinching as they bind my wrists.

"This is it, Runner," Griss says, brandishing a torch. I wince at the bright light and unsettling warmth. "I hope you had a good night's sleep; there is quite the crowd waiting for you."

"Must be a slow day," I say, grimacing as the guards finish tying me and grip my arm firmly.

They escort me out of the cell and down the tunnel back toward the gaol entrance. We ascend to the surface, the worn steps proving a trial for my tired legs. The gate guard waits by the front door and I notice that the bruise on his head is now fully healed. He pushes open the heavy door and I am instantly blinded.

I blink as I am pulled out of the shadows and into the sunlight. The powerful rays cloud my vision, shocking after so many days spent below ground. I am dimly aware of our direction, recognizing it as the same route I took when escorting Marc and the other prisoners to freedom. Unfortunately, my solo journey will be considerably shorter.

Gradually, the world swims into focus. I first become aware of the chatter of seemingly hundreds of people, all crowded into one place. There is a path cleared for our procession, leading up to the centre of the square. Guards are stationed on all sides of the expansive yard, ever stoic as they keep the way clear from the surging mass of nobility.

My eyes dart from side to side as I am dragged forward; I search wildly for a familiar face. I catch sight of the ladies-in-waiting, many of whom hold lace handkerchiefs delicately to their lips while they stare at me in wide-eyed disbelief. Among them is Hawk Nose, her pointed snout trained directly on me and a knowing look of satisfaction etched across her narrow features.

I tear my eyes away from the crowd and look straight ahead. A scaffold has been raised in the centre of the courtyard, surrounded on all sides by what seems to be every courtier in the City. I vaguely recall walking this path with Meg, clutching her arm and giggling as we shared confidences. Now, I draw my shoulders back and raise my chin as we march, holding onto the small shred of dignity I have left in knowing that my habit of betraying my friends ended on the day I destroyed the library.

The steps to the scaffold shudder from the impact of the guards' heavy tread. When we reach the top, I am pulled roughly into place. Ahead of me is another raised platform, shielded from the afternoon sun by an embroidered, blood-coloured canopy. The King and his advisors are granted the best seat in the house.

The King is in fine form today, swathed in ceremonial robes and with an ostentatious gold crown circling his high forehead. The medals decorating his vest have been polished to a fine sheen and wink boastfully in the bright sunlight. He sits rigid in his seat, positively seething while Griss steps up next to me, joined shortly thereafter by Harmen's ramrod-straight figure and a gold-bedecked herald.

Shadowed between the guards, Harmen and Griss, I stare out across the square, every one of my sore muscles contracted in an effort to make myself appear as tall and solid as possible. I lock my knees and clench my teeth, forcing myself to stop trembling.

The sheer number of people is overwhelming. Members of a sophisticated, genteel faction, all of them shifting and jostling for position as they crane to get a better look at the accused. My eyes flick back and forth over the swell, scanning the upturned faces in a vain effort to locate a friend. The eyes staring back at me are at times blank, curious or horrified, but every person is firmly rooted in place, prepared to watch the show but unwilling to take part.

The King rises slowly, causing the elderly Board members to scramble to their feet. Gradually, the murmurs subside and an eerie silence falls over the crowd. With ceremony, the herald steps to the front of our platform, facing the King and unfurling a parchment in a dramatic flourish. He clears his throat once before projecting his strong voice across the square.

"Kay Knight, commoner. Accused of treason, conspiracy, destruction of crown property, assault, impersonating a noble, obstruction of justice, kidnapping and theft. The prisoner has been found guilty of all crimes and is hereby sentenced to death, by the will of his Majesty, King Francis." His part complete, the herald takes a solemn step back.

My weak knee begins to shake at the prolonged standing and I fight to keep it straight. I glance down at my feet, for the first time noticing the wooden block placed before me. The pierced surface is pocked with dozens of chips and stained with a brown, tacky substance.

"Kay Knight."

I slowly raise my head. The King has risen to his feet, his cold, black eyes boring into mine from his place above the crowd.

"The acts you have committed against the crown and its people are unforgivable. It is with a heavy heart that I must sentence you to a traitor's death." His booming voice drips with benevolence and from the corner of my eye I can see several members of the crowd nodding their heads in grim agreement.

"May you die with a dignity that so eluded you in life," he continues, clearly revelling in this moment. "Wherever you end up, I hope most assuredly that it is a place of peace."

My hands clench into tight fists behind my back as I swallow the urge to spew a litany of curses straight to his remorseless, arrogant face. Instead, I conduct another sweep of the gathered spectators in a last-ditch effort to spot something, anything, that could suggest I'm not alone.

The King lowers himself back into his chair, sitting regally as he nods his assent. My arms are gripped and I am pushed to my knees, crouched above the block.

This is it.

No one is coming.

I fight instinctively when they try to position my neck over the rough surface of the block. Adrenalin courses through my veins, disguising the pain in my back and shoulders as I am wrestled into position. My every muscle is tensed while my heart beats with the desperation of a bird rattling its wings against a cage.

The hum of the crowd rises to a feverish level in my upturned ear. Someone gathers my hair and brushes it to the side, allowing a conspicuously cool breeze to brush the sensitive skin of my neck.

With my eyes trained on the floor of the platform, I spy Harmen's familiar shiny boots. He moves to stand in front of me, exchanging a few words with Griss. Their conversation is lost as I become awash with a high, buzzing noise, feeling nothing but the furious, heavy pounding in my chest.

Something cold touches my neck, lightly. That must be Harmen's axe, testing the placement. Taking one last, deep breath, I ready myself and squeeze my eyes shut. I think of Will, Meg, my parents, my brother, my friends.

Moments pass and I feel nothing. There is no pain, no oblivion. I remain perfectly still, waiting.

After what seems like an eternity, I crack an eye open. The ringing in my ears fades as I fight to focus and bring myself back to the present. From somewhere in the distance I can hear Griss shouting orders and I become aware of the pounding of feet on the platform beneath me. The arm holding me down against the block has slackened and I chance rising back to my knees, blinking in confusion and struggling to take in the scene.

The people in the crowd are pushing against one another, panicked looks on their faces as they stampede back to the Palace. The guards have withdrawn their weapons and are fighting their way through the current of screaming courtiers. Across from me and high above the swelling crowd, I can see the King being hurriedly escorted down from his throne.

A shadow passes over my head and the guards' grip digs painfully into my shoulder. I crane my neck upward, squinting at the massive shape floating slowly across the sky and blocking out the sun. Griss yells something indistinguishable and several guards loose their arrows at the airship. There are more screams from the scattered crowd, lost among the chaos of hundreds of terrified people trampling through the courtyard.

I blink the spots of light from my vision, my head spinning. The great silver airship is now directly overhead and moving lower. I can make out the arrows bouncing harmlessly off its hard exterior and in the recesses of my mind register Griss shouting something about fetching anti-air weapons. I ignore him, my gaze completely focused on the giant hatch attached to the airship's underbelly. It has opened and several ropes have dropped through the hole, dangling around us.

Harmen reacts immediately, jumping off the platform and scurrying back toward the Palace. The guard holding me seems to fare somewhat better, recovering his wits and yanking me to my feet. I stumble, my eyes never leaving the sky. A single, unidentifiable object falls from the open hatch down to the ground and all at once we are enveloped in a thick, choking cloud of smoke.

The unfortunate people still on the ground hack and cough, their panicked footsteps increasing in fervour as they claw their way indoors. My lungs burn and I force myself to take slow, shallow breaths through my nose, thankful that the raised platform allows for a low ceiling of fresh air. I watch as people appear above the ropes and start rappelling down from the airship. The strangers are dressed in dark clothes with black scarves pulled up high over their faces.

"Hold her!" Griss orders from somewhere below me, his voice hoarse among the smoky chaos. I am pulled roughly back toward the platform steps and I dig my heels in, struggling against the guards' grip. Someone grabs my other arm and I thrash, kicking out at them as I fight to stay in place.

The platform reverberates violently in reaction to the airship-rappelers' landing. The invaders advance on us, swords drawn. My bad knee twists painfully and I am dragged further back. One of the guards releases me to unsheathe his sword and swing at the attackers. His thrust is blocked easily and he is promptly thrown from the platform into the cloud of smoke.

I look back up. One of the strangers has reached us, his sharp gaze darting toward me. I instantly recognize the pair of steely grey eyes above his black scarf. He brings his sword up and I duck, throwing myself to the side just as the guard's grip on me loosens and a choked moan escapes his lips. I land painfully on my arm and roll instinctively out of the way of the falling guard. He crashes to the platform, his eyes wide, staring at me in an expression of utter shock as a small line of blood trickles from his mouth.

Someone grasps my arm gently and helps me to my feet. The bonds circling my wrists are cut and I gasp at the sudden sensation of circulation returning to my extremities. All around us, people are rappelling down from the airship, touching down on the platform with a practiced precision and jumping to the smoke-filled ground. The sounds of battle ring out below me, stemming from every direction. From the way the rebels expertly wield their swords, I can guess that these are Will's comrades from his time spent in the Wastelands.

I whirl to face the man behind me, feeling a relieved smile stretch across my bruised face. He pulls his scarf loose, gently wrapping it around my head so my mouth and nose are protected.

"Quite the entrance," I tell him. "I never took you for a showman."

That half-grin. "It's not my show, Runner. It's yours."

Will hands me my father's dagger and throws an arm around me, covering me as we rush down the steps of the platform. We descend into the thinning cloud of smoke, joining Marc at the base of the platform. Marc holds off the guards easily, thrusting and parrying expertly. From here, I realize there is a full-scale battle exploding on all sides of us, airship soldiers engaged with Palace guards in savage fights for their lives.

What the rebels gain in skill they lose in numbers. I turn in place, realizing with a heavy sense of dread that we will soon be overpowered.

"Can you run?" Will yells to me over the din.

"Always," I reply.

He nods grimly, drawing his sword and joining Marc as they fight back to back, forcing a path for me back toward the Palace. Too weak to do much more than clutch my dagger and stick close, I crouch and duck my way over the spilled bodies, averting my eyes from their anguished faces.

The air stings with the lingering effects of the smoke bomb. The battle presses in closer and closer, sending us off route. Someone knocks into me and I fall to my hands and knees, crying out as my bad leg collides with the hard stone path. Will appears at my side instantly, pulling me to my feet while Marc shouts something incomprehensible, his words disappearing into the swelling fight. I gasp again, hissing through the pain, as Will's arm snakes around my back.

There are too many guards. A sea of crimson overwhelms the sparse amounts of black. I can tell Will has noticed as well, by the way his arm tightens around me. This time, I don't notice my injuries, lost amid the sinking sensation of inevitable defeat.

"Where are they?" Will murmurs.

I glance up at him, confused.

At that moment, there is an almighty banging from somewhere within the Palace. My gaze snaps over to the glass walls of the Great Hall. Shouts and hollers echo from inside, rising to a deafening volume until there is a sudden, earth-shattering crash. The beautiful glass walls of the Hall splinter and break, exploding outward as a swell of people spill forth.

My eyes widen at the sight. Common men and women flood the courtyard, roughshod weapons raised savagely as they run into the foray.

Members of the King's guard continue to file out from every corner of the Palace, pooling together in the courtyard and crashing into the wave of rebels like oil meeting water. The air fills with screams and the iron taste of blood.

Our people carry an assortment of weapons, mostly pitchforks and shovels but ranging up to all manner of swords. My eyes search wildly, terrified that at any moment I will witness the death of someone I know.

"In here!" Marc yells, slashing a man and shoving him to the side as he beckons us through an archway and into one of the Palace halls. I stumble on the tiled surface and Will adjusts his grip. I tug my scarf down to breathe in the fresh air while I concentrate on moving forward.

"We need to get her out of here," Will shouts at Marc.

The cavernous halls ring with the sounds of people screaming and running for safety. I am jostled painfully as we make our way against the flow of the crowd, Will's hold tightening as he pulls me forward determinedly.

Eventually, we arrive at the grand staircases. I recognize the formerly beautiful white couches where Vitrola once greeted myself and Will. The pristine furniture now lies trampled and broken.

"Shit, they're coming," Marc curses over his shoulder, looking back down the hall.

"There's a servants' passage over there." I gesture vaguely. "You can stash me in it."

"That's not a bad idea," Marc agrees, looking to Will.

"Absolutely not. I'm not leaving her again." Will shakes his head furiously, his sword tense in his free hand.

"You won't stand a chance against them with me slowing you down," I reason, straightening and standing on shaky legs. "Use your head, Will. I'll be fine—I've made it this far."

"Make up your minds!" Marc's voice is tight, his shoulders bunched as his gaze darts between us and the approaching footsteps.

A growl of frustration tears from Will's throat and he hobbles with me over to the tunnel, gently pulling my arm from around his neck as he helps me into the passage.

"Stay here," he orders. "I mean it."

Obediently, I step around the corner. I catch one last glimpse of his concerned grey eyes before he draws away, back down the hallway where the sounds of battle ring out.

I stand with my back to the wall, quaking unsteadily as I listen to the fight. The riot seems to be coming from all sides of me, echoing off of every nook and cranny.

There is the sound of heavy footsteps behind me and I whip my head around to look over my shoulder, straining to see through the darkness. Silently, I shuffle further into the tunnel, ears perked. I poke my head around the corner, widening my eyes when I see the pair of figures near the dead end.

The King has his back turned to me, his hulking frame stooped in the narrow space. Harmen is with him, hurrying the King along, a short sword clutched in his hand. When the men reach the end of the corridor, the King reaches out, seemingly searching for something in the brickwork before he presses on a protruding bit of stone. To my astonishment, the wall swings inward with surprising force, revealing a darkened passageway beyond.

"Quickly, your Majesty." Harmen ushers the King through the hidden door.

He makes to follow but the King puts out a hand, pushing the Inquisitor back.

"Where do you think you're going?" The King is careful to keep his voice low. "My Palace is overrun with traitors, Harmen. Your duty is to take care of them."

"With all due respect, Sire, I should remain with you. For protection." Harmen speaks uneasily.

I press myself flush against the wall behind me, willing the shadows to swallow me whole. If I didn't know any better, I'd say my parents' murderer is scared. My fingers furl more securely around the hilt of my dagger, my injuries forgotten.

"Don't be a coward. You were my captain of the guard not so long ago, weren't you? Get out there and fight. That's an order." There is a rustling of clothing as the King pushes his way through the narrow pathway. "Harmen?"

"Yes, Sire?"

"The Runner cannot leave this Palace. Make sure she is dead, or don't bother finding me."

"Yes, Sire."

A deafening slam fills my ears as the door swings shut. I wait, counting my breaths while I listen for the echo of Harmen's approaching footsteps. My dagger-wielding hand trembles as adrenalin courses through my veins, readying me and igniting me with a heat I have not felt since the night of the fire.

An eternity passes and finally I hear the slow shuffle of hard-soled boots striking floor. Harmen draws closer and closer to my hiding place, his ragged breaths now reaching my ears. I remain as still as my battered body will allow, my every sense honed in on the ever-lessening distance between us.

A shadow passes my shoulder and I lash out, aiming for his neck.

Harmen reacts quickly, his mouth opening wide in shock as he twists away. I stumble, thrown off balance by my badly overestimated strike. The narrow tunnel keeps me upright, but now I find myself in plain sight of my opponent.

The point of his sword glints in the low light. I use the small space to my advantage and duck down low, throwing myself into his knees as sparks fly overhead from the impact of blade striking stone. We tumble to the ground and I shout out in pain, feeling my back tear as he fights to throw me off him, both of us scrambling for the sword in his outstretched hand.

I swipe blindly with my dagger, lacking the purchase to deliver a blow but managing to distract Harmen for long enough to pin his wrist beneath my knee. He is clutching the hilt of his sword in a vice-like grip and I try fruitlessly to pry his fingers loose, making another wild jab with my dagger.

Blackness, and then a powerful ringing fills my ear, followed by a white-hot pain. I collapse onto the floor, hands clutching my head as Harmen pushes me off him and scrambles to his feet.

I barely regain my senses in time to roll out of the way, yelling out when my back collides with the wall. Harmen spins in place as I push myself up; I stumble in my haste to clear the reach of his blade. I feel the rush of air against my face as I fall back a step, then another.

Even if I could outrun him, this tunnel will eventually end and I'll be trapped against a solid wall.

Or rather, not quite solid.

Harmen also seems to have realized that my options are steadily depleting. His mouth stretches into a tight sneer, his shiny teeth catching the last of the flickering torchlight. He takes his time in planning his next strike, angling his body and preparing to swoop a wide arc.

I take advantage of his exposed side and kick out, connecting solidly with his ribs. He utters a grunt of pain as I turn and sprint toward the dead end, my mind working feverishly to conjure a plan.

There's nowhere to run.

I glance over my shoulder, eyes widening as Harmen hurtles toward me. I sidestep, faltering on my bad leg, and slam into the false wall. My arm stings and I register the sticky feeling of blood trickling down my skin; in the next moment, I release a startled gasp as strong hands wrap themselves around my throat.

Harmen's sword clatters to the ground as he chokes me, his eyes bulging and his teeth gnashing. I struggle desperately in his grip, clawing at his wrists while my vision spots. He dodges the pathetic swipes of my dagger easily, his creepy smile growing wider and tighter with each passing second.

The Inquisitor's face swims before me, morphing from one type of psychosis to another. Before there was the measured sureness of a captain sent to execute my family. Now there is a madman wearing the triumphant look of someone who knows he's already won.

"I should have killed you down in the dungeon," his voice growls near my ear. "Kind of you to grant me the opportunity to correct my mistake."

I grope blindly at the unforgiving stone behind me, searching, unable to utter a sound.

"How disappointing. Five years of waiting for revenge and now you're going to die at my hands. Just like your parents." Harmen's grip turns impossibly tight and I feel my knees crumple. Blackness encroaches on all sides, coaxing me down into the inky abyss. "I've wasted too many chances to kill you, Kay. Not this time."

Not this time.

My palm finds the loose brick and I press down hard, angling my dagger while a mechanical *click* sounds from the secret room behind us.

Harmen's eyes widen as the hidden door springs open and the force hurtles us into the wall. I keep his gaze locked with mine, watching at the moment of impact.

"Another difference between you and me," I rasp. "I only needed one chance to kill you."

He stares at me, confusion and fear written across his face. Gradually, the light dims and he slumps forward, staring blankly at my dagger, buried up to the hilt in his stomach. His hands slip from my neck and fall to his sides, dangling limply as the life leaves his body.

I gradually become aware of my own breathing, the ragged inhales turning into great hacking coughs. I yank my dagger free and slide out from between the Inquisitor and the door, collapsing to my hands and knees. This time there is no cloud of red, no all-encompassing rage to drive me past the point of no return. Instead I feel nothing, only a cold indifference and newfound resolve. Wiping my blood-soaked hand on my ruined tunic, I glance up, looking directly into the blackened entryway to the King's secret tunnel.

I should go back. I should find Will and the others, tell them that the King has come through here.

But he could be long gone by then, vanished into the Wastelands or any number of underground passageways. I have already wasted precious minutes grappling with Harmen; time spent fetching help could mean the difference between the King's escape and his most deserved end.

The shouts and clamour of the fight reverberate in the distance as I make up my mind. I get to my feet and ease my way over to the hidden entrance, averting my eyes from the crumpled body of the former Inquisitor. If the King escapes justice tonight, then this will all have been for nothing.

Clutching the dagger tightly in my shaking hand, I take a single step forward into the darkness.

chapter 42

The wall is cold, rough under my outstretched fingers. The darkness presses in on all sides, but through the gloom I can make out a weak, flickering light. I keep my eyes trained straight ahead as I cautiously force one foot in front of another, placing them gingerly on the stairs and trying to keep my unsteady steps as silent as possible. With one hand I clutch my dagger against an aching rib and with the other I lean on the wall, trailing my fingers against it for balance.

The battle fades behind me as I sink deeper and deeper below the Palace. I attempt to orient myself as I descend, trying and failing to gauge the distance. I should have guessed that the King would have an alternate escape plan in case of uprisings; likely, this tunnel has been in place for more than a hundred years. I kick myself for not having thought to seek it out beforehand. This is exactly the type of information I should have brought back to Will.

At the thought, I suddenly startle; I just left Will and Marc completely in the lurch. When they come back and find me missing, what will they think? I didn't even take a moment to leave a trail. Stupid, Kay. I stop in my tracks, for the briefest of moments considering going back up. What madness is this, voluntarily returning belowground after finally making it back up to the surface?

If the past days have taught me anything, it's that my madness knows no limits.

As if acting of their own accord, my legs awaken and continue to lead me down the stairs. My fingers furl more securely around the hilt of my dagger, but I am all too aware that I am hardly in any shape for hand-to-hand combat. My left knee trembles uncontrollably, my back is freshly torn from the fight up above, and the time spent with limited food and water has caused my vision to swim and my breath to hitch in my throat. It was blind chance that I defeated Harmen but I would be a fool to think I could be so lucky a second time.

I utter a silent prayer to the gods of fortune and combat, then offer up a plea to the protector of the underworld as an afterthought. Tonight, the King will pay.

Finally, my foot hits the bottom of the stairs and I find myself in a low-ceilinged hallway. The stone walls cast eerie shadows, their bumpy surfaces appearing razor-sharp in the weak torchlight. I pause momentarily, listening intently before I take a step forward, still trailing my fingers for balance. The tunnel seems to curve gradually to my right and I hug the wall as I sidle along, fighting to keep my breaths shallow and my footsteps light.

The faint glow up ahead intensifies as I move down the path. My heart is thumping so loudly I can almost hear it echoing off the stone walls surrounding me. After what seems like an eternity of breathless silence, I finally reach the end of the tunnel and a room comes into view. I press myself against the wall and wait, ears perked for any sounds coming from within. Hearing nothing, I lean cautiously around the arched entranceway, letting my eyes adjust to the darkness of the space beyond.

When I spy no movement, I wipe my sweaty and bloodstained palms on my thighs and adjust my grip on the hilt of my dagger. Steeling my breath, I hold my weapon upright and slowly ease around the corner.

The room is dim, lit only by a few scattered torches. It is completely bare but for a couple of low beds pushed against one wall and an assortment of wooden trunks resting opposite. I'd wager this bunker has been set up in preparation for a lengthy stay.

At the furthest end of the room, I can dimly make out the continuation of the tunnel. Feeling exposed, I creep across the bunker toward the gaping maw. The unwavering darkness up ahead ebbs ever closer and I feel all of my senses on high alert for any disturbances.

Finally reaching the lip of the tunnel, I place one hand on the archway and peer into the gloom. There is nothing: not the faint glow of torchlight, nor the echo of a footstep retreating down the passage. Holding my breath, I cautiously take a step inside.

At once, a gasp of pain escapes my lips and I stagger back.

The point of a sword is lodged in my shoulder. As I watch, it is slowly withdrawn and I marvel in wide-eyed fascination at the patch of blood that forms. I look up, taking another step back as the King emerges from the shadows. His broad form slips free of the passage, trapping me in the bunker.

I lurch backward, clutching my injured arm. My fingers come away covered in blood. I stare past my blood-soaked hand and up at the King, tall and imposing as he moves purposely toward me, the red-tipped sword grasped tightly in his fist.

"I might have known you would find me down here." His pupil-less eyes are cold, bulging wide and filled with fury. "You couldn't leave well enough alone, could you?"

I stumble on my weak leg and my back smacks hard against a wall. I stretch out my arm and grapple madly for the entrance, wincing when I find it out of reach. The King glances over at the rust-coloured stain my blood-drenched fingers leave on the stone, licking his fleshy lips.

"Why won't you just *die* already?" he snarls. "I can't understand it. How is it that an ignorant commoner has come to be the greatest bane of my existence?" He adjusts the sword in his hand, levelling the deadly tip at me. "Tell me, Runner. What do I have to do in order to finally be rid of you?"

My eyes flick down and up again. "My family is dead because of you."

His nostrils flare, the ends of his grey moustache pulling tight across his cheeks. "You will join them."

"It doesn't matter," I tell him. "You can kill me, but I promise you that it won't make a bit of difference. The people have revolted; they don't want you anymore. Get used to this tomb, Francis. It is the only place you are welcome." Behind my back, I grip my dagger in a trembling hand.

The point of the sword rotates at my throat but I keep my eyes trained on his, directing every ounce of hate and pain within me into his soulless eyes.

"Insolent peasant," he rasps.

I note with satisfaction that some of the colour has drained from his face.

"You don't realize what it is you have done." His deep voice is strained. "You are ignorant of this world. The people need a leader. Without me, they are *nothing*. You have unleashed a roving pack of mindless drones on this city, and sooner or later they will turn on each other; it is only a matter of time."

"You misunderstand me." I grimace and clutch more tightly at my shoulder, ignoring the sensation of something running between my fingers. "They will have a leader—it just won't be you." I draw a breath, gathering my strength. "You have been revealed for who you truly are: a failure. You're a heartless coward, hiding in the cellar of a ruined Palace. Your own people have cast you out and will kill you on sight. This is what your cruelty and selfishness has wrought. You have no one to blame for your downfall but yourself."

An inhuman cry escapes his lips and he lunges at me, arcing the sword toward my heart. I bring my dagger up and parry his blade, sidestepping him and diving to the ground. He stumbles, tripping over my flayed legs before he rights himself and stabs downward madly.

I turn onto my back and parry again, bringing my elbow up and smashing it into his cheekbone. My shoulder tears painfully at the movement and I roll away, desperately trying to scramble out from under him.

"You bitch." He staggers back, recovers quickly and swipes again, raking the sword across my side.

I kick out, connecting with something solid as I fight to get back on my feet. My hands lose purchase on the slick stone and I switch tactics, trying to use my back as leverage against the wall in order to rise. I look up to see the King limping back in my direction, his sword raised and glinting in the dim light.

I barely manage to duck out of the way before he lashes out; dodging, I feel an unmistakable rush of air against my bare arm. Bringing my weapon across the floor, I summon every last ounce of strength I have left and thrust the pointed end of the dagger into the King's ankle.

He howls in pain, clutching his foot in one hand and hobbling a couple of steps away from me. Now weaponless, I scrabble against the floor, using my one uninjured arm to try and push up onto my feet.

Across the room, I see him grasp the hilt of my dagger and wrench it from his leg, a savage yell tearing from his throat. There is the sound of metal striking stone as he hurls my paltry weapon away from him and whirls back to face me. He takes a shuddering step forward, a river of blood dripping freely from his ankle as he drags the useless foot across the floor.

I feel my back press against the unforgiving stone wall and will myself to stand, fighting a surge of panic as the energy ebbs from my body. I begin to feel lightheaded from the loss of blood and shake my head to clear it, managing to register the image of the King, hunched, his fine ceremonial robes torn and stained, stalking heavily toward me. His face is twisted, the blood-covered sword poised and ready.

This time, I truly am out of luck.

"*Die*, Runner." The sword levels with my throat and I shut my eyes, awaiting the final blow.

"*Wait.*"

Time freezes. I ease my eyes open, first noticing the point of the sword inches from my neck, and then a stranger standing behind the King. A tall, shadowy figure has just emerged from the far tunnel.

No one moves. My heart thuds heavily in my chest and I have the clarity to realize each beat is leaking more of my life force out of my wounds.

"Megra?" The King is the first to break the silence. His sword stays trained on me as he rotates slightly, stumbling on his injured leg. "What are you doing here?"

"I've come for you, Father," she says calmly, moving further into the room. Torchlight drenches her, illuminating her slim frame so that she appears almost otherworldly.

I clutch my shoulder, drawing shallow breaths.

Meg is dressed in pants and a tunic, her coal-black hair pulled back from her face and woven into a tight braid. In her hand she clutches a sword, long and elegant and gleaming brilliantly in the flickering light. Her eyes dart to me momentarily before they come back to rest on the King.

The blade at my throat lowers until it scrapes against the ground. "I don't understand," the King sputters. "I thought they kidnapped you. Did you escape?"

His voice trails off as realization slowly dawns.

"You're...with *them*?" he finally chokes out, visibly quaking with rage.

She shakes her head. "No, Father. They're with me."

The King whips back around, staring at me in disbelief. I loll my head against the wall to look up, shrugging my one good shoulder, apologetically. "I told you we had a leader."

Meg's face remains impassive as he turns to face her. "It's over, Father. The time has come for you to step aside. Your reign has ended."

His whole body begins to tremble with anger. From my position on the ground, I can see his knuckles flexing as he grips his sword even tighter.

"I don't have to kill you," Meg continues. There is the barest trace of emotion in her measured tone, but she straightens her slender shoulders and continues. "You can surrender, support the new policies that I will be instituting and live out the rest of your days in the Wastelands. I cannot pardon your crimes, Father, but as a daughter I wish to show you an act of mercy."

"*You* wish to show *me* mercy?" he snarls. "I am your *father*. You will do as *I* say. Now, stand down."

She shakes her head, slowly. "I am afraid I cannot let you leave. Lower your sword and you will still have a chance of redeeming yourself."

"I am the *King*," he shouts, his great, booming voice echoing off the walls of the stone bunker. "Do you understand me? This is *my* city and neither I, nor it, will be brought down by a couple of common…*girls*." He whirls on me and raises his sword in the air, arching it toward my throat.

"*Father, don't!*"

I gasp and jerk back against the wall, my shoulders slamming painfully into the rock behind me.

The King's eyes bulge and his mouth drops open in surprise. My gaze darts from his face to his raised sword, watching wide-eyed as it clatters to the ground.

The King glances down, touches his fingers lightly to his chest, then brings them up to look at the red coating. His dark eyes glaze over and come back up to look at me, indignation written across his face.

He slumps down to his knees on the floor, rocking once before he pitches face first onto the stone. A heavy coating of blood oozes from a wound in his back and drips onto the floor.

Eventually, I manage to tear my eyes away from the King and bring them back to Meg.

She stands a step behind him, her sword lowered impassively. She stares down at her father's body, a look of sadness and grim determination etched across her elegant features.

"Meg?" I rasp.

The spell is broken and she looks up, recognition dawning. She sheathes her sword and moves toward me, delicately stepping over the King's splayed legs before lowering herself into a crouch.

"Gods, Kay. Are you sure that you're alive?"

Relief ebbs through my body and I laugh, immediately regretting it when the action tugs at my shoulder wound.

"I can't believe you're here," I say, when I have recovered my breath.

"I figured he would try to come through this way," she says, anticipating my next question and relieving me of having to speak more than I have to. "I came alone because I thought I might have a chance of reasoning with him." She glances back toward his fallen figure. "I should have known better."

"You saved my life," I tell her.

A sad smile tugs at her lips. "I suppose that makes us even."

"I'm so sorry. About all of it."

She shakes her head furiously. “You don’t have anything to apologize for. Will explained everything.” One cool hand comes up to my cheek, feeling marvellous against the hot, flaming skin. “You went through so much in order to protect me. You believed in me when no one else would. I owe you everything.”

I grin, feeling my bruises pull against the tender skin. “A true lady is loyal to her queen.”

A sudden spasm of pain shudders through me and I clutch my shoulder, grimacing. Meg makes a low tutting noise in her throat and gently helps manoeuvre my uninjured arm around her neck, then eases me to my feet.

“We should get you somewhere safe,” she says, looking to the tunnel she emerged from, back toward the City.

I shake my head. “No, we need to go up to the Palace. Will is still there. I need to find him.”

She shakes her head but dutifully turns us toward the stairs. “Each of you is as impossible as the other. You should have seen Will when we received word about your arrest; I thought he would tear the entire city down brick by brick until he brought you back.”

We move down the tunnel back toward the stairs, our progress slow as Meg helps my feet find purchase on each of the steps.

“What do you think we’ll discover when we get up there?” I ask as we ascend, listening for the sounds of the battle above.

I can’t see much in the darkness, but I imagine my friend’s face scrunched up in serious thought. “I suppose we will find the new world.”

chapter 43

Meg shoves the hidden door open, grunting as she struggles to support me with her free arm. Together, we make our way through the servants' passageway and back toward the entrance where I last left Will. There is the faint clatter of swords reverberating out in the main hallway; the battle seems to have receded.

We reach the entry to the main corridor and, with Meg's help, I manage to prop myself up against the wall. She peers out into the foyer, looking left and right.

"Do you see anyone?" I ask.

"No. I can hear fighting back toward the courtyard, though." She draws her head back in, biting her lip at the sight of me clutching my shoulder and breathing heavily. "For gods' sake, Kay. You're an absolute disaster."

"What else is new." I grit my teeth.

"I need to get help." She checks that her sword is secure in its scabbard and makes to step into the hall again.

"Don't leave me here." I cringe as the words fall out of my mouth. My hand is tacky with blood where it grips my shoulder and my left leg trembles. Weaponless and gradually losing the ability to focus, I'm terrified at the idea of being abandoned once again in a small space.

Her brow softens. "It will be fine, I promise. I'll be right back."

My leg gives out, making me sink to the floor. Meg rushes to catch me as I fall and eases me down gently.

"I can't take you with me, Kay," she says softly, brushing the matted strands of hair off my forehead. "Look at you, you can barely move."

"Right. You're right." I nearly choke on the words, the sensation of being touched so tenderly overwhelming me after days of cruelty. My vision swims again and I blink forcefully. "I understand. I'll be all right."

"Yes, you will." She forces my eyes to hers. Her expression is calm and determined and I feel myself trusting her implicitly. "You're still here. You're still with us. Just hold on a little bit longer; we're almost home."

I nod, my head feeling loose on my neck. I let it fall backward, reclining against the tunnel wall and allowing my eyes to flutter closed. I am suddenly so incredibly tired.

There is a stinging slap against my cheek and I start, my eyes flying open.

"Do *not* fall asleep," Meg scolds and I nearly laugh. "Do you understand me?"

"Yes, my Queen," I murmur.

"I mean it, Kay. You need to do this for me, understand? Stay here and count to one hundred. No sleeping under *any* circumstances." I hear her sword being unsheathed and shoo her away with my good arm.

"One," I say, for her benefit. "Two. Three."

Her footsteps echo down the hall and I settle back into my reclined position. "Four...Five...." The stone wall is lovely and cool against my injured shoulder.

I have lost my place in my counting when I hear someone sprinting in my direction. Heavy footsteps reverberate down the hallway, a familiar string of curses falling in their wake.

"*There* you are." He sounds furious. "What part of 'stay here' did you fail to understand?"

"You're not in charge of me," I mumble. I feel Will's warm arms around me, gently easing me to my feet, and I groan when my shoulder wound pulls. "Watch it."

"When did *that* happen?" he exclaims, exasperated. "Gods' sake, where were you?"

"You ask a lot of questions."

He taps my cheeks lightly and I grunt, forcing my eyes open. His gaze bores into mine, his expression concerned.

"Stay with me, Kay. It's time to go." His grip tightens around my waist. "Can you walk?"

"I can run," I tell him, shuffling my feet forward as I concentrate on matching his stride. "I'm the Runner."

"That you are." I think I hear a hint of amusement in his voice. "Let's concentrate on the walking for now, though." I expect him to steer us toward the outer gates and frown in confusion when instead he points us back in the direction of the courtyard.

"Don't we need to leave?" I ask. Walking helps me focus and my head begins to clear.

"No, we don't." Will glances down at me meaningfully, a tired half-grin tugging at the side of his mouth.

My brow furrows and I concentrate on listening for any signs of the fight. There is no sound but for our own footsteps against the tiled floor and a distant murmuring up ahead. Slowly, realization begins to dawn and I look back up Will, questioning.

His smile broadens, his grey eyes weary but satisfied. Something catches in my throat and I direct my gaze forward again, my heart swelling as we draw closer and closer to the courtyard. From the corners of my vision, I register the unfortunate fallen. They lie crumpled on the floor, pools of blood stagnating beneath them. I avoid looking into their poor faces, offering up a silent prayer to the god of the underworld instead.

Glass litters the ground where the pristine walls bordering the courtyard used to stand. The image of hundreds of commoners shattering the glass and pouring into the yard with their weapons raised would seem like something of a dream if it wasn't for the evidence lying directly in front of me. The yard is still crowded with rebels, men and women standing bloodied and dirtied. Their weapons are lowered and they are all looking expectantly toward the centre of the square. The black-clad soldiers from the airship stand among the commoners, waiting patiently.

Will manoeuvres me toward the back of the throng, where earlier (could it have been mere hours ago?) I stood flanked by guards with my hands bound, awaiting the walk to my death. As we move around the crowd, I catch sight of something impossible and dig my heels in to get a better look, halting Will.

The Palace guards are still alive, standing unbothered in the spaces between the rebels, their weapons also lowered as they stare toward the execution platform. More than that, the noblemen and women have begun to file out of the Palace's corridors and gather in the courtyard. Courtiers, their fine clothes and perfectly coiffed hair askew, waiting timidly among the commoners.

"I know," Will whispers into my ear. "Come on."

I let him lead me into the crowd. Commoners and courtiers step aside when they notice me, giving us a wide berth.

We stop moving forward when the scaffold comes into view. I sag against Will, thankful for the break. The shadows have grown long in the open space, jagged in places where the sun reflects broken glass. I stare up at the wooden platform, my eyes trailing Meg as she ascends the steps, unaccompanied.

She strides smoothly across the scaffold, centering herself, then turns to face the gathered nobles, servants, rebels, soldiers and guards. The waning sun glints magnificently off the metal inlaid in her leather vest and scabbard, illuminating her. The crowd falls silent as she widens her stance and raises her hands.

"Friends!" Her voice rings out; she's clear and poised where her father was loud and forceful. "Today, we have won ourselves a great victory. From today forth, every citizen of this city will have the freedom to choose their own path. We have taken back our humanity from the clutches of a tyrant and returned it to our citizens. This is our triumph! It is through our blood and our tears that this great gift was extracted and I, for one, will never forget that."

I think back to the fallen bodies littering the Hall. To the heartbroken look on Meg's face as her father fell. To my parents and brother. To Edmun. All perished in the name of the City.

"We won today because we are survivors. Humans have *always* been survivors. Two hundred years ago we exploited our gifts, and in retaliation,

Nature turned its back on us. Yet, still we remain. When we should have perished, we instead persisted. We adapted, we changed. We accepted our new earth and respected its power. We broke down to our most basic roles and cobbled together a society. We worked together and we *survived*. Now, that time has passed, and we must enter a new era of humanity."

She draws her sword from her scabbard and holds it up, turning the weapon so that golden rays bounce off the polished blade.

"This new era will not be ruled by violence or force. The new city will be a home where our citizens have a voice and are heard. Today, the people have spoken."

She lays her sword down at her feet, standing back and thrusting her chin into the air, looking around at all of us.

"I will lead you, but I need you to help me. I need you to work for us, to fight for us, to trust in us as a species. As courtiers and commoners, we were a divided people. Together, we are stronger. We are wiser. We are *humans*." Her voice rises in a mighty bellow and a cry rips from my throat, joining the crescendo of whoops and cheers as person after person drops their weapon and hails Meg.

I feel Will's hand squeezing mine tightly and return the gesture with fervour, all of my pain and tiredness forgotten.

"There are dark days behind us, my friends, but also, dark days ahead. Today, we have won a battle and tomorrow we will fight the war. It won't be easy; there are many trials that we have yet to pass. I cannot promise you that there will be no more suffering, but I *can* promise that the struggles we face will not be faced by one faction alone. We are a singular people, with the same rights and the same goals. If you fight, I fight. Your needs are my needs. Your heartaches are my heartaches. We are one. Rest easy knowing that our unity shall be our greatest weapon in the days to come!"

The air around us sparks with promise as every person gathered in the bloody courtyard raises their voices to the Queen, our shouts joining together to create one earth-shattering cry of triumph. I taste salt on my lips, my heart beating so loudly I feel as though it may burst through my chest.

I think of my parents and Frye, feeling a great weight evaporate from my shoulders. We've done it. Their deaths were not in vain. Their sacrifice was the ember fanned into flame.

There is a great reverberation through the crowd as Meg lifts her fist into the air, standing tall and strong amid our acclaim. Not so long ago she was a naive princess, locked away behind the walls of a glass palace. Now, she has emerged and proven herself a true queen. She has inspired hope and peace in the hearts of a broken people. She has shown a sense of honesty, justice and courage in the face of doubt. For the first time in my life, I believe in our monarchy.

"We should go." Will's breath is warm in my ear as he shouts over the din. "You need to get to the infirmary."

"I don't want to miss this!" I yell back.

Meg's voice rises over the fervour. "I ask now that you return to your homes and rest. Tomorrow, I will send word of how we will fairly distribute the City's wealth. As a sign of good faith, I invite you to visit the Palace's storerooms and take what supplies you need for yourself and your family. Thank you, friends. There is much to be done, but for now we must pay our respects to our fallen and mourn for our dead. Stay here if you can assist, or return to your families if you must. I must see to one final matter." Meg salutes to another round of cheers and strides back down the steps of the platform.

"There, she's done. Come on, now." Will nudges me and secures a hold around my waist, turning me back toward the Palace. The movement jolts me and awakens my injuries but I barely notice them, still buzzing with the heady enthusiasm over what has just taken place.

The crowd parts to let us through. We are halfway across the yard when someone appears at my side, laying her hand gently on my back.

"It's to the infirmary with you, then, is it? About time."

With Meg's help, Will manages to steer me through the gathered rebels and soldiers, all of whom offer me an encouraging smile or a thankful hand to my friends. My vision begins to swim as we pass through the shattered wall and turn toward Will's office. Miraculously, this wing appears to have been untouched by the battle.

"Right then, here we go. Easy does it."

A simple cot covered in white linen appears in front of me. It is the most beautiful thing I have ever seen.

With my friends' help I manage to lie down, curling into a fetal position on the bed and breathing in the scent of fresh laundry.

Will busies himself mixing some concoction while Meg crouches down next to me, smoothing the knotted hair back from my face.

"You were wonderful," I tell her.

Meg's eyes sparkle with a new light. "So were you."

"You should get back out there." I gesture to the door. "Your people need you."

She shakes her head, firmly. "You need me." She glances up at Will. "Will, could you go out there and start organizing the wounded? Once Kay is asleep, you can stitch her up; I'll stay here with her until then."

"All right. Here, Red. Drink this."

A warm mug is pressed into my hand and I drink greedily. Almost immediately, I feel my aches begin to ease.

"Better?" Will asks.

I nod, blinking sleepily at him, unable to wipe the smile from my face. He chuckles softly at my expression and brushes my cheek with his thumb before he leaves, closing the door of the infirmary softly behind him.

My mind is still a flurry of questions, despite the effects of the medicine.

"Where did the airship come from?" I ask.

Meg gives an indelicate snort of laughter. "That was all Will. He convinced the airfield soldiers to join our cause some time ago, and they lifted the ship this morning."

"How industrious," I murmur, marvelling at Will's ability to surprise me.

"He has quite the aptitude for battle," Meg remarks, stroking my arm absently. "I was thinking I should give him command of the army. I would like to take a negotiation tactic with the Wastelanders, but we could use someone like him if we had to fight. What do you think?"

I blink, wondering what I missed. Of course, Will would make a fantastic commander, but I am only just now registering the fact that by killing the King, we have taken on a war. The thought terrifies me but Meg, with all the responsibility on her slim shoulders, seems to be taking it in stride, already soldiering toward the next phase.

"I think that is a great idea," I tell her, meaning it.

The pillow is cool and soft beneath my cheek and I begin to slip into a comfortable darkness. There is the lightest brush of Meg's lips against my hot forehead and I sigh in contentment.

"Thank you. For everything," she whispers.

I murmur my own thanks and nestle snugly into the clean sheets, finally home.

chapter 44

My shoulder hisses and spits, spewing fire. I scream and thrash on the bed, my hands flailing blindly and sometimes connecting with one of the faceless figures hovering over me.

Someone places a hand on my brow and I bat them away. My every sinew calls out for escape, urges me to run, but my traitorous limbs feel strangely heavy and weak. My legs kick and tangle in the sheets, dampening them with my continual sweating.

I exist between fits of terrifying consciousness and burning darkness. From somewhere in the recesses of my mind, memories stir. I fight to grasp onto them while I sleep, slowly piecing myself back together. I wake, and for the briefest of moments I am aware of Meg's voice, or of Will's touch. I remember my friends, our fight. I remember why I have to wake up.

Gradually, the fear recedes and the haze clears. I briefly register someone spooning food and water into my mouth, rubbing my back when I cough and murmuring kind words as I drift back to sleep.

When I finally find the strength to ease my eyes open, the light is almost piercing in its brightness. I try again and eventually, the room swims into focus.

I am still in the bed Meg tucked me into, though I am clean and someone has changed my clothes. White, breezy curtains are tucked around my cot, blocking my view of the infirmary. I try to raise myself into a sitting position and groan when my shoulder protests. Collapsing back onto the soft cushions, I ease the neck of my shift down, poking at a thick, padded bandage before I examine the rest of my body. A cursory check reveals that my entire torso has been swathed in linen bandages but my various bruises have already begun to fade. I throw the covers aside and find that my left knee has also been wrapped heavily and is propped up on a cushion.

I hear the curtain being pulled back and look up. Will steps through, his eyes widening when he sees me looking at him. A smile breaks out over his face, both sides of his mouth lifting simultaneously.

"You're awake," he says simply, keeping his voice low. There must be more patients outside.

"I think so."

He sinks onto the edge of my bed and helps me sit up, offering a glass of water once I'm comfortable.

We sit in companionable silence while I drink; at some point I realize that Will has taken hold of my hand. A small part of me wishes to pull back, but I remain still, content to just have him with me, alive and whole.

"How are you feeling?" he asks, eventually.

I sigh contentedly. "The best I've been in days."

"I'm glad to hear it. Some people have been extremely concerned about you."

"Some people?" I tilt my head, raising an eyebrow. "Not you?"

"Not for a moment. After everything you've been through, I refused to believe that you'd be taken down by anything as ordinary as a fever." He smirks but I notice the unsightly shadows bordering his grey eyes.

"So long as I have your vote of confidence, Will Cain, I shall remain standing," I tease.

He laces his fingers more securely with mine and squeezes my hand tightly.

"How long was I out?" I ask, wrinkling my brow as I try to remember.

"Five days," he replies. "I had to stitch up your shoulder and parts of your back, so you're going to feel some tenderness back there."

I grimace, suddenly remembering the ugly network of scars that will surely mark my body forever. Deep in the gaol, it didn't matter, but out here it is difficult to keep at bay the anger I feel, knowing the King's cruelty will always be a part of my skin.

"You'll be scarred, yes."

I start at the sound of Will's voice, for a moment thinking I have spoken my thoughts aloud. His thick brows are lowered and he looks directly into my eyes, his gaze determined.

"Don't think of them as punishment: let them be a symbol of what you've overcome."

I think back to the sight of Will's own scarred back, the taut skin riddled with his father's hateful lessons. When I see Will's scars, I don't see his weakness; I see his strength. That is what my own marks will be for me.

I nod. "Thank you. For coming back."

"Kay, I…" He looks down at our intertwined fingers and back up at me. "I'm sorry that I didn't come sooner."

Something constricts in my chest and I tug my hand free, avoiding his gaze. "We don't have to talk about it."

"You have to understand, I never wanted to leave you down there. As soon as we received word of your arrest, Meg and I set about trying to rescue you."

I can hear the urgency in his voice, but I still can't bring myself to look at him, instead concentrating on picking at the bandage circling my knee.

The horrible feeling of isolation creeps up on me. Left to rot in that dungeon, dragged back and forth between a cell and a torture chamber, seeing no one but my tormentor until I was finally, mercifully granted execution. The scars may not permit me to forget the experience, but gods help me, I'm going to try anyway.

"I was implicated as a conspirator as soon as they caught you," Will continues. "I couldn't go near the Palace. They closed the gates and increased security. It wasn't even safe to step out into the streets—the King had his guards combing every square inch of the City in search of Meg."

I pick more furiously at the bandage. "It's fine, Will, really. I understand."

"I don't." His large hand comes down on top of mine, ceasing my fidgeting. "I put you in danger; I broke your trust. You should hate me."

"It's not your fault, what happened." I finally manage to drag my eyes up to him. "I'm not angry. Not anymore."

The muscles in his jaw flex. "I should have protected you. I should have been there."

"I didn't want you to. What I wanted was for you to finish what we started." I hold his gaze with mine, wanting to be as clear as possible. "And you did, Will. So don't think for a moment that you ever let me down. Nothing could be further from the truth."

The relief that crosses his strong features tugs at my heart. I know what it is to feel a burden lift from your shoulders, and I am glad to help him alleviate some of his lingering guilt.

"Besides," I say, remembering the words he said to me on a rooftop, long ago, "it's difficult to be angry, when I'm so impressed."

He smiles in that small way and leans in toward me.

I stiffen, but he simply peels back the bandage on my shoulder and begins to examine my stitches, prodding gently.

"The dramatics were quite unlike you," I tell him, registering how close our faces are. "Waiting until the eleventh hour and then showing up with airships. You really know how to make a girl sweat."

He laughs lightly as he replaces my bandage. "We had to hold off until they brought you above ground. I was afraid I wouldn't be able to get to you otherwise."

"I never doubted you for an instant." I allow a trace of sarcasm to slip into my tone.

"Your execution provided the ideal opportunity to attack. You managed to get the King and his advisors, together with all the highest-ranking courtiers, gathered together out in the open. We couldn't have asked for a more perfect setup."

"Ah, yes. You have my natural ability to draw a crowd to thank for that."

His smile disappears as his brow furrows. His eyes scan my face carefully, as though searching for something.

"What is it?" I ask.

"I can't believe how close I came to losing you."

"Will..."

"You're everything to me, Kay," he interrupts me, and my mouth snaps closed; I bite down hard on this inside of my cheek. "When you left me in that alley, it was as though some part of myself had been torn suddenly away. Then, when I heard you were arrested..." He shakes his head as his jaw clenches. "I've had some horrible experiences, but none of them compare to what I felt when you were taken from me."

I stare at him, waiting.

"I can't imagine my life without you in it."

"Why are you telling me this?" I whisper, feeling my heart twist in my chest.

"I'm sorry, I know I've never had...a soft touch," he says clumsily. "Please, just let me get through this."

I nod, dumbly.

"I've tried to make up for my past mistakes." He clears his throat and starts again. "This rebellion became an obsession and—if I'm being completely honest—it was more to me than just a cause." He tilts his head up, imploring me to understand. "It was also a way to redeem myself. To make up for everything I've done wrong."

There's a sentiment I can understand.

"I used you, Kay," he continues, speaking quickly. "I put your life in danger so I could further my plans. You were always my greatest ally and I let my own issues get in the way of us trusting each other. When I think back to how different things could have been..." He runs a hand over his scruffy head, his voice breaking. "I could have kept you from getting hurt."

I reach forward, slipping my hand around the back of his neck and forcing his gaze into mine, barely noticing the pain in my shoulder when it pulls at the movement.

"Listen to me," I tell him firmly. "I am here. You are here. The City is still standing. The past might be a part of who we are, but it doesn't define us. What has happened will make us stronger, will make us better." I draw back. "We've been hurt but we aren't broken."

"I love you," he says, simply.

My heart neglects its beat.

"I always have, since I first spoke to you in my father's library. I don't deserve your forgiveness, Kay, let alone your love. Frankly, I think you would be better off without me." He takes a breath. "I know I've probably ruined my chance to be with you, but I thought I lost you once already and..." He trails off, his grey eyes searching my face as he gently pushes a strand of hair back behind my ear. "I just needed you to know."

I bite my lip, studying him. My sore arm lifts to caress his bearded cheek, slowly moving up to smooth the worried lines between his thick brows.

After a moment, a smile slowly spreads over my face, echoing the cautious lift at the side of his mouth.

Wordlessly, he cups my chin with his hand and brings his mouth down on mine, kissing me deeply. I feel no pain as I wrap my arms around him, drawing him as close as my battered body will allow, fitting perfectly against him like a brick to mortar.

When we draw apart, we are both grinning crazily at each other.

"I love you, too," I tell him plainly. "You're it for me, Will."

He kisses me again, pushing the unruly curls back from my face.

"I'm so glad you're here," he whispers, pressing his forehead against mine.

"I thought you weren't worried about me?"

He shakes his head. "All I can do is try not to worry. Gods know that you're always going to do exactly what you please, regardless."

"I don't know about that." I roll my shoulder back, grimacing. "I've been thinking lately that there might be something to your philosophy of taking a more careful approach to problems."

His brows shoot up in surprise. "Is that so?"

"Don't get me wrong," I say, quickly. "I still think you take entirely too long to act. Luckily, you have me to push you in the right direction."

"I don't know if 'push' is the right word. Perhaps 'bully' is more accurate."

"Regardless of all that, I can't deny that your overly complicated and meticulously organized rebellion completely worked." I grasp his hand. "You did it, Will."

"*We* did it." His grip tightens. "The people have rallied behind Meg, and it's all thanks to you. It was you who saw Meg's potential to be queen. Your intuition led to us taking back the City while keeping the monarchy intact." He prods my leg gently. "You saved lives. I hope you realize that."

I have to look away from him for a few moments, swallowing the lump rising in my throat. Meg. I am so incredibly proud of her, so grateful for the sacrifices she made in order to free us. My heart constricts in my chest at the thought of my queen, scarcely believing that I can also consider her my friend.

Eventually, I am able to speak. "What are we going to do now? I've never really thought past this part."

He chortles softly. "Meg has everything pretty well in hand. Her first act as Queen was to abolish the separate sectors."

"No more Court and Commons?" I have imagined this moment countless times, but now that it has finally happened, I find myself unable to comprehend the change

"That's right."

I shake my head, still disbelieving. "What else did I miss?"

"The people injured during the Runner's Rebellion are being cared for here at the Palace, and the dead have been buried with full honours."

"Wait, what was that?" I blink.

"The Runner's Rebellion." He laughs at my shocked expression. "It's the name we've given to a great historical event. You've been absent for quite a while, Red. You may find that people regard you a little differently now."

"Different, how?"

"You're a hero." He says it as though it's the most obvious thing in the world. "How do you think we finally managed to persuade the commoners to take up arms and storm the Palace? News of your arrest stirred something within people. Word spread about how you had infiltrated the Palace and openly defied the King. You inspired them."

I fall back against the pillow, staring blankly at my bandaged knee. "This is mad."

"Now, don't go getting a big head," he mock-scolds. "There's still a lot to be done. Queen Megra has ordered that she be informed the minute you wake up. In truth, I could be tempting a charge of high treason for keeping you to myself for so long."

"What a risk-taker you are," I tease before he pulls me to him again.

chapter 45

My breath hitches in my throat, choked by the pelting sand and the pure exhilaration of the run. Adrenalin courses through my veins, feeding my limbs and heart with all the nourishment I could ever need. I race onward, delighting in the feeling of a solid roof beneath my feet and the newfound strength in my knee, mostly healed after an exhaustive regime of salves and exercises prescribed by Will.

The roof ends and I throw myself into the air, closing my eyes and grinning at the sensation of hot desert air beating against my skin. After the days spent trapped belowground, even the faultless glass walls of the Palace feel restrictive. It is only here, flying high above the City streets, that I am truly free. When I land on the next roof, I pause barely a moment, pushing myself harder, running faster and faster until I feel my lungs and heart will burst.

Rays of setting sun bounce off the Palace's glass spire, nearly blinding me with orange and yellow light. I race toward it, relying on my instincts and memory to guide me safely to my friends. Shouts and the sounds of celebration rush up to greet me, the bells of the coronation chiming endlessly from the abbey and calling every member of the City into the courtyard for the feast.

I slow and stop on the final roof, taking a few tentative steps toward the ledge, shoulders heaving as I struggle to catch my breath. From my vantage point, I can see down into the Palace courtyard, already teeming with guests as the maids and stewards light the lanterns and set the tables. I spot Harry, Gordy and the rest of my crew from the Beacon making their way through the gates and toward a table set high with food and drink. I wonder briefly where Lara is and how she is faring. After the rebellion and Meg's abolition of the sectors, several former courtiers abdicated to the Wastelands. Having not seen heads nor tail of Lara since the fall of the King, I assume she was among them. I shake my head to clear it, focusing on the party below again. Lara's welfare is no longer my concern—just as I was never any concern of hers.

Lifting my hair off the back of my neck to cool it, I stand with one foot on the ledge, poised to jump down and join the festivities. The crowd below swells ever larger, seemingly packed with every man, woman and child in the City. The sight is a far cry from the overstuffed splendour I'm accustomed to seeing at Palace events. Under Meg's rule, there is no hierarchy, no *us* and *them*. The people seem happy. They seem at peace.

I glance back behind me, toward the distant wall and the Wastelands beyond. One battle may have ended, but the war outside our borders has barely begun. Without the draft and with Will as the new Commander of Meg's army, we have an entirely new fight to contend with. I imagine the shadowy Wastelanders sharpening their spears, preparing to launch an attack on our walls; reflexively, I reach for the dagger at my belt, wiped clean of blood but ready for action all the same.

Crouching, I make to climb down but pause when my hand touches the first brick. I glance up again, watching as Meg and Will enter the courtyard through the door of the Great Hall. Meg is resplendent in a spun ivory gown, tall and regal as the queen she was always meant to be. Will walks alongside her, maddeningly handsome in his sand-coloured commander's uniform. Hope blooms within me as the clanging of the bells increases in fervour, nearly drowned out by the people's cheers. A path is cleared and Meg makes her way to a simple wooden throne, turning and smiling widely as one of her elected regents places a gold band atop her head.

I straighten, taking one step back, then another. The feast continues below, carrying on without me, despite me. The old Kay would not have hesitated to join in the ceremony, would have welcomed a drink with friends and revelled in the success of the rebellion.

The truth is that the girl who returned from belowground is not the same as the girl who first descended. The world before the gaol was black and white, made up of rich and poor, good and evil. Now, I see the varying shades brought about by our choices; I've heard the mumblings of the dissatisfied former courtiers. This is not a city made perfect by the death of a tyrant. Despite the sounds of celebration thundering from the courtyard, I know that our troubles have barely begun.

The carefree street-rat is gone. In her place is a girl unused to fame, who has been to the Burn and back, who will not hesitate to kill when threatened.

I finger the hilt of my dagger again. No, I am not the same as I once was. None of us are. The rebellion has given us a new beginning, a chance to right the wrongs of our past. We can't know what lies ahead, but at least we now have the wisdom of a true queen to guide us.

The sun dips below the horizon, inviting a cool desert breeze from the Wastelands. I shiver, my limbs once again buzzing with a familiar restlessness. I spin on my heel, turning my scarred back to the party, and return to the cascade of rooftops. The thrill of the run sings through me, pulling me into the depths of the city and beyond, toward the very stars above.

An old constellation twinkles to life, making itself known in the darkening night sky. I glance up at the Fireline as I race onward, my father's words pushing me to run ever faster, to leap ever higher.

Soaring above the streets, halfway between my old and new worlds, a clarifying certainty hammers home a reminder of what I have fought for and who I am meant to be.

The Runner.

THE END

acknowledgements

A very special thank you to the following people, who believed in this story before I did.

Mom and Dad
Janie B.
Melissa B.
Michael B.
Maurice Delaney
Greta Grace
Kirsten H.
Jonathon
Katy J.
Sarah Joyner
AJ L.
Paul L.
Laurel Mellin
Sierra Moon
Bree Moore
Pryia Moses
Shreya R.
Tony

Vicky Bell
For helping to create something out of nothing.

Kay's adventures continue in Book 2 of the Runner Series.

Turn the page for a sneak peek.

THE WASTELANDS

BOOK 2 OF THE RUNNER SERIES

chapter 1

The sun bakes down across my shoulders as I sprint from rooftop to rooftop. My legs burn with exertion and my heart pounds steadily in my chest. My breaths are slow and even, falling into a natural rhythm.

My feet land securely on the ledges and I push out across the alleyways, clearing the gaps effortlessly. My trained eyes scan the landscape in front of me, registering the familiar layout of the City and charting my course toward the Palace.

I move from the depths of what was once the Commons and into the former Court. As I run I note how it is becoming increasingly difficult to distinguish between the two districts. The excessive displays of wealth that used to be displayed prominently in the windows and storefronts have dissipated and migrated closer to our outer Wall. Now, the City streets blend together in a cacophony of colour. Sun-bleached buildings boast brightly painted shutters and richly dyed fabrics dangle on clotheslines between the alleyways.

The glass Palace swims into view and I have to blink to clear my vision, at the same time absentmindedly swiping the tendrils of red hair from my forehead. The sun has risen to its highest point and I am hard pressed to find a direction to approach from which the reflective walls of the Palace don't blind me. I curse myself for letting the hour grow late and increase my speed, relying on my instincts rather than my eyesight to direct me across the roofs.

Finally, I reach the edge of the Court nearest the royal grounds. I swing myself down over the ledge and drop window by window until I reach the ground, dusting the sand from my hands as I straighten.

This street marks the barrier between the City buildings and the wall surrounding the army compound. I turn to jog in the direction of the compound's front gate but am immediately halted in my tracks when something adorning the wall catches my eye.

I step closer, feeling a frown pull at my mouth as I read the propaganda someone has posted.

Meg's serene face smiles out at me from the parchment, marred by the words "Queen of Extinction" scrawled crudely across her features. Scowling, I reach up and tear the poster away, balling it in my fists before I rip down three more posters.

Cursing under my breath I turn and run to the front gate, smoothly dodging the carriages and people crowding the street.

The gate guard has already opened the gate to admit me and I call out my thanks as I tear past him. I run through the gate and toward the training field, bypassing the airships in the hangar and the barracks. Up ahead, I can hear the sounds of multiple booted feet marching in formation as Will runs his drills, his familiar, deep voice carrying across the open grounds.

I circle around the rear of the field and hop the fence, then duck down behind the marching soldiers, looking for an inconspicuous opening. I nudge my way into position next to my friend, Marc, adopting his stance and stepping in time with the drills. Marc throws me a knowing wink, stepping helpfully to the side.

Will's voice sounds from the front of the pack, counting off our steps as we turn and march across the field. I chance a look to the front of the line, catching sight of his scruffy head and trimmed beard, his square jaw clenched tightly in concentration. My heartbeat picks up and I force myself to focus on the back of the woman in front of me, copying her movements.

"Nicely done." Will finally calls a halt.

I suppress a sigh, covertly rubbing my lower back. Even after running these drills countless times, the practice of following orders still rankles me. The fact that it is Will calling out commands is all the more annoying.

“All right, soldiers, let's partner up for a bit of sparring. Everyone, grab a weapon," Will instructs and the soldiers disperse, heading toward the rack of swords lined up at the far end of the field.

Finally, here’s a bit of training that I can actually use. I select a sword of hammered steel, testing its weight; stepping back, I take a few experimental swings. Only a couple of months have passed since I began training, but the deadly movements are already beginning to feel natural—an intuitive step up from my street tussles. Rotating in place, I try a couple more sequences. I bring my sword up and swipe it vertically across my chest, then jump when the blade is suddenly blocked by opposing steel.

Will pushes my sword aside with his, his steely eyes dark with challenge.

I correct my stance, meeting his eye and raising an eyebrow.

Will's blade meets mine over and over with practised precision, challenging my weak side intermittently and forcing me to block. The sounds of metal striking metal reverberate through the dusty air as we join the other soldiers.

"You're still too tense across your shoulders. Relax—follow your weapon."

I fight the urge to roll my eyes as I sidestep him and block again, changing tactics abruptly and forcing him to defend. He counters my manoeuvres easily, not bothering to hide his smirk.

"Find something funny?" I ask, my voice hoarse from the exercise.

"When you're annoyed you stop using your head."

He shoves my blade aside again, deliberately using enough force to send me stumbling backwards.

"Don't let your emotions dictate your fight." He shoots me a meaningful look before he turns to shout directions over his shoulder. "You can't defend all day, Grifin. Attack him!"

At once, I hear the sound of one soldier viciously attacking another with a renewed sense of vigor. Grifin's opponent desperately defends himself against the blows, at the same time releasing a string of colourful curses.

"How are you able to see Grifin and still fight me?" I ask, buying myself a few moments to catch my breath.

"I see everything." A familiar dimple dots his cheek. "I also saw you sneak in late. You missed drills. Again."

"I caught the gist of it." I switch the sword to my left hand and wait for him to do the same.

"If you want to train with my army, then you need to stick to our rules." Will's voice has taken on that note of condescension and I feel myself prickle.

I channel my anger and aim my sword for his undefended side, letting out a grunt of annoyance when he blocks. "When I told you I wanted to train, what I meant was that I wanted to learn to fight, not to march."

"It's all part of a larger picture. Fighting is about more than just strength and technique." He parries patiently, his tone measured. "It's also about discipline."

I strike again, intending to catch him by surprise. I overcompensate and Will takes full advantage of my loss of balance, bringing his sword down on mine and sending me crashing to the ground.

I roll over onto my back, scowling at the blade pointed toward my neck.

"Most importantly, it's about attacking with your head and not your heart." That half-grin eases my annoyance a bit and I knock his sword away, accepting his hand and letting him pull me to my feet.

“I can't say I've missed your approach to teaching,” I grumble, rubbing my sore arm.

“Perhaps not, but you have to admit that this is infinitely more fun than learning names and manners.” He picks up my sword and tosses it back to me. “Now, let's try it again.”

The daylight has begun to wane by the time we are finally released from training. I joke with Marc and the other soldiers as we cross the shadowed training field to replace our weapons, then wave goodbye and hang back when they troop off toward the barracks.

I rock back and forth on my heels, stretching my arms and legs in an effort to loosen the tight muscles. I watch the soldiers retreating figures as I wait, only half-listening to their companionable chatter.

The dreaded draft was abolished when Meg came into power. Soon after, Will left the Palace medical practice and accepted the position of Commander. Enlistment was open to anyone interested, men and women alike. The ever-present threat of the Wastelanders and the army's fair pay attracted more people than we anticipated, prompting Will to organize a training camp.

Though I am not an official soldier, my newfound status within the City has afforded me the opportunity to train with the new recruits. I figured my experience on the street would translate easily to sword fighting but as Will has helpfully pointed out time and time again, I lack the discipline needed to be considered a truly fierce opponent. These thoughts set my blood boiling again and I am scowling by the time Will draws up next to me.

"You did well today," he says as we fall into step. He is wearing his official sand-coloured jacket and has affixed his sword to his waist. "You're definitely improving."

I am in no mood to discuss training and instead change the subject, remarking, "You're dressed quite formally for supper."

"We are banqueting with the Queen. Some of us still wish to uphold royal standards." As he speaks, his gaze rakes over my figure.

I glance down at my clothes. My pants and tunic are made of quality fabrics and my light, sturdy boots were crafted specially for me by Meg's personal tanner. My afternoon bouts in the training field have left me coated with patches of dust and dirt but compared to my street rat days, I think I appear quite decent.

"Would you prefer I wear a gown of spun gold?" I ask.

"I would prefer you wear nothing at all." He slips a hand around my waist and pulls me to him. At once, I melt into the familiar cocoon of his body, kissing him deeply as my hands reach up behind his neck to urge him closer.

I feel his mouth smile against mine and at once the pressures of the day lift from my shoulders. As frustrated as he makes me, there is no denying that there is little I would deny this ridiculous man.

He growls low in his throat, pulling away reluctantly. "We should go—we have responsibilities to attend to."

"I never asked for them." I sigh. The prospect of a meal at the Palace pales in comparison to a stolen night with Will.

"You did, when you brought a rebellion." He pulls me back into step with him. "Or have you forgotten that, already?"

"Of course I haven't. I just didn't think that afterward, I would be expected to assist with running the City."

"What did you suppose you would do? There isn't much call for thievery these days."

I nudge him playfully with my elbow. "I know that. To be honest, I never really figured anything past taking down the King."

"Such little faith for a revolutionary."

I laugh. "It wasn't a lack of faith, it was a lack of foresight."

"I think we could agree what you lack in foresight I more than make up for." He nudges me back, quickly offering a hand to catch me when I stumble on my tired legs. "Some would say to a fault."

"Were it left up to you, Commander Cain, humans would have burned sitting in the desert before making the decision to stand."

He chuckles, hugging me to his side as we exit the compound. We bid goodnight to the gate guard and Will flags down a carriage, offering me a hand to help me into my seat. I smile at our formal manners, leftover from the days when he was a Palace physician and I was a lady-in-waiting to the Princess. To be fair, I was really just a common street thief and merely pretending to be a lady at the time, but still, his simple gestures never fail to touch my heart.

We disembark at the Palace and are immediately waved through the doors. I glance up at the beautiful glass facade as we pass beneath the entryway, marveling at the way the faultless glass walls reflect the starry night sky.

The Great Hall is at the far end of the Palace, past the open foyer and the main staircases. The ornate decorations that used to line these walls have largely migrated to the Palace treasury, but colourful mosaics and patterns still blink cheerfully in the lantern light. Priceless tapestries and plush settees decorate the cavernous space, boasting our City's legendary craftsmanship. We move through the crowd of people milling about the foyer, their conversations ebbing and flowing as they walk to and from the Great Hall.

When I lived at the Palace as a lady, meals were a starched and formal event. White-gloved Commoners served the decadent courses atop gold plates as we sat straight-backed in our chairs and murmured stiffly in low voices.

Meg's meals are a more laid-back affair. The food is laid out on a single table in the Hall for guests to serve themselves while Palace workers move seamlessly through the room, tidying up and offering drinks.

I crane my neck as I scan the crowd, searching for a familiar face. Someone claps Will on the back and he turns to shake the man's hand, laughing. I take the opportunity to slip away, making my way into the Hall.

Meg sits at one of the tables, poised and listening raptly to a white-haired man. Our queen is resplendent tonight, dressed in a violet gown with her raven hair brushed to a high sheen and knotted elegantly at the nape of her neck. I watch her carefully as I move toward the spread. The man is gesticulating grandly as he speaks and my eyes flick over to the ever-present guards standing behind Meg. They eye the speaker warily but appear unconcerned, so I take my time in preparing a plate of food before I pick my way toward my friend. I sink down into the chair nearest her, placing myself directly in the white-haired man's line of sight.

His eyes flick to me and an ugly flush creeps up his splotchy neck. I raise my eyebrows questioningly, inviting him to continue as I take a bite of my dinner.

"All I am saying, your Majesty, is that those of us accustomed to having live-in help should not be punished."

"And as I have already explained, Mr. Helmes, you are not being punished. If you require assistance, there are people willing to work for you, for a fair compensation." Meg's voice is calm, betraying nothing.

"But how can I be expected to afford that, as well as my taxes?" Helmes' face colours further and he deliberately avoids my gaze.

"If you cannot afford both, Mr. Helmes, you will need to procure employment for yourself."

"I am an old man!"

"Everyone can be of use. It is a selfish person who says otherwise." Meg tilts her head up at him. Despite the fact that she is sitting and he is standing, she still manages to convey the sense that she is towering above him. "As I see it, you have two options. You can visit the Palace tomorrow morning and inquire about a work placement, or otherwise you can learn a new word."

Nearly all the blood has drained from his face and the red splotches on his neck stand out unattractively. "What word?"

"'Budget', Mr. Helmes."

I snort and my fork clatters noisily against my plate. Meg kicks me under the table, her brown eyes narrowed in warning.

"Sorry," I murmur, then stuff another forkful into my mouth.

She turns around again. "Now if you will excuse me, Mr. Helmes. I wish to share a meal with my friend."

He shuffles away, muttering as he pulls on his cap over his sparse hair.

"I suppose you can't please everyone," I say sarcastically, watching his retreating figure.

Meg poises a fork delicately over my plate and samples some of my meal. "I doubt very much that Mr. Helmes has been pleased a day in his life."

"You may be right about that." I spear my last carrot before she can take it. "Good meal tonight."

"Do you think so? Rations have been a bit...sparse lately."

"The oasis is just going through a slow season," I say, reassuringly. "It happens occasionally and we've survived worse."

"Of course." She nods readily. "Take as much as you need, in any case. Rumour has it that Will's training camp is ruthlessly taxing."

"Leave it to Will to over-prepare." I push my plate away and lean back in my chair, stretching my legs. From the corner of my eye I can see Meg rolling her shoulders back and I am grateful to the hovering guests and guards for giving us some space. Meg tries not to show her strain, but I know how acutely she feels every one of the City's worries.

"He has proven to be an extremely thorough Commander," she agrees, sounding distracted.

"How are you doing?" I ask, keeping my voice low.

She sighs wearily. "I'm holding up. It's difficult to make decisions when no matter what I choose, people inevitably get angry."

"That implies you are making the rest happy."

"Am I?" She leans back in her chair. "Things seem to be more or less improving, but even with an open forum, I know they are whispering about me."

"People will always talk. It doesn't mean anything."

"I wonder how often the snakes said the same thing to my father," she says, drily. "Don't coddle me, Kay. Tell me the truth. I don't want to be completely oblivious to the needs of my City the way he was."

I pause, considering. "I can tell you the things that are being said about you, but I don't think it would do you any good to know them."

"I don't care. Tell me anyway."

"There are posters of you up around the City with crude slogans on them." I watch her carefully. "'Queen of Treason,, 'Queen of Liars,' cleverness of that nature."

"Lovely." She twirls a tendril of hair absentmindedly. "Anything else?"

"It's mostly Courtiers talking. They complain about jobs meant for them going to Commoners." For the sake of brevity I forgo the politically correct terms of "former Commoner" and "former Courtier". "They complain about not having enough food and money."

"You mean, they don't have the same amount of money and food they had before the rebellion." She closes her eyes briefly. "So, no one is actually starving in the street?"

"Far from it. There are a few outliers, of course, but it's a big City and a new system. The best thing you ever did was turn the Palace into a place where we could come and ask for help. If people don't want to take advantage of your offerings, that's their problem." I try to keep my voice measured, fighting the frustration bubbling up inside me. These Courtiers have no concept of what it actually is to be poor and hungry. I cannot stand to hear them grumble about Meg's policies when she has done nothing but amazing things for us.

She senses my aggravation and places her cool hand over mine. "Thank you for telling me, Kay. It means a lot to me, to have you working with the citizens on my behalf."

I shrug. "I'm happy to do it." Being the go-between for Meg and the people means that I get to split my time between the Palace and my old friends in the Commons—really no job at all.

Just as she's opened her mouth to say something else, a low murmur sounds from near the doors to the Hall. Meg's brow furrows as she rises to her feet, standing to greet the messenger racing through the surprised crowd toward her.

"What is it?" she demands before he can properly catch his breath.

"The outer gate," he pants, referring to the Wall separating the City from the Wastelands, "is under attack." He sucks in a great lungful of air as he looks fearfully up at Meg. "The Wastelanders are breaking through."

chapter 2

The room has fallen deathly silent. My eyes dart immediately toward Will standing over the messenger's shoulder. His steely gaze meets mine; his jaw clenches.

"Your Majesty," he calls out to Meg, "we should dispatch all our available troops to the Wall at once."

Some of the colour has drained from the Queen's face, but her command is nonetheless decisive. "Do whatever you must to protect our people." Her hand squeezes mine once before I release her to leap over the table and join the people streaming toward the front door.

I shoulder my way through the crowd and catch up with Will at the front of the group, falling into a half-run alongside him.

"We will get there quickest if we travel by roof," I tell him.

He glances down at me and back at the crowd behind him. I follow his gaze, noting that we are joined not only by the guards stationed at the Palace, but also by plainclothes citizens, their faces etched with similar looks of grim determination. It occurs to me suddenly that the rebellion isn't so far behind us.

"I need to stay with my troops," he says, his voice low.

"You will lose precious minutes if you stay on the ground. You heard him, Will. The Wastelanders are already breaking through the gate; we need to head them off as soon as possible."

"I am the commander of this army—I can't abandon them at the first threat of war."

"You aren't abandoning them. We'll meet them at the Wall—you'll just have a few minutes head start."

"Don't be foolish, Kay. You don't know what's out there. Stay with the group."

We have reached the sweeping drive in front of the Palace and Will turns away to direct the crowd into the armoury. The keepers have already begun unloading various weapons and are handing them out to the grasping hands. The stables have been opened and the grooms lead the great, stamping horses toward their riders.

I shoulder my way to the armoury and select a bow and quiver, figuring that I'll want something I can use from a distance. With the weapons slung on my back I turn away from the preparation and sweep my gaze to the South. Squinting, I can just make out the low burn of fire stemming from the base of the City. I scan the tightly packed roofs ahead as I mentally calculate my route, estimating the time it would take me to reach the Wall.

"Kay, come on!" I tear my eyes away from the ominous, flickering light in time to see Will swing up into the saddle of his horse. He grasps the reins of another and holds them out to me expectantly.

I take one step back. "I'll meet you there."

"No, Kay." His voice is low with warning and I feel a spurt of indignation, taking another step back almost involuntarily. I watch Will's expression harden as I consider his words and the utter senselessness of rushing headlong into the Wasteland.

Yet, still I take another step back.

"Stay with the group, Kay. That's an order." The reins are thrust out once more.

And in that instant, I make up my mind

I whip around and sprint full throttle through the gate; somewhere in the recesses of my mind, I register a stream of curses in my wake.

I cross the wide street and leap at the wall in front of me, heaving myself up onto the roof in a matter of seconds. Below me, I can hear the sound of hoofbeats stampeding down the Palace drive. I glance over the side of the building in time to watch Will's army charging past, the few dozen horses followed closely by a grim-faced crowd, clutching their various weapons tightly as they hurry toward the Wall.

The soreness in my legs is at once forgotten as I turn and take off full tilt toward the roof ledge. In the next instant I am hurtling through the air, flying high and free before I land seamlessly, and spring into another run upon impact. I urge myself to run faster as the torchlight beyond the Wall grows brighter, the exhilaration of hot desert air against my face and limbs doing little to alleviate the ugly warning thrumming its way through my mind.

My gods, they are really here.

The hoofbeats below me recede into the twisting alleyways and slowly fade into a distant rumbling. While I run, I tune my ears to the sounds up ahead.

My heart freezes in my chest when I realize what I'm hearing.

Drums, and panicked screaming.

I redouble my speed and clear the next several alleyways at a reckless pace, my throat constricting as I fight to breathe. I barely notice when the buildings around me degrade into states of disrepair and I nearly trip on the loose stones littering the roofs of the old Common flats.

The screams suddenly reach a fevered pitch and a mighty reverberation shakes the earth below. The structure under my feet shakes and I stumble, my palms and knees scraping against the rough stone of the roof. Cursing, I right myself and lurch onwards.

The mighty Wall looms ahead of me. I expect to see our patrollers gathered on the scaffolding at the top of the wall but find it empty, abandoned but for the occasional body slouched over the ledge or lying in in a crumpled heap on the platform.

Ignoring the churning of my stomach I abruptly change course and approach from the side. I leap from the roof to the scaffolding behind the Wall, my landing nearly soundless. The wooden platforms run around the Wall's entire inner perimeter, hidden from view other than the occasional lookout tower.

I stay crouched, ears and eyes straining as I attempt to gauge the situation. The terrified screams of the City citizens are punctuated by the angry shouts on the other side of the Wall. I chance a glance into the desert and my eyes widen at the sight.

A mob has gathered outside the Wall, yelling and waving weapons, their war cries combining together to create a terrifying roar. My gaze darts to the giant, wheeled contraption the Wasters have dragged over in front the Wall. Several Wastelanders dart around the machine while others continuously nock their arrows and shoot them blindly over our gate, effectively keeping anyone on our side from looking over.

The machine is made of wood and affixed to wheels. I am harbouring a guess that it's an oversized carriage before I notice the boulders the Wasters are struggling to load into the back.

I frown as I try to piece the information together. What good would a boulder do inside this cart?

A Waster crouches behind the machinery and I watch as he secures a taut rope from the back of the cart to the ground. Someone comes over to help him tighten the rope and the boulder rolls back in its seat as the cart tilts backward.

Oh, my gods.

I spring into action, darting along the scaffolding toward the bodies of the guards. As I run, I glance down to the City below, cursing when I take in the number of people gathered near the Wall, directly in the line of fire. Something whizzes by my head and I nearly stumble, registering that an arrow just missed me by mere inches.

"Get away from the Wall!" I yell over the din.

A few people below me glance up and I signal desperately for them to get back as I continue to sprint across the platform.

I reach the first pair of fallen patrollers and examine them quickly, swallowing heavily when I find an arrow buried in the chest of one and the neck of the other. I look away from their faces, running to the next fallen and searching desperately for any signs of life.

I roll a man over and he groans. I am so on edge that I nearly tumble off the platform from shock. I sling his arm around my neck, remaining crouched as I chance another look over the Wall.

The Wasters appear even fiercer at this distance, tall and broad, their faces covered by earth-coloured scarves and protective strips of leather crossing their bodies. The torchlight dances ominously over the mob, casting dark shadows across their imposing statures. No one has backed away from the war machine, yet I can't be certain that the boulder won't be released at any moment. The word *catapult* sits on the tip of my tongue, my readings of ancient weaponry sending a terrifying premonition down my spine. There isn't time to dwell; I need to get off this Wall and far away from its base.

I manage to hobble partway down the platform steps before the shouts behind fall to a low, rumbling murmur. My time is up. I stumble as I hurry toward the stairs, spouting curses and other such encouragement to the injured man at my side, half-dragging him down the few steps before someone runs up to help us.

As the weight of the guard lifts from my shoulders I look straight out into the City, searching for any signs of Will and his reinforcements. The ground below me is a chaotic ensemble of terrified people running back and forth but there are no signs yet of the soldiers.

"We need to get away from the Wall!" I yell again, grabbing hold of people as they stream by me, steering them uphill and into the City. "Tell everyone you can; move away from the Wall!"

I tear up and down the street, shouting like a crazed woman. The screams around me increase with my own desperation as the Wasters' rhythmic chant grows conspicuously louder.

"This is it!" I shout, snatching a woman's hand and dragging her with me away from the stone barricade. We join the crowd of people streaming uphill, fighting to put as much distance between ourselves and the Wasters as possible.

Then there is a deafening impact and I am knocked to the ground. I cover my head with my hands and yank my knees up to my chest, shielding myself as sharp fragments of stone pelt me. Something clips my arm and I wince, my ears ringing.

Moments or hours of terrifying blackness pass before the world gradually swims back into focus and I register the voices crying out around me. Shaking my head to clear it I sit up and stare back down the hill toward the Wall, scarcely believing my eyes.

A cloud of sand floats up around the great, gaping hole in our outer defense. A few stragglers stumble backward, their clothes coated in blood as they hold their arms over their mouths. The dust slowly settles and I can make out the flickering torchlight beyond as the Wasters march forward, their fierce shouts ten times louder and more bone-chilling without the Wall to protect us.

They're here.

chapter 3

I rise unsteadily to my feet, sand and rubble cascading off me. I pull my scarf up over my nose to protect my airway and try to force my mind into motion as I take in the situation.

Where in the eternal Burn is Will?

I leap at the building nearest me, traversing its facade, my hands and feet slipping on the loosened bricks. I reach the roof and heave myself up onto it, running in the direction of a still-standing portion of the Wall as I swing my bow out from around my back.

Until Will and the rest of the army show up there is little I can do but try to keep as many of the Wasters on the other side of the Wall for as long as possible.

The platform sways dangerously below my feet as I run toward the gap, halting just shy of the impact zone. I crouch down low and nock an arrow, sighting along the length of the weapon just as Will taught me.

My hands tremble slightly and I fight to clear my mind, staying focused on the area where the Wasters will soon be passing through. I think back to my training and try to concentrate on the mechanics of hitting my target, rather than who will be on the receiving end of my shot. I breathe slowly, watching and waiting.

From the depths of my trance I can dimly make out the sounds of our approaching army. Will's coming. He'll be here soon.

The swirling sand clears and a shadowed form moves through the dust. I adjust my aim and release the arrow before I can second-guess myself, my heart stopping in my chest in the next moment.

Amongst the shouting and screaming I register a low utterance of pain and the form falls still. Instinctively I reach behind me and ready another arrow, loosing it the instant I get a clear shot on the next Waster. I fall back as an object flies past my shoulder; the platform below my feet sways and cracks at the sudden movement.

I grip the platform tightly and scramble to my feet. My heart lurches back to life and pounds heavily against my ribcage as I leap from the scaffolding back to a building, where I duck and crouch behind the ledge.

In the fervor of battle I had almost completely forgotten that I had left myself entirely exposed to the enemy. I listen again for the sound of the horses and will myself up again to peer over the edge, nocking another arrow as I spy the few Waster front-runners scrambling over the rubble. I release my bowstring, cursing when the arrow bounces off the rocks. Taking a deep breath, I aim my next arrow more carefully. I will time to slow before firing, wincing when it hits its mark.

Something pings off the ledge behind me. I remain crouched as I scramble to the side of the building and leap across the street to the next ledge, landing in a roll so that I remain low.

I peer up and into the street, feeling a rush of relief when our army finally appears around the corner, Will at their head. The City dwellers rush headlong into the pile of rubble, swords drawn as they are met with the encroaching Wastelanders. I make my way across and to the platform on the other side of the gap, taking advantage of the distraction below and unleashing a couple more arrows over the Wasteland side of the Wall, cringing a little less each time one of my shots finds its target.

The horses push the Wastelanders back until the battle is fully within the desert. More and more of our citizens flood into the Wastelands, meeting the enemy with their weapons and torches raised. From my vantage point I can see how Will directs his troops to flank the Wasters from all sides, fanning out around them and cutting off their chances to circle around and attack us from behind.

The cool night air rings with the sound of clashing steel, arrows and spears, mingled continuously with the shouts of angry men and women screaming with pain and attacking savagely.

When I run out of arrows I dash to the fallen patrollers, gathering what arrows I can scavenge from where they lie scattered. I leap back and forth above the gap, changing position often and picking off stragglers. I miss more often than not, but even I can see that this battle is over.

Finally, someone calls for retreat and the Wasters scatter away, rotating in perfect synchronicity and disappearing almost instantly into the night, their dark forms swallowed by the desert shadows.

I remain poised on the wall, lowering my bow slowly as I watch them disappear, amazed at the Wastelanders' level of organization. Soon, all that remains on the other side of the Wall are the horses and our troops, circling the area as they gather the wounded and dead.

I search instinctively for Will, spying him leading a group over to the Wastelanders' now-abandoned wheeled contraption. I throw my bow back behind me and lift myself over the wall, picking my way down the facade and landing in the soft sand.

As I rise out of my crouch and stare out across the endless landscape I realize this is the first time I have ever stepped foot outside the City walls. The world suddenly gives off a great impression of infinity, similar to the feeling of staring up at the blackened sky and into the depths of the stars. My stomach flips once and I take a moment to collect myself before I step forward, toward the machine.

It looms over me as I walk closer, the wheels nearly as tall as my shoulder. The great, wooden arm that heaved the boulder at our walls now dangles listlessly over the front of the cart. I run my hand over its rough surface as I pass, wincing when I catch a splinter. Unlike our carriages, this was built entirely for function and not for style.

I catch up with Will near the back wheels. He stands regarding the mechanism, discussing its workings with Marc and a couple of the other soldiers; they all have grim expressions on their faces.

He glances up as I come closer, a mixture of relief and exasperation crossing his features. I offer him a small smile as I join the group, grateful that the gathered crowd offers me a reprieve from his lectures.

"How did they manage it?" someone wonders aloud, marvelling at the underbelly. "It's massive."

"It must have taken twenty of them just to push it," Marc agrees. "How does it work?"

"They loaded a boulder into that arm, over there." I gesture toward the front of the cart. "It was pulled down to where we're standing and strapped down tight."

"You saw them use this?" Will asks, his tone clipped.

I nod. "I didn't see it go off, exactly, but I caught the gist of it."

"I'd say you caught some of it." Marc gestures to my arm and I glance down, noticing for the first time that I've been cut, probably by a piece of rubble during the explosion. I realize that covered in grime and blood I must look like I just came out of a warzone.

Which, I suppose I did.

I shoot Marc a look, annoyed that he should point out my injury to Will. My friend shrugs half-heartedly and turns his attention back to the catapult.

Will's eyes flicker down to my arm and back up again. "How did they fire it?"

"They tied it with a rope and wrenched it taut. Over here, look." I lead him back a few paces and point out a stake driven into the ground and tied with a piece of rope. Will stoops to examine the rope, holding the end out to the torchlight.

"It's been cut. They must fire it by striking the rope with an axe." He looks over his shoulder back toward the Wall, at the hole aligning with the path of the contraption. The line is as sure and true as an arrow's. There is no denying that the level of which this machine has wrought is truly devastating. Never had I considered our wall capable of falling.

Until tonight.

Will mutters a curse under his breath, running a hand across his shorn hair before straightening and signalling to Marc. "They'll be coming back for this weapon. Find a way to get this inside our walls and if it cannot be done, I want engineers out here to take whatever notes and schematics they need as quickly as possible, then I want it burned. Can you take care of that?"

"Yes, Commander." Marc salutes and scurries to comply.

Will turns and strides back toward the Wall. I follow, stumbling slightly on the uneven terrain.

I help to lead the injured men and women back over the rubble and load them into the Palace carriages Meg supplied for transportation back to the infirmary. Working quickly and efficiently with the rest of the gathered citizens I can't help but feel a sense of camaraderie despite the tragedy of the situation. Here around me, helping one another, are people I can no longer distinguish as either Common or Courtier.

The destruction of the Wall and the victims it left behind did not distinguish between classes. Neither do we.

As I scramble back and forth over the rubble and down the streets I regard Will in his element. He orders the guardianship of the Wall and the collection of the dead and injured with a calm efficiency, answering questions and directing people who have been left homeless back to the Palace for shelter.

I feel my heart swell with pride as I watch him. He was born for this role. The City is lucky to have him. I am lucky to have him.

Eventually, we manage to get everyone off the streets. I slump down against the side of a damaged building, leaning my head back as I become fully aware of just how tired and sore I am.

I sense Will crouching down next to me before I crack my eyes open and regard him. Wordlessly, he offers me a hand and pulls me to my feet.

"You should probably get that arm checked out at the infirmary," he says.

I shrug. "The cut isn't deep. I'll just clean it myself and wrap it."

"If you say so." He cocks his head down the street. "Are you going to ride with me? Or will you be taking your own route again?" The way he says it holds no trace of humour and I feel myself bristle.

I follow him toward the horses, too tired to argue. We swing up onto our saddles and ride back uphill in the direction of the Palace. I glance over my shoulder once before we turn the corner and note the amount of troops Will has left behind. I wonder if the abundance of soldiers guarding the gap is because Will thinks the Wastelanders will return, or if they have been left for the peace of mind of the citizens.

Knowing Will and that his decisions carry multiple agendas, I am guessing he is protecting us from a combination of afflictions.

The sky has turned from black to grey by the time we make it back to the Palace gates. I stifle a yawn as I hand over the reins of my horse to the groom. Meg is standing at the open door, wearing the same dress as the night before, her hands clasped tightly in front of her.

"Thank gods you're all right." She pulls me into a hug as I walk up to her and I wince, less from the pain than regret that my grubby and blood-stained clothes will leave a mark on her beautiful dress.

Will joins us and she grips his hand. "Tell me, how bad is it?"

"It's bad." Will doesn't mince words. "They blew a hole in our Wall, large enough to climb through. We held them back and they eventually retreated, but they're probably regrouping as we speak."

"Will they attack again?"

"Undoubtedly," he answers and I flinch despite myself. "We have recovered the weapon they used to damage the wall but who knows how many more they have."

Meg closes her eyes for a moment, visibly drawing a breath. "How much time do we have?"

"I can't say. I doubt they will attack again tonight. We did some damage to their numbers and many are injured; they will need some time to recover."

"As do we," Meg says, a little sadly. "You should rest now, my friends. Tomorrow we will discuss how to reconcile tonight's tragedy." She turns to walk down the hall into the Palace, Will and I falling into step behind her.

"Meg, we must consider sending our troops outside the Wall." Will drops the formalities and speaks urgently as we walk. "It is no longer enough that we simply defend ourselves."

"We will discuss tomorrow, Will." We reach the stairs and Meg turns to face us. "Rest assured that I do not plan on sitting passively behind our defences. You say that the Wastelanders will return." She raises one perfectly arched eyebrow. "I intend to go out and meet them."

about the author

Katie Baker is a web developer and sometimes-writer from Ottawa, Canada. Accustomed to long, wintery months, she occupies herself with skiing, reading and snuggling up with a fuzzy dog or a fuzzy husband.

Printed in Great Britain
by Amazon

60666291R00237